truths & lies

DUET

USA TODAY BESTSELLING AUTHORS

K WEBSTER
NIKKI ASH

To our readers, thank you for continuing to trust us
with your hearts.

hidden truths

chapter one

Kostas

THE DARK BLUE WATERS OF MIRABELLO BAY ARE CALM THIS evening. Unlike the storm brewing inside me. Where the sea before me shimmers in a serene way beneath the moonlight, the one I hold claim to is raging.

Skoulíki.

I lift my tumbler to my lips and sip the ouzo, relishing the burn that races down my throat when I swallow. It only adds fuel to the anger flickering inside me, threatening to spread like wildfire. When my wrath has been unleashed, men who wrong me—who shit on the Demetriou name—get burned.

Someone clears their throat. Just once. Quietly. A reminder to move the fuck on.

Yes, Father.

Reluctantly tearing my gaze from the bay, I regard my new guest with cold, barely contained contempt. A *skoulíki* in our rich, fruitful soil. A man so slimy and dirty, I can barely look at him. He doesn't belong here, tainting the exquisite room he's sitting in.

Niles Nikolaides.

Nothing but a filthy worm in dire need of being plucked from the dirt and fed to a fucking bird. Ignoring the piece of shit who's sitting uncomfortably in a leather armchair, with all eyes on him, I skim my gaze around the room. They're all waiting for me to make a move, especially Father.

The move I want to make is to grab Niles by the throat and throw him off the goddamn balcony. Too easy. Too fucking easy for a man like him. A man who has been stealing from right under our noses. Allowing passage into Thessaloniki without paying the Demetriou tax.

"You think because we are in Crete we don't see what it is you're up to at our port?" I ask, my tone icy and condescending.

Niles clenches his jaw and sits up, shaking his head. His good looks won't help him in a room full of men who hate him. And while my father has never come out and stated why, I can see pure hatred for Niles flickering in his hazel eyes.

Father leans back on the leather sofa, and a small smirk tugs at his lips. He's enjoying seeing Niles in the hot seat, the center of my thunderous attention. Beside him, my brother, Aris, grins. While forcing Niles to squirm some more—like the worm he is—as he waits for me to continue, I study my brother.

Aris is so different from Father and me with our dark hair, calculating eyes, and permanent scowls.

Ezio Demetriou and I could pass for brothers rather than father and son. It's Aris who stands out with his golden skin, light brown hair, and playful brown eyes. He is soft to our hard. Warm to our cold. Weak to our strong. Aris is my mother made over, much to my father's disappointment.

"Sir," Niles starts unwisely.

I sear him with a glare. "You are here to listen, *fíle.*" *Friend.*

Aris snorts, earning a sharp look from our father. We all know Niles is no friend.

Motioning with a quick flick of my fingers, two of my most trusted men approach from the shadows of the room. They're dressed in black suits, hiding enough weapons to take out a small army beneath their jackets. Adrian and Basil are the largest men in this room. Imposing, threatening, cruel. All it takes is one nod of my head and they'll drag Niles, the *skoulíki* from Thessaloniki, to the *kelári* for a proper punishment. A punishment extracted with his blood. He must sense the violent storm churning in my eyes because he does what they all do.

Spews more bullshit.

"I can make this right, Kostas," Niles pleads, eyeing Adrian and

Basil warily. "I was in a bad place. Everything is better now. Think of it as a loan."

Ignoring him, I walk over to the table where the expensive bottle of ouzo sits and refill my glass. I pour two fingers' worth of the clear liquor into the glass of ice and then splash in some water from a decanter. Like oil trying to mix with water, the ouzo becomes cloudy, but never truly mixes. I give the tumbler a shake before draining the glass and setting it back down.

"*Ena macheri*," I demand coolly to Basil, holding out my hand.

Basil pulls a sharp Benchmade Nimravus knife from inside his jacket. At just four and a half inches, it's small enough to conceal, but long enough to do lethal damage. Niles knows this because he starts shaking his head.

"No, Kostas, listen," he pleads. "It was all part of my plan. To get into better graces with the Demetriou name."

I take the knife from Basil and study the pointy tip of the blade. "Explain how *you* taking *our* taxes and keeping them for yourself, when it is *us* who allows the ships passage into the ports, gets *you* into good graces with *us*." I dart my gaze to my brother. "Aris may be the numbers whiz here, but I must say, even I know something isn't adding up."

Niles, known for his killer smile and charm, pales as a frown wrinkles his brow. He ages ten years before me. His green eyes that usually light up with a calculating glint have dulled. A man knows when death is knocking on his door. He may not want to answer, but we're fucking here whether he likes it or not.

The negotiator slides back into the pilot seat as Niles's eyes light up with their usual devious glow. "The numbers didn't add up when you started tripling the taxes I owed a decade ago," Niles says without meeting my father's barely hidden murderous stare. "And yet I didn't argue. I paid my dues to the Demetrious."

Father's eyes narrow and a vein jumps in his neck. Aris frowns, shooting me a questioning look. It's rare for my father to show emotion. He hates Niles. Always has. It's always been clear to me, although I've never understood why. Nor have I asked.

Niles is smarmy.

That's enough for me to have my father's back.

"Your point?" I demand in a bored tone, picking at my nail with the tip of Basil's knife. "I feel as though you're unsuccessfully trying to make one."

"My point is I've been paying more and more over the years without argument. The taxes I collect on your behalf at the port are being underutilized. All I did was gain new contracts. I didn't take from your current ones." His face breaks out in a grin, as though his new reasoning will somehow save him from my wrath.

"The territory still belongs to us," I snap, no longer able to keep my fury on a leash.

Aris smirks at my outburst, while Father's brows furl together in an irritated way.

Sorry, Father, but this prick is pissing me off.

Taking a deep breath, I regain some composure before I speak again. "The territory is *ours*. Therefore, new contracts are *ours*. That fucking means new taxes are *ours*."

"And you'll get your money," Niles lies smoothly. "You always do. I've simply invested it in other ventures. When I earn it back, which is soon, you'll be paid back for the taxes. Plus interest."

I can tell Father wants to take over. He doesn't like that I'm allowing Niles to continue to plead his case. The worm needs to die.

"What are these other ventures?" I ask, ignoring the anger rolling from my father in waves.

"Mostly trafficking," Niles says, his green eyes flaring with wickedness. "Of the human variety."

My stomach roils in disgust. Not because of what he's chosen to traffic, but the fact he's allowing these vermin to pass through our ports. The Demetrious aren't the mafia or cartel. No, we're a dominant crime organization. Masters of power, influence, and wealth. We manipulate it to our advantage without having to scrape the bottom of the barrel ever.

Niles lives there.

In the dirty, dank bottom with all the other worms.

I want to fucking drown him.

"Basil," I boom, no longer interested in speaking with this lowlife. "Take him to the *kelári*." I point the blade at Niles. "I'll finish this conversation when we're alone." And when I'm cutting his useless tongue from his mouth.

Father rises from the sofa, giving me a subtle shake of his head. Aris sees and lifts his brows in surprise. To any other man, this is nothing. To our family, it's a crushing blow.

He's undermining my authority.

My father doesn't like my choice to kill him.

Rather than arguing with my father—something Aris would do—I clench my teeth and take a step back to give him the limelight. White-hot fury blazes inside me. Why doesn't he want this asshole dead tonight? He fucking stole from us. Lied to us. Whatever decade long hard-on for punishment my father has against Niles is getting old. It goes against everything he's taught me.

Loyalty is everything.

Niles is far from loyal. He's as disloyal as one can get. The motherfucker has blatantly admitted to stealing from us for his own agenda. Any other fool would be in the *kelári*, paying for his crimes with flesh and blood and screams.

Not Niles.

Never Niles.

Why do you keep him around, Father?

"Take a walk with me," Father tells Niles. "You too, Kostas."

Aris's jaw clenches at being left behind. As he should be. The men are talking. Niles rises, his green eyes darting between my father and me in confusion. When my father walks out onto the balcony, Niles and I follow suit. I close the door behind us and inhale the salty sea air.

Father leans against the balcony wrought iron railing and regards Niles as though he is a fungus. A fungus he's devoted his life to trying to destroy. Not kill, destroy. I've observed my father enough to learn to read his eyes. He says very little, but his eyes are telling if you're watching. He enjoys ruining Niles, but never ending him.

"You owe our family something far more valuable than your worthless life," Father tells him, his voice cold and cruel. "Do you agree?"

Niles, clearly eager to save his ass from death, nods emphatically. "I do. I'll get you your money. Soon, Ezio."

Father's nostrils flare, his only tell at how disgusted he is to have to deal with Niles. "Money is of no issue. It's a way we control people like you." He sneers. "What I want is priceless to a man like you."

Niles frowns, and his body stiffens. "And what is that?"

When Father glances my way, his eyes quickly assessing me, a cold chill numbs me to my bone. I don't like feeling as though I'm a pawn in this game. I'm a power player. I own the fucking board right along with my father. His telling eyes state otherwise.

"Pérasma Hotel & Villas could use a little sunshine," Father says, smirking at Niles. "I know my son could use a little warmth."

Our Greek resort that's a gateway to the Aegean Sea is known for its warm, picturesque location. While we may run darker business under our bright resort face, it's never for a lack of sun. My father is talking in riddles and it infuriates me. We're practically partners, and whatever game he's been playing with Niles for years, I'm not on his team. It's man against man, and I'm simply a weapon to be used.

Niles sucks in a sharp breath. "No."

Father's brow lifts high up his forehead. "No?"

No is not in Father's vocabulary. I learned that from an early age.

"I, uh," Niles stammers. "You know that's unfair."

The malevolence in my father's eyes is enough to have Niles taking a step back. "Life is unfair," Father tells Niles. "But at least you'll have one. I believe this is the best you could ever hope for."

And like a worm caught in a hawk's beak, Niles squirms with unease.

He'll devour you one day.

One simple nod is all it takes from Niles to seal their deal. Niles Nikolaides will live to see another day because he just negotiated something that is clearly very important to him.

Fucking fool.

chapter
two

Talia

"What's here? A cup, closed in my true love's hand?" I pluck the metal tumbler out of Alex's still hand and bring it to my nose, sniffing the contents. "Poison, I see, hath been his timeless end. O churl! Drunk all, and left no friendly drop to help me after?"

I drop to my knees on the hardwood floor and bow my head in a position of prayer. Tears prick my eyes as I glance up at the man before me, lying still in the tomb. "I will kiss thy lips. Haply some poison yet doth hang on them to make me die with a restorative."

Crawling into the tomb with Alex, I snuggle up next to him and place a soft, chaste kiss to his lips. His tongue darts out playfully, and I have to stifle a laugh. "Thy lips are warm!"

From a distance, a masculine voice calls out, "Lead, boy. Which way?"

"Yeah, noise?" I ask no one. "Then I'll be brief."

Reaching over Alex's body, I find his dagger and pull it out. The silver metal glistens in the light. "O, happy dagger! This is my sheath." With tears trailing down my cheeks, I stab myself in the stomach and let my body fall limply against Alex's.

With my eyes closed, I lie in the tomb, listening as the guards speak around me, trying to figure out what has happened. Next my mother and father enter. My mother screams and cries and begs for answers, while my father demands to know what's happened. Alex and I continue to lie still while the friar explains everything from our love, to our death. My parents cry and mourn the loss of their daughter.

And then the prince speaks. "A glooming peace this morning with it brings. The sun, for sorrow, will not show his head. Go hence to have more talk of these sad things. Some shall be pardoned, and some punished. For never was a story more woe than this of Juliet and her Romeo."

The curtains close, and the auditorium booms with applause.

"You are such a beautiful Juliet," Alex says, lifting onto his forearms and caging me in.

"And you are a handsome Romeo," I say back.

Alex's lips curl into a boyish grin. His face comes down, about to kiss me, but before our lips meet, we hear, "Not now! Not now! Out! Out!" Professor Marino chides. "We have curtain call! Come!"

Alex steps out of the tomb first and then helps me to my feet, lifting and setting me down. "Later," he murmurs into my ear. Blush creeps up my neck and cheeks, heating my skin.

We form a line, and the curtains open. Everyone bows and curtsies, and the applause starts up once more. My eyes dart across the people and land on my family. My mom's face splits into a huge smile. Our eyes meet, and she mouths, *I love you.*

I love you more, I mouth back.

My eyes land on my brother next. With his fingers between his lips, he's whistling so loud, the sound overpowers the applause. My eyes roll of their own accord, but deep down, I'm happy to see him here. When I was ten, and he was fifteen, our parents divorced. I moved to Rome to live with my mom and her parents, but my brother, Phoenix, stayed with our father in Thessaloniki. I hate the distance between us, but there was no way of going around it. I wasn't about to stay in Greece without our mom, and Phoenix couldn't leave. Running the family business with our father was never not an option.

My eyes leave my brother's and roam over to my stepdad, Stefano. Then, I smile when I see my grandfather and grandmother, Emilio and Vera, still affectionately referred to as Nonno and Nonna. They're all clapping and beaming with pride.

The curtain closes once again and everyone cheers. "Magnifico!" Professor Marino exclaims. "What a wonderful way to end the semester.

Go now and greet your families. I will see all of you in August. Enjoy your summer…but not too much." She winks playfully, and we all laugh.

"Come," I say, grabbing Alex's hand. "I can't wait for you to meet my family." I already know his family isn't here. His parents live in the States and weren't able to fly over. Instead, Alex will be visiting them this summer, and he's invited me to join him.

"Talia!" My mom wraps me in a hug and kisses my cheek. "There was no Juliet better than you." She pulls her face back and frames my cheeks. "You did a marvelous job."

"Thank you, Mom."

"Talia, you did a wonderful job," my grandfather says. "You both did." His eyes flicker from me to Alex, and I take that as my cue to introduce Alex to everyone. "Alex, this is my family. My mom, Melody, my stepdad, Stefano. This is my brother, Phoenix, and my grandparents, Emilio and Vera."

Alex gives my mom and grandmother a kiss on their cheeks and then shakes each of the guys' hands. "It's a pleasure to meet all of you."

"Oh, you are American," my grandfather states when he hears Alex's American accent, even though he already knows as much. I've spoken to my family several times about Alex since we met in our Performing Arts class this semester when he transferred here to study abroad for his last year and a half of college.

"I am, sir," Alex says. "Italian-American. I came here to learn about my roots."

My grandfather gives him a nod of approval. "Will you be joining my granddaughter this summer?"

Alex gives me a confused look. I haven't told my family that I've decided to join Alex in the States instead of spending my entire summer at home like I usually do.

"Actually, I'm going to Chicago with Alex for the first half of the summer," I admit.

Nonno's lips turn down into a frown as I knew they would, but it's my mom's face I'm more concerned with. Her brows are knitted together, and her lips are pursed. I know I shouldn't have sprung this on her, but it was last-minute. I only found out a few days ago and felt it would be best to tell her in person. Aside from my one week with my father at the end of every summer, my vacations are always spent with my mom. She's my best friend, and moving to Florence to attend school was one of the hardest decisions I've had to make. Living three hours from her hasn't been easy.

"I'm sorry, *cara mia*, but that won't be possible," my mom says. "You've been summoned by your *father*." She spits out the title like it's a curse word. She doesn't talk about why she and my father divorced, but whatever happened, I know it was bad because even after all these years, she still refuses to see or talk about him.

"What? No!" I shake my head in confusion. "I always visit him the last week of the summer. You know this."

"Why am I just now hearing about this?" Nonno asks, his voice filled with concern.

"I only just found out last night," Mom explains. "Your brother will be taking you back with him."

"So, that's why you came?" I hiss, choosing to hide my hurt with anger. "Not to see my final performance, but to drag me back to Thessaloniki?"

"I came here to watch you," Phoenix says slowly, "but yes, I also came to escort you to Dad."

"I'm not going." My chin lifts in defiance and my arms cross over my chest. "I'll see him at the end of the summer like I do every year. Besides, I already purchased my plane ticket to Chicago."

"*Cara mia*, why don't we discuss this in private?" my mom suggests. Her tone hints she's trying to be polite in front of Alex, but the way she quirks one brow up tells me there will be no discussion.

Whether I like it or not, I will be going with Phoenix to visit our dad.

We go to dinner as planned, but the entire meal is filled with tension. Everyone is being polite, but there's a giant elephant in the room. When dessert is served—my favorite, crème brûlée—I finally address what nobody wants to talk about. "Why am I going to visit Dad now?"

"I'm not sure," Phoenix says. "I've only been told to bring you to him."

"And if I refuse to go?"

Phoenix hits me with a *don't make this difficult* glare. "You don't have a choice."

"Mom," I plead. She always has my back when it comes to my father. If anyone can keep me from having to go, it's her.

"I told you we would discuss this later," she says, taking a bite of her dessert.

"I have to take her from here," Phoenix says.

My mom's eyes widen. "Now? I thought we could return home first."

"We're flying out of Peretola," he states. "The plane leaves at seven o'clock."

"Maybe I can go first and then you can follow after," Alex suggests, ever the peacemaker.

When we met, I was arguing with another student about a performance we were working on. She felt I was being too dramatic for the character, and I felt I wasn't being dramatic enough. Alex walked over and played mediator—agreeing with her instead of me. Afterward, he introduced himself, to which I gave him the cold shoulder, upset he didn't agree with me. He laughed and told me he would never be anything but honest with me, and he's been a part of our group ever since. What started out as friendship eventually grew into more, and about two months ago, we made our relationship official. He's sweet and thoughtful and caring, and I can see a future with him.

"I wanted to go with you," I whine, annoyed that once again my father is messing up my plans. This is just so typical of him. He is such a mess, and it always spills over onto his family. Last summer I made plans to visit Cambridge with some friends. We set up our flights and made our hotel reservations, but because my father had issues with his business, he had to push my trip to visit him back, and I couldn't go to Cambridge.

"Go see your dad, and once you're done, we'll transfer your plane ticket over so you can fly from there to Chicago," Alex says. He reaches his hand under the table and squeezes mine gently.

"Can I do that?" I ask Phoenix.

"I don't see why not." He shrugs then glances at his watch. "We really need to get going, though."

"I haven't had time to pack."

"I've been told it will all be handled," Phoenix says.

"How long is the flight?" Alex asks.

"Five hours," I say, slumping into my seat, frustrated. I'm twenty-one years old. My dad shouldn't be able to dictate my life anymore. And if I were more of a bitch, I would put up a fight. But it's just not worth it to argue. Growing up, I've witnessed on more than one occasion the way he treats those who argue with him. The last thing I want is to get on his bad side. My father and I have a weird relationship. When I was younger, I was his little girl. His *sunshine*. But once my parents divorced, it was as if I was made to choose sides. And I chose my mom's. Ever since then, our relationship has become strained. He's changed so much over the years. He used to be a man I could go to with my problems, but over time, his own problems have taken over his life, leaving little to no room for me. I miss him and hate him and love him all at the same time.

"Call me as soon as you arrive." Alex presses a soft kiss to my lips. "The time will fly by and soon you will be in Chicago with me. I can't wait to show you around."

Everyone stands and exchanges hugs and kisses. Reluctantly, I go with Phoenix, while my mom and grandparents head back to Rome, and Alex heads back to his apartment to pack for Chicago.

The town car takes us to the airport, but where I expect us to be dropped off so we can check in and go through security, we're instead driven around the back and onto the tarmac.

The driver pulls up to a huge sleek silver plane. Across the tail reads Global 8000 with a large letter D across the side.

"We're flying on that?" I ask, confused. There's no way our father can afford a seat on this plane, let alone chartering it to pick me up.

"It was given to us on loan," Phoenix says, stepping out of the car and then taking my hand to help me out.

We are greeted by two pretty flight attendants who hand us each a glass flute filled with champagne and welcome us on board. The captain and co-captain also introduce themselves and let us know we'll be taking off shortly. As we walk through the plane, I am stunned by the extravagance and luxury that fills the inside. Gray leather seats line the entire left side with a large flat screen television hanging on the wall. The right side has several recliners with glossy mahogany tables separating them. If it weren't for the circular windows, I would think I was standing inside an expensive apartment.

"If you need to take a shower or wish to take a nap, there's a bedroom and full bathroom in the back," one of the attendants informs us, and my jaw drops. There's an entire bedroom on this plane?

"Phoenix," I hiss, pulling him to the side. "There's no way Dad can afford this."

"I already told you it's on loan." The way he says it sends a shiver racing down my spine.

"Nobody *loans* something like this for free! He couldn't even afford the home we grew up in anymore and had to sell it!" *Something is going on here...*

Just as Phoenix is about to say something, the captain comes over the intercom and asks that we have a seat and buckle in since we'll be taking off in five minutes. "The skies are clear, and the flight to Heraklion will be four hours and nine minutes."

"Heraklion?" I shriek. "Isn't that in...Crete?"

Phoenix sits on one of the leather couches and nods. "Yes, have a seat."

"No! I thought you were taking me to Thessaloniki. What the hell is going on?" My eyes find the door where we came from and see it's already shut.

"You can't leave," Phoenix says, reading my thoughts. "They're not going to open it now. We're about to take off. So, please, just sit."

"First tell me why we're going to Crete."

Phoenix sighs. "Dad is visiting with the Demetrious, a family he does business with. They own the ports Dad rents from. He's requested for us to come and join them."

I drop onto my seat with a huff. I can tell by the way Phoenix is answering my questions, he either doesn't know much or he's purposely being vague. Either way, it doesn't take a rocket scientist to know whatever is going on can't be good.

Once upon a time, my mom said our dad used to be successful, but greed got to him, and little by little he got in over his head. Every time I visit him, his homes get smaller. His clothes become more ragged. The restaurants we go to aren't as expensive. He's sold his yacht and no longer has a driver. Instead, he drives a cheap American car.

He always tells me it's just a minor setback and everything is going to be okay, but I've learned over the years, my dad is a pathological liar. I've begged him to get out of whatever he's in, but he won't. I don't know exactly what he does for a living, or what Phoenix does by his side, but

I've overheard my grandfather and mom talking enough to know whatever they're doing isn't exactly legal.

"You know this can't be good, right?"

Phoenix doesn't agree or disagree. "Why don't you take a nap in the bedroom? I imagine you've had a long day."

We arrive in Crete four hours later, and waiting for us is a black limo. I took Phoenix up on his suggestion and slept the entire flight, so now I'm wide awake. *Should be a fun, sleepless night…* The drive to wherever we're going takes about an hour. I text Alex to let him know I've arrived safely, and he texts back he'll call me once he's settled in Chicago.

Because it's almost midnight, everything is dark outside, making it hard to see. It's not until we pull up to a large wrought iron gate, which reads Pérasma Hotel & Villas, that I can finally make out what's around us. As the limo drives down the windy road, I take in my surroundings. Palm trees line each side of the road until we get to the front of the hotel. My God, it's gorgeous! The entire front is lit up with soft honey-colored lights. The split-level buildings are white and sleek with large picture windows. It's the perfect combination of chic and contemporary.

The driver opens my door and helps me out, and the first thing I smell is the salt water. We must be near the beach.

"It's late," Phoenix says, eyeing his phone. "I've been told there are rooms waiting for us, and we'll meet up with Dad in the morning."

"I don't have clothes," I remind him as we step up to the front desk.

"Good evening," a brown-haired petite woman says sweetly. "You must be Talia and Phoenix Nikolaides."

"We are," Phoenix says, hitting her with his best smile that always has women turning into disgusting piles of goo at his feet. My guess is within an hour she'll be in his room *personally* turning down his sheets. Gag!

"Great, we've been expecting you. Everything you will need, including clothes and toiletries, is in your rooms. If there is anything that isn't to your liking, please call the front desk and we will get it for you. Breakfast will be served at ten, and it will take place on the first floor in the banquet hall." She hands us each a card and explains how to get to our rooms. The way she holds on to Phoenix's card for an extra second doesn't go unnoticed. I seriously hope our rooms don't share a wall. If I have to listen to him screwing her all night, I will lose it.

As we walk down the wooden pathway she told us to take, my head moves from left to right, taking everything in. The hotel is literally sitting on the side of a cliff overlooking Mirabello Bay. I've seen this area in pictures but never in person. It's absolutely stunning.

As we continue to walk to our building, I notice the hotel is split into several areas—each having its own pool, restaurant, and pathway that looks to lead down to the water. I wonder if I'll have a chance to check it all out while I'm here. I'm not happy about being here, but if I'm going to be forced to be somewhere, at least I can enjoy the sights. While Thessaloniki is on the water, it's nothing like Crete. The water isn't as pretty as it is here, and the entire area smells like fish because of the ships bringing in loads from the sea.

We arrive at our building, and Phoenix tells me to get some sleep before heading into his room. Using my card, I place it over the black circle on the door and a lock clicks open. I enter the room and am almost knocked on my ass by the sheer luxury of my suite…no, not a suite, it's more like a home! The extravagant king-sized bed sits catty cornered with plush white sheets trimmed with gold and matching pillows fluffed on top. I open the large cherry wood armoire and spot several gorgeous dresses. The tags indicate they're all my size and expensive brands. I open a drawer and find various bras and panties, all with tags on them—again in my size. The next drawer contains silky pajamas in several different colors. The material glides through my fingertips.

I step into the bathroom and find a huge egg-shaped freestanding spa tub and a shower that could probably fit ten people inside. The walls, floors, and counters are all various shades of onyx, gray, and white marble.

Walking past the bed, I step up to the large window that makes up the entire west wall. It's too dark to see much of anything, but I can almost make out the water down below.

Sitting on the end of the bed, I lie backward onto the mattress and am swallowed up by the comfy down blanket. I've been raised in homes with wealth. When I was little, before my father began his descent, and then when my mom married Stefano, I grew up in expensive homes. Have been given all of the luxuries life has to offer. I attended one of the best private schools in Italy—my university tuition costs more than most make in ten years. But lying here in this bed, thinking about the plane I was brought here on, and glancing around at the furniture and décor and clothes that surround me, I realize I've never experienced this level of wealth.

None of this makes any sense. I've visited my father every summer for the past eleven years, and every time, his situation was worse. I expected to be taken to him in coach on a shitty plane and then driven in by cab to whatever apartment he's living in now.

Knowing there's no way I'll be able to fall asleep right away, I decide to go for a walk. I should probably tell Phoenix, but then he'll just tell me no or insist on tagging along. Plus, he's probably already getting it on with that woman from the front desk.

After changing into a pair of shorts and a flowy top, I grab my phone and room key and put them in my back pocket. I take the wooden path down a little ways until I come to a bridge that forks. Under the bridge is flowing water and what appears to be different kinds of fish. I go left and it leads me to a courtyard that's filled with beautiful outdoor daybeds with plush mattresses and pillows. I walk a little farther and find several mocha-colored wicker sectionals in the shape of half-moons. I imagine during the day people come out here and lounge out, reading a good book or even taking a peaceful afternoon nap.

I'm about to sit on one of the sectionals when I notice the exquisite stone fountain in the center of the courtyard. "Bernini's *Rape of Proserpina*," I say out loud.

"You know your art," a masculine voice says.

I turn to find a gorgeous man standing in front of me. He's dressed in a pair of khaki shorts and a white button-down shirt, his sleeves rolled to his elbows, exposing a hint of tattoos. It's hard to tell in the dark, but his hair appears to be a dark shade of brown. At one point it looks like it was gelled neatly, but now it's messy as if he's been running his fingers through it. He's sporting a pair of brown leather Sperry boat shoes. He's the perfect mix of casual meets elegance.

"It's a rather controversial piece," I tell him. It would be hard to major in art and not know about a piece like this. One of my favorite classes I've taken was Classical mythology.

"Some say controversial, some say exquisite." He shrugs, taking a step forward.

"If you can call rape exquisite."

Stepping closer, the gentleman flashes me a brief wicked grin, and I'm able to get a better look at him. His hair is in fact the color of creamy hot chocolate on a cold day. His eyes are a beautiful shade of hazel, but they're hard. Unforgiving. One side of his mouth is quirked up into a smirk I imagine has women falling at his feet. Hell, it almost has me falling. *Almost.*

"That's one way of looking at it."

"That's the only way," I argue.

The gentleman raises his hand to his face and strokes his stubbled chin. "The scene screams of passion, frenzy, a mixture of tenderness and harshness. It's the climax of the moment. They're teetering between hate and love." Hmm…so he believes *that* version of the story.

"She's trying to get away. She's pushing at his face, begging him to let her go."

"Or maybe she's just scared."

"Exactly," I say, now confused. Wasn't he just disagreeing with me?

"Scared of wanting him," he clarifies. "Scared of what she might feel. She wants to hate him, but she still *wants* him. What's that saying?" He tilts his head to the side slightly and smirks. The simple gesture makes him appear even more handsome. "There's a thin line between love and hate."

"How cliché." I roll my eyes, annoyed that he's trying to turn a serious work of art into an erotic sexual experience. "There's nothing passionate about this piece. It's about a god kidnapping a woman and forcing her to be his wife."

The gentleman barks out a harsh laugh. "If she didn't want to remain with him, she wouldn't have eaten those seeds." He steps another few feet toward me, until he's so close I can smell his cologne. It's fresh and masculine with a hint of danger. My heartbeat becomes erratic, suddenly remembering I'm on this island and standing here with a man I don't know in the dark of the night.

"Have you ever been in love?" he asks without giving me a chance to respond to his last statement.

His question throws me off for a second, but then I nod, thinking of Alex. We haven't exchanged the words, but I believe I'm falling in love with him.

"And this person you've loved, have you ever been mad at him? Hated him?"

My eyes lock with his, and I imagine I give him a look of confusion because he doesn't wait for my answer but instead continues to speak.

"Hate and love are shared passions. They pull you in and take over your body, your heart, your mind. They are both powerful emotions. It's why some say the best kind of sex is hate sex and the next is make-up sex." He smirks darkly, and my stomach knots. "The first is two people who've built up anger festering inside of them, which turns into passion and arousal. The second is two people who are still mad at each other but are trying to forgive one another. The anger still runs through their veins, but the love and forgiveness is slowly seeping in."

He nods toward the statue. "That is the perfect depiction of hate and love mixing."

I hear what he's saying, but I can't imagine having sex with someone I hate and enjoying it. That's why it's called making love. You're supposed to be with the person you love.

"Have you ever been in love?" I ask, turning his question around on him.

"No," he states matter-of-factly. "But I've had plenty of hate sex."

I turn my eyes back to the statue, but I can't see what he's saying. The man is forcing her into his clutch, while she's pushing him away. I just can't imagine at any point she would enjoy being with him.

"If you've never been in love then how do you know how it feels? How can you compare love to hate?"

"I've witnessed it firsthand. Read about it. You don't have to be in love to recognize what it looks like. To understand it."

He makes a valid point, but I still don't agree with his analysis. "I guess we'll have to agree to disagree." I shrug noncommittedly. "It's late, and I have an early morning, so I better get back to my room."

"I never got your name," the gentleman says.

"No, you didn't."

His shoulders shake up and down in silent laughter, but he doesn't say anything else. I turn and walk back toward my room, unable to get what he said about the sculpture off my mind. Just before I get back to the building where my room is, I decide to take a detour. This hotel is like nothing I've ever experienced, and I'm curious if there are any other statues or décor like the one in the courtyard.

I take a left and head down a wooden walkway. A few people are walking in various directions. A couple holding hands. A group of people laughing and talking. As I continue in my direction, I hear the light thumping of bass. I follow it until I get to a well-lit area. There's a pool and wet bar, where at least a dozen people are lounging around. Some are swimming, and others are sitting along the edge of the pool. A few people are sitting on the stools in the water at the bar, having a drink.

Opening the gate, I step inside and head to the back of the bar, the one on land and not in the pool, to grab a drink. Maybe it will help me wind down and get some sleep.

"What can I get you to drink?" the bartender asks, and it's then I remember I don't have any money on me since I left my purse in my room.

"I didn't bring any money. Is there any way you can charge it to my room?"

"I got this," a gentleman says. He gets off the stool and walks around behind the bar. The first thing I notice is he's shirtless and has several intricate tattoos along his chest. My eyes glide down to his perfectly sculpted abs, but I can't see any farther because of the bar being in the way.

When my eyes ascend and meet his, I notice they're a dark brown and match his hair. Both the color of espresso. *What's up with these sexy men on this island?* Unlike the guy I spoke to about the statue, this guy's smile is less deviant and more playful. His eyes, even though the color is dark, don't *scream* dangerous, but instead scream light and laughter. Quite the contradiction.

"What's your poison?" he asks, holding up a bottle of alcohol in each hand.

"White wine, please."

He tilts his head to the side, reminding me of the gentleman from earlier, and groans. "Bo-ring."

A giggle escapes my lips, and I shrug, sitting on the stool he just got up from. "I know, but it's been a long day and I'm hoping to get some sleep soon."

He grabs a wine glass and pours me a drink. When I take a sip, I notice it's light and fruity. "This is delicious."

"Santorini. It's the best."

I take another sip and have to agree.

"So, what brings you to Pérasma?" he asks, popping a cap on a beer and taking a long gulp.

"My father…he's *summoned* me," I say, trying, and failing, to withhold the annoyance in my tone.

The gentleman's brows rise, but he doesn't say anything, so I continue.

"I have no clue how he can even afford to stay here, but I guess I'm going to enjoy it while I can, since I have no choice."

I take a long sip of my wine and enjoy the coolness as it descends down my throat.

"And you?" I ask in return. "Do you work here?" He must be in close with the place to be allowed to get behind the bar and serve me.

"Something like that." He winks playfully then pours some more wine into my glass. "I was just about to go for a swim. Would you like to join me?"

I glance down at my outfit. "I don't have a suit." A yawn escapes me, and I cover my mouth with a giggle. Clearly, the wine is already doing what I was hoping it would do. "And I have an early morning," I say, repeating the same thing I told the other gentleman a little while ago. "Some breakfast with my dad and brother."

Standing from my stool, I down the rest of the wine in the glass. "Can you charge the wine to my room? I'm in four-nineteen."

His eyes widen a fraction, and then he grins. "It's on the house."

"Oh, okay. Thank you. Maybe I'll see you again during my stay…"

"Maybe."

I wake to the sound of knocking on my door. I glance at my phone and it reads nine thirty. And then it hits me, we're supposed to meet for breakfast at ten. Shit! I overslept. When I got back to my room last night, the wine knocked me out and I never set my alarm.

"Coming!" I yell. I swing the door open and Phoenix is standing there in a black three-piece suit.

"Wow, look at you. I thought we were just meeting Dad for breakfast." I step back so he can enter.

"It's more of a business meeting. We're meeting with the Demetrious. I told you about them yesterday." He's right. He did. I just forgot. "They own this hotel…well, really this island. Go get ready," he instructs. "They don't do well with tardiness."

"Since when do I attend business meetings?" I ask, snagging a simple floral dress from the armoire. Then I pull the drawer open and grab a matching set of white lace bra and panties.

"Since now, I guess. Go. Shower."

After taking a quick shower and blow-drying my hair just enough so it's not soaking wet but hanging in loose waves, I get dressed. I find various pairs of shoes in the closet, from heels to flip-flops, and decide on a cute pair of wedges.

"Ready?" Phoenix asks from the living room. "It's two minutes till ten."

"Yes, sorry!" I grab my phone off the nightstand but realize I don't have anywhere to put it, so I grab my purse, stuffing my phone and room key in it.

"Let's go."

We walk down the long pathway, back toward the courtyard. As we pass the statue from last night, I think back to my conversation—more like debate—with the gentleman. How he can see anything other than a woman scared and trying to escape a man who is kidnapping her is just crazy. Passion doesn't stem from anger. It stems from love. I can't imagine having sex with someone I don't love, let alone with someone I hate. While the majority of my friends enjoy hooking up, I've never seen the appeal. Sex should be intimate with the person you love and trust and want to spend your life with. It shouldn't be casual, and it definitely shouldn't be done out of anger.

We enter the building and there's a hostess waiting at the door. "Good morning, Mr. and Miss Nikolaides. Everyone is already inside."

I'm taken aback for a moment that she already knows who we are. "Thank you," Phoenix says.

We walk past the hostess stand and enter the dining room, and standing around the table are several men. The first one I spot is my dad, dressed in a suit similar to Phoenix's. My initial thought is maybe, for the first time, he's actually gotten himself together. But then his eyes meet mine, and I see the stress and nervousness in them, telling me nothing has changed.

He cuts across the room and pulls me into a tight hug. "My sunshine," he murmurs, and my heartstrings tug at the nickname he gave me when I was little. He used to tell me I was the light in his darkness. "I'm so sorry. Please forgive me. Please," he begs.

"What?" I ask, confused. "Forgive you for what?" What's going on here? Why is he begging me to forgive him? "Dad, what did you do?"

I pull out of his embrace and glance around the room. I'm shocked by what—or I guess, I should say *who*—I see. The gentleman from last night. The man I argued with over the statue. He's standing there, no longer dressed casual, but in a suit. Unlike the suits my brother and dad are wearing, which give off a formal vibe like one would wear to a dinner party, this man's screams power and wealth. His hair is gelled perfectly in place, and his eyes… How can eyes so light appear so dark? His jaw is ticking as he stares back at me, as if the simple fact of me existing offends him.

"And so we meet again," another voice says, tearing me away from the scary gentleman. *The man from the bar.* He, too, is dressed to the nines, but even in a suit, he appears playful and happy. It's almost hard to take him seriously.

"Dad, what's going on?"

chapter three

Kostas

I DART MY HARD GAZE TO MY FATHER, WHO REFUSES TO LOOK MY way. His entire focus is on Niles and the woman. A satisfied smirk plays on his lips. I want to drag my father out of the room and demand answers. What the hell kind of beef does he have with Niles that he'd rope the man's family into this as well?

Aris's brown eyes meet mine, questions dancing in them. As though I have the answers. I don't think Father would convince Niles to bring his family here just to kill them, but this whole thing feels out of my depth. At this point, I'm not sure what my father is capable of.

Killing people is a dirty necessity.

Killing people who've fucked you over is imperative.

Niles and his son, Phoenix, by default since he's his right-hand man, have stolen from the most powerful family in Greece. They need to pay. They *will* pay.

But the woman?

Glittering blue eyes. Sexy, wavy blond hair. Poutiest fucking lips I've ever seen on a woman. Full, perfect tits that strain against the fabric of her dress. Tan legs for goddamn miles. I'm not certain if she's his daughter, but they look similar enough to draw that conclusion. She's a spitting image of Phoenix. I want to know why Niles would willingly bring her here.

"Niles," my father booms, a wicked smile turning his lips up. "Please don't be rude. Introduce us to this beauty."

The beauty in question purses her full lips together and her cheeks blaze crimson.

"This, Ezio, is my darling daughter, Talia." Niles's features are tight, but he smiles anyway. "Talia, this is Ezio Demetriou. He owns this hotel."

We own everything, motherfucker.

"And," Niles continues, "these are Ezio's sons Aris and Kostas." He flicks his wrist at me like someone might swat at a fly trying to land on his fucking ice cream. It makes me want to break his goddamn hand.

It's then that her blue eyes lock with mine, flickering with emotion as though they glow. She's pissed. Confused. Upset. Hell, I would be too if Niles Nikolaides were my father. Last night, I'd been taken by the blond goddess who seemingly appeared out of nowhere, surprising me with her knowledge of the sculpture. Sassing me—Kostas Demetriou—over the meaning of the art. For a few short minutes, I'd enjoyed a rare moment of pleasure in my cold, hard life.

Clearly, the time for pleasure has come and gone.

Now, I'm staring back at the daughter of my father's mortal enemy.

And Niles has brought her here to bargain with.

When Aris leans in to say something to her, her stiff posture relaxes slightly. Irritation coils in the pit of my stomach like a snake. If it were up to Aris, he'd gladly sleep with the enemy, as long as it was fun. Everything's all about the fucking fun with him. Unfortunately for him, Father has his own agenda, and allowing Aris to bang the woman isn't a part of that plan.

"Please," Father says. "Sit."

My father takes a seat at one end of the table and I take the other. Niles sits to my father's left and Phoenix takes the seat beside him at my right. Aris escorts Talia with his hand on the small of her back to the seat beside me on my left. Once she's seated, he sits next to her. I can feel her staring at me, her anger at the situation projected my way, but I disregard her with my usual cool aloofness. I glower directly at my father, demanding an explanation.

It's what we do—speak without speaking. I've observed my father for so long that we can do it without even trying. We're an incredible team because of it too.

So why the fuck is he avoiding eye contact?

But I know that answer. He's got an ace up his sleeve for the hand he's holding. My father intends to win this game, and I'm stuck with a handful of cards in a game I didn't know I was playing. Last night, he bailed before I had a chance to corner him. He left me to pace around the hotel, lost in my brooding thoughts. After breakfast, we're going to have a good long conversation about whatever the fuck is happening right now.

I cut my eyes to the left when the servers start placing plates of breakfast down in front of everyone. Even the savory scent of bacon can't distract me from staring at her. Her cheeks are still pink and a strand of golden-blond hair hides her eyes from me as she focuses her attention on her plate. She reaches for a glass of ice water, a slight tremble in her hand. Poor thing is nervous as fuck.

With good reason, too.

Niles is a weak piece of shit who's brought her willingly into a den of wolves.

But why is she here?

As though clued into my thoughts, Father clears his throat, demanding everyone's attention. His eyes are hard as he stares straight at me. Eyes that usually communicate with me are closed off from any sort of negotiation. Whatever he says will be law in his eyes.

Don't kill her.

I don't know where the thought comes from, but it's there. She's too innocent to be in our world. I knew that last night when she breathlessly tried to hold her own in a conversation with me. I would destroy a woman like her in bed. For one moment, I considered pursuing her when she left. Fuck, how I wanted to. But even a monster has limits. Monsters aren't monsters all the time. Sometimes we're just hungry men who make decisions with our dicks. For her sake, I decided wisely. I let her walk away, much to my dick's disappointment, only for her father to bring her right back to me.

Foolish motherfucker.

"As you all can see, we're here for more than just pleasure," my father says slowly, taking his sweet ass time. "We also have some business to attend to." He stares pointedly at Talia before shooting Niles a smug grin. "Niles, I understand she's unaware of why she's here?"

Niles squirms, which makes my father's grin grow wider.

"Dad," Talia utters, a mixture of fury and hurt in her one word.

I clench my fist, wishing Father would have just let me kill the asshole last night. Could have avoided all this shit.

"Sunshine," Niles says, his voice weak and whiny. "I'm sorry. If there were any other way…"

Phoenix, from beside Niles, glowers at my father. Aris simply watches the entire ordeal with amusement. I want to know why the fuck my father would clue Niles in on business while leaving me in the dark. Whatever bullshit is going on will be the last. I won't sit idly while stuff is flung my way without any warning. My father is going to get the bitch-out of a lifetime once this breakfast is over.

"Talia, darling," my father croons. "Your father and I go way back." His jaw clenches and darkness shrouds his expression before he smiles it away. "And we've come to an agreement."

"What sort of agreement?" Talia breathes. Her hand trembles when she reaches for her water again.

"You are to marry my son," Father states with a devious glint in his eyes.

Her head turns sharply to regard Aris, who's frowning in confusion. Meanwhile, I'm about to explode with fucking rage. *If only it were that easy, Talia.*

"My eldest," Father corrects, searing his hard eyes into mine, daring me to argue.

Even as the volcano within me spills with fury, I don't speak a word against my father. Never. Not in front of weak, worthless pieces of shit like Niles Nikolaides.

Talia's head jerks my way so fast, I'm worried she'll give herself whiplash. Her blue eyes glow with accusation—as though I knew this all along. I meet her glare with one of my own. A glare filled with contempt for the Nikolaides name. She withers beneath my fierce stare.

"An arranged marriage," I state in a bored way. "Lovely. Can someone pass me the pepper before my eggs get cold?"

Phoenix grabs the pepper shaker and slams it on the table in front of me, making everyone's glasses slosh. "What the hell are you thinking, Dad?" he demands in a furious tone. "Talia? You negotiated Talia?"

My father's smile is victorious.

I want to ram my fist right into his face.

How dare he do this to me without warning?

"I fucked up," Niles admits. "I thought I could pay them back in time."

Father picks up his fork and begins stabbing at the eggs on his plate, clearly overjoyed at my emotionless response to the bomb he just dropped in my lap.

"Four point six million," Aris states, unusual anger tightening his voice. "Is that what your daughter is worth to you? A few million euros?"

"She's worth everything to me." Niles shoots his daughter a pleading look. She won't look at him. She won't speak. She's taken to wringing her hands in her lap, her bottom lip slightly wobbling.

"I have a life," she utters so softly, I almost think it's meant just for me. "I can't just leave to marry some stranger because my father is a bad businessman."

"You have to," Niles says, hanging his head in shame. "They'll kill me if you don't."

Once again, she glowers at me. As though all of this is my fault. It pisses me off.

"You'd kill my father if I don't marry you?" she hisses, anger making her face turn red again.

"I'll kill your father if he doesn't pay," I bite out in a cold tone. "And since he put a four-point-six-million-dollar price tag around your pretty neck, it looks like I'm getting my payment in full."

She stands abruptly from the table. Furious tears well in her blue eyes, reminding me of the blue waters of the Aegean Sea. "Fuck you all," she snaps. "I'm not marrying anyone. I'm going home."

As soon as she rushes from the table, Phoenix bolts after her. I give a slight nod to Basil and Adrian. They follow after them. My *fiancée* isn't going anywhere. The sooner she realizes this, the better.

"Really, Dad?" Aris mutters, the muscle in his neck flexing. "A girl as payment? That's a new low."

Father's nostrils flare at his blatant disrespect. I flick my chin up at Aris, silently telling him to leave before he fucks things up. With a grumble, he loudly scrapes his chair back and storms off.

"Please don't hurt her," Niles pleads. "Promise me."

I have to refrain from rolling my eyes. Since when do worms negotiate with sharks? Fucking never.

"I'll promise nothing of the sort," I tell him sharply. "Say your goodbyes to her. I want you and your son off Crete and heading back to Thessaloniki by noon."

"Kostas," he croaks. "Please."

Ignoring his pleas, I grab the small bottle of jam and begin smearing some all over my toast with a knife that would go to better use cutting this motherfucker's throat.

"Kostas," he says once more.

"Noon, Niles. I suggest you not waste another moment with your *sunshine*. Your world is about to get really fucking dark."

I'm waiting inside my office that overlooks the bay when Father decides to grace me with his presence. He walks in, his features impassive. It's a much different look than from earlier where he was almost gleeful. Rather than sitting across from me, he walks over to the open door to the veranda.

"You know everything I do is for a reason, *agóri mou*." *My boy*. Not anymore. I've long grown into a man—a business partner. Someone worthy of being told about a plan before it's enacted, not after. To say I feel betrayed is an understatement.

"Of course, *Patéras*."

He turns to regard me, a wistful smile on his face. If he wants to play a game of calling me his boy like he did when I was six or seven, then I will take to calling him Father in the same way I would at that age.

"She is beautiful," he mutters. "At least you have that."

"At least."

He lets out a heavy sigh. "I didn't do this to anger you, Kostas."

No, this was all about his beef with Niles.

"Then what was it about?" I demand, my voice cracking, a clear indicator of how pissed I am.

"Niles owes me in ways you'll never understand," he practically growls. "Giving up his daughter to my son is—"

"Much more difficult than just killing him," I grit out. "Why not kill him and be done with it? Why drag his family into it?"

Father shrugs and steps out onto the veranda, silently indicating he wants me to continue the conversation out there. With a frustrated sigh, I rise from my leather desk chair and stalk after him. He leans over the railing, staring out onto the sparkly bay that's dotted with sailboats.

"It's too easy," he tells me with a shrug. "Niles deserves to pay in every way he can."

"But why?"

Rather than answering, he remains seemingly lost in thought. I'm growing bored of this nostalgic power games shit he seems to be playing.

"Do I really need to marry her?" I ask in an exasperated tone. "For how long? When will this be over and I can go back to the way things were?"

Father turns my way, his features dark with hate. "I don't mean for you to think of this as a punishment, Kostas. She'll be a wife in name only. Keep whores on the side if you wish."

My lip curls up at his words. He says that as though he truly believes that. If I've learned anything from my father, it's that loyalty is everything. His marriage to my mother is solid and unbreakable, bordering on obsession. If Ezio Demetriou can keep his dick in one woman for nearly four decades, then so can I.

"Until when?" I ask, ignoring his words.

"As long as it takes to satisfy me."

Selfish fucking bastard.

I'm used to him treating everyone, even Aris, this way, but not me. It's a brutal blow that I'm at a loss for how to get over.

"Don't look at me as though I've killed your puppy," Father snaps. "She's one woman. A beautiful woman you'll no doubt enjoy every second with once you break her in. Hell, give me some grandkids for all I care. But I need this transaction to take place. I want to destroy Niles."

"Why?" I bark out. "Why do you hate that weasel bastard so much? I get it, he's fucking weak. But why? You've always been straight with me."

Father shakes his head. "Every man has secrets he holds onto. My hate for Niles is one of those. Just trust in my judgment. Do what you have to do when it comes to Talia, but make sure you dangle her in Niles's face whenever you can. Don't let her charm her way off this island. You'll marry her, and I'll continue to torment her father in every way I see fit. Are we clear?"

"Absolutely," I growl, fisting my hands, barely keeping my anger in check. "Perhaps you should go home, Father. I have important matters to deal with."

"You'll understand one day, Kostas."

Unlikely.

"Of course, Father."

He sighs and exits the veranda, slamming the office door closed on his way out. I look up and watch a plane jet across the bright, cloudless sky. After a few moments, I make my way back inside and place a call to a Greek jeweler. My beloved fiancée will need an engagement ring.

Jesus Christ, I could kill my father over this shit.

A sinister part of me, though, takes silent pleasure in the fact I'll soon own the gorgeous, innocent blond. She may be a Nikolaides, but soon she'll be a Demetriou. I have a feral need to chase this woman much like Pluto did with Proserpina, so I may pin her down, shove her pretty dress up her thighs, and sink my cock into her warm depths. I love when life imitates art.

A monster wouldn't be a true monster if he didn't hungrily sink his teeth into the offering he's been given by the lesser mortals. And, fuck, do I ever want to sink my teeth into her.

Talia.

Sweet Talia.

You'll learn to like it rough.

Proserpina sure did.

chapter four

Talia

THIS HAS GOT TO BE A GODDAMN DREAM…NO, A NIGHTMARE. THIS can't be real. There's no way anything that was said during that bullshit breakfast can possibly hold any merit. We no longer live in the eighteenth century, for crying out loud! One cannot simply tell someone *who* she is to marry. We have rights!

A manic laugh escapes my lips as I remember my conversation with Kostas last night. Oh, the irony, that not even twelve hours ago we were debating over *The Rape of Proserpina*, and now here we are in a similar situation. My father giving his consent for me to marry a man who is apparently hell-bent on kidnapping me and forcing me into some underworld! I might not know everything that goes on in my father's business, but I've overheard enough over the years to know the men he does business with are part of some illegal crime organization. And my father is literally handing me over to them on a silver platter! As if I'm available for the taking. And to save his own ass. It's one thing for him to get himself into trouble, but now he's involving me in his mess.

Grabbing my phone off the nightstand, I consider calling Alex but stop myself. As much as I want to hear his voice and seek comfort in his words, how do I explain to him the ridiculousness of the situation I've found myself in? What would I even say? *Hey, Alex! I have a slight problem. My father screwed over some crime boss and has handed me over as payment.*

Ugh! No, there's only one person to call. I pull Mom's name up on my contact list, but just as I'm about to hit call, there's a knock on my door.

Without even bothering to look, I swing the door open and find Dad and Phoenix standing on the other side. My father at least has the decency to look upset. Phoenix looks pissed, which tells me he didn't know any of this was going down.

"What do you want?" I hiss.

"Can I please come in, sunshine?" Dad begs. He takes a step forward, without waiting for me to answer, and I block the entrance.

"No, you can't," I tell him, clenching my fists at my sides. I am not a violent person, but right now, I'm desperately trying to keep from pummeling my father to the ground. And judging by the way Phoenix's jaw is clenching, I bet he'd hold him down for me.

"Please, I'm so sorry," Dad says. "If you would just let me in, I will explain."

"What the hell is there to explain?" I seethe, my tone dropping low as venom drips from it. "You sold your own flesh and blood to pay off a debt!"

Dad's back goes straight. "Don't you speak to me like that. I am sorry for what's happened, but I'm still your father. You will speak to me with respect."

"Respect?" I yell, fury bubbling up inside of me like a volcano preparing to erupt. "Fuck you and your respect!"

Before I see it coming, Dad raises his hand and slaps me across my cheek. My face whips to the side from the sheer force behind his slap. Instinctively, my hand comes up and rubs the sore spot.

"Dad! What the hell!" Phoenix roars. He shoves our dad up against the wall and gets in his face. "You did this shit! You lied about how much you owed and how bad it was. You don't get to demand respect, and you sure as fuck don't get to lay a goddamn hand on her." Phoenix cocks his fist back and punches Dad square in the jaw. Blood spurts from Dad's lip, and he folds himself over in pain.

"I'm sorry," he cries. "I'm sorry!" He glances up at me and wipes the blood off his chin. "Please forgive me, sunshine. You are everything to me."

Everything?

He thinks I'm *everything*?

Apparently so since he sold me.

Well, *Dad*, I hope it was worth it. I hope you can buy a new yacht or a bigger home or whatever it is you chose over your own daughter.

"I am nothing to you," I say, my tone flat, defeated. There's no denying his betrayal runs deep. "And you are nothing to me."

I turn to Phoenix, not giving *that man* another glance. "Is there any way of me getting out of this?"

Phoenix's eyes gloss over, and I already know my answer. He bridges the gap between us and pulls me into his arms. "I'm going to do everything I can to try to figure this out. I promise you. I won't stop until they let you come home."

I nod into his chest. "Thank you," I whisper, my voice overcome with emotion.

When he pulls back, he gives me a sad smile. "I love you. Be strong."

"Sunshine, please," Dad begs again.

"Take him away," I tell Phoenix. "I never want to see him again."

Phoenix nods in understanding, then grabbing Niles by his arm, pulls him down the pathway and out of my life.

Closing the door behind me, I press my back against the hard wood and take several deep breaths, needing to calm myself. My face falls into my hands, and my cheek throbs, reminding me I was just hit. I walk into the bathroom where the mirror is and check it out. My cheek is bright pink but doesn't show any signs of bruising.

With my heart thundering inside my chest like a war drum and my head pounding to the beat, I head back to the main room, needing to call the one person who's always had my back. My mom.

She answers on the first ring. "*Cara mia*! How are you? I've been waiting for your call."

The sound of her voice has me falling onto my bed in tears. "Mom," I sob uncontrollably, all of the built up adrenaline hitting me hard. "I need your help. I need you to come get me."

By the time I finish telling her all that's happened, and the little I know, she's crying as well. "I'm going to call your grandfather. He'll know what to do."

"Please hurry, Mom," I beg.

I hang up the phone and curl into a ball on the bed, hugging the soft pillows. I'm not sure how long I cry for, but when there's a knock on the door, my head is pounding, and my eyes are burning from the little bit of mascara I put on that's now running.

Thinking it's Phoenix coming back to check on me, I swing the door open, only to find it's Aris, Kostas's brother, the playful flirt I met at the bar last night. I shoot him a glare, and he flinches. Good!

"What the hell do you want?"

Aris raises his hands in mock surrender. "I didn't know."

"So, you're telling me when we were talking, you had no idea who I was?" I tilt my head to the side and throw a hand on my hip. "You didn't know I was my father's daughter?"

"At first, no, but once we started talking, I put two and two together…"

I grab the edge of the door, about to slam it in his face, when he slides his foot in the doorway to prevent it from closing. His eyes land on my cheek, and he steps closer, widening the door.

"Who did this to you?" His fingers come up to touch my face, but I take a step back. "Who did this to you?" he repeats.

"My—Niles," I say, refusing to ever refer to him as my dad again.

Aris's jaw ticks. "He's lucky he already got on that plane."

"He may have physically hurt me, but what you guys are doing is even worse."

Aris flinches at my words, as though I've slapped him like my father slapped me. His eyes plead with me to understand. Understand what? That he's not the same monster as they are? But when his gaze softens, I find my heart does too.

"I didn't know what my father and Kostas were planning," he utters in a tone that begs for me to understand. "I swear. I only came by to see if you're okay."

I assess his features in an attempt to get a read on him, and for some reason, I believe him. His brows are furrowed in worry, and his lips are pursed in a concerned frown. I think back to earlier, during breakfast. When Ezio announced I was to marry his son, I had assumed he meant Aris. When I looked over at him, he genuinely looked as confused and shocked as I did. And then when his father clarified it would be his eldest son I would be marrying, Aris looked almost…angry.

"I'm not marrying your brother," I state. "So, if you're here to try to talk me into going along with this craziness, you can leave now."

"That's not why I'm here. I told you…I came by to see if you're okay. Why don't we walk down to the bar and get a drink?"

Figuring it's probably better to have Aris as an ally than an enemy, I nod once. "Let me grab my phone." I need to make sure I'm available when my mom calls back.

After grabbing my phone, I take a quick detour back into the bathroom to clean up my face and hair, so I don't look like a hot mess. Then I slip on my wedges and grab my purse. It's probably best if I bring it everywhere with me in case I need to run at any moment. It's all I came with, and it holds everything I have. A little bit of cash, my credit cards, my license, and my passport. *My passport!* Why didn't I think about that before? It won't be easy, but at least I know I have a backup plan.

"You ready?" Aris asks.

"Yep."

In the light of the day, the hotel is even more gorgeous. It was exquisite last night, but with the sun shining, I'm able to see every detail of the place. The pool is kidney-shaped, with a bar on one end and a beautiful rock waterfall on the other. Several people are already swimming in the pool and lying out in the loungers with drinks in their hands.

"Wine?" Aris asks, lifting the bottle from last night.

I shake my head. I need to keep a clear head.

"Just a lemonade if you have it. If not, water."

He pours my drink then pops a top on a beer for himself. We take our drinks over to two empty loungers that are under an umbrella and have a seat.

"You're from Italy, right?" he asks after a few minutes of silence.

"Yes, Rome, but I go to school in Florence at the Florence Art Institute." And then it hits me. If somehow Kostas and his dad get their way, will I be allowed to go back to school in the fall? Or will he force me to stay here with him? Away from my mom, my family, my life.

"What's wrong?" Aris asks.

"I was just thinking about school. I'm supposed to be starting my senior year. I hope this all gets sorted out before then."

"Talia, I don't think you understand—"

His words are cut off by the sound of my phone ringing. "I need to take this," I say before I answer the call. "Mom."

"No, Talia, it's your grandfather."

"Nonno!" A sob escapes my lips. "Please tell me I can go home."

There's a deafening silence on the other line that causes my body to grow cold with fear. "Nonno," I repeat.

"Talia, you need to listen to me," he says, his tone unlike anything I've ever heard. It's flat and cold, devoid of all emotion. "Your father made some terrible choices, and because of that, the Demetrious have decided the way for him to pay is through you. I've spoken to Ezio, and the decision has been made. You will marry his eldest son, Kostas, and become his wife."

"No!" With a shaky hand, I set my drink on the table next to me. "Please, Nonno, I can't marry him. I have a life. A boyfriend. I have my senior year! I didn't agree to this." Another wave of fury spreads through my veins like wildfire. How dare my father—No! Niles! How dare Niles use me to pay his debt! He's a selfish bastard! "I'm not marrying him," I tell my grandfather. "I don't care if they kill Niles." My eyes swing over to Aris, who is staring at me with pity in his eyes.

"You don't have a choice," my grandfather says so nonchalantly one would think he was discussing the weather and not the fate of my future. "The decision is final."

At his words, I nearly drop my phone. My hands are trembling with fury, and I have to clasp the device tightly. "Ezio told me if I don't marry Kostas, Niles will die. Well, fuck him! He did this to himself. Let. Him. Rot." Without thinking about where I am or what I'm doing, I lean forward and swipe the glass off the table. It smashes against the ground, shards of glass flying in every direction. It's not enough to tame the rage rolling through me, but it helps tamper it down a notch.

"Talia," Nonno snaps. "Do not take up that language with me. I understand you are upset, and you have every right to be. But you will not speak to me with such disrespect."

Seriously? All of these men want to jerk me around and dictate my life, then demand respect? Respect is earned. And as far as I'm concerned, they've all lost mine.

"Now, you will listen to me," my grandfather continues. "The Demetrious family is not one you go against. The only way to get out of this would be death…for you. They've already decided, and once they make a decision, it's law."

My body falls back onto the lounge chair. My shoulders sag, and my head lulls forward in defeat. "So, that's it then? My life is being taken from

me? I'm being kidnapped against my will and being forced to marry that…
that man." I can't think of anything to call him at the moment that would
be fitting. "I would rather die," I cry out.

"Oh, Talia, don't be dramatic."

"Dramatic?" I pop my head back up. "Dramatic? You aren't the one
stuck on this island with complete strangers. What about my school? And
my friends? What about Alex? My apartment?"

"Your life will be wherever Kostas decides. I'm sorry, Talia. I tried to
speak to them, but they made it clear this marriage will happen."

A gut-wrenching sob tears through my chest. Complete hopelessness
converts into tears that rain down my cheeks at lightning speed. If I don't
find a way out, I'm going to be sentenced to a life underground, just like
Proserpina. But unlike her—who at least was stuck with Pluto, who in
some versions of the story appeared to be a decent husband, despite beginning their marriage in such a horrible way—I'm being taken by Kostas.
The man who found dark humor in Proserpina's rape. The man who tried
to argue that she enjoyed it. That the statue screamed passion.

I'm once again overcome with rage as the realization strikes that I have
no one I can count on but myself. My own father was the one to hand me
over. The rest of my family has their hands tied behind their backs. The
only chance I have at getting out of this is me. I need to formulate a plan.
And to do that I need to be alone.

When I stand, ready to flee back to my room, Aris says my name.

"Are you okay?" he asks, worry dripping in his words.

"No," I tell him honestly, "but I will be."

"I'm really sorry your grandfather wasn't able to get you out of this
mess." Even though it's his family who is causing all of this to happen, I
feel like, to an extent, he might genuinely mean that.

"It's not your fault. Thank you for being so kind to me." I kneel to pick
up the pieces of glass, but Aris stops me.

"Someone will clean that up. Would you like to go for a walk? The
bay is beautiful at this time."

"Raincheck?" I ask, even though I don't plan to be here for him to
collect. I don't care how I have to do it, I will be getting the hell off this island. "I think I need some time to myself."

"Sure." His lips curl into a soft smile. "Let me see your phone."

I hold it closer to my chest. If he takes my phone from me, it will mess up my plan.

"I'm just going to input my number into your contacts in case you need something or someone to talk to."

Reluctantly, I type in my code then hand my phone over to him. After a few seconds, he hands it back.

"The restaurants serve all day. Just let them know your name and they'll serve you anything you want."

"Okay, thank you."

On my way back to my room, my phone pings with a text, reminding me I don't want to just change his contact from Dad to Niles, but to block his number altogether.

Dad: I'm so sorry, sunshine. I hope one day you can forgive me. There was just no other way.

And with that text, my anger is back with a vengeance. The second I step into my room, I allow myself to lose it. Picking up the crystal vase from the end table, I imagine it's my dad's head as I cock my arm back and throw it as hard as I can. It bounces off the wall and shatters when it hits the wood floor.

Damn, that felt good.

I grab something else—this time, a lamp—and chuck it across the room. It smashes against the wall, fragments raining down and landing on top of the broken crystal.

I take a deep breath. And then I grab the other lamp and throw it.

Item after item, I throw everything I can get my hands on until my arm is dead and there's nothing left to throw. Until my anger has dissipated enough that I can form a coherent thought.

And then I formulate my plan.

I pull up my airline ticket and call the airline. After my flight is booked, I call Alex.

"Talia, how are you?" Alex asks when he answers the phone. His voice is groggy, and it's then I remember there's an eight-hour time difference between Chicago and Greece.

"I'm good. I'm sorry to wake you, but I have great news. My father is letting me come visit you after all. My flight leaves in a few hours."

"That's fabulous!" he exclaims, his voice brighter and more awake. "I'll pick you up at the airport. What time will your flight arrive?"

"It's a twelve-hour flight, so I should be there at six o'clock your time."

"Once you find out your gate number, call me so I know where to meet you."

"I will. I can't wait to see you."

After we hang up, I make sure I have everything I need in my purse, and then, leaving my room key on the nightstand, I slip out. I head up the path and find a side exit. I thought about snagging a cab from here, but then they could track me. So instead, my plan is to walk as far as I can go and then hail a cab outside of the hotel.

My plan works. After walking the mile down the long roadway, I sneak behind a guard gate and exit along the back. When I step out of the trees, I'm standing on the sidewalk facing a busy street. Several cabs drive up and down the road, and not even a second after I've waved my hand, one pulls to the side.

"Heraklion airport."

The driver nods once and takes off. Fifty minutes later, I swipe my credit card and exit the cab. I find the airline I'm flying with and check in. Because I don't have any bags to check, I'm pushed through the line quickly. As I watch the line to go through security move forward, my heart pounds against my ribcage. I'm almost in the clear. Just a few more people and then I'll be on the other side.

Three more people.

Two.

One.

"Put your belongings in the bin, then step through," the guard instructs.

"That won't be necessary," a cold, menacing voice says. "She won't be going anywhere."

Like ice straight to my veins, my body freezes in its place. I don't have to turn around to know who is standing behind me.

Pluto…and he's here to drag me back into the Underworld against my will.

chapter five

Kostas

SHE LEFT. JUST LIKE I KNEW SHE FUCKING WOULD. GRABBED her purse and waltzed right out the door. I have to give her credit. Sneaking away rather than taking a cab from the front entrance of the hotel was clever. Not clever enough, though. I anticipated her move. She's a Nikolaides after all.

Not for long.

Every person we pass ignores her fuming. Around these parts, they see me and they move the fuck on. Nobody messes with my family. Not locals, not airport workers, not cab drivers, not even goddamn tourists. Everyone sees the blinking neon sign above my head that says: Don't fuck with me.

Or else.

Those who fuck with me and my family—like Niles Nikolaides— learn what else we have in store for them. In his case, he forfeited over his blond vixen of a daughter. Others pay with their blood. I prefer blood, but in this instance, I'm not unhappy about getting this furious woman into my bed.

Forever.

The thought is equal parts disturbing and thrilling. I'd never admit to my father I'm a lonely bastard who wishes he had someone to come home to every night. He's happy with Mamá, and has been for my entire life, so it's only natural I crave the same for myself.

We exit the airport without incident. My charcoal-gray Maserati

GranTurismo sits parked in the fire lane. No one writes a ticket. They just ignore me as it should be.

"Get in," I bite out, my voice cold and commanding as I open the passenger side door.

Her plump lips press together as though she's thinking desperately of arguing, but in the end, she lets out an exaggerated huff before throwing herself into the car. I close the door and catch the eye of a security guard.

"Women," he mutters, chuckling at me.

"Women," I agree. I smirk at him before climbing in my car.

She's quiet as I drive away from the airport and onto the main road. Her thoughts are loud, though. A cacophony of accusations and hate bouncing around inside the vehicle as though they can physically harm me.

I'm untouchable, moró mou.

I shift through the gears and fly down the road, passing cars along the way. She clutches the side of the door and the console as though that will help her if we were to crash. It won't. Lucky for her, we won't crash either. Next to crushing the bones of motherfuckers who cross me, I love to drive and I'm good at it. My father and brother prefer drivers, but not me. I'll take one of my many cars for a ride any day to escape the stifling responsibilities that weigh on me continuously.

"Am I in trouble?" she finally asks after a few minutes, darting her worried gaze my way.

"For trying to flee the country and hide from me?"

She nods, fear gleaming in her blue eyes.

"I didn't make the rules clear, so I suppose not," I tell her, catching her gaze briefly before I turn my attention back on the road. "However, if you run from me again, you'll be punished. Severely."

"You'll kill me?"

"My punishments are never so simple."

She doesn't try for more conversation, and I offer none. The drive takes less time than it should because I drive like a bat out of hell. When I finally pull into the hotel, I drive around to the back and down a long road that's far from tourists' eyes.

"Where are we going?" she demands, as though she has every right to make demands of me. "I thought you were bringing me back."

Ignoring her, I climb out of my car and make my way over to her side. I open the door and gesture for her to get out.

"Are you going to hurt me?" she asks, the bravado in her tone gone without a trace.

"Not at the moment."

Her lips press together, but she exits the vehicle. I grip her bicep and guide her to the groundskeeper's house on the corner of the property. The groundskeeper nods when we enter his small home unannounced. My barging in with someone in tow is nothing new. I haul her through the living room and into the kitchen. Pushing through the cellar door, I walk her down the narrow, steep stairs into the *kelári*.

But there is no wine in this cellar.

Only sad attempts for mercy.

There's no mercy here either.

Adrian sits on the sofa in the corner with his feet perched on the coffee table. In the center of the room, tied to a chair, is a man. Not just any man, but a man who thought he could lie to me.

"Cy," I greet. "Did you miss me?"

His brown eyes are wild and he whimpers from behind the red scarf that's stuffed inside his mouth. Sweat pours down his forehead and his T-shirt is soaked through. His feet are a mess, just like I left him.

When Adrian sees Talia, he sits upright and pats the sofa, understanding washing over him. She is to watch. She needs to see. "Come sit, miss," he urges.

As though he is the villain in this dank cellar, she takes a step nearer to me. Rather than allowing her any comfort, I release her arm and swat her ass. "Go, Talia."

She shoots me a venomous look over her shoulder. I bite back a chuckle. Fiery, even when fearful. Impressive. Once she sits as far away from Adrian as she can get, I remove my jacket and drape it over a chair.

"Talia, *moró mou*," I rumble. "Meet Cy. Cy, meet my fiancée."

Cy cries, but no one cares.

"Cy is a bad man," I tell her. "A bad man who must be punished. Do you want to know what he did that was so heinous to be tied to that chair?"

She shakes her head furiously, tears welling in her blue eyes. "No."

So brave this woman. Challenges me continuously.

"Allow me to regale you anyway," I say with a smile. "Cy here was asked where his brother Bakken was. Bakken is a thief and a killer. A pirate of sorts. An Aegean Sea asshole who boards ships that do not belong to him and cuts throats of innocent people. Bakken thinks if he kills people in my territory, that the Hellenic police will come after me and my family."

Her brows furrow as she waits for me to continue, her eyes glued to Cy's bloody feet.

I roll my sleeves up before whistling at Adrian. "Give me your sock."

He groans but kicks off his shoe. The big brute pulls off his black sock and tosses it to me. I set the sock down on the table and place my hands on my hips.

"Talia, Cy was wrong. The Hellenic police are my father's friends. They'll be at our wedding. There's a blurred line between good and bad. You'll soon learn to straddle it with me." I turn my head to regard Cy. "We burned your brother alive on his own ship. We found him no thanks to you."

Cy whimpers and shakes his head. He isn't allowed to speak anymore. There was a time when I allowed him to, and he lied. Told me his brother had fled to Istanbul. In reality, his brother was floating around in my territory, fucking with what's mine.

"Know what happens to liars, Talia?" I demand, my attention once again on her.

She flinches and shakes her head.

"Use that pretty head of yours," I growl. "Amuse me and guess."

"T-They lose their tongue?" she asks, her bottom lip trembling.

Adrian snorts out a laugh.

"I suppose that'd make sense," I say as I squat in front of Cy. "But a madman doesn't make sense. Therefore, liars get a different treatment around here."

I pick up the knife from the floor. Earlier, when my father left my office, I came straight down to the cellar to work on Cy. I'd barely started when Basil told me that my fiancée had fled. Cy's been waiting all this time.

The stench of piss permeates the air, but it's to be expected. I inspect my blood-crusted blade and flash Talia a wide smile. When I continue my sawing through his leg, just above his ankle, he screams through his scarf. I can hear Talia gagging from nearby. The knife is sharp, but it still takes me a good half hour to saw through the bone. Blood gushes everywhere, and I'll have to throw out these shoes, unfortunately. Eventually, I break through the bone and finish sawing through the muscle until I've completely removed his foot. Cy's head lolls to the side, but he's still awake. Good.

Adrian leans forward and picks up the sock from the table before tossing it to me. I stuff the hacked off foot into the sock. As I stand, I seek out Talia's face. She's buried her face in her hands as she sobs.

"Make her watch," I command in a cold tone. "Make her see."

She cries out when Adrian grips her wrists and pulls them away.

I tie a knot in the sock close to the severed foot and then hold the tube end in my grip. With a hard pop, I whack Cy in the head.

"You're s-sick," she croaks out. "A fucking sick monster!"

Whack! Whack! Whack!

I ignore her as I beat the shit out of Cy with his own goddamn foot. He groans and gurgles.

Whack! Whack! Whack!

When I hit him just right across his nose, it pops as it breaks. Blood gushes down his front like a river of crimson. I whack him in the face again, his blood splattering everywhere.

Whack! Whack! Whack!

I nail him hard in the throat, making him gag. Enough whacks to his throat and I'll crush his windpipe. Yanking on his hair with one hand to tilt his head back, I swing with the other over and over against his Adam's apple with his severed foot. A nasty crunching sound can be heard and then raspy wheezing. I continue nailing him with the foot until the sock rips and the foot flings out. Blood covers my front and I'm breathing heavily with exertion.

"I hate liars," I snarl, my eyes locking with Talia's blue, terror-filled ones. "People loyal to me don't lie. I expect you'll learn to be quite loyal."

I move to stand behind Cy, staring at the Nikolaides woman, who seems to want to learn lessons the hard way. Gripping Cy's head, I twist hard to the right, snapping his neck and ending his miserable existence.

"Call Franco to clean this up," I bark out to Adrian as I head over to the sink. "And give me your shoes." I unbutton my shirt and peel it off before tossing it over to where Cy's body sits. I kick off my shoes and step into the clean ones Adrian offers to me. Then, I start washing what I can of the blood off me. "Tell Phynn I'll want my car detailed by tomorrow. This shit will stain."

Adrian is already on the phone to Franco. Franco owns a funeral home and crematory. For his aid in disposing of bodies, he receives preferential treatment from our family and handsome payments.

"Be a doll, will you, and grab my jacket," I instruct to Talia.

When she makes no moves to get up, her body trembling violently, I whistle sharply.

"Now, *moró mou.*"

She rises and stumbles over to the chair with my jacket before snagging it up. It gets tossed to me as she storms up the stairs. I pull it on along the way up and grab her before she's made it out of the door. Pinning her to the wall, I glower down at her.

So small.

Breakable.

Mine now.

"Your attitude fucking sucks," I growl. "Learn to keep it in check."

"Or what?" she hisses. "You'll beat me with my own foot?"

Smirking, I release her. "I'm sure I'll come up with something clever to teach you a lesson should you disobey."

Her blue eyes flare as she pulls away from me. "I hate you."

"You wouldn't be the first." I give her ass a swat. "Pick up the pace. We have dinner reservations at six. I imagine you'd like a shower and a nap before then."

"I'm not going to dinner with you," she chokes out, turning on her heel in the kitchen to glower at me. "I can't stand to look at you."

Reaching forward, I delicately twirl a strand of her blond hair around my finger and tug. "This is where you seem to be confused. You think you have a say…" I lean forward and rest my forehead to hers. "You. Have. No. Say."

She pulls away from me and rushes out. I stalk after her, pleased to find her getting back inside my car. *Good girl. May as well learn your place in the Demetriou world right away.*

Once inside my vehicle, I reach over and take her trembling hand. She attempts to pull it away, but I'm stronger.

"What size ring do you wear?"

"Fuck you," she breathes, hate dripping from her words.

"Soon, *moró mou*. Don't worry." I chuckle when she hisses at me. "Size six?"

She stubbornly refuses to speak. I pull her hand toward me and inhale her skin before nipping at the back of it.

"Tell me," I warn. "You don't want to learn how persuasive my teeth are when I am needing information." I catch her flesh between my teeth and bite hard enough to make her squirm, but not hard enough to leave a bruise.

"Seven," she chokes out. "I'm a seven."

I release her skin and kiss the back of her hand. "Thank you. You'll learn," I explain with a smile. "Do as I say and I'll reward you. Refuse me and I'll punish you. Understand?"

She nods rapidly, tears streaking down her cheeks.

"Good girl."

chapter
six

Talia

"WHERE ARE WE?" I ASK AS KOSTAS PARKS HIS CAR IN what looks like a private underground carport. "I think my room is on the other side."

The hotel is huge, but I've explored enough of it to know my room is on the south side of the property, and we're currently on the north side.

"We're at my place," Kostas states coldly. "Your stuff has been moved here."

He exits his vehicle, and without waiting for me, stalks down the walkway. I consider, for a brief second, running in the opposite direction, but then flashbacks to only a few minutes ago surface: of the bloodied man. Kostas sawing off his foot and then beating him with it. Kostas snapping his neck like it was a chicken bone. And I follow behind Kostas.

It's not that I'm giving up on escaping, but I'm not stupid enough to be careless about it anymore. I underestimated him. I lumped him into the same category as my father and the men I've met over the years who work for him. Kostas is *not* my father. He's on an entirely different level. Leaving is going to require extensive planning because if he catches me the next time, I have no doubt he will make me suffer the way he made that man suffer in the cellar.

I shiver at the thought of what he would do to me if he caught me trying to leave again. No, the next time I leave, I have to make sure I completely disappear.

When we step through the threshold of Kostas's place, I realize that while the outside looks similar to the hotel rooms, inside is vastly different. For one, it's massive. Just the foyer and living room are at least twice the size of the entire room I was staying in. I thought my room was exquisite, but his puts my room to shame.

Brown and white marble flooring expands across the entire area. Plush coffee-colored leather couches, a mahogany wood coffee table, and a beautiful fireplace make up the living room. The walls are different shades of brown with a few strategically placed pieces of art hanging up. It's clearly a typical bachelor pad, but upgraded to fit Kostas's level of wealth.

I follow him past the expansive kitchen that matches the living room perfectly, with its mahogany wood cabinets and marble countertops. Complete with stainless steel appliances. As I walk through Kostas's home, I quickly come to the realization that my family's money couldn't even afford to have a conversation with Kostas's family's money. This is why Nonno said their decision is law. They can afford to make things go their way.

Kostas stops when he enters what appears to be the master bedroom. The same color scheme has continued into his room, but to soften it a bit, cream has been added to the mix. In the center of the room is a king-sized four-poster bed. If in any other standard master bedroom it would appear overwhelming, in this room it fits perfectly. The bed is solid wood and has intricate designs running up each of the poles. When my eyes land on the cream-colored sheets, it hits me. I'm expected to sleep in this bed with Kostas. The man who just singlehandedly took the life of another man.

"We're not married yet," I blurt out, terrified all over again. "Shouldn't I sleep somewhere else until we are?"

Kostas, who has already stripped down to his boxers, raises a single brow. "If you're afraid of me stealing your virtue, don't worry. I have no intention of touching you until we're married. My mother raised me to be a gentleman." He smirks. "But later tonight, you *will* be sleeping in this bed with me."

My eyes rake over Kostas's body. Various tattoos cover his chiseled chest, rock-hard abs, and corded biceps and forearms. He's not overly muscular, but it's apparent he works out and keeps in shape. *It's probably all from sawing off body parts and then beating people with them...*

The only man's body I've ever paid any attention to was Alex's, and the vast difference between the two men is evident. Where Alex is toned and lean, his body is clearly that of a boy, while Kostas's body...it's all man...and scary.

"You like what you see, *moró mou?*" Kostas asks when he catches me checking him out. My eyes swing back up to meet his hazel ones. They're no longer dark like they were in the cellar. No longer angry. Now, they're softer, taking on a beautiful honey color. For a moment, I'm mesmerized by the way his eyes change according to his mood. Earlier, it's clear he was angry, but right now, I can't quite figure out what his mood is.

"I asked you a question," he utters, his eyes brightening just a tad.

"No," I say, answering his question, "and stop calling me *moró mou.* I'm *not* your baby. I'm not your anything." I flinch as soon as the words are out, afraid of what his reaction will be. I've never been good at simply obeying. My mother always told me I'm stubborn and strong-willed, and I can do anything I put my mind to because I'm not the kind of person to give up. I always considered those traits a good thing, but now, those same traits may be what gets me killed...or worse.

Kostas cuts across the room and is in my face before I can apologize. He pushes me against the dresser, the carved wood digging into my back. His hands come down on either side of my body, caging me in, his face only a hairbreadth away from mine. His gaze locks with mine.

"You. Are. Mine," he growls. "And the sooner you accept that, the better off you'll be. This time next week you will be my wife. The type of life you want is up to you. You can play nice, and I will give you the world. The sun, the stars, and the motherfucking sky. Or you can make shit difficult, and I will take it all away, leaving you with nothing but darkness."

His eyes drop to my mouth, and his tongue darts out, wetting his lips. And suddenly the look in his eyes makes sense. Lust. He's turned on. And he's going to kiss me. He's testing me. Wanting to see if I'll play nice.

I haven't made my decision yet when his tongue traces my top lip, then my bottom one. My eyes close of their own accord, clearly making the choice for me, when a jolt of pain sears through me. My eyes pop open, shocked. It takes me a second to figure out what just happened.

The asshole bit me! I suck in my bottom lip and can taste the metallic liquid. He fucking bit me and drew blood! Kostas's lips curl into a devious smile that pisses me off because I was actually going to let him kiss me.

"Real nice," I hiss, trying to hide my embarrassment.

I attempt to push his arm out of my way so I can escape—to where, I have no idea—but he doesn't budge. Instead, his chin dips down and he captures my bleeding lip with his mouth. My hands push against his chest, but it's futile. He's stronger. His sturdy yet surprisingly soft lips suck in my own, and he licks across my flesh. I stop pushing against him, frozen in place. Unsure of what to do. And then his lips descend on mine. His tongue pushes through my parted lips, and I can taste my blood mixed with something else…something minty.

And it's as if my body has a mind of its own, because before I can give it any more thought, my lips are moving in sync with his. Every swipe of his tongue is controlled, deliberate. I've never felt so exposed. I'm fully clothed, and the only part of my body he's touching is my mouth, yet I feel like he's able to see all of me. Every hidden and private part of me.

Suddenly, it's all too much. This isn't right. I shouldn't be kissing him. He's still wearing the blood of the man he just tortured and killed. But I can't stop it. His mouth dominates mine, and I'm defenseless to end it. So, instead, I just let it happen.

When Kostas pulls back, and his eyes meet mine, they're blazing with an emotion I can't quite pinpoint. He doesn't quite look mad. Maybe confused. *That makes two of us…*

He steps back and draws his bottom lip into his mouth as if he's still tasting me. "I need to shower. Be ready at five thirty." And with that, he turns on his heel and stalks into the bathroom, slamming the door behind him—leaving me to wonder what the hell just happened, and if maybe Kostas was right. Maybe there was more to Proserpina's feelings. Maybe she was scared of wanting him. Scared of what she felt for him. It would make sense. Because right now, even though I don't want to admit it, I can completely relate to how Kostas described Proserpina. And I've never been more scared.

Ring...Ring...Ring...

My eyes pop open, and I glance around the room, taking in my surroundings. I'm in Kostas's master bedroom, in his bed. He kissed me. And I *might've* enjoyed it. But then he walked away. Despite not wanting to do as he instructed, I was exhausted, and after fighting sleep for a few minutes, I ended up passing out.

"An *Alex* is calling you," a deep voice says. I whip my head around to see Kostas standing next to the bed with my cell phone in his hand. I reach out to take it from him, remembering I never called Alex to let him know what my gate number would be, but Kostas pulls it back before I can grab it. "Who's Alex?"

"Nobody," I say before I can think about it.

Kostas kneels so he's eye level with me, his features darkening and confirming what I noticed earlier: his eyes change according to his mood. "Did you already forget what happens when people lie to me?" he asks. "Let's try this again. Who. Is. Alex?"

Sitting up, so I don't feel at such a disadvantage, I tell him the truth. "He's my boyfriend."

I gauge Kostas's features to see how he's going to react to my truth. Outwardly, he gives nothing away. But his eyes—they're all too telling in the way they blaze with anger, so hot, that with one strike, they could catch the room we're in on fire.

The phone rings in his hand again, and he silences it. "I will not have my wife spreading her legs for anyone but me. I suggest you handle this problem. Otherwise, I will handle it for you."

I don't need to ask to know his way of handling it, will end with someone—Alex—dying.

The phone rings once again, and this time he lets me take it. "I have work to do. I'll be back at five thirty to get you. Be ready."

I wait until he's out of the room before I call Alex back.

"Talia, are you okay?" Alex asks, worry in his voice. "You told me you would call me with the gate number and you never did. You should have already been on your way, so I was worried."

I close my eyes, refusing to let the tears fall. I can't do this to him. I can't have him worrying about me. Who knows when or if I'll be able to get away. And if I do, going to Alex will mean putting a huge target on his chest. Kostas killed that guy earlier without a second thought, and I don't doubt he will do the same to Alex if he views him as a problem.

"Alex, I'm not coming."

"Why? What's wrong?" His concern solidifies my decision. If I leave him hanging, he's going to continue to worry, and I can't have him involved in any of this.

"I can't be with you anymore. I'm sorry, but I'm with someone else now."

The line is silent for a long beat before Alex finally responds. "I don't understand." Of course he doesn't. We were just making plans to spend the summer together and now I'm breaking up with him. I have to cut ties completely, though. I have to make it clear it's over so he doesn't try to contact me.

"I'm back together with my ex. I'm sorry, but you were nothing more than a rebound. I thought I was over him, but then I saw him again and realized I still loved him." I swallow the large lump in my throat and then add, "We're engaged to be married."

"This doesn't make any sense!" Alex shouts through the phone. "You were just coming here."

"You don't have to understand," I tell him. "You just need to know it's over and that I don't want you to ever contact me again. Goodbye." I hang up before he can argue and then block his number from being able to call or text me.

For a moment, I sit and stare at the wall, trying to figure out how my life has come to this. Not even twenty-four hours ago, I was on top of the world. I was excelling in school, had a loving boyfriend. I had my entire future planned out. Now, I've lost my father...no, I take that back. I didn't lose him. He lost me. He handed me over. And by consequence, I've lost my entire life. Will Kostas even let me see my mother? In the blink of an eye, I've lost *everything* that means anything to me, and there's a good chance I'm never going to get any of it back.

A sudden wave of anxiety hits me, and I reach up to my throat, struggling to breathe. It's all just too much. This can't be real. I keep hoping that I'm going to wake up and it will all be a horrible dream. But deep down, I know…this isn't a dream at all. This is my reality.

I close my eyes and count to ten, trying to even out my breathing. When that doesn't work, I get up and head into the bathroom to splash some water on my face. Checking myself out in the mirror, I see the pink is gone from the cheek where I was slapped. I also notice I'm all wrinkled. I'm going to need to change for dinner. Change…Kostas said all of my stuff was brought here.

Stepping back into the bedroom, I spot an armoire similar to the one in the room I was staying in. Opening it up, I find the outfits that were in my room are now in this one. I move to the dresser and open each of the drawers: bras, panties, silk pajamas. Oh my God, he really did have all my stuff moved. When the hell did he find the time?

It's as though he planned this all along.

Predicted my moves before I made them.

He's a genuine nut job.

Curious, I open the closet door to see if there's anything of mine in there as well. It's a huge walk-in closet. When I step inside, I notice the back wall first. It has floor-to-ceiling shelves filled with various styles of shoes. The top half are all men's, but the bottom half are women's. I pick one up and see it's a size eight. My size. As if it's burned me, I drop it back down where I got it from.

He's a psychopath.

What kind of person does this?!

Turning around, I take in the two side walls. Each are filled wall-to-wall with clothes. On one side are men's clothes. From suits, to collared shirts, to a couple hoodies, with a few pairs of jeans hanging up at the end. On the other side are all women's clothes. There must be thousands of euros' worth of clothes in here. Needing to confirm they're for me, I check out a few of the tags. All my size.

Psycho. Creep. Stalker.

Oh my God. I have got to get away from this man.

Backing up slightly, I bump into a dresser island in the middle of the room—yes, his closet is the size of a freaking room. It has several drawers, and on the end there's a bench where you can sit to put on your shoes.

With a deep breath, I try to steady my nerves and calm myself. I grab an off the shoulder sweater and a pair of shorts and quickly change into them, needing to get out of here. Out of this closet. Out of this room. Out of this fucking house.

Since I have some time before dinner, I leave the villa, desperate for fresh air and to clear my head, but as the door closes behind me, I realize I don't have a key. "Shit!" I try to turn the handle, but it's locked. Unlike the room I stayed in last night, Kostas's door has a number pad on it, and I don't know the code. Nor do I know his phone number. "Just great." I groan.

"Locked out?" a masculine voice asks. Unlike Kostas's dark, cold tone, this voice is melodic and playful. Aris. I turn around and find him leaning against the wall, in a pair of board shorts and boat shoes, with his leg propped up, and his arms crossed over his shirtless chest.

"Do you know the code?" I ask, nodding toward the offending panel.

Aris laughs, light and throaty. I haven't heard Kostas laugh yet, but I imagine it would sound the complete opposite. I don't really know either of them, but from what I've seen, they seem to be polar opposites.

"It's not funny," I snap. "Your brother told me to be ready at five thirty. The last thing I need is him…punishing me." I mumble the last two words.

"Ahh…" Aris grins. "So, you've already had a chance to get to know my brother."

"If you call watching him torture a man with his own limb that he cut off using a knife, getting to know him, then sure, I know him *real* well," I smart. My words come out harsh and sarcastic, but my voice cracks at the end, giving away how overwhelmed and scared I am.

Aris steps off the wall and stalks toward me. "Come here." His voice, so sweet and soft, is my breaking point. A single tear squeezes past my flimsy barrier and rolls down my cheek. Aris, not missing a beat, swipes his thumb across my flesh and catches it. And then another falls, and another. And the next thing I know, I'm in Aris's arms, crying onto his shoulder.

"Shh," he coos. "It's okay. It's going to be okay."

I don't know how, but without even asking him, I know Aris is nothing like his brother. They both might work for their father, but Aris isn't stone cold like Kostas. He's different. Softer.

"How can you say that?" I murmur. "I'm being forced to marry a man who made me watch him take another man's life to show me what he's capable of. How can anything ever be all right?"

It can't.

It won't.

"What can I do?" he asks, but before I can answer, someone else answers for me.

"You can get your fucking hands off my fiancée for starters."

chapter seven

ARIS MEETS MY GLARE OVER TALIA'S BLOND HEAD WITH A MADdening smirk that used to get his ass beat when we were kids. I swear he lives to taunt me. Wisely, he drops his arms.

Talia jerks away from him and crosses her arms over her chest. My gaze flits to her smooth, sexy shoulder that's exposed. Golden like honey. I bet it tastes sweet too.

"I don't know the code to get back in," she mutters, not meeting my gaze.

"You were supposed to stay put," I say, stepping closer.

"What *is* the code?" Aris implores just to fuck with me. He sure as hell isn't welcome in my villa.

Shaking my head at him, I bite out my words. "Don't you have some errands to run for Daddy?"

All humor is wiped off his fucking face. If anyone has daddy issues, it's my brother. It boils his blood that he's a glorified errand boy and I'm the heir to the Demetriou kingdom. Instead of losing his cool like I wish he would, he straightens his spine and shoots me a nasty glare.

"Excuse me, Talia," he mutters. "I have work to do. See you at dinner."

As soon as he's gone, she frowns at me. "He'll be at dinner with us?"

I walk over to her and grip her wrist. She smells like lavender, a pleasing scent that simmers some of my rage at seeing Aris swooping in on her like a fucking hawk. "It's a family dinner," I explain, studying her plump lips. "My father and mother will be there as well."

Her blue eyes widen. "I'm going to meet your mother?"

"You're my fiancée," I remind her with a smirk. "Of course you'll meet her. She's been told about you and will be helping to plan our wedding." My voice drops to a low octave as I reach up to brush a blond strand of hair from her eyes. "You'll respect my mother, yes?"

The unspoken threat lingers in the air between us.

Ignoring my words, she narrows her eyes at me and huffs out, "You're sure taking this marriage debt seriously."

Sliding my hand to her throat, I gently caress her soft skin. My thumb lingers on her fat vein that throbs wildly. I make her nervous. Good. "I'm a successful businessman. I take *all* business seriously," I utter, my eyes locked with her flaring blue ones. "And, like my father, I take marriage even more seriously."

She swallows and her throat moves against my palm. This woman is so delicate. A butterfly caught in a spider's web—her wings about to be tied down indefinitely.

"Come now, *moró mou*. We have important matters to see to."

I release her neck but not her wrist. She hesitates for a fraction of a second when I pull her with me, but I'm stronger and she's forced to follow along. Soon, she falls into step beside me and I release my grip on her. We walk down the stone pathway between other private villas until we come to the side entrance of the hotel. Her curiosity and apparent appreciation of our hotel gets the better of her once we step inside. When we pass a painting I had flown in from Portugal recently, I sense her hesitation. She wants to look at it but is afraid to ask.

If she is to be my wife, she'll have to tap into that bravery sooner rather than later.

Animals can sense fear. They thirst for it. Can scent it in the air. Hunt it down. Humans are no different. She wants to be hunted? I'll fucking hunt her.

"This way, *mikró kounéli*." *Little rabbit.*

She shoots me a venomous glare—one that's better suited for a reptile that eats little rabbits. Her sudden flare of animosity has heat coursing through me straight to my dick. I let out a dark chuckle before guiding her to my office where Faustus and his team await.

Once inside my office, she stumbles slightly. I place my palm on the small of her back to steady her. Faustus—a world-renowned jeweler from Athens—has set up my office with his best pieces. Several men stand in corners, their black suits and impassive features meant to blend in. In reality, they're there to keep anyone from robbing Faustus blind of his precious treasures.

"Faustus," I greet, reaching to shake hands with the short, white-haired man.

"Mr. Demetriou." He shakes my hand and then offers his to Talia. She's been brought up to be a lady, apparently, because she smiles and takes his hand. "Lovely woman."

"Thank you," she utters. "What's all this?" She shoots me a questioning look.

"This," Faustus answers for me, "is the finest gold, platinum, silver, and stones in the entire world." He grins wide at her, his white mustache stretching across his face. "Only the finest for a Demetriou."

I can tell it's on the tip of her tongue to argue that she's still a Nikolaides, but she wisely keeps her mouth shut.

"Come," Faustus tells her. "Sit."

I sit in my desk chair while he sits in the chair next to her, opposite my desk. Faustus pulls one of the jewel-covered black trays over to her lap. As he explains the quality of each piece, I study my fiancée. Her brows are furled and her nostrils flare. She'd love to be anywhere but here, no doubt, but that's too fucking bad. After seeing Aris with his arms wrapped around her, I'd nearly exploded with fury. She needs a heavy, priceless ring on her finger so the whole fucking world knows who she belongs to.

Touching my woman will have consequences.

Aris knows this and yet he tests my patience.

Because he's my brother, he's allowed a small sliver of leniency. But my graciousness toward my flesh and blood has been eliminated. I won't cut him with words next time. No, I'll cut him with something much sharper.

"You prefer pink?" Faustus asks her, offering her a rather large pink diamond to inspect.

Her face sours and she shakes her head. "These are all too big."

Faustus snorts. "Nonsense. No diamond is too big for a beautiful woman."

"Pick the one you like," I instruct. "You're not leaving here until you do. Choose wisely."

She rolls her eyes, making her seem younger and less overwhelmed. That, too, gets my dick hard. I smirk as she takes the pink diamond. I can tell she doesn't like it.

"No pink," I tell Faustus. "Perhaps something to match her eyes."

I nod to the small tray that's covered by a black cloth. Jewelers like him are all the same. They tease and tease until they get to the truly priceless gems. I don't have all day. I want a ring on her finger by the time we leave this room. Preferably the most valuable one.

Faustus, clearly peeved that I've cut short his show, frowns at me before reaching for the tray. He swaps out the one on her lap for the new one.

"This is as rare as they come," he explains, his voice turning to a whisper as he foreshadows what must be the best diamond here. "Priceless."

He pulls away the cloth to reveal a square light blue diamond already set in a platinum band. It sparkles from the sun streaming in the window, nearly blinding me. This will do. This will do nicely. Her eyes have locked onto the ring and she can't hide her appreciation for it. The blues in her eyes sparkle exactly like that of the diamond.

"This is a 24.18 carat emerald-cut vivid blue diamond called the Aster Blue. It comes from a South African mine and is the largest of five gems cut from a 122.52 carat rough blue diamond unearthed in 2001." He smiles at her. "Blue diamonds are among the rarest this world has ever seen. This diamond even rarer due to the size and cut. The jeweler who first owned it selfishly kept it for his wife, but eventually sold it in an auction seven years ago."

She looks up at Faustus. "Why did he sell it?"

Faustus's smile falters and he shoots me a panicked look. I, too, am curious about how a man would give his wife a priceless stone and then sell it.

"Is it important? Look at the way it catches the light," Faustus tells her.

Her head bows to inspect it, but irritation churns in my gut at his blatant refusal to answer her question. All it takes is for me to lean forward in my chair, my gaze burning into him, for him to give up the goods.

"He sold it because his wife left him. Ran away with his brother." He cringes, shooting me an apologetic look. "She left the ring and a note. His broken heart could only be soothed by the hefty amount the diamond brought in."

"Do you ever plan to leave me, *moró mou*?" I taunt, my voice dropping to a deadly low level.

Her blue eyes snap to mine, fear gleaming in them. With one hard stare, I challenge her to lie to me. We both know this morning, she'd done just that.

"I would like to try it on," she says, ignoring my question and holding out her dainty hand to Faustus.

Beads of perspiration dot his forehead as he eagerly takes her hand, clearly desperate to change the line of conversation. He slides the massive light blue diamond on her slender finger. Possessiveness claws its way around my heart at seeing it on her hand. She'd be a fool to not choose it. It's perfect on her.

"How much is it?" she asks, her nose scrunching as she regards him.

"Priceless." He grins at her, before glancing my way. "Nothing a Demetriou can't afford."

"I guess I'll take this one then," she says in a breathy voice.

"You guess?" Faustus chokes out. "My lovely lady, this blue diamond is worth fifty-seven point seven million euros."

Talia jerks her hand back, snapping her gaze my way, horror in her blue eyes. "That's insane!"

"It is the one," I tell Faustus blandly as I pick up my desk phone and dial Aris's secretary, Carlene. When she answers, I bark out my request for her to wire the money to Faustus. By the time I hang up, Faustus is beaming and Talia looks as though she swallowed something poisonous. "I thank you for your time, Faustus." With a nod, I dismiss them.

Talia remains still, the shiny diamond ring sparkling, as the men pack up the jewelry. They work quickly and quietly. After a brief hand-shake with Faustus, I rise and see them to the door.

"Talia, come," I bark out.

She jolts at my words and stands. Crimson paints her neck red, making me wonder what it is she's embarrassed about.

"Bring me the ring," I order, holding out my palm.

Her nostrils flare, but she obeys, stalking over to me. She plucks the ring from her finger and hands it over. Once it's safely encased in my fist, I grip her wrist and walk her out to my veranda.

"Talia Nikolaides," I say, pulling her hand up and kissing her knuckle. "You are to be my wife." I'm not asking for her hand in marriage, I'm taking it. I slide on the impressive ring, enjoying the way it shimmers in the sun. "And if you leave me like the poor man who first owned this ring, I will extract all fifty-seven point seven million from you. Blood, sweat, tears. However I can get my payment." I thread our fingers together. Her eyes flare with worry. "You know this, yes?"

"Yes," she breathes, her bottom lip wobbling wildly.

"Good." I kiss the back of her hand. "Four. Seven. Seven. One. That's the code to our villa. Don't share it with anyone."

She nods emphatically. "Of course not."

I lean in and kiss her cheek. "Run along and get ready for dinner. Dress nicely."

As soon as she plucks her hand from my grip, she hightails it out of my presence. I'm staring out at the bay when a little while later some-one approaches me from behind. Familiar fingernails scratch down my spine, making me smile.

"Look how handsome you are."

I turn to take in a pair of brown eyes that shine with love for me. Her face is youthful despite her age. Red-painted lips curl into a smile.

Pulling her into my arms, I hug her tight and inhale her hair that smells of oranges.

"Is it true?" she asks, pulling away to search my face, tears shining in her eyes. "You've found someone?"

I found her at the bottom of a Nikolaides hole. Like the priceless diamond, I unearthed her and made her mine. Unlike the jeweler, I'll make sure she wears that ring until her very last breath.

"It is," I grunt. Guilt niggles at me when her brown eyes flood and then spill over with her emotion.

"Oh, Kos," she chokes out. "Is it love?"

"It's something." I smile at her. "You look beautiful. Did you come alone?"

Her face pinches. "No, he's here, too." Worry flickers in her eyes. "Are you happy?"

I'm as happy as a man like me can get.

"Of course, Mamá."

I'm marrying the most beautiful woman in Greece and she's the daughter of an enemy. Of course I'm fucking happy.

The woman who raised us to be kind, honorable men hugs me once more.

Sometimes I almost feel sorry for her. Because for every good thing she taught us, my father taught us three more bad ones.

I'm not a good man.

Good men don't turn good women into Demetrious.

Only bad men do.

Mamá, of all women, should know that.

chapter eight

Talia

"Hēdonē?" My eyes flicker from the seductively lit sign above the restaurant we're about to enter, to Kostas. His expression is cold and emotionless, but I'm learning his eyes don't lie. The hazel seems to flicker with amusement. I imagine he's thinking the same thing I am. *Another goddess. Another story.* He arches a brow as though to say, "And your point?"

"Your restaurant is seriously named after the Goddess of Pleasure?" It'd be romantic coming from anyone but the man who is taking me as his wife in exchange for a debt. Speaking of which…

Don't look at it.

Don't look at it.

I have no choice. I sneak a peek at the massive diamond on my finger. It's heavy and sparkling. It's a beautiful ring, but it's ridiculous and over the top, especially for a marriage that's not even real.

This is forced imprisonment, where he's the warden and I'm in unseen shackles with the walls around me rising higher by the minute.

I'll never get away from him.

Kostas doesn't give me a response, just tugs on my arm to keep me moving. We're halted by a familiar voice.

"Don't let the name fool you," Aris says as he approaches. "My brother prefers pain over pleasure. Isn't that right, Kostas?" Aris pats his brother on the shoulder, and Kostas's entire body visibly stiffens. Darkness gleams in his eyes, not much different from the violent look on his face when he tortured that man. "It was our mother who named the restaurant. She's the romantic in the family."

Aris shoots a playful wink my way. Taunting his brother on purpose. I may not like Kostas, but Aris is practically signing my death warrant. In an effort to show I'm not encouraging things, I lean into Kostas.

"Unless you want to learn firsthand about the pain I prefer, I suggest you shut your fucking mouth," Kostas snarls, stepping away from me and toward Aris.

The air crackles with electricity—two storms about to collide. Unfortunately, from experience, I know one storm is more violent than the other.

Aris laughs as if Kostas is joking, but I can see it in his posture, he's preparing for the possibility of a fight. And with Kostas, it could end deadly.

"Oh, boys," a female voice says. "No fighting tonight. We have much to celebrate." A beautiful, smiling woman steps into view, and both Aris and Kostas immediately stand down, giving her a sincere smile. The animosity still lingers in the air, but for this woman, they've put a lid on it for now.

Her brown hair is down in waves, and her lips are painted a bright red. She's dressed in a gorgeous black cocktail gown with a matching pair of stilettos. She looks like the female version of Aris, and I know right away, she's their mother. She gives each of them a kiss on their cheek, and then she places her attention on me.

"I'm Nora," she says, giving me a kiss on each cheek before she steps back. "And you must be Kostas's fiancée." She beams. "I'm ashamed to admit that while I've heard about you, Kostas and his father neglected to tell me your name."

"Oh, my dear wife," Ezio purrs in a somewhat condescending tone. "I was going to wait until we were all seated to make introductions."

He's dressed in a black suit similar to the one he wore this morning. He wraps his arm around her waist and grins wide. Unlike Kostas's smile, which comes across dangerous with a hint of seductiveness, or Aris's, which gives off a playful vibe, Ezio's smile screams barely hidden malice. It's the kind of smile that sends chills up your spine and leaves you afraid of what's to come.

"This is Talia…Talia Nikolaides." He draws out my last name slowly, and his grin grows wider, making the tiny hairs on the back of my neck stand at attention.

Nora's bright smile falters for a split second before it's back and even brighter than before. "It's nice to meet you, Talia," she says. "Shall we go in?" She nods toward the restaurant. "We can get to know each other over dinner."

What's there to know?

I'm a captive on this island, forced to marry a monster.

The end.

Happily fucking ever after, lady.

Rather than going off on this poor woman who doesn't fit in with these malevolent men, I plaster on a fake, polite smile that would make my grandfather proud.

"Come," Kostas instructs, his voice low and commanding.

Placing his palm against my lower back, Kostas guides us through the door and past the hostess stand. Like everything else at this hotel, the restaurant is over the top gorgeous. The walls are an off white with wrought iron lamps hanging every few feet apart, casting yellow and orange hues onto the walls, making it appear as if the walls are on fire. There's a large stone fireplace that takes up the entire back wall. The tables are a soft white, and the chairs are all black leather and wood wingback with orange cushions. The floor is made up of red and orange swirls.

Like fire licking up from Hell.

Who knew Hell could look so pretty?

The Devil sure is…

I know without asking he had something to do with designing this restaurant.

When we arrive at our table, Kostas pulls my chair out for me. "Thank you," I whisper, still in awe of my surroundings.

"I thought you might like this restaurant," Kostas says, sitting next to me.

For one moment, he seems as though he might be genuine. As though he's a dutiful boyfriend who knows what his girlfriend likes. But he doesn't know. He's an actor. Not unlike Alex. Difference is, Alex really was the dutiful boyfriend who cared.

Was.

Sickness roils in my belly, and tears threaten, but I push them back.

"It's beautiful," I murmur, plastering on a fake smile, because apparently, I too am supposed to play a part. And I'm fearful of the consequences if I don't. "Did you help design it?"

His mother seems unaware of the awkward vibe hissing in the air. Pride shines on her pretty face.

"It was both of us," Nora admits as her husband pushes her chair in and sits next to her, on the other side of Kostas. We're at a round table that seats five people, so Aris sits in the empty seat to my right, which happens to be between his mom and me. "Do you enjoy Greek mythology?" she asks.

One quick glance at Kostas and I try not to shudder. His intense, calculating glare is on me, daring me to bark out what I want to say.

What does it matter anymore what I enjoy?

"I do." I place my napkin on my lap, forcing another smile for her. "I'm studying art at the Florence Art Institute. I prefer the performing arts, but I've taken several art classes and have taken a liking to classic mythology." Too bad I'll never get to go back and finish.

The waiter comes over and pours us each a glass of water, and Kostas orders a bottle of wine for the table.

"Florence?" Nora questions. "How was it you met my son from all the way over in Italy?" She tilts her head to the side slightly, and it hits me that she really has no clue as to why I'm here and engaged to her son.

I shift in my seat, shooting Kostas a questioning look. I may have studied theater, but I'm not a liar. Am I supposed to just make up some romantic story of how we met?

Kostas's hand lands on my thigh under the table and squeezes as he saves me from her line of questioning. "Talia was visiting with her father on vacation. We ran into each other in front of Bernini's sculpture and debated the story of Proserpina."

Nora's face pales at his answer, making me wonder if she knows more about her dark little prince and her wicked king of a husband than she lets on. She nods, as though she believes her son is a romantic. But she's half present and half lost in thought. Though her smile is steady on her face, it's not as bright as it was initially.

"How romantic," she finally says, regarding Kostas as though she truly believes that.

"Yes," I grit out. "So romantic."

I want to ask her if she thinks it's romantic the way her son defends Pluto in the sculpture. The captor. The rapist. It's on the tip of my tongue, my inner Nikolaides fire brimming to the surface.

Kostas's grip on my thigh tightens to the point of pain, reminding me of my place. He leans over, his lips grazing my earlobe, and whispers, "We can discuss it more when we get home tonight, *moró mou*. I just might be inclined to show you what else I find *romantic*."

A threat.

It coils around me and suffocates me.

Thankfully, the waiter comes over and saves us from this conversation. Kostas orders for me, which might normally grate on me, but I'm too flustered to care.

The rest of the dinner goes fairly smoothly considering I'm dining with a demon, a poor, unsuspecting woman, and Aris, who appears to be *almost* as much out of place as I am. The men discuss a new hotel they're opening up on Crete island, and Nora gives her input when asked. I remain silent, lost in my head.

While this family chatters happily with one another, all it makes me do is long for the loss of my own. If I were at dinner with Mom and Stefano, he'd be proudly talking about some new securities he's invested in while Mom gushes about a pair of shoes she recently bought. I'd order my own damn food and I'd join the conversation without fear of saying the wrong thing.

And what happens when I do step out of line?

I chance a quick glance at Kostas. His hazel eyes are sharpened as his dad speaks, but I have no doubts he's got me locked in his side eye. I'd like to convince myself he's civilized as he sips his wine and discusses potential property locations with his father.

But he's not civilized.

He cut off a man's foot and beat him to death with it, for fuck's sake.

As though clued into my thoughts, his eyes slide my way, cutting me to the bone. I've never met a man who can say so little with his mouth, but scream everything with his eyes.

Behave.

You're mine.

Buckle up, sweetheart, because this is your life now.

I tear my gaze from his and gulp down my wine, hating the way heat creeps up my neck. I'm embarrassed. A ridiculous sensation, but it's the truth. Embarrassed I was born into a family who would sell me like a head of cattle. Sold to a slaughterhouse, no less. It can't get any more embarrassing than that.

When dessert is finally brought out, Nora turns her attention to me. "I was thinking since we only have a week to plan your wedding, we could get started tomorrow."

The spoon that was almost to my mouth, filled with custard, falls from my fingers and clangs against the ceramic plate. Holy shit.

One week.

One week and I'll officially have been sold to the Devil.

Lovely.

Kostas mentioned the timeframe before, but it didn't hit me until right at this moment. I'm about to become his wife in less than a week.

I think I'm going to be sick.

As if he can sense my freaking out, Kostas makes it a point to glide his hand up my thigh and under my dress. My hand flies under the table to stop him, and he glares my way.

Mine.

He doesn't have to say it, because those beautifully horrible eyes do it for him.

I try to remove his hand, and he releases me, only to thread our fingers together. Like we're a real couple. This is the same hand he used to kill a man.

"Have you seen the ring your son bought me?" I ask Nora, using my question as an excuse to take my hand back. Reaching over Aris, I extend my arm to show her the ridiculous rock that sits on my ring finger.

As soon as I realize what I've done, a cold dread settles over me. I'm practically leaned across Aris's lap—a place I know for a fact Kostas doesn't want me to be.

"Oh, it's gorgeous!" Nora coos. "See, Aris, your brother *can* be romantic."

Aris snorts but doesn't argue with his mother.

I quickly shrink back after she's inspected the diamond and glance over at Kostas. His expression is hard and unreadable. His eyes, though, are blazing with fury.

Oh God.

My hand trembles, and he takes it again. This time, I don't pull it away. I let his thumb sweep over the back of my hand and truly pretend he's trying to comfort me.

But silly me…

The perpetrator doesn't comfort the victim.

Hot tears well in my eyes, but I quickly blink them away. My mother didn't raise a victim. She raised me to be strong and feisty and assertive.

I miss my mom.

I miss home.

"I was thinking we could go in search of the venue tomorrow," Nora says, pulling me from my near meltdown. "I've made a list of the best locations. Kostas mentioned hiring a wedding planner, but I thought it would be fun for us to do it ourselves. There are some gorgeous churches in the area. What do you think?"

I always envisioned a beautiful church wedding where my soul mate and I would exchange heartfelt vows, and afterward attend the reception filled with our closest family and friends. My husband and I would spend the evening in each other's arms until it was time to say our goodbyes and leave for our honeymoon. Now, all of my dreams have been shattered.

I'm living in a nightmare.

It doesn't matter if it's the most beautiful wedding ever put on, it'll be a hateful shame. A vengeful way to get back at my father. A lifelong sentence for a crime I didn't commit.

"Talia," Kostas rumbles from beside me, a low warning in his tone.

I don't know why her sons and husband haven't told her that this wedding isn't a romantic union of two people in love, but of a debt being paid, but I'm not going to be the one to tell her. I can guarantee, based on Kostas's behavior, that the devilish momma's boy at my side would not like that at all. So, even though I have no desire to plan any aspect of this sham of a wedding, I nod politely.

"Uh, sure," I stammer out. "That sounds like fun."

"Perfect!" She beams. "I'll be by at ten to pick you up."

She seems nice. Really nice. I wonder if she's nice enough to betray her own family and help me escape this hellish island.

"Do you live here as well?" I ask.

"No, Ezio and I live about twenty minutes just outside of town, in the home Kostas and Aris grew up in. You will have to bring her to visit soon," she says to Kostas.

"Of course, Mamá," he assures her in a gentle voice that's as fake as my smile.

We wrap up dessert and I'm spared from any more probing questions. For the most part, this family leaves me out of their seemingly common dinner conversation. All too soon, I'm broken from the most normal situation I've been in since I got here, to leave.

Off to be alone with my *fiancé*.

Wonderful.

Cue panic attack.

After we say our goodbyes, Aris heads toward the bar. Kostas places a palm on my lower back, guiding me down the hallway and out of the hotel. The night is warm with a slight breeze. I wish it'd strengthen and carry me far away from here. Unfortunately, though, my luck doesn't hold out, because before I know it, we're standing in front of Kostas's impressive villa.

The Devil's den.

And I live here now.

Terror claws its way up my throat. We'll be alone. Together. Sharing a bed. Images of what might happen in that bed claw at my mind, causing a hemorrhaging of fear to drown my every thought. One gentle push once the door is open and I'm thrust right into my living nightmare.

The door closes with a click behind us. He's quiet. Too quiet. The hairs on my arms stand on end as I anticipate his next move.

"Relax," he rumbles. "I'm not going to eat you. *Yet.*"

Anger surges up inside of me and fuels me out of my state of terror. I shoot him a scathing glare that earns me a smirk instead. This, I can do. Sparring with an asshole. I did it all the time with my father. As long as he doesn't pull out his knives or tie me to a chair, I think I can handle this.

Rather than attack me like I conjured up in my mind, Kostas heads straight for the bedroom. I follow behind, watching as he removes his jacket and unbuttons his shirt, hanging both over the back of the chair. I'm frozen in place as he toes off his shoes and slides his dress pants down each muscular thigh, leaving him in only his briefs.

I let my guard down too soon.

Is this where we role play, our own little parts in this fucked-up play?

Pluto and Proserpina.

The rapist and his victim.

"Keep eyeing me like that and I'll fulfill those dark fantasies rolling through your mind," he bites out, his intense hazel eyes searing into me. "Every last one of them. All night long."

Averting my eyes, I stare down at the floor, frozen on what to do next. He stalks over to me until his black socks come into view.

Socks.

So simple and normal.

That is, unless you're using said sock to contain a murder weapon.

His fingers grip my jaw and he lifts my chin until I'm forced to look at him. He runs his thumb along my bottom lip, dragging the flesh roughly to the side.

"This is the part where you get ready for bed also," he explains, his voice dry and condescending. "Understand?"

I swallow down the mixture of hatred and fear that have tangled inside my throat. Furious tears burn at my eyes. One escapes and slides down my cheek. He leans forward, kissing the wetness.

"You have an early morning. I suggest you move." With those words, he releases me and motions at the dresser before turning his back to me.

I focus on grabbing my own change of clothes from the drawer, but unlike Kostas, who's clearly okay with being on display, I close the bathroom door and get changed in there. When I come out, dressed in the silkiest pair of pajamas I've ever felt, Kostas is already in bed and the room is darkened. He's staring down at his phone and it illuminates his face, making him seem darker and scarier than he already is, which is quite a feat if you ask me.

When he tilts his head up, I snap my eyes down and walk around to the other side of the bed.

I've never slept in a bed with a man before, and I have no clue what

I'm supposed to do. He said we're waiting until our wedding night to have sex, but does that mean we're waiting until that night to do everything? Suddenly feeling inexperienced and sheltered and terrified out of my mind, I tug my blankets up to my neck and lie on my side, facing away from Kostas, in hope that he'll let me go to sleep without asking anything of me.

But sleeping beside a monster is easier said than done.

No matter how tightly I squeeze my eyes shut, I know he's there, lying in wait. Just waiting to sink his teeth in and take a bite.

Just as I begin to relax, I hear him set his phone on the nightstand. The bed moves slightly as he adjusts to get comfortable.

"You're shaking the bed," he rumbles, pulling me slightly into his chest. "Are you crying?"

"No," I rasp out.

He wraps his arm around my front and nuzzles his face into the crook of my neck. "Are you afraid of me?"

"Y-Yes," I admit, knowing lying to him is futile and stupid.

"Mmm," is all he says. As though my being afraid is hardly an interesting thought to him. Then, his grip around me tightens as he draws me closer, his hips slightly flexing as he rubs his very obvious erection against my butt. "Fear can be healthy. Keeps the heart pumping like it should."

I hate this man.

I hate him with everything I am.

His palm spreads out over the front of my pajama top above my breasts. He caresses me gently with his thumb.

"Your heart is certainly beating like a champ." He slides his thumb lower, grazing my nipple and causing it to harden. "This works too."

I'd burst into tears if I weren't so pissed at his arrogance.

"Fuck you," I whisper, the hate vibrating through me.

"Don't worry, *moró mou*. I will. And soon."

chapter nine

Kostas

I'M AN ASSHOLE.

The poor girl thought I'd rape her.

I am a lot of things, but I don't have to force women. My sweet little fiancée will one day beg, whether she likes it or not. I'll spread her out on the bed and bury my face in her cunt until she doesn't push me away, but instead tugs me to her.

My phone buzzes and I groan. Fucking Aris. If he knows what's good for him, he'd leave me the hell alone.

Aris: We need to talk.

Me: I'm busy.

Aris: Too bad.

I toss my phone on my desk, swallowing down my irritation. It's not like I can avoid my brother forever. He's a part of the family business. Without his incredible ability to manipulate numbers in our favor, we wouldn't have half the fortune we do. Unfortunately, Aris is a necessary part of my world.

While I wait on the smug bastard, I think about this morning. I'd left Talia sleeping. At some point in the middle of the night, she'd softened toward me. In her dreams, I'm not a total monster. Her hand had snaked up my chest and she'd held on to me. Selfishly, I'd inhaled her hair while I wondered about my future with her.

It's not real.

I ignore the words inside my head. Maybe Talia and I are forced into this arranged marriage because her father is a stupid, spineless bitch, but there's no reason I can't make this work in my favor. Talia is a fucking knockout. Exactly my type with her curvaceous body, plump dick sucking lips, and tight ass. Her mouth that she tries desperately to keep in check is more than attractive. It gets my cock achingly hard.

"Ahh," Aris chirps from the doorway. "Up bright and early this morning, dear brother."

Leaning back in my chair and crossing my arms over my chest, I watch my brother with disinterest. With one look, I convey to him that I'm more superior than he will ever be. Father chooses me as his second-in-command. I'm the one who deals with the dark, nefarious deeds that cloud around the Demetriou name. It's me who takes a wife for a business debt, because soft men like Aris would cave at a few tears.

Aris is too soft, too sweet, too passive.

But he looks at my fiancée like he might try to assert a little power over me.

Over my fucking dead body.

"Get to the point," I bite out, darting my eyes to the clock. "I need to ravish my bride-to-be before our mother whisks her away to do wedding things."

His jaw clenches and his eyes flare with anger.

One point for me, little brother.

"I didn't know rape was in your repertoire of evil deeds," he hisses, losing some of his good boy cool.

I laugh, but it's cold and heartless. "There's a lot you don't know about me."

"You're a cruel motherfucker." He drops into the seat across from me. "But she'll be your wife. You sure you want to start out a marriage with hate?"

"She didn't hate me last night when she was snuggled up against me," I taunt, loving the way his eyes flicker with rage. That's right, asshole, she's mine. Little baby brothers don't get gifts from Daddy.

His nostrils flare, and he casts his gaze out the window. Finally, he takes a calming breath, huffing out his words. "Cy and Bakken Galani's family are retaliating."

I lift a brow. "The Galanis are roaches, brother. Plentiful and difficult to kill with usual methods. That is why we drive them out of their hiding place and stomp on them."

"Your arrogance is a weakness," Aris sneers. "It'll get you killed by our enemies one day. Who knows, maybe it'll be one of the Nikolaides. Phoenix seems like he'd be quite a match for you."

"Phoenix is on his daddy's leash. And Niles is on ours," I remind him. "As long as Talia warms my bed, those rats won't try a goddamn thing."

"Perhaps not the Nikolaides," Aris concedes. "But the Galanis are fired up. My contacts state that their other brother Estevan is pissed. He's the reckless one. I wouldn't put it past that fucker to blow up the damn hotel."

"I'll send out some men to hunt him down. Get me names of anyone in Estevan's circle. We'll drive them out and stomp on them. Surely this we can agree on, brother."

Aris grimaces. "Surely."

"Now," I state as I rise, "you'll have to excuse me. I need to wake my future wife up."

His eyes narrow on me. "That ring wiped out your account."

"So move money from my offshores. By the end of third quarter, I'll have made it back. Taxes are due soon." I raise my eyebrows to dare him to challenge me more.

"Whatever, man. Just don't be a total dick to her. She's been through enough."

"But being a dick is so entertaining," I say with a smirk.

Once I'm out of my office, I stride out of the hotel to my villa. I slip in quietly and find Talia sitting at the bar eating a bowl of cereal. Her blond hair is messy and dark circles ring her eyes from stress or lack of sleep. She picks up the bowl and gulps down the milk. It's cute and shows her age. As soon as she realizes I'm looking at her, she stiffens, shooting me a hateful glare.

"My mother will be here within the hour."

She pushes away the bowl, a feral gleam in her blue eyes. "I'm not going."

"Excuse me?"

The brave woman slides off the barstool and shrugs. "I can't pretend,

Kostas. I can't and I won't. You want to treat me as your prisoner, then do it. I can't go on acting like this is something I want."

"Don't be dramatic, *moró mou*. You'll shower and dress. Quickly now." I stalk past her and into my bedroom. Once in the bathroom, I turn on the shower before walking back into the living room.

She crosses her arms over her chest in defiance.

"Go," I bark out.

Her head shakes stubbornly. "No."

Now she's really starting to piss me off.

"Do I need to remind you who I am?" I rumble, locking eyes with her.

"Haven't forgotten," she hisses. "If you're going to kill me, just do it already."

I roll my eyes and storm over to her. "If I wanted to kill you, I would've done it already. We'll have far more fun playing together. Don't quit the game now, ómorfo korítsi."

Her nostrils flare at the words *beautiful girl*. "I hate you."

"Too bad," I growl, rushing her. She shrieks when I toss her over my shoulder and stride out of the room. Her useless hands pound against my lower back. Once in the bathroom, I drop her to her feet. "Take them off or I take them off for you."

She shakes her head, backing away from me.

"Suit yourself," I snap, irritated that she's acting like a spoiled brat. I grab the front of her pajamas and yank her forward. Her hands grip my suit jacket to keep herself from falling.

"Stop!" she yells, attempting to claw at me.

I wrangle her out of her shirt easily enough, but she's wiggling too much for me to get her pants off. Flipping her around, I push her against the wall and grip her wrists behind her with one hand. She cries out when I yank her pants and underwear down in one pass. When she's naked, I swivel her around and pin her against the wall by gripping her biceps. Her tits jiggle with every breath she takes and her skin burns crimson.

"Are you going to bathe yourself?"

Her blue eyes burn into mine with challenge. "And if I don't?"

I nudge her knees apart with my knee and slide up to her cunt. "I would be more than thrilled with the husbandly duty of washing my future wife." I lean in and nuzzle the side of her neck with my nose before nipping at the side of her throat. "Just be warned. I'm very thorough."

Pulling away, I regard her with a lifted brow. Her lips press together, barely containing words she desperately wants to say. Words that will get her in trouble. I slide my palms down her arms and then take her hands in mine. She jerks them from my grip, so I clutch onto her naked hips instead. When I rub circles on her soft flesh with my thumbs, her breath hitches and her nipples harden. I'm painfully hard in my slacks, and if my mother wasn't on her way, I'd throw out my stupid waiting until marriage for sex shit and take her right now.

The eyes don't lie.

Behind her thinly veiled hate is lust. Desire. Need.

"Make the decision now, Talia."

Her eyes flutter closed when I slide my fingers along her lower stomach in a teasing way. As my knuckle runs along her slit, she sucks in a sharp breath.

"I, uh, I can do it myself," she whispers. "Please."

"Pity," I say with a faux pout. "I was looking forward to washing your dirty little body." I slide my hand back to her hip before turning her to face the shower. I smack her ass hard enough to earn me a hateful scowl over her shoulder. "Quickly now. My mother doesn't like tardiness."

She climbs into the shower and glowers at me through the glass. "You can leave now."

"Quality control," I say, holding my palms up. "It's a dirty job, but someone has to do it."

Her middle finger goes up and she spends her entire shower washing herself one-handed so that she can flip me off the whole time. I've killed men for lesser offenses.

Not her.

With her, it's fucking cute.

Keep testing me, *moró mou*. It gets my dick really goddamn hard.

The water finally shuts off and I'm waiting with a towel. She must have cooled in her shower because she won't meet my gaze. I wrap the towel around her and hug her to my chest. Her body grows stiff when my mouth brushes along her ear.

"Adrian will accompany you and my mother today. Don't try anything funny like running away. You won't get far."

She turns her head slightly toward me. My lips hover above her cheek.

"What if I tell your mother about what an awful monster you are?" she challenges, her voice breathy despite the brave words she speaks.

"She'll laugh it off because she's sweet and polite," I tell her, pressing my lips to her cheek. "And then you'll have to come back home and deal with me."

"What will you do?"

"What won't I do is a better question."

Her body trembles. "You scare me."

"You'll soon grow to love it."

"I'll never love *you*."

I slide my palms to her stomach and then up to her breasts. "You will if I *make* you." I tug away her towel, once again leaving her naked. Stepping back, I admire her perfect ass. "My mother will want to take you somewhere nice for lunch. A dress will do."

"You're an asshole."

I slap her ass hard before leaving her to get ready.

Because that's what assholes do.

chapter
ten

Talia

NORA AND I HAVE SPENT THE DAY DOING ALL THINGS WEDDING related. We've found the most gorgeous wedding gown—one I would die to wear if it wasn't Kostas I'm marrying. Ordered the bridesmaids' dresses—for bridesmaids I don't even know and won't meet until the wedding rehearsal dinner on Friday. Apparently, Kostas's parents both have extended family, who will all be a part of the wedding, and Nora confirmed all of their measurements. We confirmed the church we'll be getting married in, and the beautiful garden venue for the reception. We scheduled the catering company and designed the wedding cake—an exquisite five-tier wilted magnolia petal design. It will match the color scheme we decided on—soft pink and cream. We only stopped once for a quick lunch.

In one long, exhausting day, Nora and I have planned the wedding of my dreams. If I could wave a magic wand, this is exactly what it would all look like, except for one detail. The groom. And that one detail is what ruined every moment of the day. I tried to picture walking down the decorated aisle in my wedding dress, but only imagined Kostas scowling at me. I imagined us cutting the beautiful cake and partaking in the tradition of *feeding each other*, but all I could envision is Kostas glaring at me.

I saw several of the receipts from today, so I know this wedding is costing the Demetriou family a small fortune—not that they can't afford it—and it's all a waste. An unnecessary show. The church and reception and decorations and wedding attire might all be perfect, but none of it matters because the wedding is a sham. The vows we'll recite will be fake. The exchanging of rings will have zero meaning. And all for what? So Kostas's mom can enjoy her eldest son getting married? So my da— Niles, can have it rubbed in his face that his daughter has been bought in exchange for his debt? It doesn't make any sense. He doesn't even live anywhere near Kostas and his dad. How is it fair that he's now debt free and I have to spend the rest of my life married to a man who is hell-bent on making my life miserable?

"I was thinking we could go to dinner," Nora suggests from the back of the town car. We've just left the bakery and are heading back home. *Home.* The word leaves a sour taste in my mouth. This place will never really be home. "Aris mentioned he's just finished up a meeting and is available to join us." Nora smiles sweetly. If the circumstances were different, and I was marrying Kostas out of love and not to fulfill an obligation, I would feel lucky to have Nora as my mother-in-law. In all of the movies I've seen, the mother-in-law is always a bitch, trying to create a wedding the bride hates. But not Nora.

The entire day she has been nothing but sweet to me. When I was standing on the alteration pedestal in my wedding grown and began to cry—she assumed they were happy tears—she pulled me into a hug and whispered, "I am so happy my son has found love. It takes a strong woman to love a Demetriou man. Thank you for loving my boy."

I wanted so badly to tell her that it's impossible to love a Demetriou man, and that it would never happen, but then I remembered that she does in fact love one. How? I have no idea. But she does. So I kept my mouth shut and nodded and told her the only honest thing I could think to say. "I'm so glad you're going to be my mother-in-law."

"Talia," Nora says, bringing me back into the now. "How do you feel about dinner?"

"That sounds wonderful," I tell her truthfully. For one, I really do love her company, and it will mean less time I'm stuck at home with Kostas taunting and torturing me. Sick, sadistic asshole. It's like he gets off on messing with me. Not that it should surprise me. The guy also gets off on beating men with their own limbs. God knows what else turns him on.

My mind goes to earlier this morning, Kostas provoking me in the shower. I thought for sure he was going to force himself on me, and shockingly, while my brain screamed no, my body…my damn traitorous body reacted oppositely. My nipples hardened in want, and the area between my legs tightened in need. For a split second when I thought maybe Kostas was going to take me right then and there in the bathroom, I wasn't sure whether to beg him not to, or beg him to do it. Even now, sitting here in the car, my body shivers at the mere thought of him touching me. But I imagine, just like this fake wedding, sex with Kostas will be nothing like I've always fantasized about when I've thought about my wedding night with my husband. There won't be any love making or worshipping. He won't tenderly kiss and love on me. He'll be rough and mean and cruel. He'll hurt me…just because he can.

The town car stops in front of a small hole-in-the-wall restaurant. Alessandro's Urban Kitchen, the sign reads. The driver opens Nora's door, at the same time my door is opened. I'm momentarily taken aback, until I see Aris is standing there, holding the door open with one hand, his other extended to help me out.

"Thank you," I tell him with a soft smile. While Kostas is a cruel, heartless asshole, his brother doesn't seem to be anything like him.

"Did you ladies have a good day?" Aris asks, guiding his mother and me into the restaurant.

"We did," Nora says, beaming. "Everything is ready for Friday."

"Friday?" Aris prompts.

"The rehearsal dinner," Nora tells him. The hostess sits us at a small booth. Nora sits on one side and I sit on the other. Without thought, Aris slides in next to me. His leg bumps mine, and he grins playfully. Flush creeps up my neck. Why couldn't Kostas be more like Aris? Then maybe being forced to marry him wouldn't be so bad.

"Don't forget you need to pick up your tux," she says, picking up the wine menu. "And don't leave until you're sure it fits. We can't have you standing up as your brother's best man looking like a dressed up monkey." She and Aris laugh. It's light and playful, and it makes my heart both soar and hurt.

"When I was a teenager, Mom ordered my suit for a dance," Aris explains. "I told her I tried it on, but I lied. When I got home, it turned out I had had a growth spurt, and the arms and legs were all two inches too short."

"I told him he reminded me of those monkeys in the circus," Nora adds with a laugh.

The waiter comes over, and Nora orders us a red wine, while I eye the menu. It's Mediterranean and everything looks delicious. We spend dinner talking and laughing. Nora talks about her sons, and two things become apparent: one, she loves them with every ounce of her being, and two, she either has no clue who Kostas really is, or she's deep, deep in denial.

"Aris, *agóri mou*, would you mind bringing Talia home with you? The time has gotten away from me and I really need to get home. Your father will be home shortly, and you know how upset he gets if I'm not home to sit with him while he eats." Nora smiles, but it's not as bright as it's been all day, and I have to wonder, if maybe the reason she focuses so heavily on her relationship with her sons is because her marriage is lacking. When my parents were going through their divorce, my mom made it a point to smother me with love and affection. I didn't understand it at the time, but maybe it was out of her guilt of not giving her children the perfect family.

"Of course, Mamá." Aris stands and offers his hand to his mother as she exits the booth. The three of us walk outside, and after Nora makes me promise to not be a stranger and reminds me that she'll see me Friday evening, we part ways.

Aris's car is brought around by the valet. It's a shiny gray two-door Porsche sports car. After opening the door for me, Aris walks around to the driver side and folds himself into the car. "It's a nice evening," he says. "How about the top down?"

"Sure." I shrug. Aris's lips curl into a handsome grin as he presses a button that has the top lifting.

"Buckle up, *agapiméni*." *Sweetheart*. Aris winks, and a giggle bubbles up and flows out of me at his playfulness. Aris speeds through the streets just like his brother, wild and reckless, only it's different, because Aris's version is fun and exciting.

Too quickly we arrive back at the hotel, and my mood immediately drops. Aris gives me a speculating look, and it's as if he can read my thoughts because he says, "Why don't we go for a swim? I heard

Kostas is working late anyway…something about a business associate not cooperating."

A chill races down my spine at the last *business associate* of his I met.

"A swim sounds really good," I say, then remember I don't have a suit. At least I don't think I do. "Can we go by the shop so I can grab a bathing suit?"

"Sure," Aris says, placing his hand on my lower back. "I need to get changed, so I'll meet you over there."

After finding a cute bikini and matching cover-up and flip-flops, I head out to the pool. Aris is already there, with a beer in his hand, sitting along the edge of the pool. "I got you your favorite," he says, holding up a glass of lemonade.

"Thanks." I set the bag of my clothes next to a lounge chair, kick off my flip-flops, and take off my cover-up.

When I catch Aris eyeing my body, my neck and chest both heat up. The bikinis were all super skimpy, and even though I picked the one with the most material, it still shows off *all* of my assets.

After taking a sip of my lemonade, I glance around the area. The last time I was here I was upset and didn't really pay close attention. On one side of the pool is the tiki hut and bar. On the other side, though, is a massive rock waterfall with something running through the middle of it. "Is that a waterslide?" I ask Aris, who laughs.

"Yep, you want to go?"

I haven't been to a waterpark since I was a child. My mom and Stefano brought me, and we had a blast. "Sure!"

Aris laughs some more. "C'mon, *agipénos.*"

I can't help my grin at his new nickname for me. *Sweetheart.* It's not so different from what Kostas calls me, but when Aris says it, it feels sincere, sweet, genuine. He's not trying to taunt me with his words, or scare me with his actions.

We race up the rock steps to the top of the waterfall. I didn't realize just how tall it was, until we're standing at the top where the entrance to the slide is. My step falters slightly, and Aris chuckles. "You're not getting cold feet, are you?"

"No," I sass. "But…you go first."

Aris throws his head back in laughter, and I find myself smiling hard.

It feels good to smile. "Okay, fine," he says. He drops onto the beginning of the slide. "Come here real quick. I want to show you something."

Stepping toward him, I lean down to see inside the tunnel, but it's too dark. Before I can tell him that, he grabs my hips and throws me onto his lap. "Hold on!" he yells as we descend down the dark tube of flowing water. I scream and squeal the entire way down, and Aris laughs, holding on to me tightly.

When we reach the bottom of the slide, we fall a foot or so into the water. Our bodies splash and sink, but Aris never lets go of me. We both ascend at the same time, and my laughter can't be stopped. "You're such an ass!" My hair is a mess, all over my face, and I'm sure my makeup is running. I probably look like a drowned rat, but I don't care.

"You liked it," he says with a flirty grin. "You should see our other hotel on the other side of the island. It has an entire water park." Aris runs his fingers through his wet hair.

I don't mean to, but my eyes linger on his face. On his brown eyes, that are darker than Kostas's, yet seem so much lighter. The water drips down, and his tongue darts out to lick the liquid that's landed above his lip. His sweet lips that curl into a playful smile.

My heart pounds against my ribcage, and I have to force myself to look away. I can't be crushing on Aris. He's Kostas's brother. He's going to be the best man at our wedding in five days. I've seen what Kostas has done to a man who wasn't loyal to his family. What would he do to me if he even thought I had feelings for Aris?

"I need to go," I blurt out, and without waiting for a response from Aris, I swim over to the stairs and get out. I grab a towel and wrap it around myself. When I turn around, I find Aris standing in front of me.

"Did I do something?" he asks, his brows furrowing in confusion.

"No." I shake my head to emphasize my answer. "I just…I should probably get home."

"Okay." He nods in understanding, only he doesn't really understand. "Just let me grab my stuff and I'll walk you back."

"Oh, you don't have to do that." The last thing I need is Kostas to spot the two of us together. Something I probably should've thought about before I agreed to go swimming with Aris.

"It's no problem." Aris shrugs. "My villa is right next door." He winks, and I flinch. He's not implying what I think he is, right? He's just being his usual playful self. He doesn't mean anything by it. It's all in my head.

We grab our stuff, and I throw my cover-up over my still wet bikini. We walk in silence until we reach the door to my villa.

"I'm assuming my brother told you the code," Aris jokes.

"Yeah." I type it in, then turn around. "Thank you for…" I wave my hand toward where we came from. "I had a good time."

"You're welcome," Aris says back. He steps forward and into my space. Several long seconds pass as we stare at one another, neither of us saying a word. My breathing becomes labored. Heat radiates from him, nearly luring me closer. If it weren't for the chill of worry creeping over me that my fiancé might show up, I might just chase that warmth. But just as quickly as it came, the heat disappears as Aris takes a step back. "Anything you need…I'm here," he says before he turns and walks away.

chapter eleven

Talia

I ROLL OVER FROM MY SIDE ONTO MY STOMACH AND SEE KOSTAS'S side of the bed is empty. My hand brushes along the sheets, feeling the coolness. Every day this week it's been the same thing. He comes home after I'm asleep and leaves before I wake up. I spend my days walking the property, swimming, and hanging out with Aris when he's not working. But today is different because today is Friday. Our wedding rehearsal and dinner. A smile stretches across my face at the thought. Not because I'm going to have to walk through the steps of marrying Kostas, but because I'm going to get to see my family, specifically my mom. At that thought, I throw my covers off my body and stretch my legs, ready to get the day started. Kostas told me I could drive with Adrian to pick them up at the airport.

After taking a shower, I head over to Aphrodite's, a restaurant on the hotel property that serves the best breakfast and coffee, and eat by myself. Then I take a stroll over to the library—yes, the hotel has an actual library where one can read, and the shelves are filled with every type of book imaginable. I get comfy on the couch, reading *The Scarlet Letter* until Adrian lets me know it's time to go. I never tell him where I'm going, but somehow he always knows where to find me.

Freaking Kostas. He couldn't care less about me, yet he still has to make sure he's always in control of my life. Stupid, possessive asshole.

When we pull up to the front of the airport, it's just after two o'clock, and their flight has already arrived. Adrian insists we wait in the car, but I can't help myself, so I get out and wait on the sidewalk. Several people are exiting at the same time. My eyes dart all around in search of her, my feet bouncing in place in anticipation, and when they finally find her, tears fall.

"Mom!" I throw myself into her arms and nuzzle my face into her neck. I can smell her signature perfume she's been wearing for as far back as I can remember. It's sweet and comforting and smells like home. The bag she was carrying hits the ground and she wraps her arms around me.

"Oh, *cara mia*," she cries. "Let me see you." She pulls back slightly, but still keeps her hands in mine. "You've gotten a tan." She smiles, but it's not real. It's her version of making the best out of things. "The sun agrees with you."

"I missed you, Mom." I pull her back into a tight hug.

"We must go," Adrian points out, and I mentally roll my eyes.

After my mom and I separate, I give Stefano a hug. Nonno and Nonna each take turns giving me a hug, but it's awkward. Everything has changed. My grandfather used to be a man I thought was invincible, but not even he could save me from this forced marriage. And our last conversation ended with him yelling at me. Something he's never done before.

"I spoke with Phoenix," Mom says as we all climb into the limo. "He and your father will be arriving shortly and will meet us at the church."

I still at her words. I didn't even think about *him* coming.

"He's not my father," I hiss. "And he's not welcome anywhere near me, especially at the wedding he's forced me into."

My mom's brows rise in concern, but she doesn't argue.

Pulling my cell phone out, I send a text message to Kostas. I've had his number but have yet to call or text him.

Me: I don't want Niles at the wedding.

Not even a minute later, he replies.

Kostas: None of this is about what you want.

Ugh! He's such an asshole. I don't even bother to respond.

"Is everything ready for tomorrow?" Mom asks. She pushes a wayward strand of hair behind my ear and gives me her motherly smile. I hate that Niles will be at the wedding, but I'm so thankful my mom will at least be there.

"Yes, Nora and I got everything done. The seamstress will be available at the church in case any of the bridesmaids' dresses don't fit." I've spoken to my mom every day on the phone, so she knows how nice Nora has been to me. Nora came to the hotel yesterday and we had lunch to go over everything.

"I'm sure it will be a beautiful wedding," Mom says. "Have you spoken to Kostas about finishing school in the fall?"

I shake my head. My goal these past few days has been to speak to him as little as possible. I imagine once we're married tomorrow, everything will continue as it has been. He probably won't even notice if I go to school as long as I'm in bed at the end of the day.

Forty minutes later we arrive at Saint Nicholas's church. Several vehicles are parked in the parking lot, including Aris's Porsche and Kostas's Maserati. My stomach roils in fear and anticipation. I can't believe this is really happening. This time tomorrow I am going to be Mrs. Kostas Demetriou. The thought has me wanting to highjack this limo and take off in the other direction.

My mom must notice the sudden shift in my mood because she wraps her arm around me as we all walk toward the entrance to the church. The moment we're inside, I spot Nora. She's dressed in a simple yet elegant cream-colored dress with nude heels. When she sees we've arrived, she comes over to us.

"Talia, my darling girl, you look beautiful." Her eyes run up and down the simple floral dress and heels I'm wearing. And then her eyes look just past me and her smile falters slightly.

"Nora, this is my family," I say, making introductions. "This is my mom, Melody, my stepdad, Stefano, and my grandparents, Emilio and Vera."

"Yes, of course," Nora says. "Your grandparents and I have met at the occasional dinner. It's nice to see you both again." She gives each person an air kiss to their cheeks and a hug. "Everyone is waiting to begin. Victoria, Paulina, and Jacqueline have all tried on their dresses and they fit beautifully."

Nora guides us inside where the ceremony will be held. We've already gone over the details with the priest when we were here earlier this week, but she goes over it all again.

"Your family will sit on the left." Nora points out. "If you would like to have a seat, Father Nicholas is just going to go over what to expect during the ceremony tomorrow, and then we'll head over to Hēdonē for dinner," she says to my family, who all have a seat where she's pointed.

When I step up onto the altar, my eyes first find Aris's. He's standing next to his brother and three other men I've yet to meet. They must be family or friends of Kostas's. Aris gives me a small nod, and his lips curl into a half-smile half smirk. The familiarity and comfort his smile brings helps me to breathe just a little easier.

My eyes next land on Kostas. His eyes are gleaming and his wicked smirk does nothing to calm my nerves. He steps forward, and I almost take a step back but quickly stop myself.

He pushes a strand of hair behind my ear and whispers, "If you're done eye-fucking my brother, I'd like to get this over with so I can once and for all make you mine."

chapter twelve

Kostas

THE NERVE OF THIS WOMAN. SHE MAY BE MARRYING ME tomorrow, but it's my younger brother whom she smiles for. It's fucking Aris who she's been spending all her time with. Maybe no one else sees the way she looks at him, but I certainly do. And it pisses me right the fuck off.

Her face blanches at my words. "Kostas…"

"Yes, my bride," I say lowly, a hint of danger in my tone. "What do you have to say for yourself?"

All eyes are on us, but our voices are low enough only for us to hear.

"I, uh, you're being ridiculous," she murmurs. "I wasn't eye-fucking him."

It's like she's already forgotten what happened to the last person who lied to me. A hard look from me to her passes between us, making her tremble. Looking down, I nod at her strappy sandals.

"Lovely shoes. Did you get your toes done?"

She snaps her eyes to mine, her blue eyes flickering with horror. "I'm not a liar," she chokes out, understanding dawning on her. "You're just a jealous fiancé."

I reach up to cradle her cheek with my palm. "Perhaps."

"And an asshole," she hisses, earning a chuckle from me. "Let's get this over with."

I smirk at her. "So I'm not the only one looking forward to the honeymoon it would seem."

"Go to hell," she growls.

"Of course, Talia," I say, stepping closer, our mouths nearly touching. "But you're going with me."

The rehearsal was boring as fuck. Wedding shit always is. It doesn't matter if it's my wedding or one of my several girl cousins I've chosen for bridesmaids. Weddings are a fucking snooze. What's entertaining, though, is watching my fiancée squirm now every time Aris tries to talk to her.

That's right. I'm watching. Always fucking watching.

He finally gives up and walks over to talk to our father, who as usual, barely acknowledges he exists.

After we finished at the church, we came back to Hēdonē for a private dinner. According to Mamá, it's all part of the tradition. The two families breaking bread before the big day tomorrow. While we wait for dinner to be served, everyone enjoys a drink while they socialize amongst each other.

I watch as my father's gaze darts between Niles and Melody, as if bringing the two exes into the same room to watch their daughter be forcefully married off is the most entertaining thing he's ever seen.

It shouldn't be.

That's what has me on edge.

My marrying Talia should please Father because he loves revenge, but that's it. It shouldn't be ongoing like this. I'm pissed that I feel in the dark about the whole situation.

My eyes zero in on Mamá. At the rehearsal she seemed so happy, but right now as she sips on her cocktail and speaks to Melody, something is off. Sure, she's wearing her signature Demetriou good wife smile, but the light that's usually in her eyes is snuffed out.

Melody is probably tattling to her about how her daughter was forced to marry a horrible Demetriou man. Unfortunately for Melody, my mother knows all about bad men. And she loves her son. If she thinks she'll sway my mother, she has another thing coming. Mamá's gaze darts my way, a pained expression on her face.

Enough.

I stalk over to them and Mamá's face brightens. Melody is polite enough to end whatever line of conversation she initiated.

"Would you know I forgot my gift for Talia in the car?" Mamá says, her features tight. "I'm going to just run out and grab it real quick before dinner begins."

"What about my present?" I tease, smiling at her.

She laughs and kisses my cheek. "You're spoiled, son."

As soon as she rushes off, Melody clutches my bicep. "Kostas."

"Yes?"

"It's not too late." Her lips purse together.

Irritation burns in my gut. "Not too late for what?"

"To back out of this," she utters. "You have to know you're making a mistake."

I grit my teeth. "We both know what this marriage is."

"Yes," she bites back. "Punishment against my ex-husband for screwing your family over." She lets out a heavy sigh. "Please, Kostas, I know you're a good man. Don't make her the consequence of her father's actions."

Stepping away from her, I shake my head. "Sorry, Melody, but I'm not a good man. I'm marrying your daughter and it'd be in your best interest not to intervene."

I walk away without saying another word to her.

When Mamá gets back, we're going to need to have a chat.

I'm just seeking out Talia when someone clears their throat.

"Good evening, everyone, your table is now ready," Vince, the restaurant manager, announces. He opens the doors leading to the private dining room, and everyone herds in like cattle. My cousins, aunts, and uncles all find a seat on one side of the table, along with my brother. Father sits at the head of the table, and Mamá, who has just now returned, sits to his left, next to Aris. I notice that Niles and Phoenix are wisely standing away from the table, waiting to be asked to join.

Talia practically clings to her mother and stepfather while her grandparents remain polite and stoic beside them, on the other side of the table. I've allowed her to avoid me by riding with them from the chapel to the restaurant, but I'm done playing gracious host. I want my woman at my side. Where she belongs.

"Talia, come," I bark out, making her jolt and her stepfather glower at me. "It's time to make some toasts."

She grimaces but doesn't argue. I hold my hand out and wait for her to take it. A server walks by and begins handing out glasses of our house chardonnay. I release her hand so we can each take a glass.

"You can't hide from me forever," I taunt lowly, pressing a kiss to the top of her head.

"I'm not hiding. I was spending time with my mom. You should try it sometime."

I wince at her low blow, darting my gaze over to Mamá. Aris seems concerned as well, which has my nerves ratcheting up. When I catch my mother's gaze, I expect to see her eyes light up like usual. Instead, she tears up and looks away.

What the fuck? Is it possible she's really that upset over what Melody might've told her? She knows the score, and while she might've thought Talia and I are marrying for love, deep down she has to know nothing we do is without motive.

"Did you say something to upset her?" I demand, turning to look at Talia. Maybe it wasn't Melody, but Talia who upset her. She's gotten close to Mamá this week. If she's using her to punish me, she *will* regret it.

She seems offended because she huffs. "No, if anything, I've done the best job of convincing that poor woman that I'm madly in love with you."

"Obviously not convincing enough," I mutter, sliding my palm to her cheek. "Maybe you should practice." I press my lips to hers in a slightly provocative kiss meant to serve three purposes.

Piss off her family.

Make my mother happy.

And remind both Talia and Aris I'm the fucking fiancé.

Talia grips one lapel of my suit jacket and starts to pull away, on the verge of saying something. I deepen the kiss, lashing out at her tongue with mine. My free palm slides to her ass and I give it a little squeeze before breaking away. She shoots me a flustered, go to hell look, before draining her chardonnay. I chuckle and sip mine, assessing to see if our kiss did what it was intended.

Her family is pissed. In fact, I'd say her brother and stepfather would love to take turns pummeling my ass. And Aris looks jealous as fuck. Good. But my mother?

Hot tears roll down her cheeks as she shakes her head at me. Her bottom lip trembles. What the fuck? Is she ill? What have I done to upset her? And then her gaze darts over to Melody, confirming my suspicions. Meddling bitch. I'll have to remind her she has a reason to keep her mouth shut. I know she doesn't want her daughter to pay for her sins. Poor girl is already in a life sentence from her father.

"The toast?" Father urges, from the head of table looking regal as a king. "We're all waiting."

I clench my jaw and motion for Niles and Phoenix to join the table. Phoenix sits beside his mother in Talia's vacated seat with his father beside him. The weak Nikolaides all sitting in a row are fucking pathetic.

You're marrying one, asshole.

And she'll become a Demetriou.

Demetrious are not fucking pathetic.

"Tomorrow, Talia and I will become one," I say with a smile. "I'm sure the wedding will be a beautiful, extravagant affair because my mother has the magical touch when it comes to these things." I implore my mother to look at me, but she remains staring at her lap. Unease coils in my gut, but I continue. "I'm looking forward to marrying the most exquisite prize in all of Greece."

That jab is for Niles.

A jab that makes my mother flinch.

Fuck.

Talia grips my bicep and shoots me a stern look. As though she disapproves of my speech. But I can't help and agree with her. My mother is disgusted with me.

"I…" I trail off, unable to find the right words. Nothing is genuine because this entire thing is a fraud. Sure, I'm getting the good end of the deal, wrangling a hot-ass wife, but it's not real. And my mother knows it. Either she heard it from Melody or she can sense it. Either way she knows. This isn't some business that gets taken care of in a dank cellar with a sharp knife—business my mother never has to see. No, this business is infiltrating our personal lives. Her life.

"We just want to thank you all for coming," Talia says, saving me from utter humiliation. "Nora and I have tirelessly planned a gorgeous wedding. I'm thrilled to wear the loveliest gown to ever be created. Marrying Kostas will be quite the adventure, I am sure. Here's to adventures and new memories."

Everyone but my mother raises their glass. Since Talia's glass is empty, I hand her mine before stalking over to Mamá. I grip my mother's shoulder and lean down.

"Everything okay?" I demand, shooting Aris a worried look.

She reaches up to grab my hand and then takes my brother's hand with her other. "Just feeling a little emotional. I love you boys very much. Not a second of regret when it comes to my love for you both."

O-fucking-kay.

"We love you too, Mamá," Aris and I both say in unison.

"Good," she chokes out. "Make sure you keep on loving those who deserve it, so you don't end up like your father."

Talia's eyes meet mine from across the table where she must choose to sit beside her father or mine. In the end, her hatred over what her father has done to her wins out because she sits directly across from my mother, at my father's side. Weirded out by the whole thing, I walk back over to her and take my seat between the slimy Nikolaides and the beautiful one who'll shed that last name soon. The servers begin bringing out food. My stomach is in knots. I busy myself with a Mediterranean salad, stirring it up to coat each piece of lettuce with the dressing. Everyone is talking loudly and the restaurant buzzes with voices and laughter.

Glancing up at my mother, I realize she's left the table to stand directly behind my father. She rests a hand on his shoulder.

"Everyone," Mamá calls out. "I'd like to say something."

A polite hush falls across the table. I meet Aris's stare and he's getting the same weird-ass vibe from our mother because he's tense as fuck. Father stares directly ahead, the amusement gone from his face.

"I have something to say, and it will be in everyone's best interest to let me say it. Understood?" Mamá's eyes are slightly wild. She's normally serene and calm. Currently, she's in a manic state. Her body trembles and her face is red. Sweat beads at her temples and above her upper lip.

"Mamá," I start, but she cuts me off with a sharp look I remember from my childhood.

"Especially you, my son. You need to hear what I have to say the most."

I stiffen and slide my gaze to my father. His nostrils flare, but he remains tightlipped. Since when does my father not put my mother in her place if it means she'll embarrass him. Since he's not coming to my aid, I simply nod at her.

"You know," she says bitterly, "when I saw this beautiful woman who was to marry my son, I was thrilled. Beyond thrilled. I thought, perhaps, my boy had enough of me in him to break the horrible Demetriou curse. To be anyone but his father."

"Mamá," Aris mutters.

She shakes her head at him. "Let. Me. Finish."

Talia of all people should enjoy this and be gloating, but she's tense beside me.

"I thought things were changing for our family," Mamá says, tears welling in her eyes. "I thought we'd moved past all the hate from our past, Ezio." She edges closer to my father, patting his shoulder and making his eyes widen. "But you didn't forget the affair, did you? No, you held onto that revenge and waited all these years to get back at me."

What?

I glower at my father, who won't even look at me. Again, I'm in the fucking dark and I hate it. Aris shoots me a confused look.

"Father," I growl. "Shut this down. Now."

"Your father won't say a goddamn thing, Kostas," my mother bellows and waves a gun in the air before pushing it against my father's back.

Fuck.

No wonder he's being quiet. She's holding him at gunpoint.

"Your father tortured me for years, Kostas," Mamá explains, the tears rolling down her cheeks and ruining her makeup. "Years. While you looked up to your father and wanted to be just like him, I hated him with every ounce of my being. I stayed for my boys."

"You stayed because you had to," Father growls, consequences be damned.

Mamá pushes the gun harder against his back. "I stayed for those boys," she hisses. "Don't think for a second you had me chained to you out of fear. I don't fear you, Ezio, I hate you."

A warm hand slides into mine and I realize it's Talia offering me comfort. Her of all people. My hand is cold in hers. I can't bring myself to squeeze it back. I certainly don't pull the fuck away, though.

"I am so sorry," Mamá says, turning her attention to Melody. "I was in love with Niles for over a decade, and selfishly, I hoped I could escape from my cold marriage and into the warmth of his arms indefinitely. I didn't think about what it did to your family and your marriage. Please forgive me."

It all makes fucking sense now.

"Nothing to forgive. I have Stefano now," Melody says politely, a tremble in her voice. The woman who stole her husband has a gun. I'd be polite too.

Mamá turns her animosity on Niles. "You used me," she chokes out. "I loved you and you used me. When it came down to it, and I was ready to run off with you, you abandoned me. You allowed Ezio to find out about the affair and then you left me to deal with the aftermath alone." Mamá swipes a tear away. "He was cruel to me, Niles. He hurt me and belittled me. He punished me—alone—for crimes we committed together. And yet I took it all for my sons and for the love I still held onto for you."

"You weren't the only one punished," Niles argues like the stupid fucking fool he is. "I'm broke because of you." Being broke is going to be the least of his concerns if he doesn't shut his fucking mouth.

I catch Adrian's stare from across the room as he slowly inches closer and closer. I'm caught between wanting him to stop my mother and telling him to back the fuck away from her. Adrian is loyal to the Demetriou men, not the women.

"Talia," Mamá says sadly, ignoring Niles. "I'm so sorry. I hoped it was a coincidence when I discovered you and Kostas were to be married. My past was a shadow that was creeping up on you, ready to shroud you in darkness as well." Mamá looks pointedly at me. "Don't give up on true love. If you find it, take it, and get the hell out of here, consequences be damned."

A mixture of shame and fury rushes through my veins. Talia squeezes my hand again, and this time, I thread my fingers with hers.

"Mamá, may I speak?" I demand in a low, deadly tone.

She shakes her head. "No, you may not. You will sit and listen to every word I have to say."

I'm not a child and yet she's treating me like one. I glance at Aris, expecting a satisfied smirk on his face, but he's furious too.

"Kostas, you can't turn out like him. Your father is a monster. I know you have enough good in you that you can do better than that," Mamá chokes out, her voice pleading. "Aris will be fine. He's like me. Not so hard around the edges, but it's you I worry about. I worry you'll destroy this poor, sweet girl like your father destroyed me."

"Mamá," I snap, losing my cool. "That's enough."

Talia leans in, her shoulder brushing mine. "Kostas, calm down," she whispers, looking up at me. "She has a gun. Just let her say what she has to say. It'll all be over soon."

Absently, I kiss her lips and nod before looking at my mother. Mamá stares at me, her eyes empty and her features tired. She ages ten years before us.

"Talia and you both deserve more than this," Mamá says, her voice devoid of emotion. "You deserve to make your own choices about love, not be forced into it because of the actions of your parents." She regards Aris with a soft look that used to bother me when we were kids because I assumed it meant he was her favorite. "Aris, my boy, I'm sorry if I in-advertently hurt you by my actions. Your father enjoyed punishing me, and unfortunately, you were too much like me."

Aris clenches his jaw and his eyes glass over with tears.

"And, Kostas, my boy," Mamá utters, her eyes still soft as she regards me. "I'm sorry if I've embarrassed you or hurt you. I love you and your brother both. Equally. I always have."

Talia squeezes my hand again, a reminder that even though we're on different teams in this shit show, she's offering her support. Confusing emotions war within me, but gratitude that she can put down our differ-ences to comfort me wins over. Maybe this marriage will work out after all. Mamá has said her piece and embarrassed the shit out of everyone. Now, we can get back to dinner and Mamá can take a Valium.

"It's time to put an end to this," Mamá utters. "And the only way to do that is to eliminate the person who is the root cause of everyone's pain."

Pop!

Father's eyes widen as his chest blooms red.

"Mamá!" I roar, rising to my feet as Aris does.

Adrian rushes forward and several women at the table scream in horror. I'm already stalking to my mother when she mouths, "I'm sorry," before sliding the barrel of the gun between her lips. My eyes slam shut at the same time another pop is heard. Chaos ensues around us. When I reopen my eyes, my mother lies on the floor, a large pool of blood already forming around her head.

No.

No. No. Fucking no.

Something hot trickles down my cheek and I hastily swipe it away. Aris slides across the floor on his knees to pull Mamá into his arms. Her brain is blown across the wall. She's fucking dead. I turn away from the horror scene and catch Talia's horrified stare. When I see Talia's grandfather, Emilio, and Adrian hovering over my father, speaking in low, calming tones, I realize he's not dead. Yet.

"Father," I choke out, rushing over to him and kneeling.

His face is pale. Adrian holds a dinner napkin to the wound to staunch the bleeding where the bullet came through his chest. I grab my father's hand, another hot tear leaking from my eye.

"Father, don't leave me too."

He flutters his eyelids, but he doesn't close them. No, he locks his gaze with mine, harnessing his inner Demetriou strength, and holds on.

"Stay with me, *Patéras*," I plead, sounding every bit like his little boy. "Just fucking stay with me."

"An ambulance is on the way," someone shouts.

"Get everyone out of here," Emilio barks out to Stefano. "Now."

The room empties out save for the ones trying to keep my father alive and the ones sobbing over my mother's death.

My only focus is my father.

I won't lose them both.

chapter thirteen

THE VISUAL OF NORA PLACING THE GUN INTO HER MOUTH AND pulling the trigger is imbedded in my brain. Everywhere I look, all I can see is crimson. There was so much blood everywhere. The walls and the floor were all streaked with red. I've seen people shot on shows, and every time it's gory, but I had assumed it was done like that for show. To make everyone cringe. I never imagined, in real life, one gunshot could create so much red. So much blood.

I stood frozen in place, watching as Aris held his lifeless mother in his arms the same way my mom would hold me when I would scrape my knee from falling off my bike. He brushed her hair off her face, not caring that it was mangled and bloody. Almost unrecognizable. Begging her to wake up. Pleading with God to bring her back.

Kostas focused on his father, who was hanging on by a thread. He barked out orders. None of them made any sense, but it didn't matter. Kostas just needed to feel in control in a situation that was completely out of his control.

I wasn't sure who to go to. Before that moment, going to Kostas wouldn't have even been an option. The only thing I wanted to do was run from him. But as I watched the drops of grief race down his face, all I wanted to do was hold him. Tell him, even though it was a lie, that everything would be okay.

At the same time, I knew Aris needed someone. He was clutching his mother's body like she was his lifeline, and I wasn't sure he would be able to let her go on his own.

But before I could decide who to go to, my grandfather took control, demanding everyone leave. He ushered us out the door, and Phoenix walked us to the room my mom and stepdad were staying in. It wasn't until we were inside, with the door closed, and the silence overtook, that I realized I was trembling. Mom pulled me into her arms and held me while I cried into her chest. I cried for the two boys who lost their mother. For the woman who felt she had no choice but to take her own life. I didn't know her well, but from the short time we spent together, I know she loved her sons more than life itself. And when the tears began to slow, and it felt as if my tear ducts were drying out, my sadness began to turn into anger. And that was when everything Nora said hit me like a wrecking ball.

"Niles cheated on you," I say to Mom, sitting up. Her body stills, and her arms tighten around me. "He cheated on you with Kostas's mom."

My glossy eyes meet hers, and she nods once. "I didn't know it was her, though." Her voice chokes up. "It's all my fault." A waterfall of tears falls down her cheeks. "I approached Nora and begged her to speak to her husband."

A knot forms in the pit of my stomach. "About what?" I ask, but I already know the answer.

"To try to make him see reason. To stop you and Kostas from marrying." A sob breaks through, past her lips. "I didn't know she didn't know you two weren't really in love. I'm the reason she was so upset."

Oh, no. It's not my mom's fault. I should've told her. It didn't even cross my mind she would approach Nora about it. Now, though, it all makes sense. She told Nora the real reason why Kostas and I are marrying and it broke her. It broke her because our marriage wasn't just a debt to be paid. It was revenge. It was personal. Because Niles couldn't remain faithful to his wife! Because he couldn't be satisfied with what he had right in front of him. My mom wasn't enough. My brother and I weren't enough. Nothing is ever fucking enough for him. It's why he is where he is. He's a greedy, selfish asshole.

"It's not your fault," I say, trying to soothe her.

"I approached Kostas too," she adds, and the small hairs on the back of my neck rise. "I begged him not to make you marry him. He warned me not to interfere…"

"You were just trying to be a good mom," I tell her, but even as I speak the words, I know Kostas isn't going to agree. The minute he calms down and thinks, he's going to put two and two together, and he's going to want revenge. Just like his father. And when it happens, my mom can't be here.

"You need to go back to Italy," I blurt out.

Her brows knit in confusion. "With you?"

"No." I shake my head. "You need to go. Now. If Kostas finds out you were the one who told Nora about our wedding being a sham, he's going to go after you. He thought I said something to her and he was livid." I stand abruptly. "You need to go. Take Nonna and get on the first flight out." I look around, realizing Stefano isn't here. "Call Stefano and tell him you guys need to leave."

"Talia," Mom pleads. "I can't just leave you here."

"Yes, you can, and you will. I can't risk Kostas hurting you. Please." Needing her to leave right away, I grab the bags the driver left in the corner of the room and roll them to the door. "Nonna!" I call out. With everything that happened, she lay down for a nap when we got here. "Nonna, wake up!"

My hands are shaking, and my legs are trembling in fear. I've seen what my fiancé is capable of, and I don't doubt for a second he won't hesitate to torture and kill my mom if he believes she's the reason his mother shot herself.

As I'm helping my grandmother to her feet, Stefano and Nonno walk in. They both have blood on their clothes and frowns on their faces. Without waiting for them to speak, I rush over to them. "You have to leave."

Both men look at me in confusion, and Nonno speaks. "What's going on?"

I quickly explain to them what my mom said to Nora and Kostas, and my grandfather agrees it's best for them to put distance between them. "He left in the ambulance with his father," Nonno says. "I imagine he'll be there for some time."

"What about Aris?" I ask.

"The police forced him to let go of her and he took off," Stefano says. Oh, God! Poor Aris. I need to find him.

After wrapping my mom up in a tight hug and telling her to call me once she's home, I see them out and then head over to Aris's villa to find out if he went there.

After banging on the door several times and no one answering, I begin my search of the property. I check the tiki bar to see if he came here for a drink but don't find him. I dial his cell number, but he doesn't pick up. Maybe he went to the hospital…I call Kostas, but he doesn't pick up either. I spend the next couple hours combing through every inch of the hotel. The restaurants, the bars, the pools. I go by his office, but nobody's there. I check the parking garage and see his car is there, so he has to be somewhere.

Before giving up and heading home, I try his place one more time. "Aris!" I shout, banging on the door. "If you're in there, please open up. I just want to make sure…" I stop myself before I finish my sentence. Of course he isn't okay. His mom just killed herself. His father, who she blamed, was shot. He's the furthest thing from being okay. "Aris, please." I pound on the door, refusing to give up. What if he's hurt himself?

Finally the door swings open and Aris stumbles out slightly. "Talia," he slurs. The blood from his mother is still covering his entire front. "Sweet, sweet Talia." He smirks, but it's not playful. It's sad and despondent.

"Oh, Aris." I pull him into a hug, and it's then I notice he's holding a bottle of liquor. It drops to the floor with a bang, and liquid sloshes out, spraying my feet. "Let's get you cleaned up."

"She's…she's dead," Aris whispers. His mouth is so close to my ear, I can feel and smell his cool, liquor-covered breath.

"I know. I know," I tell him, having no clue what to say. Nothing I say is going to make this better. He's just lost both his parents. His mother literally, and his father…how will he ever get past it, knowing his father is why she killed herself?

"C'mon." I wrap my arm around Aris's waist and help him walk to the bathroom, so I can get him into the shower and clean him up. I let go of him momentarily to turn on the water, and he slumps against the wall, his body sliding down into a heap on the floor. His eyes close, and his head bangs against the wall.

"She's dead," he murmurs.

"Here, let me help you," I tell him, needing to get his crimson-stained clothes off him. His eyes are still closed as he extends each arm so I can pull his suit jacket off. Next, I unbutton his shirt, then peel it from his body. His limbs are limp, and his breathing is almost nonexistent. "Aris," I whisper, needing to know he's still awake. His brown eyes open. His lids are hooded over, and his pupils are slightly dilated. He looks devastated and lost, and my heart breaks for him. I can't imagine losing my mom, let alone watching her kill herself.

Reaching out, he pushes several strands of my hair out of my face and whispers, "She's gone."

"I know. I'm so sorry." I yank each of his loafers off his feet, then pull his socks off. "I need you to stand so we can get your pants off." The front of his pants, where he laid his mother's head in his lap, is drenched through from the blood.

Aris swallows thickly, and his Adam's apple bobs slightly. His eyes gloss over, and he nods once but doesn't make any move to get up. Kneeling in front of him, I position my hands under each armpit and attempt to lift him. He's too heavy and doesn't budge. "Aris, please," I beg. This time when he nods, he presses his hands against the marbled floor and stands. He's shaky on his feet, but he remains standing while I unbutton and unzip his pants. I push them down and consider removing his briefs but don't want to go there.

"The water is warm and will feel good," I tell him as I guide him into the walk-in shower. The water rains down on his face and back, dripping down his body. The clear liquid turns red as it circles the drain and empties. I'm about to go find him a towel, when his hands grip my hips and he pulls me into the shower with him.

"Aris…" I begin, but he stumbles forward, pushing me against the shower wall. His face finds the crook of my neck and he nuzzles into it. The only sound is the water hitting the marble. For a second I think maybe Aris has passed out standing up, but then I feel it. His body trembling against mine. His shoulders shaking up and down. He's crying. I don't know what to do or say, so I do the only thing I can do. I wrap my arms around his torso and I hold him tight as his silent sobs rack his body. We stay like this until the water turns cold, and then Aris lifts his head.

"Let me grab us a towel," I tell him, turning the water off. I find a couple towels under his sink and snag them. I hand one to him and keep one for myself. Without caring that I'm in the room, he pushes his briefs down and wraps his towel around his waist. Diverting my eyes, I say, "I'm going to get these wet clothes off. Can I borrow some clothes?"

"Yeah." He nods once and steps out. "I'll leave them for you on the bed."

After stripping out of my wet clothes and wringing them out in the sink, I wrap the towel around me and then walk into Aris's room. He's in there, still in his towel. He's sitting on the edge of his bed with his head bowed and his face in his hands. I've never felt so helpless.

"Hey." I step in front of him, and he lifts his head slightly. "I don't know what to say," I admit. "Do you want me to take you to the hospital? I think that's where Kostas is…"

Aris's eyes bulge out of their sockets and then form into thin slits. "He killed her," he hisses. Of course he blames his father. I don't blame him. Everything she said. She might as well have handed Ezio the gun. "No, I don't want to go to the fucking hospital, and you shouldn't either." He glares at me, and his hands grip my forearms.

"It should've been him, not her," he sneers. "He should be fucking dead."

"I know," I agree. "I hate this for you." My cell phone rings out somewhere in the villa. "Let me go grab that. It could be Kostas."

"Kostas?" Aris spits. "Who fucking cares?" We're both silent for a minute and then Aris says, "You're not thinking of still marrying him, are you?" He stands from the bed, now towering over me.

"It's…it's not up to me," I tell him. He knows this. He knows I'm being forced. He was there when my fate was sealed.

"That was before!" he roars. "Everything has fucking changed." He stalks toward me and I back up, my lower back hitting the edge of the dresser. I wince in pain. "You can't marry him, Talia! Didn't you hear my mother's dying wishes? To you? To me? To Kostas?"

"I know." I nod emphatically. He's starting to scare me. His chest is heaving in anger, and I'm trapped between him and the dresser. My phone continues to ring, but I can't answer it because it's in the other room. "I know what she said," I tell him softly, hoping to calm him. "And I want to give her what she asked. But in order to do that, I'm going to have to talk to Kostas. That might be him calling."

Aris flinches at Kostas's name. "He's not going to listen. He always does what our father says. He's going to make you marry him. And then my father will get what he wanted. You can't marry him. You can't." He shakes his head. His eyes bore into mine, and he almost appears to be possessed. My hands shake at my sides. I need to figure a way to get to my phone, or get out of here. Something's not right. Something is off.

"I understand," I say to Aris to placate him, "I will—"

Aris cuts me off. "No, there's nothing you can do. There's only one way to stop Kostas. There's only one reason he would call off this wedding." His eyes rake down my body, stopping when they get to the knot holding my towel together. Reaching forward, he tugs on it enough to loosen it, but not enough to make it fall. "If you're tainted…then he won't want you, and my dad won't get his way."

"Then I'm as good as dead too," I choke out, pushing at his chest. "You know that."

Another sob makes his entire body shake. "Fuck, Talia, I'm sorry."

Relaxing in his arms, I gently hug him. "It's okay."

"He doesn't deserve you," he murmurs, his breath hot against my ear. "He doesn't deserve you."

A shiver runs down my spine when his lips latch onto the side of my neck. He sucks on my flesh in a reverent way. My towel slides down, exposing my breasts.

"Aris," I whisper. "Aris, stop."

He pulls away enough to look me right in the eye. His are bloodshot from crying and drinking. Before I can grab the towel, his lips crash to mine in a demanding kiss. I abandon trying to keep the towel on in an effort to push him away. Turning my head, I manage to break the kiss.

"Aris," I whimper. "Please—"

His grip finds my jaw as he guides my face back to his, attacking my lips once more and silencing me. As he kisses me, all I can think about is how bad this is. If Kostas finds out his brother was kissing me, it's not going to end well for me.

He'll kill me.

My thought has me frozen in fear. Distracted. Worried. Confused. Hot skin against my own has me crying out in shock.

Holy shit.

Aris is naked and he's rubbing his erection against my stomach. This is bad. Really bad. I have to put a stop to it. My hands find his chest and I push against him to no avail. He's strong. Really strong. Oh God.

Kostas will kill me.

He. Will. Kill. Me.

Aris's strong hands bite into the backs of my thighs as he lifts me. I scream against his mouth as terror floods through me. His mouth consumes mine as he shoves my ass against the dresser.

No. No. No.

I claw my fingers down his chest, trying to stop him. My lips finally break from his and I scream. But that one small moment allows him to nudge the head of his cock between my spread thighs and he thrusts.

One thrust to destroy my world.

Another scream rasps from me as everything spins around me.

Numb. Darkness closes in on me and numbness takes over. Pain tears at me from the inside out while I try desperately to block it out.

He will kill me. Kostas will kill me.

Oh, God.

What have I done?

A loud, ugly sob rattles from me and my body goes limp.

I don't want to die. I don't want to die. I don't want to die.

"You're not going to die," Aris growls, dragging me to the heinous act, making me realize I'm chanting those words.

I squeeze my eyes shut, blocking out the way he drives into me in a painful way. I try to ignore the way he kisses my neck and grips my breast.

This can't last forever.

This. Can't. Last. Forever.

I'm crying so hard I can't breathe. Loud hiccups resound from me and snot runs down my lip. Everything aches, but it's my heart that hurts.

Why did he do this?

Why?

He makes a grunting sound and then heat floods inside me. A burst of elation rushes through me. He's done. He's fucking done.

"You're not going to die," Aris says again, swiping away the snot from my lip with his thumb. "I won't let him hurt you."

His cock softens and he pulls out of me before stumbling over to the bed, falling face first onto it. I stand staring at him, my entire body shaking uncontrollably as his semen runs down my thigh. For far too long, I gape at the man in horror, until his breathing evens out into soft snores, jarring me from my frozen state.

Oh God.

I need to get the hell out of here.

chapter fourteen

Kostas

BACK AND FORTH.

Back and forth.

My cousin Victoria yammers on the phone loudly to her husband, and I want to tell her to shut the fuck up. Instead, I grit my teeth and continue to pace the floor.

Back and forth.

Back and forth.

She's dead. My mother is dead. I'll never hear her laughter again. See her smile. I'll never be able to tease her about being the favorite son. I'll never again smell her lovely floral perfume scent she's worn since childhood.

I pause my pacing as a violent tremble shakes through me.

"Kos, hon, you okay?" Paulina, my other cousin, asks.

"I'm fine," I growl.

But I'm not fine. Everything is a fucking mess.

I need for my father to be okay. I can't lose both my parents in one day. I'm barely holding on to my sanity, which means Aris has probably gone off the deep end. He was a momma's boy, and he, like me, watched his mother blow her head off right after she shot our fucking father.

Fuck.

Paulina hands me a tissue, but I wave it off, opting to swipe at the rogue tear with the palm of my hand.

I should have pressed Father on the Nikolaides issue. I'd known something was fucking wrong, but I ignored it. I hoped Father would come out and tell me why he was obsessed with making Niles pay.

Revenge.

My mother is a cheater, and he wanted to make them all pay for it.

An ache forms in my stomach. How could I have not seen this? All these years, I thought my mother and father loved each other. Sure, he was an asshole, but he would kiss her and occasionally playfully carry her up the stairs. I took it for face value. I'd never dreamed she hated him and was only staying with him because of us. He spent years tormenting her over this shit.

I want to be angry with him, but I understand his need for revenge. He loved his wife. They had a contract—that's what marriage is after all—to love one another. She was the mother of his children. And she stepped out of the marriage. With Niles fucking Nikolaides of all people. He conned her like he tries to do everyone else.

I'm going to end that motherfucker.

String him up by his goddamn ballsack.

"Kos," Paulina says, "are you sure you're okay?"

"Fucking go away," I snarl. "I just watched my mother blow her fucking brains out. How the hell do you think I'm doing?"

Paulina gapes at me and Victoria quickly ushers her away from me. I continue my pacing. Father has to be okay. We'll get through this and make a plan to get Niles back.

My blood turns icy.

Melody.

If she'd kept her damn mouth shut, my mother may not have lost it like she did. But she didn't. Melody blabbing to my mother was the catalyst for the events that took place. As soon as I can fucking think clearly, I'll send Adrian to fetch them for me. Melody, her pussy husband, her prissy parents. I'll fucking destroy their entire line in one swoop. Phoenix too. But Niles, I'll save him to torture him slowly.

And Talia?

I stop pacing and retrieve my phone. She's tried to call me. I'm reminded of the way she held my hand at dinner. Hearing her voice might bring me some peace at the moment. I sure as fuck need it.

I dial her back.

It rings and rings and rings.

Did she leave? She better fucking not have.

I'll drag her back kicking and screaming.

She's mine.

"Mr. Demetriou," a doctor calls out, rushing over to me. "I have good news. He's stable. Your father is going to live."

I let out a heavy sigh of relief. "I want to see him. Now."

chapter fifteen

WITH NOTHING BUT A TOWEL WRAPPED AROUND MY BODY, I run home. My bare feet trip and stumble over the rocks that have been kicked up onto the pathway, but I don't stop until I'm standing outside my door. With shaky hands, it takes me four tries to get the code right so the door will unlock. The house is pitch-black, and I breathe a sigh of relief that Kostas isn't here.

My first thought is that I need to get *him* off of me. Rid myself of the evidence of what he did. Turning the shower on, I set it to as hot as it can go. I drop the towel and step inside, the steam hitting my senses and allowing me to take my first deep breath. For several minutes I just stand here. I'm not sure if I'm in shock, but I can't find it in me to move. And then I remember why I'm in here. To rid myself of him.

With my mind and body completely numb, I work the soapy loofah over my flesh. Scrubbing. Cleaning. Getting him off me. I scrub my face where he kissed me. My neck where he bit me. I scrub my arms and legs where he grabbed me. But it doesn't feel like it's enough. I scrub and scrub and scrub, but I can still feel him on me, over me, in me.

When I spread my legs and wipe between my thighs, the loofah turns a light shade of pink. And it's then the reality of what he did to me hits me full force. My already shaky hands begin to tremble, and my knees go weak. My body gives out, and I fall into a heap on the floor of the shower as grief pours down my face in a flood of uncontrollable tears that mix with the pink water. I watch as my blood and tears run down into the drain and disappear, reminding me that only a couple short hours ago I was in the shower with *him*. Trying to comfort *him*. Washing the blood off *him*.

How could he do this to me?

He took something from me I can never get back.

Something that wasn't his to take.

It was mine. Mine to give. Mine to share.

And now it's gone, and it feels as though a part of me is gone as well.

I scrub my body until my skin is bright red and hurts to touch. Until the water turns ice-cold and runs clear once again. Until I have no choice but to get out and deal with what he did to me.

Feeling exposed and wanting to hide my body—as if hiding it will make what he did to me any less real—I find a pair of sweatpants and a hoodie and throw them on. When I go back into the bathroom to brush my teeth, I spot the towel on the floor. Needing to get rid of it, *to get rid of the evidence*, I scoop it up and bring it into the bedroom with me. I light the fireplace, not caring that it's nowhere near cold enough to justify having a fire going, and when the room dances with bright reds and oranges, I throw it into the fire. Grabbing the blanket off the bed, I wrap it around my body like a cocoon, then I lie down in front of the fire and watch the fabric burn, until my eyelids can no longer stay open, and I allow myself to shut down.

chapter sixteen

Kostas

I'VE WATCHED HER SLEEP FITFULLY FOR FUCK KNOWS HOW LONG now. Hours maybe. Sometime during the early morning hours when the moon was still out, I left the hospital and came home intent on crashing. The events have worn me the hell out. But finding Talia looking so broken and fragile gave me pause. A frozen sliver in time where everything stilled and elusive peace washed over me.

I don't move.

I don't speak.

I don't do a damn thing except stare at her sleeping form as I sit on the edge of the bed. Her silky blond hair has dried into messy waves and her plump lips pout out as though her dreams are horrible. For her, they probably are. She was dragged into Greece's most ruthless family and forced into a marriage with a monster.

Monsters aren't always as horrible as they seem.

One day, maybe she'll see that.

Like Mamá did?

The thought hollows me out. My mother clearly put on a show for all of us. A show Father was a star in. I feel betrayed by them both. For my mother stepping out on my father, and for him playing this fucked up game with our lives as payback.

Would Talia eventually come to love me like I thought my mother did my father, or will she feel like she's trapped with a monster, always seeking for a chance to escape?

Irritation churns in my gut.

My instinct is to drag Talia up by her hair, force her to look deep into my eyes, and explain to her that if she even thinks about pulling a stunt like my mother, I'll destroy her in every way possible. The monstrous beast inside me begs to do just that, fueled on betrayal.

But all it takes is a little whimper in her sleep to have me backtracking.

Talia isn't my mom.

And I'm not my dad.

I scrub my palm down my face and let out a huff. I'm still marrying her because that's clearly the play destiny has set for us. It's something my parents and her parents paved the way for. Sure, it was done to us as some sort of punishment, but it doesn't mean we can't take control from here.

Rising from the bed, I make my way over to her and kneel. My fingernails are still caked with my father's blood and a shower is long overdue. But as the sun peeks in through the windows, signaling the start of a new day, I can't help but take action.

Take what's mine.

"Morning," I say, my voice rough from leftover emotion and lack of sleep. "Talia, wake up."

She jolts, a scream of terror ripping from her lips, as she tries to scramble away. I grab her shoulders and pin her down on her back.

"Calm down," I growl. "It's me."

Her lashes flutter and then a mixture of relief and worry swims in her sleepy blue eyes that are bloodshot. "Kostas," she croaks. "You're home."

Something about the way she says home has my chest tightening in response. "I am. We need to shower and get ready. I have a big day planned for us."

She furrows her brows together as she studies me. "Are we going to the hospital?"

"No, *moró mou*, we're getting married. Remember?"

"W-What?" she screeches, sitting up and looking around frantically. "We can't. Your mom just died and your dad is in the hospital. And my parents…" She trails off, more worry flashing in her eyes.

"Your parents what?"

"I sent them away," she breathes.

Smart girl. There's no telling what I'd do to Melody if I saw her right now.

"It'll be better as a private affair." I rise and walk toward my bathroom, shedding soiled clothes along the way. I've just turned on the shower when I sense her nearby.

"Kostas," she whispers, her hand touching my bare back. "Are you sure this is a good idea?"

I swivel around to look at her. Genuine concern gleams in her eyes. Her chin is lifted, and even in her disheveled state, she's beautiful. And mine. Soon, in the eyes of God and the law, legally mine.

"It was always the plan," I remind her, tucking a blond strand behind her ear.

She trembles visibly and curls her arms around her waist. A pitiful look crumples her pretty face. I really am a monster to her. A prison sentence. Torture. I grip her wrist—the hand that wears my ring shining brilliantly—and bring her palm to my bare chest where my heart thunders.

"Feel this?" I rumble, searing my gaze into hers. "This thinks it's a good idea."

Her eyes well with tears, and her bottom lip trembles. "But…"

I lean forward and kiss her soft lips. "There are no buts, Talia. Just the plan. Follow the plan."

A tear snakes down her cheek, making my heart pound harder. Everything in me screams to strip her down and tug her into the shower with me so I can give her a preview of exactly how good of a plan this is. But the utter fear on her face is enough to have me pulling back.

"Go eat some breakfast," I grunt out as I unbuckle my slacks. "We'll leave in an hour."

She bolts from my presence before I even get the words out of my mouth.

As we drive to the church, I expect Talia to argue, or ask me to check on my brother, or beg me not to make her go through with this marriage, but she doesn't. After my shower, she quickly took her own. Then, she fixed her hair and put on makeup before donning a simple, silky white dress I laid out for her. She's being ridiculously compliant, which makes me feel uneasy.

I'd thought about calling Aris, but I know how he is. He was a momma's boy. If I know him, he's gotten wasted, cried his eyes out, and fucked his way into oblivion. His villa is probably destroyed due to one of his tantrums. And with time, he'll get better. I'm not the person to help him out of his sea of grief. I'm treading water as it is. Thank fuck I have Talia as a lifeline, breathing fresh, healing water into me with every breath I take.

She's quiet when we arrive and doesn't pull away when I take her hand before walking inside. I'd called ahead to tell the priest it'd be a private wedding with just the bride and groom. I'm sure news has spread about my mother and he wisely didn't ask. I simply instructed him to be ready for us, not wanting to waste another minute.

Father Nicholas greets us once we're inside the empty cathedral that's already been decorated. Talia's heels clack along the marble floors as we follow him down the center aisle to the altar. Once up front, I take both her hands while Father Nicholas flips through his Bible.

"Ready?" I ask Talia.

A line between her brows deepens. "Not really."

I rub my thumbs over the backs of her hands. "Too bad."

Her nostrils flare, giving me a preview of the fiery woman she can be when she's not overcome by fear of her situation. One day, I'll pull her from her fear that has its steely hold on her, and into my arms, where she can be herself all the time.

One day.

"Okay," Father Nicholas chirps. "And so let us begin…"

As he recites verses from the Bible, I admire Talia's pretty features. Wide, brilliant blue eyes that say so much all at once. A petite, slightly upturned nose that begs to be kissed. It's her lips, though, that always steal the show. Full, naturally dark pink, glistening and parted as though she's desperate to be kissed.

I'm going to kiss you a lot, *moró mou.*

"Talia," Father Nicholas gently urges. "Here's where you state your vows."

Her eyes widen as she gapes at me. "I didn't know we were writing vows."

"It's okay," Father Nicholas says. "Repeat after me."

As he recites words from the Bible that Talia breathlessly repeats, her cheeks blaze red. Shame. I think she might be embarrassed that she didn't come up with her own vows. Not that I expected her to. She's made it clear she thinks this wedding is a sham. I don't hold her responsible for thinking that way. When they finish, I clear my throat.

"Talia, you were born to be a Demetriou. Fate knew it, I know it, and one day you'll know it, too. Too many things over the past decade have happened to lead to this exact moment for us to believe otherwise. At this point, we not only must accept it, but we must embrace it." I pin her with a fierce look that I hope she can feel down to her pretty toes. "I, Kostas Angelo Demetriou, vow to protect you always from yourself, from others, and from me. When you take my name, you take a part of me, and I will treat you as though you are a valued piece of me. The truth you'll come to learn is that I am yours now as much as you are mine. I vow to learn every part of you in hope you'll want to learn every part of me. If you ever lose your way, I vow to find you and guide you back to a place where we can be truly happy. By taking my ring and my name, you're taking me too. We're bound in more ways than either of us can count. For me, it will be until death. And I vow to never let you go, even then."

Tears slide down her red cheeks as she regards me with a mixture of confusion and worry. It makes me want to lick the tears right from her face and vow to her what I'll do to make her scream a little later on. But, alas, Father completes the ceremony by asking us to exchange rings. She seems surprised when he hands her my titanium band that says Demetriou carved along the outside of the band. Inside, it has our initials and today's date. Once she shakily slips my ring on my finger, I place a platinum one beside her massive diamond. Her ring, too, has the same inscriptions.

"By the powers vested in me and God, I now pronounce you Mr. and Mrs. Kostas Demetriou." He smiles at me. "You may now kiss your lovely bride."

Sliding my hands into her silky hair, I grip her and tilt her head back. Her lips part and a gasp escapes her. I brush my lips across hers in a warning kiss a second before I sear her with a claiming kiss. My tongue slides out to lash with hers. Eagerly, I devour her sweet moan of surprise. We kiss with me owning every breath and mewl until I decide we've given this old man enough of a show for today. Besides, I want to spend the entire day with my wife, making her whimper in other ways.

"Come now, wife, it's time to go home."

I hang up with room service and track Talia as she exits the bathroom. Like a good wife, she obeyed me when I told her to put on her swimsuit. Since the wedding, she's not spoken a word to me. It's like she's shut down and closed me out.

Time to open up, *zoí mou. My life.*

While she looks out the window, I quickly change into some swim trunks and then walk over to the door in my room. I open it and grab her hand before guiding her out the back of the villa, to the secluded pool. In one corner of my private yard, beside the outdoor expandable daybed, a man from the hotel staff is setting up a small table with a pitcher of ice water. I give him a nod of my head before walking Talia over to it. The daybed is shaded from the bright sun with a white canopy.

"Thirsty?" I ask, nodding to the pitcher. "They're bringing out food and some proper drinks soon."

She shakes her head. "I'm fine."

But she's not fine. The poor girl is shaking like a leaf despite the hot sun blazing down on us. I take her hand again and guide her to the stairs of the pool.

"What are we doing?" she bites out.

"We're going swimming."

"Obviously. But what are we doing? I thought…you know…"

I step in the cool water and cock my head at her. "That we'd get right to the fucking?"

She scowls at me. "You're an asshole."

"You married me."

Before she can huff and puff any more, I grip her hips and pull her back with me into the chilly water. She screeches, her hands going to my shoulders as though she can climb on top of me to keep from getting wet. A laugh rumbles from me as I dunk us both. When we reemerge, she sputters and gives me the worst go to hell look, which only makes me laugh more.

"What?" I ask innocently. "I prefer a little foreplay before I bed a woman."

"You're disgusting."

I grip her ass in a hard, punishing way as I urge her to wrap her legs around me. Fear once again contorts her features. But, with firm urging, I manage to get her to lock onto me. She's tense and her fingernails dig slightly into my shoulders.

"Relax," I croon, walking her to the edge of the pool. "You don't have to hold on so tight. I won't let you go."

She rolls her eyes, but my taunting her seems to have her losing some of her tension. Once I don't think she'll take off, I gently massage her ass.

"Kostas," she mutters. "What are we doing?" she asks again.

I lift a brow as my gaze travels to her pouty mouth, then give her the same answer I already gave her. "Swimming."

"But why?" she demands. "Your mom…your dad… You have a funeral to plan."

Gritting my teeth, I look past her to where another hotel staff member walks over with a tray of food and begins setting it on our table. "I'm trying to enjoy the moment."

Her wet palm slides to my face as she turns my attention back to her. "It won't make what happened go away."

"No," I agree, stepping closer so that she can feel my erection pressed against her. "But it can freeze time and give me a fucking break."

My harsh words make her flinch. "I'm scared," she whimpers. "I'm scared you'll hurt me."

I press my lips to hers, kissing her softly and in a teasing way. "I'll make it feel good."

She opens her mouth to accept my demanding kiss. I gently grind against her cunt, wanting to tease her in every possible way. A whimper travels through her, more fear than excitement. With a sigh, I pull away and carry her out of the pool. She frowns at me the entire walk over to the daybed. I set her to her feet and then drape a large towel over her.

"Sit," I command.

She rolls her eyes at me but curls up on the daybed. I fill up a plate with meats and olives and cheeses and crackers before handing it to her. Then, I wrap a towel around me and grab another plate. She scoots over and gives me room to sit. A warm breeze tickles around us as we eat in silence.

"I meant what I vowed," I tell her when I finish up my food and set the plate down.

She frowns and hands me her plate. "Why, though?"

"Because marriage, to me, isn't what they told me it had to be." I know I sound like a pouting schoolboy, but I don't care. I make my own destiny, not my father. Not Niles. Me.

A hotel staffer walks over to us with a chilled bottle of chardonnay. He pours us a couple of glasses. I instruct him to bring something a little more stout. I'm going to need it to get through today. After handing Talia her glass, I clink mine to hers.

"To us."

She acts like she wants to say something, but in the end, she utters out, "To us."

We spend the entire day eating, drinking, and swimming. Talia doesn't say much, and frankly, I'm not in the mood to talk. She allows me to touch and kiss her, but always freezes up when she thinks I'll do more.

"You're drunk," I state when she stumbles slightly on the way back to the daybed.

The sun is setting and the breeze has picked up. I smell rain in the air.

"No, I'm not," she sasses as she pours more ouzo into her tumbler. Someone really likes her ouzo.

I climb out of the pool, prowling after her. This time, when I touch her hips, rubbing against her from behind, she doesn't flinch. She simply sucks down her ouzo instead. I pull the drink from her lips, not allowing her to finish, and scoop her into my arms. She lets out a shriek, clawing at me, but then relaxes when I settle us on the daybed.

This time, when we kiss, she puts more effort into it. Her fingers explore my wet chest, and her breaths come out unevenly. Needy almost. I kiss her hard, twisting her until she's pinned down on the cushions. She moans when I kiss along the column of her throat. Another sound of pleasure resounds from her when my lips meet her nipple over her suit. I kiss her and then bite at the hardened nub over the fabric.

"Ohhhh," she cries out, her back arching up.

Taking that as permission, I peel her suit off to the side. She mewls when I lick her bare nipple.

"Kostas."

I smile against her nipple. She's drunk as shit. It's nice seeing her so relaxed, though. Trailing my kisses south, I linger at her belly button for a moment. The thought of filling her up with my kids is thrilling. A possessive need courses through me. She makes a garbled sound when I tug at the strings of her bikini bottoms. With a few short pulls, I reveal her pussy with trimmed, golden-blond hair.

"You smell good," I murmur, inhaling her scent of arousal.

She lifts her hips up. "I do?"

I lick her slit, causing her to groan and her fingers to latch onto my wet hair. "You taste good, too."

"Oh, God," she whispers.

"We left him back at the church," I growl. "It's just us now."

Using my thumbs, I part her lips so I can find all the delicate pink she hides beneath. Suddenly feeling starved despite the fact I've eaten all day, I lick and suck and nip at her sweetness. It doesn't take long before she detonates. Loud, explosive, without warning, like a bomb. I lick at her clit as she rides out her orgasm. When she's down from her high and can't take any more teasing, I kiss my way back up her body.

Her eyes are closed, a serene smile on her face. My pretty, drunk wife. She'll hate herself when she sobers up. Hate that she gave up control to me. I smirk, imagining how her face will turn pink. The same color as her needy cunt.

I pull her to me and drape the towel over me. Within seconds, her soft breathing evens out. My dick aches for attention, but I ignore it for now. I'll wear her down eventually.

It might take some time, but we have the rest of our lives.

She's stuck with me now.

chapter seventeen

Talia

MY EYES ARE CLOSED, BUT I CAN FEEL THE LIGHT FLOODING IN through the window. I'm no longer outside on the daybed with Kostas. I can feel the cool air in the room. The soft bedding wrapped around my body, and the plush pillows under my head. The last thing I remember was Kostas's mouth on me. Bringing me to orgasm. Making me scream in pleasure. It was the first orgasm I've experienced by the hands—or I guess I should say mouth—of a man. Why was he making me scream in pleasure? And why was I letting him? Oh, God! Because I married him. I'm his wife. I'm Mrs. Freaking Kostas Demetriou.

And he was unusually sweet. The vows he spoke, telling me he's mine as much as I'm his. Promising to protect me until the day he dies and even then after. His eyes when he spoke were warm. Sweet. Determined. Honest. As if he was a different man. Not the monster who kills, but a man capable of loving. *A man I could see myself falling in love with.* My chest tightens at the mere thought. A choked sob escaping past my lips. A throat clears, and my eyes pop open, realizing I'm not alone.

"Good morning, wife," Kostas says, his voice almost sounding playful. He's lying on his side, shirtless, with his hand holding up his head. He looks so normal like this. Like a husband. The thought makes me smile, which has Kostas eyeing me warily.

"We're married," I blurt out, the reality of yesterday hitting me again. I *married* Kostas. I am a Demetriou.

"I was there." He chuckles in amusement and holds up his hand, showing me his wedding band. The one he had engraved to match mine. He reaches over and brushes a strand of hair behind my ear. The gesture is so sweet. So unlike Kostas.

His tongue darts out to wet his lips, and I'm reminded of where that tongue was yesterday. Licking my nipples. My neck. Between my thighs. When my thighs clench together, remembering how good it felt, I feel the dull ache between my legs. The ache that wasn't caused by Kostas's mouth, but by his brother.

A cold sense of dread chases away the surprising warmth I'd been feeling. My heart rate speeds up. When my eyes meet Kostas, he's assessing me closely. I feel too vulnerable under his careful scrutiny. Like if he looks too hard, he'll see the pain that's bubbling beneath the surface. His lips are turned down in a frown. He knows my thoughts have taken a wrong turn. I need to tell him. He needs to know what his brother did to me.

"Kostas," I begin, as he sits up, throwing the blanket off his body, and then stands. For a second, I'm distracted by his hard body. He's in nothing but his boxer briefs, his full body on display. His intricate tattoos. His rock-hard abs. The trail of hair leading downward…

"As much as I'm enjoying the way you're looking at me right now," Kostas says, ending my moment of ogling, "you need to save your *eye-fucking* for later. I need to get going." He shoots me a knowing smirk and then starts for the bathroom. I cringe at the word eye-fucking. The same word he flung at me at the wedding rehearsal.

"Kostas," I yell, flinching when I realize my voice came out louder than I planned. "I need…"

Without looking at me, he says, "Whatever you need will have to wait. I need to get to the hospital to see my dad and plan my mother's funeral."

"Wait!" I shuffle out of the bed and stumble toward him. He turns around in the doorway, his eyes meeting mine. Burning fiercely. He's back to himself. The sweet man from yesterday is gone. The monster is back. He stares at me for a long beat, his eyes narrowing, and his nostrils flaring.

"I need to talk to you," I croak out. *I need to tell you that your brother raped me…please don't cut off my feet and beat me with them.*

"We can talk tonight," he says, his tone final. "Be ready at seven for dinner. We'll talk then."

Knock. Knock. Knock. Knock.

My eyes flutter open when I hear the sound of someone knocking on the front door.

Bang. Bang. Bang. Bang.

The knocking turns into banging. I rush out of bed, worried Kostas might've forgotten his key. But when I swing the door open and see it's Aris standing on the other side, I remember the door has a damn code, so Kostas can't be locked out.

Shit.

Panic swells up inside me like a tidal wave. Fast. Unexpected. Terrifying.

My heart hammers in my chest as I'm frozen in terror.

"Hmm…in my brother's shirt. Looks like you two have gotten cozy," Aris accuses with a wicked smirk that sends chills up my spine. He grips the bottom of the shirt, tugging on it slightly, and I slap his hand away. I didn't even realize I was wearing Kostas's shirt. He must've put it on me last night after I fell asleep. The last thing I remember wearing is my swimsuit. Before he removed it…

I lift my chin, facing off with the man who raped me, praying I don't burst into tears. I need him to know I'm not afraid of him. The slight wobble in my bottom lip suggests otherwise.

"I figured you would want this back," Aris says. He extends his hand, holding my phone out for me to take, but when I reach out to grab it, he brings it back in. "We need to talk." He steps forward, and I take one back, bumping into the door.

"We can talk out here." I push his chest with enough strength, he's forced to take a step back. There's no way I'm letting him anywhere in my home.

"What's wrong?" he asks, tilting his head to the side slightly. "Are you afraid to be alone with me?"

"Can you blame me?" I glare at him. "The last time we were alone, you—"

Aris cuts me off. "Had sex with you?"

"More like you raped me," I hiss.

His eyes go wide, and he takes a menacing step forward into my space. He drops his voice low to a frightening growl, as though he fears we might be overheard. "What the fuck did you just say?"

"I said you raped me." I cross my arms over my chest. "Or were you too drunk to remember?"

"Like fucking hell!" he booms, pushing me into the villa and slamming the door behind him. My back hits the table in the foyer, and Aris towers over me. "I don't know what game you're playing at, but I suggest you think twice before you make that kind of accusation."

Accusation?

He's delusional.

Not one bit of what happened was consensual.

"It's not an accusation," I choke out. "It's the truth! And we both know it." This time, I can't keep the tears at bay. They burn my eyes.

Aris's hand comes up, and I flinch, thinking he's going to hit me, but instead he grabs something on the table. A paper crinkles. "You and Kostas got married?" He holds the marriage paperwork Father Nicholas gave us in my face.

"Yes, yesterday," I admit.

Aris drops the paper back onto the table and barks out a humorless laugh. "So, let me get this straight. You fuck me Friday night, and the next day marry my brother. And now you're crying rape?"

"I'm not crying anything. You *did* rape me."

"Do you really believe my *brother* is going to believe that? I'm his flesh and blood. You're a fucking Nikolaides. You're a liar by birth. It's in your blood. You came to my villa to comfort me, we ended up having sex, and now that you're married to Kostas, you want to cry rape, so he doesn't kill you for sleeping with his brother." At his version of what happened, my bones grow cold as fear slides through me. He's right. Kostas isn't going to believe me. I'm my father's daughter. The man who had an affair with his mother.

"I like you, Talia," Aris says. "And I don't want to see you die, so you don't have to worry. I'm not going to tell him what happened between us." He leans in close, until his body is flush against mine, and then he whispers into my ear, "It will be our secret."

A shudder ripples through me. Sharing secrets with this monster is the last thing I want to do, but what choice do I have? If Kostas finds out…

He can't.

He simply can't.

Aris backs up and extends his hand, offering me my phone, but before I can grab it, he drops it onto the table. "Welcome to the family, *sis*."

The moment he leaves, I lock the door behind him, then attach the chain just to be on the safe side. The nerve of that asshole! And to think I thought he was the nice one. The one with a heart. He's nothing more than a wolf in sheep's clothing. At least Kostas owns the monster he is.

Grabbing my cell off the table, I check to see if Kostas has called or texted. He hasn't. He's busy dealing with the shitstorm that's become his life. His father is in the hospital. His mother is dead.

It's only ten in the morning, and we're not meeting for dinner until seven. I glance around the room. It's quiet. Empty. It's only me here. I consider calling my mom, but what would I say? Do I tell her I got married? Will I be able to keep it together enough that she won't know how upset I am about Aris?

Needing to calm the blood that's boiling beneath my skin, I take a cool shower, taking my time to wash and shave every part of me. My thoughts go to yesterday with Kostas. He could've easily taken advantage of the fact I was drunk, but he didn't. We've yet to consummate our marriage. At one time I would've been dreading it, but now I just want to get it over with. I want to replace the horrid images of Aris with Kostas. I wonder what kind of lover Kostas will be. I assumed he would be rough. Ungentle. But the way he made me feel by the pool was the complete opposite. Maybe I have him all wrong. Maybe he's not the monster I've made him out to be. But then I remember the way he tortured that man for lying. Would he torture me like that if he believes I'm lying about Aris raping me? A body trembling shiver runs down my spine.

Turning off the water, I step out and wrap myself in a towel. It's the same towel from Aris's villa. They all have the same towels. Because they live on the same property. The thought has my heart rate picking up and my chest heaving. I was hoping a shower would calm me, but it only had the opposite effect. Maybe I just need to get out of here. Get some fresh air. It will help me take a deep breath.

After blow drying and straightening my hair, and applying a little bit of makeup, I feel a little more like myself again.

Just as I'm finishing getting dressed, my phone rings. It's my mom. I hit ignore. At the same time, my stomach growls. I consider taking a walk to the restaurant but stop myself. The last thing I need is to run into Aris. Space. We need space. Out of sight, out of mind. Right?

Instead, I place a call to room service and order breakfast and coffee. I glance at my phone again to see if maybe Kostas has texted. He hasn't. It's only eleven o'clock. It's only been an hour. I need to get out of here.

Remembering the patio that Kostas and I passed through to get to the pool yesterday, I head out back. The patio looks out at a beautiful, private flower garden. There are two Adirondack chairs and a matching table. They look untouched. I laugh, imagining Kostas coming out here to lounge out on his day off. Does he even get a day off? I doubt crime organizations have a set of working hours.

Dropping into one of the chairs, I take a deep, calming breath and then dial my mom's number. She answers on the first ring, her frantic voice bringing tears to my eyes.

"Talia!" she screeches. "I've called you so many times, but you haven't answered. Please tell me Kostas hasn't hurt you because of me. I've been so worried!"

"Oh, Mom," I choke out. "I'm okay. I miss you. Kostas hasn't hurt me. I'm sorry I haven't called. A lot has happened. I have so much to tell you."

"Talk to me, *cara mia*. Tell me everything."

"Well, for starters, Kostas and I got married." There's a deafening silence, and for a second I wonder if she's hung up on me. But then I hear a sniffle through the line and I know she's still there. She's crying.

"Don't cry, Mom. Please don't cry."

"I just always thought I would be there when you got married. And I had hoped…with everything that happened, maybe there was a chance he would let you go." She sobs through the phone.

"It's okay," I tell her, realizing I need to hear it myself. "It will be okay."

I hear a rustling in the bushes, and a sudden sense of unease washes over me. Remembering room service will be delivering my breakfast soon, I stand to head inside, when the sound of several branches cracking sounds through the air. And then a man in a black ski mask is coming at me. With my phone still in my hand—my mom still on the line—my fight or flight instinct kicks into gear. Grabbing the chair, I kick it toward the man. It causes him to momentarily stumble, and it's enough time for me to get inside and lock the doors.

"Mom!" I scream. "Someone is here. I need to call you back." I hear her yelling over the phone, but I hit end and dial Kostas's number. The doorknob on the French doors rattle, and I know it's only a matter of time until the man gets in.

"Talia, I'm going to need to call you back," Kostas says, his voice calm.

"Kostas! Someone is here. He's wearing a mask, and I think he's trying to get to me." The nob begins to turn, and I run to the front door.

"Where are you?" Kostas demands.

"At home! He's trying to come in from the back." I stand against the front door, watching the French doors, when the front door begins to shake, causing me to jump back.

"He's at the front door!"

"There's a gun in my nightstand, Talia. Go grab it! I'm going to call Aris right now. He should be close by."

I sprint into the bedroom and find the gun he mentioned. "No, Kos, I need you! Not him," I cry. "Please come home! Please."

I can't chance going out the front or the back. So instead I find a spot in the corner of the closet to hide, and with Kostas's gun in my hand, I wait.

chapter eighteen

Kostas

"I'M SCARED."

My heart thunders in my chest as I excuse myself from the hospital room where my dad sleeps in a medically induced coma. As I talk to her on speaker, I text my men on the hotel grounds. This ski mask fucker won't touch a hair on her head.

"I know, *zoí mou*, but you're safe," I assure her. "Just stay quiet. Did you do as I told you? The safety is off?"

"I t-think so," she whispers.

"Check it again," I instruct.

"Y-Yes. It's ready to fire."

"Good, now keep it trained on the door. Aim high and for the chest if anyone comes through the door."

Her breathing is erratic. "Are you coming home? Please come home."

The terror in her voice—begging for me—claws inside me. I hate to hear her so terrified. Once the threat is eliminated, whoever thought they could try and hurt my girl will fucking pay.

"I'm coming—"

Pop! Pop! Pop!

It takes me a second to realize the gunshots aren't coming from her end, but here at the hospital. What the fuck?

"Talia, listen to me," I growl. "Hide behind the clothes and shoot anything that comes for you. There's a shooting in the hospital. I need to go."

"Kostas," she sobs.

"I'll be home soon."

Hanging up with her makes my chest ache, but I need to focus. Another shot. I take off running, drawing my H&K .45 from my holster inside my suit jacket. Nurses and employees run toward me, so I head in that direction, passing my father's room door. Two men in suits round the corner holding MP5s. A spray of bullets mows down a handful of people. I slam my back against the wall and retreat into my father's room.

Where the fuck are my men?

Pop! Pop! Pop!

Responding fire to the spray has my heart ratcheting up. My guys are out there. Shouts can be heard. I back up, putting myself between my father and the gunmen. When the door flings open, I shoot.

Pop!

The headshot sends the man flying back and the door closing again. Another loud spray of bullets shatters the door to pieces, but then I hear several pops. Moments later, Adrian flies in, disheveled and breathing heavily. That'll teach him to take a shit break.

"Sir," he barks out. "You okay?"

"Yes," I grunt and check over my father. "So is Father. Did you get them?"

"There were two and they've been eliminated. I've called for more men and the Minister of Public Order. He'll sort it out from his end," he assures me.

Thank fuck Father is friends with Josef, otherwise this shooting at the hospital would look bad on the Demetrious.

"Any word on Basil?" I demand.

Adrian pulls out his phone to check his texts. "Threat has been eliminated. Talia won't open the door, but there are no signs of forced entry into your villa. The men are in Basil's custody."

"Men?"

"The one who was trying to get to Talia was wearing a ski mask. The other two wore suits. They seem like two different operations."

Could be a coincidence. With my father on death's door, it wouldn't take long for our enemies to come up with a plan to try and take out the Demetrious while we were down. Too bad for them, we fight fucking better when we're down.

"Deal with the shitstorm here," I order as I move past him. "I'm going back to the hotel."

I slam my Maserati into park and fly out of the car on one mission. Get to Talia. My men are posted around my villa, angry scowls on their faces. This attack is personal. These people waited until we were weakened by grief and pounced. Lowlife motherfuckers. I'll hunt them all down and make them pay.

After.

Right now, I must console my frightened wife.

I punch in the code on the front door, but the chain is hooked. Good girl. Walking around to the back patio doors, I punch in the code and slip inside. The villa is quiet and I creep through it in case anyone is hiding inside. When I make it to the closet door, I call out her name as I open it.

Bam!

A huge hunk gets blown out of the door, sending me stumbling back.

Bam!

Another blast.

"Talia!" I roar. "It's me, Kostas!"

Bam!

Enough of this shit. I crawl on my knees and yank open the door. Pressed against the far wall with her knees to her chest and the Glock wobbling in her hand is Talia. Crying, terrified, trembling. Her eyes are wild as she aims for me. Not giving her a chance, I pounce on her, grabbing for the gun as she fires again. I wrestle the gun away from her and toss it away. Then, I grab her ankles, dragging her toward me. She screams and kicks until I pin her body with mine. I hold her wrists together with one hand and grip her jaw with the other.

"Look at me," I demand. "It's me."

She blinks away her daze before crumbling. Heavy sobs rack through her. I release her to hug her on the closet floor, nuzzling my nose in her hair that's sweaty. I kiss her cheek and whisper assurances until she calms, no longer crying.

"I almost shot you," she whispers hoarsely. "I'm sorry."

I lift my head to look at her. "You did great, *zoí mou*."

Her fingers find my head and she pulls me closer. Our lips meet in a soft kiss that soon turns ravenous. I bite on her bottom lip and tease her tongue with mine. She whimpers when I nestle on top of her between her thighs and grind against her. My dick is aching to be inside her, but now's not the time. Not when I have to get answers. She claws at my tie and manages to loosen it. Banging can be heard at the front door, but I ignore it for a few more seconds with my wife.

"Mr. Demetriou," Basil bellows. "We heard gunfire. Are you okay?"

I groan, pulling from Talia's lips. "I'm fine," I call out. Aside from the fucking blue balls. "I'll be out in a minute."

My lips meet Talia's once more for a brief kiss. "I need to take care of business."

"What business?"

"Interrogate the man who tried to take you," I snarl.

Her brows furrow. "Like Cy the liar?"

"Probably more intense of an interrogation. Cy was a liar. This motherfucker tried to hurt my wife. It carries a heavier offense."

She nods as though she approves of my monstrous intentions. "I want to come with you."

"It's probably best if you stay and rest."

Tears flood her eyes. "Please don't leave me again."

Fuck.

"Fine," I relent. "Let's get this over with. I have a big fucking PR mess to deal with."

"Your dad?" she croaks.

"Alive. They didn't get to him, but they shot a lot of people at the hospital."

"I'm sorry."

I kiss her once more. "Come on. Let's get this over with."

Once I coaxed Talia out of the closet, I changed out of my suit into something a little more comfortable. A pair of navy shorts and a red T-shirt. No sense in dirtying up one of my good suits. Talia also changed from her dress into something that looked better suited for the beach—a pair of jean shorts and a black tank top. Now, we probably look like a tourist couple who got lost and ended up in a torture cellar.

Lucky for us, we're the torturers and not the other way around.

Three men sit in chairs, tied tight by my men. The one who tried to take Talia has his ski mask sitting in his lap. My men wanted me to know which one should get the most of my attention. This is why I pay them well. They know my preferences.

"Care to sit, *zoí mou*?" I ask, lifting a brow at her, motioning to the sofa where Aris is already seated wearing a hateful scowl.

She shakes her head and reluctantly releases my hand. "I'll stand here."

I kiss her cheek before turning to regard the hunks of shit tied to the chairs. They stink and I want them gone. But I want answers first.

"Names," I bark out. "I want your names."

Nobody responds.

Okay, I suppose we'll do this the hard way.

Walking over to the guy on the far right, I slam my fist into his throat. He gasps and chokes for air, struggling against his restraints. When I pull back my fist, he sputters out a name.

Gio.

"Next," I state in a bored tone.

The middle man, also wearing a suit, scowls at me. His body

tenses as he awaits my blow. I give Basil a hard look and he tosses a knife at me. When I catch it by the hilt, the middle man tenses.

"We both know I'll do whatever it takes to get your fucking name," I growl. "One, two—"

"Jordan," the man barks out, sweat beads racing down his forehead.

Turning my attention to the asshole who tried to take Talia, I give him an expectant look. He trembles like a motherfucking girl at a horror flick. When I'm done with him, he'll be less than a man and there'll be enough blood. I can see where he'd be confused. He must sense my malevolent intentions because he pisses on himself. The middle man, Jordan, curses in disgust.

"P-P-Pauly," the wannabe bitch cries out.

"Okay, P-P-Pauly," I taunt. "Why the fuck were you trying to steal my goddamn wife?"

He sobs. "I fucked up, man."

He fucked up.

This pussy has no motherfucking idea how badly he fucked up.

"Hmmm," is all I say as I approach him.

The man stills when I run the blade along his carotid artery, cutting just deep enough to open his skin. One wrong move and I'll puncture the vein that keeps him alive. He cries out in pain but doesn't move a muscle. Crimson runs quickly from the cut. I take a step back and admire my handiwork.

"I need more of an answer than 'I fucked up' because that's not a fucking answer. I want to know who hired you."

He trembles, his dark eyes darting all around. "Niles Nikolaides," he blurts out.

Talia gasps from nearby. Betrayal cuts deep. I cut fucking deeper. This motherfucker is about to learn: you mess with a Demetriou and you'll pay the hard way. Talia Demetriou is mine to avenge.

"Niles Nikolaides wanted you to what? Kidnap his daughter and be a hero? I'm sorry," I tell him, shaking my head. "Seems a little out of character for that worm."

"H-He thought with you d-distracted by your f-father, he could sneak in and sneak out with her."

"So he sent a pussy to do his dirty work?" I demand. "A little bitch who pisses himself in the face of true danger? A cunt of a man who thought stealing a Demetriou would make him a tough guy?"

"N-No," he whimpers. "I had other plans. I wasn't going to hurt her. I was g-going to contact you. Return her in exchange f-for more cash and offer up that N-Nikolaides was behind this."

I set my knife in his lap on top of his mask and dig my fingers into his cut. He howls in pain when I rip open his flesh, baring his veins and muscle. "So you thought you could blackmail me, bitch? Is that what you thought? A little Nikolaides errand runner thought he could go toe to fucking toe with me?"

The man screams and squirms in pain. I push my fingers into the meat of his neck, rolling my thumb over his carotid that pulses furiously. His head lolls as he nearly passes out, but when I spit in his face, he jolts awake.

"Apologize to my wife," I snarl, massaging his fat vein.

"I'm s-so sorry," he moans.

"Sorry for what?"

"F-For trying to steal her."

"Tell her you're just a little bitch who couldn't even capture a woman right. Tell her you're a fucking failure. Tell her you're a piece of shit who doesn't deserve to share the same motherfucking air she breathes," I roar, inches from his face.

"I, uh, what was the first part?"

I yank hard on his slippery vein, breaking it like a piece of liquorish. Blood sprays outward in a high arc, and I sidestep it to avoid the mess. I grip his chin and make him look at my wife.

"Talia, he's sorry."

The man twitches and convulses as his life bleeds out of him. Too easy. Too quick. But the fact he's denying me of time with Talia pisses me off.

"Now," I growl, turning toward Jordan. "I want to know why you thought you could try and kill my father. Who fucking sent you?"

Pop! Pop!

Talia screams, pressing her back against the wall. I jerk my head over to my brother, fury rising up inside me.

"What the hell, Aris?" I bark out. "I wasn't done interrogating them!"

Aris's chest heaves and his eyes are wild. "They tried to kill Father. Kostas, they tried to kill our dad." His eyes glisten with tears.

Weak.

Always so fucking weak.

"Find out who they are and who sent them," I snap at him. "And next time you interfere with one of my interrogations, it'll be your last."

He winces at my words. "Shit, man. I'm sorry. I was just so angry."

"Make sure this gets cleaned up," I hiss as I storm past him to Talia. I grab her hand with my blood-soaked one and haul her upstairs. We barely make it out of the groundskeeper's house before she mauls me.

Her lips crush to mine in a breath-stealing kiss. I grab her ass and lift her, carrying her to my car. Pressing her ass to the door, I deepen our kiss, my hands roaming all over her.

"Kostas," she pleads. "I need you."

And right now, I'd love nothing more than to rip her shorts down her tanned thighs, flip her around, and fuck her hard against the side of my Maserati.

But there are cameras and men stationed nearby and I don't fucking share.

I grind my hips against her, loving the sound of her whimper. Trailing kisses from her mouth along her jaw, I find her ear and bite hard enough on her earlobe she moans.

"I'm going to fuck you, *zoí mou*, and soon."

She squirms in my arms, her nails digging into my shoulders. My fingers bite into her ass as I rub against her until her breathing becomes shallow and ragged.

"That's it," I croon. "Come like a good girl and get it out of your system."

Her head tilts back as she lets go. I latch onto her sweaty flesh and suck hard. She convulses with an orgasm simply from being dry humped. I can only imagine how she'll explode when I'm deep inside her needy cunt. As soon as she comes down from her high, I bite her neck hard enough to leave a bruise. On the same spot I just flayed a man. My girl is brave because she slides her fingers into my hair and holds me to her, unafraid. I smile at her growing trust in me before pressing a soft kiss to the bite mark.

"Let's get cleaned up. I owe you a nice dinner."

<h1 style="text-align:center">chapter
nineteen</h1>

Talia

I WAKE TO FIND KOSTAS'S SIDE OF OUR BED EMPTY, AND I SCRAMBLE up, needing to find him. Not wanting to be alone. It's been three days since I was nearly stolen from our back patio and I'm still shaken by the events. Before that day, I never so much as touched a gun, let alone shot one. But that day I not only shot one, but almost killed my husband, who up until recently, I wouldn't have minded being shot. But now, well, things are changing at such a rapid speed, I feel as if my head is spinning and my heart is being pulled in a million directions. When I saw the way Kostas killed the man who tried to take me, two things became clear: Kostas would do everything in his power to keep me safe, and if you fuck him over, he won't hesitate to end your life. I also learned a couple things about Aris down in that cellar: he won't hesitate to shoot, either, and he's a loose cannon. A piece of information I would be stupid to ignore.

"Kostas!" I call out, my heart pumping against my ribcage. For the last few days, since I was almost taken, I haven't allowed Kostas to leave my sight, and surprisingly, he's been extremely patient about it, allowing me to stick to his side without making me feel as though I'm a burden. While he's had his father brought home from the hospital and hired a couple of nurses to care for him while he recovers, I've helped him plan his mother's funeral.

Which is today.

"Kostas!" I call out again, climbing out of bed to find him. He wouldn't have left without me, right? When I hear his commanding tone through the walls, I take a breath of relief, knowing he's here. I round the corner and find him standing in his home office, already dressed in his black suit. I swear the man practically lives in suits. Not that I'm complaining. He looks hot as hell in them.

When he sees me approach, he tilts his chin down, indicating for me to join him, without stopping his conversation. When I get over to his desk, where he's sitting, he pats the top of the oak desk, silently telling me to hop on, so I do. Coyly, I spread my legs wide, placing one foot on each arm of his chair, giving him a full view between my legs. Kostas smirks, knowing exactly what I'm up to. I swear the man has the patience and restraint of a saint. If it weren't for the way he's constantly touching and kissing me, I would have quite the complex by now.

"I will speak to my father and let you know," he tells whoever he's talking to. "Today isn't the day to discuss it." His hands run up my bare thighs and under my silky pajama short bottoms, near where I want him, without actually touching me there. When I scoot closer, trying to trick his hands into touching me, he chuckles under his breath and shakes his head. "Very well. I will see you in a couple hours."

He hangs up and sets his phone down, giving me his undivided attention.

"I got worried when I didn't see you in bed." The corners of my mouth turn down into a frown.

"I'll never be far from you, *zoí mou*." He leans in and captures my mouth with his own. When my arms wrap around his neck, and I pull him closer to me, he breathes out a laugh and backs up. "Not now, *moró mou*. We need to leave soon for the funeral." When my lips purse together in displeasure, he lifts me off the desk and swats my ass. "Go get ready. Now."

Stepping into the limo that's going to take us to the church and cemetery, where the funeral is being held, I'm momentarily taken aback when I see Aris is already in the limo waiting. I should've expected him to be here, but I've made it a point to think about the man as little as possible.

"Talia," Aris says with a wicked smirk. The same smirk I once thought was playful. How could I have been so stupid to believe he was a good guy? A man I could consider a friend?

"Aris," I say dryly, scooting to the other side of the seat.

Kostas slides in next to me and pulls me into his side. The ride there is silent. Kostas is on his phone doing business, and I'm checking out my social media accounts in an attempt to avoid Aris, but to also get caught up with my friends. As I'm scrolling through my newsfeed, I spot a picture of Alex with his arm around a pretty woman. He's grinning from ear-to-ear, and while I should be upset or jealous, I find myself smiling, happy he's having a good time in Chicago.

"Who's that?" Kostas's demanding voice asks. I jump in shock, my phone falling into my lap. I didn't realize he was paying any attention to what I'm doing. "Who. Is. That?" he asks again, his tone telling me he's about three seconds from losing his shit.

"Alex," I admit. "He's still on my social media."

"Do you still talk to him?" he asks, taking the phone from my lap and clicking on the picture.

"No, I haven't talked to anyone except my mom," I tell him, flinching slightly when I mention her. The last thing I want is for her to be on his radar.

"Hmm…" He hands me back my phone. "I don't think it's appropriate for you to have your ex on your social media. It looks bad." In other words, delete him now before I make you.

Remembering Aris is in the car with us, I glance over at him, embarrassed that Kostas is telling me what to do like I'm his puppet. I expect to find him smirking at me, enjoying Kostas giving me shit, but instead I find he has his arms crossed over his chest and his eyes are pointed narrowly at Kostas as if he's silently cursing him. It's no secret they have some weird love-hate relationship going on, but the way he's glowering at his brother looks a hell of a lot more like hate than love.

At the church, Kostas and Aris stand just inside the doors, greeting and thanking everyone for coming as each person walks through and extends their condolences. I stand by Kostas's side as he introduces me to several people as his wife. Some look shocked, but most congratulate us. He explains who some are to me, and others, who I assume aren't important enough in his eyes, he doesn't bother.

When his father arrives, a nurse wheels him up the ramp in his wheelchair and then Kostas takes over, pushing him to the front row, leaving him to sit at the end of the pew. The funeral service is being held in the same church as our wedding. Father Nicholas speaks about love and loss, and the entire time, Kostas's fingers stay intertwined with mine. He doesn't shed a single tear, but I can feel it in the way he squeezes my hand when Father Nicholas talks about her going to heaven, he's barely keeping it together. I can practically feel the sadness radiating off him, and I wonder if, at some point, he's going to finally lose it. In the short time since I've known Kostas he's never once lost it. He's the epitome of put together all the time. Aris, on the other hand, gets so upset, he ends up walking out of the church.

The funeral moves to the cemetery for the burial, and once again, Kostas pushes his father down the sidewalk to the spot where the earth is open and Nora's coffin is waiting to be lowered into the ground. There's a tent set up so everyone can stand in the shade while Father Nicholas says a few more words, and then the casket is lowered.

When Father Nicholas calls on the family to step forward to throw the dirt onto her coffin, Kostas pushes Ezio over and helps him gather a handful of dirt to throw in. Aris and I go next, and then the other family members follow. Everyone circles back around under the tent while Kostas remains in the front with his dad.

Kostas's gaze meets mine, and I try to convey through my gaze how sorry I am for his loss. As if he knows what I'm trying to say, his eyes go a little softer, and the smallest hint of a smile appears.

And then they go dark. And hard. I have no clue what's going on until I feel someone's hot breath at my ear. "I know you married him because you thought you had to…because you're afraid of him."

With my eyes locked on Kostas still, I do my best not to make a scene or show any emotion. I will not let Aris get to me.

"You can't deny we have something. From the moment I saw you in the bar, to the night we fucked…"

My chest heaves at his words, and Kostas's eyes narrow as he pushes his father's wheelchair toward us, his eyes never leaving mine.

"Just because you're married now, doesn't mean we can't explore those feelings. I could make you happier than Kostas ever could," Aris says.

And just when I think he's finally done, he grabs my ass.

Panic rises inside me.

I feel sweaty and dizzy.

I'm thrust back to the night he shoved me against the dresser and took what wasn't his to take. It's difficult to keep my emotions in check.

My lip wobbles slightly, and I pray Kostas doesn't notice.

Leave me alone! I want to scream at him. Push him away. But there are people all around us, and I don't want to cause a scene at Nora's funeral.

Unable to stand this monster's hand on me for another second, my self-preservation wins out. My eyes leave Kostas's and meet Aris's, and my hands comes out, grabbing Aris's hand to remove it off my ass. "What the hell is your problem?" I seethe. "We're at your *mother's* funeral, for God's sake."

Aris simply shrugs a shoulder and smirks, not even bothering to argue. When I scan the area to find Kostas, hoping he didn't see what Aris did, I find him standing directly behind Aris. His fists are clenched at his sides, and his eyes are pointed down at my hand, which is still holding Aris's. Oh, shit!

"Kostas," I begin, unsure how to even explain what he's seeing. But he doesn't give me a chance. Because when Aris spins around to face his brother, Kostas cocks his fist back and clocks Aris directly in the jaw. His head whips to the side, and he stumbles back. The hit is so loud, everyone turns to see what the commotion is.

"You ever put your hands on my wife again, and you will lose them," Kostas roars, his body trembling with rage.

Aris, the instigator he is, just laughs and walks away. It's like he has a death sentence he gleefully awaits.

"Kostas." I step toward him. "Please let me explain."

"Go home," he demands, his eyes cold. "I'll see you when I get there."

"But—"

"Now, Talia," he seethes, and I don't dare to argue.

I nod in understanding, and on shaky feet I walk back to the limo.

When I get there, I'm terrified Aris will be in there, waiting, but thankfully he's not. The driver returns me to the hotel, and I head straight back to our villa to wait for Kostas. The entire time I'm waiting for him, I pace the room. Back and forth. Rehearsing what I'm going to say. How I will explain. I'm not sure if he saw Aris grab my butt, or if he just saw what looked like we were holding hands. If he didn't see him grab my butt, I don't want to tattle on Aris. Based on the shit he was word vomiting, he's either seriously delusional or scarily cunning. Either way, the last thing I need is to fuel whatever is motivating him.

An hour later, the door clicks open and in walks Kostas. I stand frozen in place, waiting for him to speak first. His tie is now unknotted, the top several buttons undone, and his hair looks disheveled as if he was running his fingers through it in irritation.

His eyes meet mine, and I look to see which man I'm dealing with. Warm. Sad. Soft. I take in a breath of relief. I can deal with this man. He will see reason.

"I'm sorry about earlier," Kostas says, cupping my cheeks with his hands. My features must convey my confusion over his apology because he adds, "Aris explained that he was only asking if you were okay." He told Kostas he was seeing if I'm okay? What the hell is Aris playing at? "He seems very concerned about you almost being taken." I search his eyes to see if there's any hint of disbelief in them, yet I don't find anything but worry. Wow, Aris is fucking good. And that seriously worries me.

"I shouldn't have punched him," Kostas grumbles. "At least not at our mother's funeral. But as I told him, I don't care what the reason is, he never has the right to touch you in any way. He's lucky the only thing he was doing was holding your hand." His lips descend on mine and he kisses me deeply. "You're mine, *moró mou*. Only mine to touch."

He releases my face and steps around me. "My father was supposed to head over to the other side of the island to handle some business, but because he's out of commission, he's asked me to go. The business will probably take a week." I follow him into our bedroom as he pulls out some luggage from the closet and sets it on the bed.

"You're leaving?" My heart begins to race, and my head goes fuzzy. A heaviness in my chest weighs down on me, and I have to grab the side of the dresser to steady myself.

Kostas is leaving me here.
For a week.
Alone.
No, not alone.
With Aris.

"Kostas, you can't leave me." I cut across the room and grab ahold of his hand, yanking him toward me. "Please," I choke out. "Take me with you." Hot, wet tears fill my lids.

Kostas brows dip low. Still allowing me to hold on to his one hand, he lifts the other to wipe the liquid from my cheeks. "Calm down, *moró mou*. Of course you're coming. You don't really think I'd leave you alone again, do you?"

chapter twenty

Kostas

THE FARTHER AWAY WE GET FROM AGIOS NIKOLAOS, THE LIGHTER I feel. I opted to take my Range Rover versus the Maserati because after the shit that went down a few days ago, there's no way I'd go anywhere without bringing a small arsenal with me. The hour plus drive has flown by because Talia's mindless chatter passes time in the best possible way.

"I think I can see the ocean," Talia says, leaning forward toward the windshield. "Where are we going again?"

"Agia Fotia Beach. And we're close. The cliffside home I reserved is about five minutes away."

She smiles at me. "Will you have to work right away or can we explore?"

"Work can wait until tomorrow." I'm chasing down a lead per my father's request. He's certain Estevan Galanis was behind the attempt on his life. Estevan has been known to hole up in one of the hotels on Agia Fotia Beach when things heat up. I'm about to bring motherfucking hellfire to his doorstep.

She sits back and returns to looking out the window, a pleased smile on her face. I don't think I've ever seen her so relaxed and happy. Getting away is exactly what we both needed.

"Kostas," she chokes out. "Someone's following us."

I glance in the rearview mirror to see a black SUV behind us. "It's Adrian and a few of my men. Basil is holding down the fort back home."

"Oh," she mutters. "Duh. Wherever we go, they go."

Reaching over, I clutch her thigh over her dress. "Not everywhere."

She lets out a breathy laugh before covering my hand with hers. "I can live with that."

Adrian is droning on about the hotel Estevan is staying at and I'm trying to stay focused. It's just Talia has changed into a skimpy bikini and is rooting around in the refrigerator looking for something. Adrian, a wise man, keeps his gaze averted. I, however, can't take my eyes off her ass that's barely covered in the white fabric. When she finds a bottle of water and closes the door with her hip, making her tits jiggle in the tiny triangles, I've had enough.

"Time to go, Adrian," I growl.

"Yes, sir," he responds with a chuckle and slips from the kitchen without another word.

"Can we go swimming now?" Talia asks, her blue eyes flickering with wickedness despite the innocent look she has plastered on her face. As if she didn't just seduce my dick into canceling my meeting to go chase after her fine ass.

"We can," I say as I stand. "I need to change first."

The dirty girl watches me with rapt fascination as I trade my three-piece suit for a swimsuit. It's fucking cute when her cheeks burn bright red when I give her a preview of my dick.

"Keep looking at me like that and we'll never get to swim."

She bites on her bottom lip. Adorable as hell. "I mean, we can swim later."

"Nah, it'll get cool. Let's go down to the ocean before the sun sets."

Grabbing her hand, I guide her out of the small house and down the series of wooden staircases on the side of the cliff. As soon as our feet hit the small round rocks, I inhale the salty air and exhale the past week's worth of stress.

Even villains need a fucking vacation.

Talia kicks off her flip-flops and gingerly runs along the rock-covered beach to the cerulean water. The waves lap at the shore in a soft, rhythmic way. Her blond hair flutters in the wind and she looks over her shoulder, smiling at me. I wish I could capture this moment. Freeze it into a frame to look at when the world is weighing heavily.

She makes me soft.

Inside.

My dick is achingly hard.

But my heart? I'm drawn to her. I want to own and spend hours exploring her. I'm happy as fuck that she's mine now.

"Come on, Kostas," she calls out before turning back to stare at the Mediterranean Sea.

I kick off my boat shoes and prowl after her, the rocks making me wince each time I step on a sharp one. She's already knee-deep in the ocean by the time I make it to her.

"It's warm," she tells me when I wrap my arms around her from behind.

"Want me to make it hotter?"

She laughs, tilting her head to allow me access to her bare neck. I kiss her soft flesh. "By all means, make it hotter."

I nip at her throat as my palms slide to her breasts. Her breath hitches when I pull the tiny triangles of fabric down to reveal her hard nipples. A small moan escapes her when my thumbs run over the hardened nubs.

"It would seem that we're both very hard for one another," I tease as I pinch her nipples and rub my erection against her ass.

"Very," she breathes.

"Your body is practically begging for mine." I bite her neck again. "Don't you think?"

"It is. But you never give in. In a couple of days, if you still haven't, it'll be too late."

I slide a palm down her flat stomach and inch my middle finger down into the fabric of her bikini bottoms. She sucks in a harsh breath of anticipation. Before I go any farther, I find her ear with my mouth.

"Why will it be too late, wife?"

She groans, rubbing her ass against me as if to encourage me. "B-Because."

I slide my finger farther down, just between the lips of her pussy to tease at her clit. "Hmmm?"

"I'll be on my period then," she murmurs. "You can't have sex with me then."

Biting on her earlobe, I sink my finger farther down and push into her soaked opening. A kitten-like mewl purrs from her. Fuck, she's tight around my finger. She's going to strangle my cock.

"You think a little blood scares me off?" I rumble, finger-fucking her in a teasing way.

"I, uh…"

I slide my finger out of her and rub the wet tip over her clit again. Her hips rock in tandem with my movements as she eagerly seeks release.

"What, Mrs. Demetriou? Please enlighten me with your answer."

"It doesn't gross you out?"

"Nothing with you will gross me out. I already wiped away the only gross thing about you when I wed you in that chapel. Your last name. The new one is pretty fucking fabulous if I do say so myself." I suck on her neck and then let go with a loud popping sound. "I'm going to fuck you whenever the need arises, *zoí mou*."

She whimpers when I bring her right into an orgasm. Her body trembles and shakes so much that I have to keep her standing with my free arm. When she finally comes down, I slide my hand from her bottoms and twist her to face me.

"I'm going to fuck you now," I growl.

She blinks rapidly at me. "Now, now?"

I point at the never-ending staircase. "I don't have the energy for that shit right now. I'm going to fuck you on those rocks, Talia. It's going to hurt."

Her brows furrow and she looks away, a slight tremble wracking through her. "Will I bleed again?"

I sense a shift in her mood. True fear practically seeps from her pores. If I find out this Alex fucker hurt her taking her virginity, I'll drag him to my cellar and make him bleed.

"You bled your first time?" I ask, gripping her chin and tilting her face to meet mine.

She blinks away tears and tries to avert her gaze. I keep her pinned so I can study her face. "Y-Yes. My, uh, my first time was painful and traumatic."

I suppress a growl low in my throat. "That first time…did you want it?"

Her head shakes from side to side vehemently. "No, Kostas. I didn't."

Fury swells up inside of me. One day she'll tell me who the motherfucker was who hurt her. "Listen," I say harshly. "If you didn't want it, it doesn't fucking count. Understand? What we're about to do fucking counts. That's your first time. Are we clear?"

Relief floods her features. "But you said it would hurt."

I smile wolfishly at her. "Because I'm going to fuck you on a beach of rocks. Your back is going to be pissed."

"Oh," she utters, a shy smile on her lips.

Grabbing her ass, I pick her up and carry her to a part on the shore where the rocks are smaller and finer. Gently, I lay her back as the ocean laps at our feet. With my eyes searing into hers, I peel away her bottoms, revealing her sweet cunt to me. Once they're gone, I toss them farther up the beach. She unties her bikini top at her neck first and then undoes the one at her back. The moment it loosens, I rid her of that too. I stare at her perfect body, drinking in every tanned curve of her.

"Beautiful," I praise, skimming my palm down her thigh. "Mine."

A sweet smile tugs at her lips. "Your turn, husband."

My dick does a jolt at her words. I untie the top of my trunks and shed them faster than a teenage boy about to get laid for the first time. When I fling them up the beach, she laughs, her tits jiggling in a delicious way.

"Come here, wife," I growl, pouncing on her.

Her laughter fades to uneven breaths as I kiss her hard. My cock rubs against her clit. At first, she's stiff, but the more I rub on her, the more eager for it she is. Her legs gingerly hook around my waist and soon she's digging her heels in, silently begging for it.

"It's not supposed to hurt," I whisper on her supple lips. "It's supposed to feel good."

"I want to feel good," she pleads.

"Are you wet enough?"

She nods rapidly.

"We'll see," I mutter with a wicked grin.

I grip my dick and tease her slick opening. She's more than wet. Her body practically weeps with need. I rub the tip of my dick up and down along her slit from her clit damn near to her asshole. Up and down. Up and down. Up and down.

"Kostas!" she cries out, the need making her fussy.

"Yes, *zoí mou*?"

"I need you."

Her breath sucks in sharply when I press slightly into her. Our eyes meet, and though hers are wild and frantic, they're begging me to erase whatever fuckface who hurt her before. Fucking gladly. I thrust into her deep, loving the way her eyes bulge in shock. My lips meet hers and I kiss her deeply, keeping my hips still so she'll adjust to my size.

I kiss along her cheek to her ear. When I nibble her lobe, her cunt clenches around me.

"Ahhh," I croon against her ear and then nip at her throat. Her body tightens around me once more. "You like being bitten as much as I like to bite. What a match made in hell we are, woman."

I slide my palm to her hip, gripping her tightly. Possessively. I'll never let her go. Not now. Not after I've had her as mine.

One of her hands claws at the rocks as though she's trying to get away, but we both know she loves being in my grip.

"Do you believe Pluto was hurting Proserpina now, my wife?"

"Kostas," she whines.

"He couldn't let her go," I murmur, clutching her hip hard enough it'll certainly bruise. "But he would never hurt her."

"You think?" she chokes out. "You think he loved her?"

"I think she loved him too."

She moans and digs her nails into my shoulders when I thrust hard. Again and again. Her slick juices provide the most delicious lubricant. I want her coming with me, though, and with rocks digging into her spine, I don't know if she'll reach that height by my dick alone. My hand slides between us and I rub at her throbbing clit, loving the way she clenches around me with each rub. It doesn't take long until she's squirming and screaming my name. As soon as she comes, I buck into her wild and hard. When my nuts seize up, I latch onto her neck with my teeth and growl against her flesh as my release floods inside her. My hips flex a few more times until she's milked every ounce of cum from my dick. Feeling boneless, I relax against her and kiss her neck.

"I'm going to have to carry you up those motherfucking stairs, aren't I?"

She laughs, breathless. "That's what good husbands do."

"What if I'm a bad husband?"

"Save being bad for when we make it to the hot tub on the deck. Then you can be the bad husband all you want." Her fingers thread into my hair, making my softening cock twitch back to life. "Now carry me out into the ocean so we can swim. I have about four hundred rocks that need removing from my ass."

Sassy fucking girl.

chapter twenty-one

Talia

THE EGGS ARE FRYING IN THE PAN, THE BACON IS SIZZLING IN THE oven, and the bread is toasting in the toaster. While I move the eggs from one side of the pan to the other, my eyes are stuck on the window just above the stove. The one that overlooks Agia Fotia Beach. The crystal clear blue water turns darker and darker the farther out it goes until it's the darkest shade of blue-black. Not quite black, but not blue either. The perfect mixture of dark and light.

It reminds me of my life. In Italy, it was the lightest shade of blue. The shallow parts of the ocean, where you can see. Where it's safe. My mom. Alex. School. My friends.

Here, in Crete, I'm swimming in the black waters. The darkest, deepest part. Where you can't see inside the water. Where it's dangerous. Aris. Niles. Ezio.

And then there's Kostas. He's the blue-black. The mixture. Not quite dark, but not light either. He's the part just after the shallow waters, where you step down and are shocked by just how deep it is, but you're still able to stand. Your head is just above the water, and you can still breathe. It's the best part of the ocean. The water is warm, and you're fully emerged. You're comfortable. Far enough out to make you feel like you're dangerous, but still knowing you're safe.

That's what Kostas does to me. He makes me feel safe.

"Your eggs are burning," a deep, throaty voice says from behind me, bringing me back to what I was doing. Kostas's hands encircle my waist, and his lips find my neck. Nibbling on the sensitive part of my flesh. I find myself leaning into him, soaking up his warmth, his depth. "Good morning," he rasps before stepping back and leaving me alone in the shallow end, where it's cold. I used to like the shallow end. It was safe. Now, I suddenly find myself craving deeper, warmer waters.

Clicking the stove and oven off, I move the pan of eggs off the heat and take the bacon out of the oven. Grabbing the toast out of the toaster, I make us both a plate of food and set them on the table, along with two coffees and orange juice.

"Good morning," I say back.

Kostas finds his seat first, and when I'm about to sit across from him, he grips the curve of my hip and pulls me into his lap.

"Kostas!" I squeal at his playfulness. He situates me so I'm sitting bridal style with my arm around his neck. Taking a forkful of eggs, he brings them to my lips before he takes the fork away and takes the bite of food, moaning dramatically.

"Give me some!" I smack his chest, and he chuckles darkly. The sound does strange things to my body. He piles some more onto his fork and this time slides the fork past my lips.

"I have some business I need to take care of today," he says, taking a piece of bacon and running it along my bottom lip before I take a playful bite, nipping at the tips of his fingers. He growls lowly but also smirks playfully. *The perfect mix of blue-black.*

"How long will you be gone for?" I ask, picking up a piece of bacon and feeding it to him. He takes the entire slice into his mouth like the damn caveman he is.

"I should be back by dinner time. Adrian will be around watching you." He pulls my face toward his and traps my bottom lip between his teeth before he licks across my flesh. "Behave, and I'll take you to dinner when I return."

After cleaning up after breakfast, I throw on my bathing suit, a pair of cut-off jean shorts, and flip-flops, then head down to the beach for a walk.

With Kostas renting us this home, the beach we're on is private, cut off from the rest of the world. With the only sound coming from the waves crashing against the shore, it's serene and peaceful. My own little piece of heaven.

Unrolling the towel from the bag I've packed, I lie down on it and pull up my Kindle app on my phone so I can get some reading in. The sky is shining down, and the wind is whipping around my face, calming my heartrate, and before I know it, my eyes are fluttering shut.

Ring. Ring. Ring. Ring.

My eyes pop open, and for a second I forget where I am. That is until I feel the salt sticking to my limbs and remember I'm on the beach in southeast Crete.

Ring. Ring. Ring. Ring.

Grabbing my phone from where I left it next to me, I answer the call without looking to see who it is. "Hello."

"Talia, *cara mia*. How are you? How was the funeral?" My mom. I spoke to her briefly after I was almost taken so she knew I was okay. She cried and begged me to come home, but she knew it wasn't happening. I haven't spoken to her since the funeral, and I know she's concerned about Kostas. More about his reaction than how he's handling his feelings toward his mother's death. I haven't brought my mom up to him, and he hasn't either. I don't know if that's a good or bad thing. Eventually, I'm going to want to visit my mom, or have her visit me, so I imagine I'm going to have to broach the subject and see where he stands, but right now, it's too soon. His wound is still too deep.

"It was okay," I tell her. "Sad, of course. How are you? How's Stefano?"

Mom breathes out a sigh, her telltale sign she's about to tell me something I'm not going to like. "We're okay. But…we…umm…received your bill for your classes for next semester." The classes I signed up for just before I was taken to Crete and told I would be marrying Kostas.

"I'll go online and cancel them," I say, each word getting caught in my throat. "I don't want to waste your money when we know I won't be back." *And I won't be graduating.* Tears of hopelessness fill my eyes.

"I looked online," Mom says. "Did you know there's a college near you in Agios Nikolaos?"

My chest blooms with hope. I didn't even think to look at colleges here. I was too busy fighting off psycho rapists and potential kidnappers.

"I can email you the info," she adds.

"That would be great. Thank you, Mom." I miss her so much. Her hugs and kisses. Her comfort.

We talk for a few minutes about the school, and the more information she gives me, the more I want to check it out. After we hang up, I click on the email she sent and browse the online catalogue. It has all the classes I need to finish my degree. Now it's just a matter of convincing my thick-headed husband to let me go.

And then an idea blooms…

The door slams shut, and I quickly light the candles I found at the market to create a romantic ambiance. Standing, I run my sweaty palms down my tiny black dress—another find at the market—and quickly fluff my hair as I wait for Kostas.

There's a crash and a bang and then a "Fuck!" followed by "Talia! Why the fuck is it so dark in here?" Kostas enters the dining room and stops in his place. The brightness of the candles hit his eyes and I can see the irritation in them. He's had a bad day. And my heart sinks. This isn't going to go over well.

"What's all this for?" he asks, taking in the candles and dinner and me in my dress.

"Surprise." I shrug, attempting to smile even though my nerves are getting the best of me and my entire body is now trembling. "I made you dinner." I lift the metal lid, exposing the chicken parmesan, pasta, and broccoli. Kostas eyes me speculatively but doesn't say a word, sitting in his seat.

"It's Italian," I tell him, taking his lid off, and then filling his glass with an Italian white wine I found.

"It smells good," he says with a small smile. "Thank you."

I sit adjacent to him and we begin eating in silence. When I can't take it anymore, feeling as if this night is going to shit, I break the silence. "How was your day?"

His fork, which was halfway to his mouth, stops, and he sets it down. His jaw ticking. "Talia, what is this all about?" he asks, waving his hand over the table and ignoring my question.

I could lie and tell him this was just my way of being romantic, but something tells me that Kostas will appreciate my truth more than my lie. "I spoke with my mom today," I say, watching his face for any reaction. His hazel eyes go the tiniest bit darker, and his teeth clench together. Both signs he's not a fan of my mom. Both signs it's probably best to keep her out of our conversation for the time being.

"And?" he prompts dryly.

"There's a college—"

"No," he says, cutting me off.

"You didn't even let me finish!" I screech, already losing my patience.

"I don't need to. You're not leaving me, ever. End of conversation."

"Well"—my eyes narrow on his, hitting him with my fiercest glare—"if you would let me finish, I was about to say the college is in Crete."

Kostas's eyes soften a notch, and I take in a deep breath.

"I only have one year of school left. I've already completed three years, and I would really like to finish. It would mean a lot to me."

I wait with bated breath for him to say something. Anything. But when he finally does, I want to reach over the table and choke him.

"We'll see."

We'll see? *We'll see?* Is he freaking serious right now?

"That's what my mom used to tell me when I was a child and she didn't want me to throw a temper tantrum over her telling me no."

Kostas lifts his gaze from his plate, raising his brows slightly, and then goes back to eating, as if that look is the end of the conversation.

"That's it?" I hiss. "You have nothing else to say? Just 'we'll see?'"

Kostas drops his fork onto his plate, and it makes a loud clanging sound that causes me to flinch. "I've had a shit day, and the only thing I want to think about right now is sinking my cock into your tight cunt and getting lost in you. But you made this dinner, so I'm trying to enjoy it so I don't hurt your feelings. So, yes, Talia. 'We'll see' is the only answer you're getting from me right now."

I'm not sure whether to gasp at his dirty words, or swoon over the fact that even after he's had a bad day, and the last thing he wants to do is sit at this table and eat dinner with me, he is just for the sake of my feelings.

Leaning across the table, I blow out the candle, then stand, making my way around the table and extending my hand. "How about we skip the dinner and move onto the dessert?" I hit him with my most dramatic Marilyn Monroe wink, and Kostas grants me the smallest smile.

With our hands entwined, I walk us outside and onto the deck where I've already turned on the hot tub and have the jets and bubbles going. Kostas stands near the edge, eyeing me with lust-filled eyes as I shimmy off my dress, leaving me in only a super-tiny white bikini that *barely* covers the important parts.

"Did you wear that anywhere other than under that dress?" he asks, his lids hooded over. For a brief moment I want to lie and tell him I have, just to see what he'll do, but instead I go for the truth. My goal is to calm him down, not rile him up more.

"Nope, only for you." I saunter over to him, adding a bit more sway in my hips, and he groans lowly, liking what he sees. "Your turn." He's dressed more casual than usual, in a button-down shirt and dress pants. No tie or jacket. And he's barefoot. He must've taken his shoes off at the door.

After removing his shirt and pants, and setting them on the lounge chair, I reach for his briefs. Hooking them around my thumbs, I pull them down slowly, bending with them until my face is eye level to his dick. And holy hell, is it a nice dick. It's the only one I've ever seen—Aris doesn't count because he never gave me the opportunity to take a look before he brutally shoved it inside me—so I have nothing to compare it to. But Kostas's is neatly trimmed and smooth. He's already hard, and a tiny pebble of pre-cum is lingering on the tip of his mushroom head.

According to my Cosmopolitan article online, the key to giving good head is to tease, so that's exactly what I plan to do.

I back up until I'm at the edge of the hot tub, and then I step down inside, taking a few seconds to adjust to the hot water. I pat the edge of the porcelain, indicating for Kostas to join me. Once he's sitting on the edge, with only his feet in the water, I spread his thighs and grip his shaft lightly with my fingers. He watches me intently but doesn't say a word as I lift up until I'm hovering over the top of his dick and then take him all the way into my mouth. Remembering the article said to use tongue, I run my tongue along his smooth skin. He tastes like a mixture of salt and soap.

"Jesus, woman," he groans. His fingers weave into my hair, but he doesn't push down. Instead, he grips my hair tightly and lifts my chin so I'm forced to look at him. "Keep that up and your 'we'll see' may be upgraded to a maybe." He smirks devilishly, and my thighs clench in need.

He releases my hair, and I go back to what I was doing. My tongue darts out and swipes across the tiny slit of his swollen head, the saltiness of his pre-cum hitting all of my senses. I lick and suck. Taste and tease. And then wrapping my lips around him, I take him all the way down. Kostas groans, then pulls me off his dick, my lips making a popping sound from the saliva.

"I wasn't done," I whine, at the same time Kostas growls, "Need to be in you. Now," as he lifts me by my hips and drops his body into the water. His hand finds the material of my bottoms, and with one tug, he yanks them off my body and pulls me directly onto his dick, filling me to the hilt.

"Fuck. Yes." His head goes back, and his eyes close. His hands are still holding on to my hips, but he doesn't move, seeming content to just sit here with his dick buried inside me.

After a long beat, his head lifts, and his eyes meet mine, reminding me of the ocean this morning. Warm honey around the edges with cool shades of green mixed in. Dark meets light. Dangerous meets safe.

"Ride me, baby," he demands, and even though I have no clue what the hell I'm doing, I do exactly what he asks, suddenly wanting—no, needing—to please him. Not so he'll say yes to me going to school. Not to calm him down after his shitty day. I need to please him because pleasing him means pleasing myself.

With my hands firmly gripped onto Kostas's shoulders, I begin to ride him. Up and down. Side to side. I get lost in the feeling of Kostas deep inside of me. He nuzzles his face into my hair, biting and nibbling on my neck. And then his thumb is at my clit, and with a couple of swipes to my already swollen nub, I'm exploding around him. My head falls onto his shoulder, and he takes over, his fingers digging into my hips as he pumps into me from the bottom until he finds his own release.

"Congratulations, *zoí mou*, you just earned yourself a definite maybe."

chapter twenty-two

School. She wants to go to fucking school. It's like she forgets who I am. The enemies who lie in wait, desperate to grab something precious to me and tarnish it. Talia is a good girl. Sheltered despite being born to a shady Nikolaides. I'm the bad guy... *whom she fucks.* So the lines are blurred for her and the threat is confusing at best.

She doesn't understand what's out there.

What they'd do to her if she slipped from my grip.

Fuck.

But what am I supposed to do? Keep her holed away like a fucking princess in a castle?

Yes.

Of course that's what I'll do because she's safer that way.

Irritation churns in my gut. It's hard to stick to my guns with her because then she prances by in her tiny shred of a bathing suit, flashing me her fuck me eyes, and I'm giving in to her.

She makes me weak.

Weak never felt so fucking amazing.

Focus, Kostas.

Estevan. We've sniffed him out, and as it turns out, he's hiding in an apartment complex not far from the hotel. Either his money has run out, or he thinks he's clever. Either way, we have eyes on him, and I'm coming for him.

"Where are you going?" Talia asks, looking up from her phone.

I wish nowhere.

She looks hot as hell in my T-shirt and a pair of tiny shorts as she scrolls through her phone.

"To work."

"I want to come."

Is she fucking serious right now?

"No," I bark out, stalking from the room.

She huffs in exasperation and storms after me. "Kostas, stop."

"I'm going to get answers from Estevan. It's dangerous, Talia. Understand?"

Her nostrils flare. "Maybe I need a little danger in my life. You leave every day to go hunt *badder* bad guys and leave me to do what?" Her voice rises several octaves. "Watch fucking sunsets while I wait for you to come home? What century are we in?"

"Jesus, woman," I snap. "I said no."

She gapes at me, her blue eyes filling with tears, but anger makes her neck turn bright red. "Kostas…"

"Do you need more chocolate?"

Her lashes blink rapidly in confusion. "W-What?"

"To get over your hormones."

She fucking attacks me. Claws bared. Hissing. A little roar of fury ripping from her. "You fucking asshole! How dare you blame this on my period!"

I catch her before she claws my eyes out and twist her around, pinning her to the wall. Her body heaves as she breathes heavily, her cheek smashed against the wall.

"What the fuck is your problem?" I demand, holding her tighter when she tries to escape.

"You!" she cries out. "You think I'm good for nothing but a good fuck or a blow job when the need arises." A loud sob escapes her. "You don't care about what I want, though."

Jesus fucking Christ.

"You said you wanted to go to school and I said fine—"

"You didn't say fine," she argues.

"And after breakfast this morning, we decided—"

"We decided nothing!"

"—that we'd go to dinner somewhere fancy—"

"I'm tired of eating and fucking and goddamn walks!"

When she starts to sob, I groan. Leaning my hips forward, I release her hand and reach up to brush her hair away from her neck. I kiss her sweaty flesh. "I've never been married before, Talia. I'm not good at this."

Her body relaxes. "I'm not good at it either, but I know most normal marriages don't work this way. The husband doesn't lock away his bride and not expect her to go crazy from boredom."

I nuzzle her hair with my nose. "Then what do you want to do?"

"Feel normal. Nothing about this feels normal."

Sliding my palms to her waist, I pull away to twist her around. Her blue eyes glimmer with a myriad of emotions. "We're not normal, Talia. You're married to me. A fucking mobster. People hate me. People want to destroy what's mine. You saw this firsthand at the hotel when that asshole tried to take you."

Her brows furl together. "Staying locked up by myself all day long isn't safe either."

"And why not?" I demand, scowling.

"Because I can't be happy that way. If I can't be happy…if I don't have family or friends…if I can't go to school or fulfill my sense of purpose, why am I even here?"

I grip her jaw and glower at her. "What does that mean?"

"It means nothing," she says gently. "But your mother was unhappy. Unhappiness is a poison that eventually will kill."

As though she's struck me, I stumble back. She lifts her chin, not backing down on her stance. I pace the floor, glaring at her. So what? She'd fucking off herself like my mother did? Because she's fucking bored?

"We'll talk about this later," I snarl, stalking toward the door.

A loud crashing sound fills the room. When I glance over, I see pieces of ceramic shattered across the floor. She threw a fucking vase. At my head. Luckily for her, she missed.

"Kostas, so help me, if you walk out now…"

She doesn't finish that statement.

"I don't take lightly to threats." I turn and narrow my gaze on her. "Are you threatening me?"

"I'm educating you."

"Go to fucking school. You happy?"

"In August I will be," she says softly. "But what about now? Today?"

Thunder rumbles in the distance as though pleading her case.

"And, Kostas, so help me if you tell me to watch the storm roll in…"

I smirk. "Thunderstorms are beautiful."

"So are long walks on the beach." She smiles. "Maybe I want to see something not so beautiful."

"You're serious about going with me?"

"It sure beats sitting here by myself."

I scrub my palm over my face. Adrian will give me his stupid little smirk when he sees I've given in to Talia and taken her on business. Women don't go on business. But Adrian likes her sassy mouth, and if he were here right now, he'd probably help plead her case.

"Fine."

"Fine?"

"You can go with me," I agree. "But you listen to me. You don't step out of line. It's dangerous."

She suppresses a squeal like torturing fucking Estevan is an exciting item on the honeymoon itinerary. "And then?"

"Dinner," I growl. "I'll take you to dinner where we can discuss whatever it is you did for enjoyment back in Italy that kept you from driving the ones around you crazy." It would seem I need to spend a little more time getting inside that pretty head of hers that apparently runs constantly with all the things she'd rather be doing than being treated like a mafia queen who wants for nothing.

"I enjoyed pickling," she deadpans, the corners of her lips twitching.

Cute, fucking sassy as hell girl.

"Go get dressed, smartass."

"You don't believe me?"

"Five minutes, Talia, and I'm leaving you."

"Fourth floor," Adrian says from the passenger side.

Talia remains quiet in the backseat, but I can hear her fingernails tapping on her phone. I look in the rearview mirror. Her blond hair is pulled up in a neat bun. She wears a black T-shirt, jeans, and tennis shoes. Hot as fuck wannabe bad guy killer who's going to sit in the car and play Candy Crush. As though she senses me watching her, she lifts her big eyes to mine.

"I'm not sitting in the car," she sasses.

I roll my eyes and Adrian chuckles.

"Give her a gun, Adrian," I growl out. "She knows how to use one."

"I do," she assures Adrian.

"Yeah, I heard. Basil said you almost took out our boss."

"Save your girl talk for later, ladies. We have an interrogation to attend. Are Felix and the team inside yet?"

Adrian nods. "They've staked out the whole building and have it surrounded. We have a clear shot to go inside on your call, Kostas. Room 414."

"Let's go," I command, climbing out of the car and pulling out my H&K .45. The wind is whistling harder now as the storm rolls in, and rain sprinkles on my face.

Adrian stalks forward and I step aside to let Talia come between us. Her eyes are wide and worried, but she's also eager too. I guess she really was bored as fuck if she'd rather come do this. As we creep down the hallway toward the stairwell, I can't help but replay our fight.

My parents never fought.

At least not that I knew of.

Clearly, their fight was more like a war. Long lasting, no one wins, everyone damn near dies.

Mother is dead, Father nearly died, and Niles will die.

Whatever my parents had wasn't normal. A small glimmer of delight flitters through me. The stupid as shit argument Talia and I had was as normal as they come. My entire life I've lived an extraordinary life—one written in other men's blood and my father's endless supply of money. I used to watch the kids who'd come to the hotel with their families and they were happy. They were free to splash around at the pool, surf, and play sports. Aris and I? We watched as our father lectured about the importance of organized crime, dressed in our expensive-ass suits, and secretly wished for one day to be normal kids.

I never thought much about my future or my own kids. But the more I allow my mind to wander there, now that I have Talia as my wife, I can't help but want them to have some normalcy. Talia grew up with her mom and was happy. I'm sure she did what all teenage girls did—crushed over boys, went shopping at the mall, and watched rom-coms. She very well could have been one of the carefree girls at the hotel diving into the pool hunting for plastic rings at the bottom.

I'm tired of being an outsider.

I want something genuine.

Fighting with Talia is both maddening and refreshing. She runs her mouth in ways that would get most men killed, but with her? I fucking stare at her, imagining all the naughty things I could do to her sassy mouth.

What was I thinking bringing her here?

As we reach the fourth floor, she smiles over her shoulder at me. So out of place. She looks like a fucking college girl on her way to toilet paper a frat house. Fuck. This is a mistake. I grab her bicep, ready to turn her back around, when Adrian wastes no time kicking the apartment door in.

"Stay close," I bark at Talia, shoving her right behind me as I raise my weapon.

Her fingers clutch the back of my shirt as we stalk along the hallway toward the doorway where Adrian went inside. As soon as I creep around the corner, I see he's in a scuffle with a tubby fucker.

They're grunting, but Adrian has two hundred pounds of solid muscle on this big boy. Adrian clocks him hard in the jaw, sending the man stumbling back onto the bed.

"That's Estevan?" I ask, walking inside the room, curling my lip at him.

"Yep," Adrian grunts out.

Estevan swipes blood from his lip and glowers at me. For a man in his position, he should be begging, knowing what's coming to him. "You killed my brothers," Estevan sneers, confirming his identity.

"Fire killed Bakken," I say, holding up one palm in defense, my gun still trained on him.

"Fire that *you* ordered," Estevan hisses. His eyes dart just past me and his brows furrow. "Who the fuck is this bitch?"

I tense and crack my neck. "A ghost. Someone you can't fucking see or talk to. You keep looking at her and I'll relieve you of your goddamn eyes."

Estevan snorts out a laugh, his attention back on me. "You're going to kill me anyway, Demetriou."

"I might let you live," I taunt. "For the right information."

"You. Killed. My. Brothers."

"Technically, Cy did it to himself," I say with a smirk.

Talia makes a small choking sound behind me, earning Estevan's creepy stare.

"Listen," I say as I walk into the room, nearing the bed. If he moves, I'll put a bullet through his throat. "I just want answers."

"I'm not talking to you."

Petulant fucking man-child.

"Tell him what I did to Cy, *moró mou*." I turn and give her a nod.

"He, uh," she stammers. "H-He cut off his foot and beat him to death with it."

Estevan's face turns purple. "You motherfucker."

"*The* motherfucker," I correct. "*The* motherfucker who can end you with a bullet to the head before you can even glance at my wife one more time. But I'm giving you a chance here, man. Tell me who put the hit out on my father. You do that and I'll let you go." I motion toward the balcony.

"Your *wife*," he grunts, licking his lips as he eye-fucks her just to piss me off. "It may not be me, but someone is going to use that to your disadvantage." He lifts his hips in a salacious way as he stares her down. "And it's going to hurt, baby. So goddamn—"

His words are cut off when I fire a round into his crotch. Blood blooms from where his hopefully mutilated cock lies in his jeans. He clutches the area in horror.

"Y-You shot my dick, you sick fuck!"

"I know it was the Galanis behind the hit, but I want to know who ordered it," I bark out, stalking right up to him. "Tell me and I'll allow you to die quickly unlike your rotten brothers. Keep evading the fucking question and you can live as a cockless roach never to fuck again."

"You're fucking blind, Demetriou," he hisses. "Blind and a damn fool dragging your motherfucking wife here."

I put another bullet in his thigh. He screams in pain, clutching both his thigh and his dick. "Tell me who ordered the hit."

"Fuck you."

Cocking my head at Adrian, I point at Estevan with my gun. "Pull his intestines out through the hole I made in his crotch. Then hang him with them."

Talia gapes in horror, stumbling back a few feet.

Adrian starts forward and Estevan shakes his head.

"Just shoot me," Estevan howls, waving his bloody hand in the air at us. "Fucking psychopaths."

"Okay, then." I pop off another round, blowing out a huge hunk of flesh in the middle of his palm. "Any more requests, Galani?"

He rolls on his side, writhing in pain. Felix stomps through the door, scowling. "Police are on the way."

I nod at him. "Deal with them."

"Sir," he says before rushing out.

"You're lucky they're on their way," I tell Estevan. "I was going to make you scream a little more before I put you out of your misery."

"Just s-shoot me," Estevan says through gritted teeth. "In the fucking head."

"Tell me what I want to know," I growl. "And the police won't have to wonder how to put your mangled cock back together. I imagine they'll be able to staunch the bleeding and get you to a hospital in time."

"No," Estevan moans.

"They'll try to put it back together, but what a fucking mess, man. You really want to live your life with that messy meat show in your trousers?"

Estevan sobs. "P-Please, Demetriou."

"Tell. Me."

"Nikolaides," he says, darting his eyes to Talia.

She gasps behind me, but I'm not easily fooled.

I won't be played. So he figured out who she was. Big fucking deal. Not rocket science. She looks just like Niles. I'm not stupid like Estevan thinks.

"Have it your way," I tell him. "Come, *moró mou*. Let's go."

"No! Kill me, motherfucker! KILL ME!" Estevan cries out. "I told you what you wanted to hear!"

I glower at him. "Exactly. I didn't want you to tell me what I wanted to hear. I wanted you to tell me the fucking truth."

He can bleed out or live for all I care. Estevan Galani is a roach. I will squash him eventually, but right now, I'm hunting a rat.

chapter twenty-three

Talia

"WHAT CAN I GET YOU TO DRINK?" THE BARTENDER ASKS with a flirty grin. Kostas and I have been back home for three days and I've had enough of hiding from Aris and being stuck in that damn villa, so I've ventured out. The hotel has six pools, each one with its own tiki bar. Aris favors the one on the east side, so I'm at the one on the west side.

"Can you make a strawberry lemonade vodka?" Maybe adding some alcohol to my usual lemonade will help to suppress the constant sense of boredom.

"I can make anything you'd like," he says.

"And you'll do it without ogling my *wife*, or I'll fire you and then kill you," Kostas says, having a seat next to me.

The bartender's eyes widen, and he nods several times. "I'm sorry, sir. I didn't know she was yours."

He stumbles over something behind the bar and then goes about making my drink.

"Must you threaten every man who speaks to me?" I twist my head to the side, narrowing my eyes at Kostas. "At this rate, I'll have nobody to talk to but you."

"Is it really wise to start drinking at ten in the morning?" he asks, ignoring my question as the bartender sets my drink on the coaster in front of me.

"Would you like anything, sir?" he asks Kostas, who simply waves him off.

"What else do I have to do but drink?" I stand, and taking my drink with me, walk down the cobblestone walkway. I hear Kostas groan in irritation behind me, but I pay him no attention.

"I'm bringing in your father later to speak to him. Would you like to join me?"

"He's not my father," I correct. "And yes, I would like to join. Do you believe he put the hit out on your father like that fat man said?" I take a sip of my fruity drink. It's delicious.

"No, I don't believe Niles is stupid enough to do something like that. Try to steal you, yes? That was his way of trying to apologize to you. But hire men to try and kill my father, no. However, I would be a stupid man not to consider all the possibilities."

"It's too late for him to apologize," I say. "I'll never forgive him for what he did."

We walk down a pathway I've yet to take, along the side of the cliff. The hotel is so big, I could probably take a different direction every day for a month and still not cover the whole property.

"Is being married to me so bad, *moró mou*?" Kostas asks.

I glance over at him, and for the first time, his eyes scream something that looks like vulnerability, maybe even insecurity. I must be seeing things because Kostas is the strongest man I know.

"It's not the point," I tell him truthfully, stopping and facing him. "If I had a child, I would do everything in my power to protect him or her. If I was dumb enough to have an affair with a powerful man's wife and then drum up a debt worth millions of euros, I would *never* hand my child, my own flesh and blood, over to him to save myself." I don't realize tears have begun to fall down my cheeks until Kostas steps closer and swipes one away. "I would protect my child," I say through a sob. "A parent is supposed to protect their child." And then I add, "Like what your mom did for you."

Kostas flinches. "She killed herself. How is that protecting her children?"

"Didn't you hear everything she said, Kostas?" I take his hand in mine and he lets me. "Her warnings and apologies? It might've not been right the way she went about it, but it was her way of putting you first. All she wanted was for you to fall in love and be happy. While she wanted more for you than this life, mine was handing me over to it."

"This life is all I know, Talia. You understand that, right?" Kostas's eyes plead with me to understand. "What my mother said. It's not going to happen. I will live and die in this life, and now as my wife you will too."

The burning in his eyes tells me what he says is the truth. And at one time, this life would've scared me, but now, I've accepted my fate. "I'm okay with that," I tell him honestly. "I just…I'm just trying to find out who I am in this life. Before you, I was Talia, the college student in Italy. During the week, I attended classes and studied. On the weekends, I attended parties and shows and visited art museums. I just don't know where I fit in, in this world. Your world." I raise my barely drunk glass. "I'm not a girl who drinks at ten in the morning."

Kostas stares at me for a long moment before he takes my glass out of my hand and sets it down on a table. "Come with me," he commands. Pulling me down the sidewalk, we end up in front of an area of the hotel I haven't been to yet. It's quieter over here. The pool isn't open. The rooms look as if they're all empty. "Come." He unlocks a door to the building, and just like the outside, it's quiet on the inside. Empty.

"Before my mother died, we were expanding. She handled all of the interior design. The rooms are just about done, but the restaurant isn't yet. We were planning to open in the fall, but we'll need every-thing to be finished before we do."

Confused as to why he's brought me here, I ask, "What does this have to do with me?"

"You're an art major, right?" he asks. "You know style, and you're educated about Greek mythology. You said you're bored. I'm giving you something to do." When my brows rise, still needing further clar-ification, Kostas adds, "I want you to finish what my mother started. The restaurant. You can design it however you want. Money is no object."

My heart expands at his words. Finish what his mother started. Sure, he could hire someone to finish it, but he listened to me. I told him I needed a purpose and he gave me a solution. I turn in a circle, taking the massive empty space in. It's filled with so much potential. I can make it anything I want. I can spend my summer creating a masterpiece.

"So," he prompts. "What do you say?"

"Yes." I nod emphatically. "I'll do it."

"Good." He threads his fingers into mine and walks us back out, locking the door behind us. "I have time before my meeting, so we can quickly go over the details."

When we get back to the main hotel, he stops in front of his office but doesn't go in. Instead, he makes a left and…walks into Aris's office. Oh my God. Why are we going in there? It's been over a week since I've last seen him. I've done a stellar job at avoiding him since we've been back.

"Aris," Kostas greets his brother, gesturing for me to have a seat.

"What can I do for you?" Aris asks, tilting his head to the side in annoyance. "I'm busy…working."

"As I am." Kostas grins. "Meet our new interior designer. Talia has agreed to finish the restaurant Mamá had started. The unfinished expansion on the west side that's due to open in the fall."

Aris glances from Kostas to me, a sly grin splaying upon his lips, and my heart sinks. What does Aris have to do with the expansion? The only time the guy leaves his office is to go to the bar near his villa.

As if Kostas can hear my thoughts, he says, "Aris is in charge of the money."

"I thought you said I don't have a budget," I choke out as all the pieces slowly come together.

"You don't, but Aris is who you will get all your money from. He also knows who all the vendors are. Anything you need to get the restaurant done, just ask him and he'll be able to help you." In other words, I'm going to be forced to go to Aris every time I need money. And I can't change my mind now because that will raise a red flag.

"Okay, will do," I say. "If you don't mind, I'm going to head home to think about what I would like to do with the restaurant, and then I'll meet with you."

"I look forward to it," Aris says with a knowing smirk tugging on the corner of his lips.

"Can you see yourself back, Talia? I have some things to discuss with my brother. I'll meet you at home."

I nod my understanding. Just as I'm about to exit Aris's office, I'm gently tugged into Kostas's arms. He cups my cheeks in his strong hands, and his mouth, oh so gently, presses against mine. "I'll be home in a little bit, and then we can spend the afternoon together…in bed." He sucks my lower lip into his mouth and bites down, not enough to cause any pain, but enough to send shivers down my spine, momentarily making me forget we're standing in front of Aris.

And then a throat clears, reminding me that we are in fact in Aris's office. I will my eyes not to glance over at Aris, but I can't help it, and when I do, I see he's staring at us, his jaw clenching, his smirk wiped clean off his face. I need to get out of here, away from him.

Pulling out of Kostas's arms, I give him one last chaste kiss before I turn around and leave. I practically run the entire way home. Only slowing down once I'm safely back in our villa, with the door locked. I don't know how I'm going to get out of this, but I can't work with Aris. I can't sit in his office and have meetings with him. I have to find a way around this.

As I climb into bed, curling up into a fetal position, I think about everything Aris has said to me. It's clear he's jealous of his brother. He wants what Kostas has. Kostas is closer to his father. He runs the majority of their business. He was chosen to marry me. And the entire time, for the most part, Aris keeps his mouth shut. He didn't threaten to tell Kostas that we, according to him, slept together. No, he agreed to keep it a secret. And then it hits me. Even if Kostas believed Aris didn't rape me, and what happened between us was consensual, Kostas would kill his brother for having sex with me. Aris knew we were supposed to marry. We were engaged. And yet he still went behind his brother's back and had sex with his now-wife.

And now, every time I see him, he gets off on my being scared of him. Of Kostas finding out. Well, fuck that, and fuck him. I'm not going to let him victimize me. We both know what he did, and if I told Kostas, sure, he might not believe me, but regardless he would end Aris's life. Which is why Aris will never tell him himself.

I'm going to design that restaurant, and I'm going to go to those meetings with my head held high, knowing Aris is a piece of shit, coward rapist. And I'm going to turn the table on him. He wants to threaten me, well, two can play this game.

No more scared Talia. I'm the wife of Kostas Demetriou, the biggest mobster in Greece, and it's time I start acting like it.

The door opens and in walks Kostas. Once he's in our bedroom, he sheds each article of clothing from his body until he's naked. His beautiful, masculine body completely on display. "I see you're waiting in bed for me, *zoí mou*." Kostas grins devilishly as he stalks over to the bed, his thick cock bobbing between his muscular legs. I find myself salivating like Pavlov's dog at the sight of him. "I don't have a lot of time before my meeting, but we have just enough for me to make you come a couple of times."

And with his words, all thoughts of Aris are pushed out of my head. I'm back in the warm, safe waters with my husband, right where I want to be.

chapter twenty-four

Kostas

"I'M COMING WITH YOU."

I stare at my wife with her mussed up blond hair and swollen lips. I thought I could distract her into staying, but I should have known better. She looks good in my bed. Sated, just-fucked, relaxed. Her tits are on full display, proudly showing off the red and purple marks I left on her with my mouth.

Claimed.

She looks claimed and owned.

The possessive animal within me roars with pride. It also wants to chain her to the bed and leave her there until I'm ready for her again.

But Talia has an animal of her own and it hates to be caged. Her animal likes to prowl about trying to see what sort of trouble she can drum up. If she's going to be out of my bed, then she may as well be with me.

"It could get messy," I challenge with a hard glare. No matter how much she thinks she wants to watch her father suffer, it's always different when it comes down to it. My methods are brutal and unconventional. I won't go easy on him.

"I've seen messy," she huffs out as she climbs from the bed.

My dick jumps in my slacks at seeing her naked body prancing in front of me like a little treat just begging to be devoured.

"You've seen messy with work shit. But you haven't seen messy from personal shit," I grind out, my eyes fixated on her ass as she bends to pull underwear from her drawer. Red marks from my fingertips still dot her tanned skin at her hips where I held on tight as I fucked her hard.

She slides on the silky white panties that look virginal on her, and she frowns at me. "He put me in this situation and then paid to have me kidnapped. If you're going to interrogate him, I want to come with. I have questions of my own." Her chin lifts in a regal way that makes me want to kiss the fire out of her.

"Fine, little badass. Get dressed and let's go." I cock my head to the side as I admire her marked flesh since it's proudly being shown to me. "He won't get any favors from me simply because he's your dad. You do realize this."

She pulls on some yoga pants, still leaving her tits for me to salivate over. "Kostas, I know you. I know what you're capable of. And I'm still going."

Sadly, she pulls on a bra and then a tank top. Her sexy curves are not hidden behind fabric. If I didn't have this motherfucker waiting on me, I'd rip her clothes off again and fuck her until she passes out.

"Stop looking at me like you're going to eat me," she grumbles. "My thighs are raw from your scruff. No more eating."

I snort and motion for the door. "That's a promise I can't make. When it comes to you, I'll never get enough."

She slides on her tennis shoes and shakes her head at me before taking my hand. "You say that super sweetly, but it's kind of psychotic if we're being honest."

"What you see is what you get with me," I remind her. "Psychopath and all. And if you're not only married to me, but also enjoy getting fucked all hours of the day by said psychopath, what does that make you, hmmm?"

"Dumb."

I let out a chuckle as we step outside. "It makes you a psychopath too, *zoí mou*. Own it. You're not the same woman who stepped onto Crete." I give her hand a squeeze. "You're one of us now."

She doesn't argue, simply rests her head against my arm as we walk.

The drive to the groundskeeper's house isn't long, and soon we're walking down into the cellar hand in hand. When we reach the bottom, anger bursts up inside me to find the chair empty and no one tied to it.

"What the fuck?" I roar, my fury aimed at Basil.

Basil scowls and points to the corner where Phoenix stands smoking a cigarette. "I said I had Nikolaides."

"You implied it was Niles," I snarl. I yank my hand from Talia's grip, eager to fuck someone up.

"Good afternoon to you too, Kostas," Phoenix says coldly, dropping his cigarette to his feet and stubbing it out with his shoe. "Talia. Good to see you. Do I get a hug?"

Before I can forbid her to see him, she rushes over to him and hugs him. Jealousy lashes at me, which is fucking stupid. She's his sister. They're not long lost lovers finally reunited. Not one single thing about their hug should I be jealous about.

And yet I am.

I grit my teeth and level Basil with a hard glare. "You know better than this shit," I growl at my family's long-time bodyguard.

Basil has the sense to look ashamed. "He wanted to talk to you and—"

"You report to him now?" I demand, a tsunami of rage consuming me.

"No," Basil grits out.

"He reports to me," Aris says, clomping down the stairs. "I told him to keep it vague. We need answers, and you'd be pissed if you learned we didn't have Niles. This conversation still needed to happen, and if you knew we didn't have Niles, you would've stayed holed away doing your husbandly duties." He smirks at the last part.

Talia clings to her brother, frowning at me.

"Then start fucking talking," I bite out, my eyes on Phoenix. "Where's your father?"

Phoenix's eyes flare with anger. "Underground."

"Where?" I seethe.

"That, I don't know," Phoenix grumbles. "He won't even tell me."

"Put him in the chair," I bark at Basil.

Basil starts for them, but Talia clings harder to Phoenix.

"No, Kostas," she begs. "He's telling the truth!"

Fucking woman.

I knew I should have left her fine ass in bed where she fucking belongs.

"He's telling the truth," Aris agrees. "Two of our guys have been tracking Phoenix's activity and can confirm this."

"Then what the fuck is the point of this meeting?" I hiss, seconds away from yanking Talia from Phoenix so I can pummel his smug face just for the goddamn fun of it.

Aris scrubs his face in frustration. "We need him to draw out Niles. Something he's agreed to do as long as he has contact with his sister."

The hairs on my arms rise. I don't take fucking lightly to people making plans behind my back. Basil keeps his gaze averted to the ground. He fucked up and he knows it. I'll let Adrian deal with his misstep.

"I'm supposed to believe you'd sell your father out?" I demand, glowering at Phoenix.

"I'm not selling him out," Phoenix snaps. "I'm telling you I don't know where he is and I'll give whatever information I have, which isn't much, so you can find him."

Anger rolls off me in waves hot enough to burn everyone in the room. "Why are you being so compliant?"

"Jesus, Kostas," Aris grumbles. "It's right in your face."

Phoenix tightens his hold around his sister. "I don't want to be cut off from Talia. I shouldn't have to pay for the sins of my father and neither should she."

I crack my neck, desperate to relieve some tension. "They're paying taxes to the Demetrious now?" I ask Aris. "Every penny plus interest?"

Aris nods. "Now that Niles is gone, Phoenix has been doing damage control. The money is flowing in from Thessaloniki as it should be. Numbers look good now that Niles is no longer dipping his greedy fingers in the pot."

"No more games," I growl, darting my eyes from Aris to Basil. Then, I land my eyes on Phoenix. "I want you to do whatever it takes to get Niles out of hiding."

"I will," Phoenix agrees. "And I want to freely see my sister."

The fact that *this* Nikolaides thinks he can negotiate with *my wife* has me wanting to choke the life out of him.

"Phoenix," Talia finally says. "We can have dinner together or you can come swim every now and again. But 'freely' is a little overboard. Even before all this, we didn't see much of each other."

Her brother grits his teeth. She hugs him, standing on her toes, and whispers something to him that has him relaxing. I want to rip them apart, but I keep my emotions in check.

"I want him found," I say coldly, not agreeing to his terms. "And until we find him, you can deal with me. I'll collect the taxes."

Aris scowls at me. "I can handle it. You've got enough going on now that our father is out of commission."

I'm tired of him being the middle man. The power is going to his head. My brother isn't cut out to sniff out lies and find hidden truths. I'll do this shit my damn self.

"This isn't up for discussion," I utter in a low tone.

Once Talia realizes I'm not going to kill her beloved brother, she smiles at me and pulls from his embrace to walk over to me. I'm stiff when she hugs me, still thrumming with wild energy to make someone pay.

"I'll call you and we can make a date to do something," Phoenix tells his sister as he makes his way to the stairs. "And I'll let you know if I hear word on my father."

As soon as he's gone, Aris opens his mouth, but I wave him on. "Not now. We can talk later."

Aris's jaw flexes as he bites back his words and gives me a clipped nod. He storms up the stairs. I pull from Talia and walk over to Basil. When I poke him in the chest, he glares back at me.

"Loyalty is everything," I remind him.

His brown eyes gleam fiercely. "I'm always loyal to you, Kostas."

Not my brother. Not my father. Not the Demetrious. Me.

"That's what I thought," I grind out, dismissing him with a nod.

Basil leaves without another word.

"Kostas…" Talia's hand clutches my shoulder from behind.

I shake off her hold and turn to stare at her, my icy gaze freezing her where she stands.

"You can't undermine me like that," I hiss, my anger still needing an outlet. I'd come here hoping to fuck up Niles. Instead, I made an alliance with his fucking son.

Her plump pink lips part. "I wasn't undermining you. I was protecting my brother."

"From your husband!" I roar, making her flinch. "You're mine, not his!"

She recovers from my outburst and bravely walks up to me. Her hands are warm over my dress shirt as she runs them up over my pecks. "I'm yours," she breathes, her blue eyes glimmering with conviction. "I took those vows, albeit against my better judgment, but I stand by them now. We weren't meant to care about one another, but we do, Kostas. And because you care about me, you'll protect the ones I care about too."

I clench my jaw, burning my glare into her. She's so fucking confident that I care enough about her that I'll take care of the people she loves too.

Weak.

She makes me so fucking weak.

"Underneath all this fury and aggression, you're gentle and loving. Beneath the mob boss is my husband." She stands on her toes and kisses me.

Some of the anger melts away as my palms find her ass. I squeeze her hard enough that she gasps against my lips. When her hand slides down to my cock that's hardening by the second, I groan. Too quickly she's learning to play my body against me to get what she wants.

I've killed men for much less.

With Talia, it's like she's a seductress who gets inside my mind, no matter how dark and fucked up it is, and fills me with her sweet light. It's maddening. And exhilarating too.

"I know you hate giving in to those who've angered you, but unfortunately, these people are a part of me." She grips my dick and kisses me deeply before pulling her lips away. "Like my mother." When she starts to kneel, her motive on giving me a blow job evident, I grip her hair tight to prevent her from moving.

"No," I say lowly. "You're not going to suck my cock into getting your way. It doesn't work like that, Talia. I'm on to you."

Rather than seeming afraid or panicked, she frowns at me. "So you don't want a blow job?"

Why does she have to look so fucking cute when I'm pissed at her?

"Of course I want a blow job. But not when you're trying to secretly get your way. You want your way then you negotiate for it like a real Demetriou. Out with what you want and what you're willing to give for it." I nip at her bottom lip before giving her a sinister smile. "Let's make a deal, *zoí mou*."

She purses her lips, studying my face for a moment. "Fine. I want contact with my mom."

Anger coils inside me like a snake. "Your mother—"

"I know exactly what she did," she breathes. "And I'm sorry. I'm sorry it was her who was the catalyst for what happened to Nora. But my mom was still a victim. She'd been cheated on."

"You can't go see her," I bite out.

"I want her to come see me." She lifts her chin, fire burning in her blue eyes. "Freely."

"I don't care to see that woman," I growl.

"She's my mom," Talia bites out. "And if you care about me, you'll give this to me."

I narrow my eyes. "In exchange for what? We're negotiating. I might bite. But I want to know what I get. And don't offer me a fucking blow job."

Her lips curve up into a half smile. "I'm inviting her to the grand opening of the restaurant when it's done."

"In. Exchange. For. What?"

"I don't know," she purrs, backing away from me. "I think you're a smart man, *Pluto*, and can come up with that answer."

A chase.

She'll let me chase her down and fuck her like a god does for the one he's laid claim to.

"I agree to your terms, *Proserpina*," I growl. "But you better run fast. When I catch you, I'm going to fuck you hard, wild, and rough."

She grins and flashes me a wink.

And then she's gone.

Watching her ass bounce up those stairs, knowing I'll be ripping her yoga pants off very soon, is worth the shitty meeting I just endured.

Talia's ass makes everything better.

chapter twenty-five

Talia

Sitting at Kostas's desk in his home office, double-checking my book of ideas a.k.a. my restaurant proposal to present to Aris, my mind wanders to a recent conversation with him. When I approached Aris a couple weeks ago regarding the budget, he explained I wasn't prepared, and once I was, to schedule an appointment. Asshole.

After taking fifteen calming breaths, I knock on Aris's door and wait for him to grant me access.

"Talia, what can I do for you?" He closes his laptop and gives me his undivided attention. My heart is beating so fast you would think it was in a race, but luckily, Aris's door is open and is surrounded by other offices. Including Kostas's.

"I'm here to speak to you regarding the budget for the restaurant." I stay standing, hoping this will be quick and painless.

Aris's lips curl into a smile, and I'm taken aback. It's just like the smiles he would grant me before… "Okay. What do you need from me?"

"I guess I just need to know who I order from and how to pay for things." I shuffle from one foot to the other nervously.

Aris laughs and then starts firing questions off at me. "Have you decided what the theme will be? What the menu will look like? Contacted any chefs for interviews? Have you put together a plan? How about an estimated budget?"

When I don't say anything, shocked and dumbfounded at how

formal he's behaving, he says, "I take it you didn't think about any of that?" Aris stands and walks around to the front of his desk. Instinctively, I back up so I'm almost out of the office, afraid he's going to try to close the door and trap me in here. He stops and leans against the desk, completely unfazed by my actions. "In the world of business, Talia, one must come prepared to a meeting with all the information needed. I know my brother told you there's no budget, but that doesn't mean you view it as a shopping spree. The Pérasma Hotel has a reputation to up-hold. The restaurant needs to be cohesive with the rest of the wing, which will be finalized at the same time, and Hilda, who is in charge of that, actually has a budget. She's going to need to know what your intentions are so she can work alongside you. And while my brother doesn't seem to care how much you spend, we still need to turn a profit. It is a business after all."

I refrain from rolling my eyes. We both know damn well this restaurant, hell, this hotel is nothing but a front. Sure, they turn a profit, but Aris doesn't really give a shit about how much I spend. He's only doing this to stick it to me.

"Once you have all your ducks in a row, give my secretary a call to schedule an appointment and we'll sit down and discuss it." He steps toward the door, opening it wider, silently indicating he'd like for me to leave. So, this is how he wants to play this game... Fine. He might've won this round, but I will win the war.

After leaving his office, I was more determined than ever to make this restaurant a success. First step, I had to come up with a theme. Once I figured that out, I started researching everything. From paint, to décor, the restaurant kitchen appliances. I've created an item analysis of everything I'm planning to purchase and what the estimated cost of labor will be. I'll be damned if I'm not prepared for the meeting today.

Going over everything one last time, I gather everything I'm going to need for our meeting, including my big girl panties and five-inch heels, and head over to Aris's office. His secretary has rescheduled me twice now, so hopefully this meeting sticks. I could've told Kostas the games Aris is playing, but I almost think that's exactly what he wants me to do—run crying to my husband, who I know will tell

Aris to stop his shit. So, I haven't told Kostas anything, except that I'm, as Aris said, 'Getting my ducks in a row.'

"Talia, how are you?" Carlene, Aris's secretary greets me.

"I'm good. How are you?"

"Ready for five o'clock to come." She laughs good-naturedly. "I have a date tonight." She winks playfully, reminding me of my friends back in Italy. Maybe Carlene and I can hang out some time. "Mr. Demetriou is ready for you. Just go on back."

"Thanks, Carlene. Have fun on your date tonight."

When I get to Aris's door, it's slightly ajar, but I still knock, not wanting him to give me another lecture on business etiquette.

"Come in."

When I enter, he stands and gives me a sincere smile. *I swear the man is bipolar.* "Have a seat, Talia. I can't wait to hear what you have for me."

Against my better judgement, I have a seat, and Aris sits back in his. I hand him my business projection binder—I made three copies—and he starts flipping through it. He stops at the restaurant name but doesn't ask questions. Unlike Kostas, he's not educated in Greek mythology, so he won't get it. I wait with bated breath as he flips through the pages until he gets to the end. Then he closes it and grins.

"I see you've come more prepared, Talia. This is great work. We'll need to make a copy for Hilda—"

"Actually, I made one." I hand him one of the other copies I made, and he chuckles.

"Very good." He types something on his laptop and then the printer starts up. He grabs the papers and hands them to me. "These are the billing instructions and credit card info. Everything gets charged to this card, unless it's over ten thousand, then it needs to be submitted and I'll use our business account."

He circles the information, then says, "Your estimated opening date is at the end of August. That's only eight weeks. We'll need to meet every couple weeks to make sure you're on track to finish on time. We can't open the reservations if the work isn't going to be completed on time."

Mother. Fucking. Asshole. Of course he wants to meet every two damn weeks. So he can kill me with kindness.

Not letting him see that my blood is boiling, I plaster on my sweetest smile and say, "Sounds good."

After we finish our meeting, I head straight over to the restaurant to take another look at the place and begin placing orders. If I'm honest, this part of the hotel is my favorite. Unlike the other parts of the hotel, which are built up with pools and gyms and walkways, this side has a more natural feel to it. The trees cover the entire area, giving it privacy. Nora had started designing the area, so there's a few hammocks hanging from palm trees, which overlook Mirabello Bay. While I've been working on designing the restaurant, lying in these hammocks has become my new favorite pastime.

After spending the next few hours calling various places to get things scheduled, I call the contractor I've chosen to confirm a walkthrough with him and his team. I need to make sure everything can be done in time.

"Tomorrow at noon is perfect," Mr. DeSantis says.

"Thank you. I will see you then." Just as I'm hitting end on our call, a masculine voice speaks into my ear, and I jump slightly in the hammock, almost tipping it over.

"There's my wife," Kostas says, his voice deep but playful. "I was beginning to forget what you looked like." He leans down and gives me a soft kiss. "Were you planning to come home tonight?"

I glance at my phone and see it's already almost six o'clock. "I didn't realize how late it was. And you just saw me this morning…in bed…naked."

Kostas leans against the wall that separates the hotel from the bay. "I can't help that I can't get enough of my wife." Kostas hits me with a boyish grin, the one I'm beginning to think he saves only for me. It never ceases to amaze me how Kostas can be so cruel and cold one minute, and then turn around and say something so sweet.

"Who were you speaking to on the phone?" he asks, changing the subject.

"The contractor. We begin construction on Pomegranate tomorrow."

Kostas smirks wickedly at the name of the restaurant. Of course he gets it. "That's what you're calling it? Pomegranate."

I climb out of the hammock and step in between Kostas's legs. "It seems fitting." After all, pomegranate was what the Greek god, Pluto, of the Underworld conned Proserpina into eating to keep her by his side for all eternity.

"I would happen to agree with you. Come, wife, I'm taking you to dinner." He grips the curves of my hips and pulls me in closer, his lips finding mine. My body sinks into his and he deepens the kiss before he pulls back and whispers, "And then I'm going to have you for dessert."

chapter twenty-six

Kostas

IT'S BEEN A WEEK SINCE CONSTRUCTION STARTED ON Pomegranate. A week too long of losing my wife to the leering stares of workers as she flits about bossing everyone around in a way that gets my dick hard. She fought me on working late tonight too, but I pulled rank and told her we're dining with my family whether she wants to or not.

"You don't have to be so smug about it," she sasses from the passenger seat.

I reach over and grip her silky, tanned thigh just below the hem of her sparkly navy dress. "About what, *zoí mou*?"

She shakes her head but doesn't push my hand away. I smirk as I pull into the driveway at my father's estate. Aris's gray 911 GT2 RS sits parked crooked in front of the six-bay garage. It makes me want to park close enough that Talia's door dings the car he adores. In the end, I'm an adult and choose to park directly behind him instead to block him in.

"Close enough?" Talia asks, laughing.

"He worships that stupid Porsche. He's lucky I don't do worse just to fuck with him."

She simply smirks and climbs out. I follow after her, drinking in how goddamn hot she is today. After being on site all day, she'd scrubbed away the grime, ditched the jeans, and dolled up for me. Her long blond locks hang in messy beach waves down her back, nearly coming to her ass that has my full attention. The dress is just short enough on her long legs to seem risqué. I'm torn between wanting her to change and demanding she bend over so I can see what color panties she's wearing.

I do neither because Aris steps out to greet us. One look at the proximity of my car and the murderous scowl on his face is enough to send satisfaction thrumming through me. My pleasure at his annoyance is cut short when he rakes his gaze up and down my wife. She stalls to a stop. I prowl up behind her and wrap a possessive arm around her middle.

Aris, the little bitch, laughs. "Calm down, killer. I wasn't checking out your wife. I was thinking she and Selene must have shopped at the same boutique for their dresses."

Selene?

Who the fuck is Selene?

As though on cue, a redhead with fat lips and wide green eyes clacks over to Aris in her high heels. She's wearing a navy dress as well, but unlike Talia's classy one, Selene's looks to be painted on her curvy body. And it looks like they missed some paint on her big tits.

"Kostas, this is my girl, Selene," Aris introduces. "Selene, that's my brother, and his wife, Talia."

Selene offers her hand. Talia politely shakes it, but I don't offer my hand, just a nod of my head. Gingers aren't usually my brother's type—blondes are—but I can't say I'm complaining. Maybe he's moving on from eye-fucking my wife all the time, something I'm glad to see.

"How's Father?" I grunt out as I usher Talia past them.

"Chipper as fuck. You know Dad." Aris's dry, sarcastic tone has Selene giggling at his humor.

Ignoring her annoying laugh, I guide Talia into the house I grew up in. Since my mother died, I've tried not to get caught up in the emotions and memories. I stay singularly focused when I visit. Make sure Father is cared for and doesn't hurt for anything.

I find Father seated in the dining room. Despite the pain meds he's been on since the accident, he still remains sharp and aware. He watches us enter, irritation marring his features. I've avoided bringing

Talia here because Father has no problem in telling me how much he despises her and her family. And while I can tune it out, I don't want to see how his words might affect her.

"Good evening," I greet, nodding to him.

Talia clutches my hand like a lifeline. I guide her to a seat and pull out the chair. Once she's settled, I take a seat between her and Father. Aris escorts Selene to the other side of the table, planting her beside Father, and then sitting across from Talia, much to my aggravation.

"We're in beautiful company tonight," Father says, turning his smile on for Selene's benefit.

Aris straightens, seemingly surprised and simultaneously proud that Father approves of his flavor of the week. "I certainly agree," Aris says, offering our father a smile.

I simply grunt. Talia is hot as fuck. Selene is a cheap wannabe who won't last until Saturday. She's insignificant to the Demetrious.

Before dinner starts, Father asks us to say a small prayer for our mother. I bow my head and try not to let her absence claw at my heart. His words float through the air, but I don't hear them. Talia clutches my thigh and squeezes. I grab her hand and bring it to my lips, kissing her skin.

At first, dinner is polite and conversational. We steer away from Father's "condition" even though I can tell Talia is curious. Talia sucks down the wine nearly as fast as Aris and Selene. I keep my eye on the clock, waiting for the moment we can wrap up and bail. Things between my father and me are strained. His power and influence have waned, and in his inability to lead, I've been forced to take over all aspects of the Demetriou business. It pisses him off, but there's nothing he can do about it.

"Any word on the men behind the attempt on my life?" Father grits out.

Aris lifts a brow at me. Both women are quiet as they listen for the answer.

"It's being handled, Father," I reply in a bored, dismissive tone.

"And the taxes?" Father demands.

"They're being collected, Father."

"And the Aegean Sea fleets?"

"Still floating, Father."

"And Niles?"

"We're hunting him down, Father."

"And the hotel?"

"Running flawlessly, Father."

Father slams his fist down on the table, his rage making his face burn bright red. "Stop dismissing me like I'm your fucking wife, Kostas. I want answers. Tell me what's going on with my empire."

Aris sucks down another glass of wine, too much of a wussy to get involved. Selene obviously gropes him underneath the table because he hisses at the contact.

"It's all being handled, Father," I tell him, tearing my gaze from my brother.

"You're being a disrespectful shit," Father seethes.

Aris shoves Selene's hand away, his eyes gleaming with delight to see our father and me arguing. Usually he's the one in the hot seat.

"You're acting like an old man who needs a nap." I narrow my eyes at my father. "Does the doctor need to change your medications? It's unlike you to snap and lose your cool in front of the ladies."

"I don't give a flying fuck about your fake wife and your brother's whore," Father rages. "I want to know what's going on with my businesses!"

Rising from my chair, I shake my head. "We'll talk when your head is clear," I say in a placating tone. Then, to Aris, I order him to stay. "Keep Father company through dessert and then see to it he's put to bed early. I'll call Dr. Newman in the morning."

Father huffs and puffs but wisely shuts his mouth as I escort Talia from the dining room. When we make it back outside, I let out a breath of relief. Slowly, I've had to take over in all aspects. It's what I was trained to do. Of course, we didn't expect for me to take over so soon, but that was before my mother offed herself and nearly took out my father in the process. Now, I'm forced into the position, but I'm ready. And I can't allow my invalid father to keep calling the shots from his bedroom. The Demetriou name has ruled efficiently and powerfully because we are an active participant in our business dealings. We don't send men to do the jobs we can easily do ourselves. My father is beyond that. He's no longer the King of Crete. I am.

"You okay?" Talia asks, stopping in front of Aris's car.

"Better now," I admit, brushing a strand of blond hair from her face.

"Good." She stands on her toes and plants a kiss on my mouth.

I nip at her lip and grab her ass through her dress. "Be better if I were inside of you."

Her blue eyes darken with lust. "No one's stopping you."

A shriek escapes her when I lift her by gripping the globes of her ass. Her legs hook at my waist, and her hands latch at my neck.

"I've always wanted to fuck you on the side of my brother's precious car," I rumble, nipping at her jaw and then tugging at her earlobe with my teeth. "You going to let me fuck you on his pretty Porsche?"

Her answer comes in the way of her unbuckling my slacks. I smirk as she pulls my cock into her hand.

"It'll have to be quick, *zoí mou*. He'll have a shit fit if he catches us out here doing this."

"You're the one stalling, Kos."

I grin wolfishly at her. "Pull your panties to the side and show me how wet you are."

With her eyes fiery with desire, she pushes up her dress and tugs at the tiny scrap of blue panties revealing her pink center. In the moonlight, her cunt glistens with her need. Nice and juicy, ready to take my cock. Greedy girl. I tease her opening with the tip of my cock until she's squirming, begging for every hot inch. Without warning, I push hard into her with a forceful thrust.

"Kostas!"

"Shhh," I rumble. "You'll get us caught. I don't want to have to slit my own brother's throat for accidentally seeing my wife's pussy."

Her cunt clenches around me, encouraging me to pound harder into her. I grip her breast hard through her dress as I ravish her mouth with mine. I devour each needy moan until she's trembling with a near orgasm.

"Put your foot there," I instruct, nodding to the hood of the car right beside us. "I want your pussy wide open so you can take every inch, Talia."

She unpeels her leg from my waist and spreads herself. I grip her knee and push it, stretching her. The heel of her shoe finds purchase on the hood. Her head tilts back as she breathes heavily.

"I'm so close," she moans. "Touch me."

Her hand holding her panties to the side trembles. I reach between us and finger her needy nub that's warm to the touch. My cock slides in and out of her easily as she becomes juicy as fuck.

"You're so fucking hot," I growl, pinching her clit.

"Mmm," she moans. "Oh, God. So close."

I rub her until she spirals out of control. Then, I slam into her hard. Over and over and over until she's clawing the shit out of my neck and her arousal is soaking me. She shudders again, signaling another climax, which sets me off with my own. I groan as my cum jets deep inside her. The moment my dick stops twitching, I slide out of her heat and pull away.

What a fucking sight.

My wife spread open with my cum running down her thigh, her eyes hooded with lust. I step closer and bend so I can run my fingers through our combined juices running down her leg. Slowly, with my eyes locked on hers, I run them back up her leg to her pussy. She lets out a sharp gasp when I push the cum back inside her.

"It belongs right here," I growl. "Right fucking here."

She bites on her bottom swollen lip and nods.

"Now put your panties in place like a good little wifey and keep my cum inside you."

Her fingers release her panties and then she adjusts them so they cover her again. I hook my arm under her knee and ease it down so that her feet are once again planted on the pavement. Her entire body trembles.

"Oh, naughty Talia," I rumble, glancing at the hood of my brother's car. "You've scratched his car." Gouges from the heel of her shoe mar the shiny surface. He's going to be so fucking pissed.

Her eyes flash with evil wickedness I'm sure she's learned from me. "Oops."

I grip her jaw in a punishing grip and kiss her hard until she's panting and clawing at me for more. Pulling away slightly, I grin at her.

"Are we going to fuck on your car next?" she purrs, her voice breathless.

"My car cost a helluva lot more than his." I stroke her hair. "But you can suck me off on the way home, dirty wife."

"And then you can have your dessert by the pool when we get home," she challenges back.

I reach between us and feel her up, loving how soaked her panties are as my cum drains out of her.

"A good marriage is about compromise," I tell her with a sinister smile. "And we're getting really fucking good at it."

chapter twenty-seven

Talia

"Looks like you've been busy." Aris steps through the doors of Pomegranate and eyes the place speculatively. My gaze follows his, trying to see through an outsider's eyes the finished restaurant. The rich crimson, dark brown, and black color scheme flows throughout the place. Mahogany tables and chairs matched with blood red centerpieces, which hold tiny candles that flicker against the dark walls, giving it a sensual and mystical feel. A large cut-open pomegranate custom designed and created out of crystal and wrought iron is hung on the center of the back wall to represent the symbolic meaning of the restaurant's name. It's hung just above the large stone fireplace, which was created to give the restaurant a warm and cozy feel to it.

"I gotta be honest," he continues, assessing the expansive bar just off the dining room, "I didn't really think you'd be able to pull it off, but it seems I underestimated you." His eyes land on mine, his one brow rising in a challenging way.

Every time Aris speaks to me, as if he hadn't forced himself on me only a couple short months ago—stealing the most precious part of myself, as if it were his to steal—my stomach roils in disgust. Instead of meeting with him, like he advised, I managed to find a loophole by sending weekly emails to update him. I was shocked when I sent the first one and he replied with a simple "Thank you." My only thought is maybe having Selene around is keeping him occupied. I've seen them around the hotel on several occasions: having a drink at the bar, coming and going out of Aris's villa, going out to dinner at the restaurants on the grounds—Kostas and I even got roped into joining them once. Yuck! Maybe he's done antagonizing me. It would definitely make things easier if that were the case. Nothing is harder than trying to move forward with Kostas, while having his brother lurking in the shadows.

"What are you doing here?" I ask Aris, ignoring his backhanded compliment. With the restaurant set to open in less than two weeks, I'm meeting Rosie, who I've hired to manage the restaurant, and Angelo, the head chef, to finalize the menu. I could've left it up to Rosie to handle it since she's more than capable, with twenty years of restaurant management experience under her belt, but Pomegranate has become my baby, and I want to see it through to the final detail.

"Do I need to remind you that this restaurant is owned by the Demetrious, and therefore obligates me to make sure it meets the standards our name represents?"

I should've known when I emailed Aris to let him know the restaurant is done, and that I would be confirming the menu today for opening night, he would show up.

"My brother may be pussy-whipped and not care what you do," he continues, "but I'm not waiting until opening night to make sure everything is in order."

My stomach heaves at the mention of the word pussy out of Aris's mouth, but I choke it down. I need to get this meeting over with and then I can go home to my husband and get lost in him, erasing every part of Aris once again from my mind.

Just as I'm about to tell him to go fuck himself, the door opens again, and in walks Rosie, dressed in a professional royal blue pantsuit. Her heels *click-clack* against the wood floor. She smiles wide at me and waves as she approaches Aris and me.

"I hope I'm not late," she says, glancing at Aris, who is now standing by the table where my tablet and cell phone are at. I was working on a couple final details while I was waiting for Rosie to arrive and the chef to finish.

"Nope, you're right on time." I want nothing more than to pretend Aris isn't here, but when he clears his throat, silently indicating to make introductions, my manners win out. "Aris," I say, gesturing toward the man I despise, "this is Rosie, the restaurant manager. Rosie, this is Aris, the *bookkeeper*."

Aris's nostrils flare at my little dig. Everyone knows how jealous and resentful he is toward Kostas, especially since Kostas has formally taken over the entire organization in his father's indefinite absence.

"Aris, is there anything else you need?" I ask, hoping he'll get the hint and leave.

"Nah." He tilts his head to the side slightly and swipes his tongue across his bottom lip, hitting me with a hard stare. My stomach knots, worried I've crossed the line and angered the beast.

He smiles, his signature boyish smile I once upon a time fell for, walks around the table, and pulls my chair out for me. "If it's okay with you, I think I'll stay to try the food. I haven't had lunch yet."

"Fine," I choke out as I begrudgingly accept his gesture and sit in my seat, allowing him to push it in. He does the same thing for Rosie before he has a seat as well.

While we wait for the food to be ready, Rosie and Aris make small talk. He's sweet and polite and professional, and it makes me want to stab him in the eye with my salad fork.

The chef finally brings the sample of food out, and after going through each item—I've gone with an Italian menu—he places the tray in the middle of the table.

"Thank you, Angelo, this all looks delectable," I tell the chef. With a smile donning his face, he nods once and waits for us to each take an item from the tray. The veal parmesan looks delicious, so I decide to go with that. Bringing it up to my nose to smell it, the delicious aroma wafts in the air, and my stomach gurgles in hunger. Aris takes a piece of the chicken marsala and Rosie forks a piece of the crab stuffed parmesan shrimp.

Bringing the veal to my lips, I take a small bite, wanting to make sure I leave room to try everything else. It's scrumptious. The sauce is flavorful, the veal is tender, and the cheese is gooey.

"Angelo," I say, needing to praise him. "This is perfect."

"Agreed," Aris says.

"This shrimp is to die for," Rosie adds. "Here, try it." She forks another piece of the shrimp onto my plate. Without hesitation, I pop the shrimp into my mouth, but unlike the veal that appealed to all of my senses, the shrimp does the opposite. The moment it lands on my tongue, my stomach rolls, and then, when I force myself to swallow it down, my stomach revolts, refusing to accept the food.

Quickly excusing myself, I bolt straight to the bathroom and throw up. Just when I think I'm okay, I throw up again, losing whatever is left in my belly.

My head is halfway into the toilet when a masculine hand lands on my shoulder. Thinking it's Aris, I jump back, smacking the back of my head on the marble wall.

"*Zoí mou*, it's just me," Kostas says, his brows drawn together in worry. "Are you okay?" He kneels next to me, and lifting me in his arms, carries me over to the sink, setting me on the countertop. "I wanted to surprise you, but I got held up at a meeting. When I arrived, Aris said you ran to the bathroom." He takes a paper towel from the dispenser and wets it, then dabs it along my forehead.

"I'm okay. I think it was the shrimp." I take in a deep breath. My stomach no longer hurts. "I feel better now."

Kostas eyes me carefully. "I think Rosie and Aris can handle the rest of the menu. Let's get you home."

When we get back to the table, Aris eyes me speculatively. "Everything okay?"

"Yeah," Kostas says for me. "Talia isn't feeling well, though, so I'm going to get her home."

Not wanting Angelo to think his food was bad, I explain to him that I'm not much of a seafood person. Thankfully, he doesn't appear to be too offended. It helps that Rosie is working her way through almost every item on the tray and swears everything is perfection.

"Let's go, wife," Kostas says as he guides me down the pathway toward our home. "I was going to offer to run you a relaxing bath, but now that you're feeling better, I think a hot shower is in order." His wicked smirk makes me feel *tons* better.

chapter
twenty-eight

Kostas

I PACE OUR BEDROOM, SLIGHTLY ANNOYED BY THE FACT I'M WEARING a tux rather than one of my usual Armani suits. But this is Talia's doing. The entire grand opening of Pomegranate is an over the top affair that she singlehandedly orchestrated herself. Pride chases away my irritation as I think about all the work she's put into the restaurant. It's by far the most unique restaurant at Pérasma Hotel. She's put an incredible amount of effort into it. My mother would be so proud.

Thunder rumbles in the distance. We've had nice weather all week. Of course it'd wait to rain until when we have guests coming in from all over Greece to help celebrate opening night.

"We better get a move on," I call out. "Weather's looking shitty."

She exits the bathroom in a pair of nude-colored panties and nothing else. Instantly, all thoughts of the event are erased as my hunger for her takes center place.

"No," she grumbles. "My stomach is in knots with nerves, and I need to get dressed. We can't be late." She purses her juicy lips that have been painted the color of the skin of a pomegranate and frowns. If we didn't have this shit to go to, I'd suck every bit of the color off those perfect lips like she was my very own fruit to devour. "No," she huffs once more.

I roll my eyes but follow her into the large closet. Her long blond hair has been curled and hangs loose down her back. She locates her dress on a hanger and unzips the back. Then, she pulls it off the hanger before stepping into it. Her ass gets hugged by the material before it disappears when she pulls it up. I stride over to her and push her hair over one shoulder so I can zip it up. A tremble rattles through her.

"Don't be nervous," I tell her, kissing the top of her head. "You've done the hard part. Now it's time to enjoy it."

She turns and presses her lips to mine. "Thank you."

I step away and admire the way the crystal-studded dress hugs her luscious curves. When she'd seen the dress in a magazine and offhandedly mentioned how much she liked it, I knew the truth. It was her subtle way of asking for it. And since I'm a giving husband, I flew the designer out for a fitting. The sheer chiffon material serves one purpose—to hold the crystals in place. But in the places the crystals don't touch, I'm rewarded with tiny glimpses of her tanned flesh. It makes me want to tear the dress from her body one crystal at a time and forbid her to ever leave my sight. Just knowing both men and women will be staring at what's mine sets my teeth on edge.

"You're growling like a dog," she teases as she bends to slide on her silver strappy sandal heels.

"You're a sparkling dick magnet," I bite back.

She laughs—sweet and carefree. "I think that's a compliment, so thank you."

I stalk over to her and place my hands on her hips so I can inspect her closely. The dress is heart-shaped at the top and strapless. Her breasts fill the cups and spill over slightly. With each breath she takes, the flesh jiggles and entices. My dick fucking loves this dress.

"Still growling," she sings, flashing me a wicked grin.

She pulls away to walk over to her jewelry drawer that I've filled with gorgeous pieces that remind me of her. As she peers into the drawer to select what she'll wear, I rake my gaze down the rest of her dress. Where the crystals stop mid-thigh, the shimmery sheer chiffon goes all the way down to her ankles with only a few crystals dotting the material here and there. A long slit cuts through the fabric and ends incredibly high up her thigh.

This dress is fucking maddening.

"Can you help me with my bracelet, Fido?"

I pierce her with a hard glare. "I swear to fuck if anyone so much as touches you tonight, I'll gut them with my fork."

"Your wickedly possessive and equal parts horrifying threats are somehow romantic in a way," she teases as she hands me the thick, sparkly diamond bracelet. "I don't want anyone touching me but you, Kostas. No one."

Settled by her fierce words, I take the jewelry and connect it around her delicate wrist. Not letting go of her hand, I draw her palm to my mouth and kiss it, my eyes searing into hers. She grins at me before pulling away to put on some diamond dangly earrings.

"I'm ready," she finally says, "and you look handsome as ever."

Gently, I grip her neck and run my thumb along her throbbing vein. "Are you sure you wouldn't rather stay here instead?"

She clutches my wrist at her throat. "I'm sure. I'm excited to do this. But I'm already tired, so maybe we can cut out early."

"Deal, wife. And then you're mine."

"I already am."

I watch Talia like a hawk as she moves about the room as though she was born to do this. Eyes follow her everywhere and they all smile for her. Irritation burns inside me each time I see her mother and stepfather, but they're wise enough to avoid me. They're proud of her and that makes me happy for her. Doesn't mean I have to fucking socialize with them, though.

Aris comes to stand beside me and follows my stare, simply sipping from his tumbler of amber liquid without saying much else. After a few moments, he points at them, still holding his glass. It sloshes slightly.

"It's her fault, you know," he says, his words sharp and furious.

"Talia?"

He turns and offers me a cruel smile. "So quick to blame your wife and you don't even know what I'm talking about."

I grit my teeth. "Out with whatever the hell you're going to say, asshole."

"Not your wife." A laugh escapes him. "Her mother." He turns back to look at them and scowls. "Our mother would still be—"

"Oh, honey," Selene coos. "There you are." She bounds over to Aris, her big boobs nearly bouncing out of her dress in the process. "Been looking everywhere for you." Her gaze follows his, which is still locked on Talia, and she huffs. "That's an awfully daring dress to wear in public."

Before I can snap at her, Aris shuts her down by snagging her wrist and pulling her to him. "That mouth always gets you in trouble. Keep it up and I'm going to find something to keep it quiet."

Rather than being intimidated, she giggles and presses her tits against him as she kisses him. When they get a little too into it, I step away from them on a hunt for Talia. A waitress walks by with a tray filled with plates of dessert—pomegranate themed—and I grab one from her. I take a small bite and lift my brows in surprise. It's delicious.

Talia's eyes catch mine as her mother speaks to her. She pales at my looming presence. I don't miss the slight wobble of her feet, and the breathy way she asks for them to excuse her. Then, she makes her way over to me, forcing a smile.

"I know this is awkward," she breathes, sounding tired and over-whelmed. "But thank you for letting them come. It means the world to me."

I give her a simple nod and then grab her elbow to lead her over to an abandoned table. Once she's seated, I set the plate down and give her thigh a squeeze.

"You did a wonderful job. I'm impressed, but not surprised," I say, smiling at her.

Her smile falters and her face seems to pale more. She blinks as though she's slightly dizzy. Now that I think about it, while everyone else was eating, she made her rounds instead. When she looks down at her lap, I pick up the fork and stab at a piece of the dessert.

"You haven't eaten a thing tonight," I tell her, offering her a bite.

She lifts her gaze and eyes the food warily before darting her attention to her mother nearby. "I'm fine," she utters with a frown, not taking the bite, but instead waving it off.

"You're nervous and overwhelmed, which is to be expected," I placate as I set the fork back down on the plate. "The next restaurant opening in November will go off even smoother."

"That'll be tricky with school and all," she mutters, reaching for an untouched glass of water in front of her. "I enrolled for a full load. But I'm pretty sure I can make it all work."

Opening this restaurant took up all her damn time.

But school too?

There's no fucking way.

"Make the new restaurant your focus. We both know school was just something to pass the time for you. You have this now." I wave in the air as if to back up my words. "Now eat this. You're about to pass out."

She eyes the forkful of pomegranate dessert like it's poison. "Something to pass the time? You're being a dick, Kostas."

I grit my teeth, darting my gaze around to see if anyone heard her. Luckily, everyone is focused on chatting and eating dessert.

"Eat the fucking food," I grit out.

Her cheeks bloom red with the first flush of color all night. "No," she says stubbornly.

"You're hungry. Eat."

"I loved doing this restaurant, but I want to finish school. Something you said I could do," she bites out. "I'll figure out a way to manage both." She swats away the fork and it's really starting to piss me off.

I pin her with a hard glare. "Eat the pomegranate, *Persephone*."

"I said I don't want any, *Hades*." Her nostrils flare and she swallows hard.

Fury rises up inside of me like fire from the depths of Hell. Is this how the fabled god felt when the one he loved refused to eat the pomegranate that would keep her bound to him for eternity?

Obstinate women.

"Fine," I snap, setting the fork down with a hard clank. "Be that way."

She flinches at my tone. "I'm not being any way, Kostas." She rises quickly from her chair, swaying slightly. "I need fresh air."

"You're not going," I lash out.

"Outside or to school?" she challenges, tears welling in her pretty eyes.

I'm an asshole.

"School," I growl. "You have the restaurants, and you have me."

A tear races down her cheek as her blue eyes flash with betrayal at my words. I never said I wasn't a liar. School is a waste of fucking time and energy. She's a Demetriou now and doesn't need it.

"Then I'm going outside, boss," she sneers, her red bottom lip wobbling.

"Get your air and dry your tears." I clench my teeth before pinning her with a hard glare. "And then come back to eat your fucking pomegranate dessert."

We both know the meaning behind my words.

You eat it. You stay.

That's the end of our motherfucking story.

Five long minutes pass before my blood runs icy cold.

Fuck this.

Fuck her attitude, too.

I stalk out of the restaurant and into the pouring rain. It's cold and immediately saturates through my tux. In the dark, I scan the buildings and trees, searching for her.

Nowhere.

"Looking for your wife?" Aris asks, pressed against the wall, just under the awning of the building. "She went that way. Said she was running away from the monsters." He snorts at his joke. "Something could happen to a woman all alone…"

I'd love nothing more than to punch his fucking face in, but his words cause my anxiety to spike. I rush out into the direction he pointed along a path that leads between some villas. My dress shoes splatter in puddles on the stone in my quest to find her. As minutes pass without finding her, I'm getting more and more pissed.

It's like she forgets who she married sometimes.

I'm a monster.

She's called me this many times. It's not my fucking fault she has a hard time remembering it. I hear sobbing nearby, ratcheting up my nerves.

"Talia," I call out. "Come here."

"No," she barks out.

I see a flash of white in the darkness and chase after it. A squeal erupts from her as she tries to outrun me, which is futile. I'll always catch her. I'll always find her.

She darts through some bushes into the backyard of someone's villa. I push through the shrubs and catch her running around their small pool. I charge after her, nearly making it to her, when she slides out of the yard on the other side. Once outside of the yard, she runs up some stone steps, but she's losing steam. I'm nearly to her when she slips and lands hard on her knee. A choked sob rattles from her, cutting me to the bone. Without a word, I scoop her soaked and trembling body into my arms. She's lost the fight.

My fight still burns inside me.

I storm back to our villa. She whimpers when I push inside and then slam the door shut with my foot. My chest heaves with fury. I just want to strip her down, fuck her senseless, and remind her who she belongs to. I've barely set her on her feet when she takes off running again. This time, she makes it into the closet where she starts angrily ripping off her jewelry.

"Calm the fuck down," I roar, stomping in after her.

Her blond hair is darker now that it's wet and plastered to her head. Black makeup runs down her cheeks and she's red-faced from crying. Lips that were once red are now looking kind of blue from the cold rain.

"Take that dress off," I command.

She needs a hot shower and a good dicking to calm her down.

"F-Fuck you," she chatters out.

I pounce on her and twist her around, bending her over the island in the closet. She screams when I unzip her dress. Forcefully, I rip the offending material off her body and it falls heavily to her feet. Her body trembles from the cold and adrenaline. I rip off her panties next and then her shoes, the entire time with her fighting me. When I've had enough, I yank her wrists back and gather them with one hand.

"Stop flipping the fuck out," I demand.

She squirms and wriggles to no avail. I press my hard dick against the crack of her ass, letting her feel through my slacks what she does to me even when she's pissing me the fuck off.

"I hate you," she sobs.

"No, you don't, goddammit."

I unbuckle my slacks and send them to the floor before kicking out of them. My boxers get shoved down my thighs and then I grip my dick before pressing into her soft, warm, and inviting body. We both hiss as I slide into her.

"I'll always be your little captive," she whimpers.

"Damn right," I growl, slamming into her.

"You're a liar," she accuses. "You lied right to my face to get your way."

I punish her hard with a thrust of my hips that makes her scream. "You said it yourself. I'm a monster."

She doesn't say anything else. Simply cries. I reach around to touch her clit. At first she flinches, but then she starts to moan when I work her into a frenzy. As soon as she reaches climax, she screams out my name, whether she wanted to or not. A sense of male pride surges through me. I groan out her name too before coming deep inside her. Her body relaxes against the island. I pull her to her feet and then turn her around.

Hopeless. Sad. Broken.

Fuck.

Maybe I'm not a monster when it comes to her.

"I'm sorry," I blurt out, cradling her cold cheeks in my palms. "I'm fucking sorry, okay."

She falls against my chest and I hug her tight. "I'm sorry too."

"You can go to school," I assure her. "I'm just a possessive asshole, is all." I kiss the top of her head. "Please don't ever run away from me again."

Her head tilts up and she kisses my lips. "I promise. Although running from you is kind of hot."

"Says the woman with blue lips and chattering teeth." I pull away and frown when I see blood from her skinned knee. "Come on. Let's get you cleaned up and warmed up and fed."

I don't let her walk to the bathroom, but instead scoop her into my arms. Her fingers push back my wet hair from my forehead as she studies me intently.

"I just didn't want that sweet dessert," she whispers, her bottom lip wobbling. "I wanted the pomegranate. I want you."

Relief floods inside me at the double meaning in her words.

She may have run, but she wants to stay.

"I know," I assure her. "I know."

Settled by my response, she smiles. I spend the rest of the night taking care of everything I fucked up.

Lucky for me, Talia's quick to forgive. She's sweet like that.

The make-up sex is even sweeter.

chapter twenty-nine

Books. Check. Schedule. Check. Pens. Check. Notebooks. Check. I triple check I have everything I need for my first day of classes. I'm taking Theatre, Creative Writing, Art History, and Modern Greek Literature. I already know Theatre will be my favorite with Modern Greek Lit coming in second. I've read over the syllabi the professors have sent and I'm as prepared as I can be for my first day.

"Talia, I have a meeting at nine. Let's go," Kostas calls from the other room.

I roll my eyes as I gather my stuff and head out to meet him. He's been cranky ever since he realized I was set on finishing my degree, but at least he's now accepting it. That crazy man seriously thought he was going to keep me locked up here and I would be okay with it.

When I step into the living room, I find two beefed up men, both dressed to the nines in suits, with buzzed cuts, standing next to Kostas. Both share a similar scowl.

"Hello," I say, greeting them. I wasn't aware we had company. When neither of them says anything back, my gaze goes straight to Kostas.

"This is Michael." He points to the man on the left. "And this is Tadd." He points to the one on the right. "They'll be escorting you whenever you leave the property, including to school." Kostas raises a single brow, daring me to argue, but I'm not stupid. He's looking for any excuse to forbid me from going, and I'm not about to give him one. "They'll remain with you at all times. Anywhere you go, they go."

"Including the bathroom?" I joke, not able to help myself.

Kostas's jaw clenches. I guess he's not in a joking mood. "Talia, if you don't want to take this seriously, I can tie your ass to the bed to keep you at home and call it a day."

My eyes dart over to Michael and Tadd. Neither of them even cracks a smile or flinches. Are they even human?

"I was only kidding," I defend.

Kostas steps toward me. "Your safety is not a joking matter," he says matter-of-factly. "I have a lot of enemies, *zoí mou.*" He fondles a strand of hair that's fallen out of my ponytail. "Men who would do anything to get their hands on what's mine." His fingers travel down the side of my neck, and my body goes limp at his touch. "To use you as a bargaining chip. To torture you for the things I've done to them."

A chill runs down my spine, remembering when I thought I was going to be kidnapped. It turned out it was Niles's doing, but at the time, I was terrified. My face must show how I'm feeling because Kostas gives me a knowing look. "Every time you step foot off the property, you are in danger. These men are trained to keep you safe. They know your schedule and will escort you to every class, every day. Understand?"

"Yes." I glance over at the men, who are still standing in place as if they aren't even really here.

"Very well," Kostas says. "I'll see you at home tonight. We'll go to dinner so you can tell me all about your day."

I find myself sighing in relief. He may not be happy about it, but he really is going to let me go.

"Have a good day," I tell him. Standing on my tiptoes, I give him a chaste kiss, unsure if he's okay with kissing me in front of my new bodyguards. Kostas must not care because he turns my quick kiss into something deeper, devouring me as if it's the last time he'll see me. For a split second, I consider skipping my first day of classes and spending the day in bed with him. But then he pulls away.

"Behave," he warns.

In the town car, I sit in the back, while Michael drives and Tadd sits shotgun. Neither of them says a word as we drive out of the resort and toward the city.

"Can you please stop for coffee?" I request when I notice we're going to be passing by my favorite coffee shop. Michael nods once. Since I'm not allowed to go anywhere alone, they both accompany me into the coffee shop. I offer to buy them something, but they shake their heads. Their loss. The coffee and pastries here are to die for.

When the barista calls my name, I grab my coffee and croissant, thanking her. I take a sip, but it tastes off, bitter, causing my stomach to churn.

"Everything okay?" Tadd asks.

"Yeah, I think the coffee is bad." I try another sip, but when the smell hits my nose, I gag, almost throwing up.

"Excuse me," I say to the barista, "I ordered an espresso, but I don't think it's good." I hand her back the cup. She apologizes and remakes it. Not wanting to be late, I take the new drink with me to the car, but when I try to drink it, it tastes and smells just as bad as the last one.

What a shame…I really liked that coffee shop. Maybe my school will have a coffee shop on campus. Otherwise, I'm going to need to get up early, so I can go to the restaurant at the hotel.

Not wanting to risk getting sick on my first day of school, I forget the coffee and just eat the croissant while I mess around on my phone, checking social media. A few of my friends in Italy have started classes and have posted about upcoming performances. I no longer have Alex as a friend, but he's tagged in a few posts.

A picture of my mom at a charity function from last night pops up on my feed, and the feeling of loneliness overtakes me. My friends and family are all in another country going about their lives, while I'm over here. Sure, the restaurant kept me busy this summer, but I need something more. Something for me. Kostas doesn't understand that because when we got married, his life pretty much stayed the same. My life, on the other hand, completely changed, and going to school means holding onto that last piece of myself I haven't handed over to my husband.

Feeling overly emotional, I put my phone away.

We arrive at school, and Tadd opens my door for me. When I get to the first building, I pull out my map to see where my Theatre class is located, but Michael grunts out, "This way," and nods toward the first hallway.

"You know where all my classes are located?" I ask, confused.

"It's our job, ma'am," Tadd says. Of course. Kostas said they knew my schedule. He probably made them scour the campus and map out where and when each of my classes are.

When we get to the door that reads Theatre, Michael opens it for me. As I step in, I notice they're following me, so I halt in my place.

"You're not, like, coming in here with me, are you?" There's no way I'm going to sit in my classes with them literally standing guard next to me.

"It's our job, ma'am," Tadd repeats. Another student walks up, and since we're blocking the doorway, I move out of the way.

"You can wait outside," I tell them, trying to keep calm.

"You'll have to take that up with Mr. Demetriou, ma'am," Michael says with zero emotion.

Pulling my phone out of my purse, I dial Kostas. He answers on the first ring. "Talia."

"Kostas, they're trying to go in my class with me," I whisper-yell, not wanting to cause a scene, as if two two-hundred-pound men in the performing arts building aren't already standing out.

"That's their job." Jesus, is that the answer of the day?

"Kostas!" I screech, letting my frustration get the best of me. "You can't do this! It's so embarrassing. I'm a grown-ass woman. I don't need a babysitter in my class, let alone two!" When the phone remains silent, I fear I've crossed the line. Scared he's going to tell the men to bring me home, not allowing me to go to school after all, I change my tone.

"Kostas, please," I beg. "Can't they scope out the place and then wait outside by the door?"

"No."

"No?" I ask dumbly.

"No," he repeats.

No. That's it. Just fucking no. No conversing. No discussing. No compromising. Just *no.* Like he really is goddamn God of the Underworld and has the final damn say in everything.

"Fine!" I hang up and throw my phone back into my purse. Stomping to the door, I swing it open, and my bodyguards follow me in, knowing I didn't get my way.

I stalk down the aisle and find a seat a couple rows back, next to a girl who is flipping through the textbook for this class. I glance back and see Michael and Tadd have at least remained in the back, standing against the wall as if they're meant to blend in.

"I'm Penelope." The girl greets me with a soft smile.

"Talia."

"Did you see the performance schedule?" she asks, holding the syllabus up for me to see.

"Yeah, it's a good list. A couple of them I've performed back home, but a few are new."

"Home?" she questions.

"I'm from Italy. This is my first semester here."

"Italy is beautiful," Penelope gushes. "My family and I visited there last summer." She tells me about everything she saw and asks me questions about where I lived and went to school, until the professor enters the room and introduces himself. He runs through the performances and when the auditions will be held. I take notes, jotting down the ones I'm interested in. Because it's a senior level course, the only requirements are that we participate in a minimum of three performances, either by acting or as part of the stage crew. The first audition is for Macbeth. I already know I'm going to try out for the role of Lady Macbeth.

The rest of the morning goes smoothly. Michael and Tadd escort me to my creative writing class and once again remain in the back. The professor gets straight to it, going over the different types of poetry and assigning us homework: to create a poem of our choosing. I meet a couple of people in this class who seem really nice and ask me to join them for lunch.

The afternoon consists of my Lit and History of Art classes. They're not as fun as my morning classes, but they fly by, and before I know it I'm back in the car heading home. My classes are Tuesdays and Thursdays with Theatre practice on Fridays. That gives me the other days to get my homework done.

As I'm walking toward the parking lot with Michael and Tadd flanking me, my brother steps into view from out of nowhere.

"Phoenix!" I'm about to throw my arms around him for a hug when Michael yanks me back. "Hey," I shriek at the same time my brother hisses, "Get your hands off her."

"Back up," Tadd commands.

Phoenix reaches behind him, for what I assume is his gun, and before he can even pull it out, Tadd has him on the ground with his hands locked behind his back.

"Stop, please," I whisper, hating the attention we're drawing from the students walking by. "I know him. He's okay."

Tadd stands, bringing Phoenix up with him. "He's not on the approved list, ma'am."

"I'm her fucking brother, asshole. I don't need to be on any fucking list."

Tadd steps toward him. "You do if you want to go anywhere near her."

In fear he'll take out my brother, I move forward, only Michael is still holding me back. "Okay, okay," I say in a placating tone. "I'll speak to Kostas tonight and get you on the approved list." I silently beg Phoenix not to argue. The last thing I need is to give Kostas a reason to kill my brother. Phoenix looks like he wants to say something, but when I shake my head, he closes his mouth.

"I'll see you soon," I tell him.

"All right." He nods once and then takes off in the opposite direction than we're heading.

By the time we're pulling through the entrance to the hotel, my blood is boiling. Damn Kostas and his need to control everything and everyone. Not sure when he'll be home, and not wanting to be here when he arrives, I opt to go for a swim in the pool to cool off. I can bring my homework with me and work on it by the pool. But when I step through the door, and am hit with a cold glare from Kostas, I know I'm not going anywhere. Setting my purse and books on the table, I shoot him what I hope is an equally pissed off expression.

"Welcome home, *wife*," Kostas greets as I stalk past him to the bedroom to change. Deciding a shower is in order, I strip down and go straight to the bathroom. I can feel Kostas behind me, but I ignore him, focusing on the temperature of the water. Once it's hot enough, I step in, only to find Kostas is also naked and following me in.

Doing my best to ignore him, I grab the body wash and squeeze some onto a loofah. But like the tyrant my husband is, he won't be ignored. Gripping the curve of my hip, he turns me around to face him, backing me against the shower wall. The loofah falls to the ground as he pins my hands above my head with one of his own. "I asked how your day was, *wife*," he seethes.

When I still refuse to answer, he leans in and bites down on my bottom lip. I screech out in pain, trying to push him away, but he's too strong, and I'm at his mercy. I'm *always* at his mercy.

"Want me to tell you how my day was?" he asks, clearly as a rhetorical question, since he doesn't wait for an answer before he continues. "It started with my wife screaming at me over the phone while I was standing in an important business meeting." My eyes go wide. Shit, I didn't think about why he was being so short over the phone. "Apparently it's more *important* for her to fit in than to be safe." His icy-hot gaze bores into mine. "Not even an hour away from here and you're already forgetting whose *wife* you are." His grip tightens on my wrists, and with his other hand, he lifts me up by my ass. My legs wrap around his torso, and then he roughly drives into me.

Everything inside me clenches.

"You." *Thrust.* "Are." *Another thrust.* "My goddamned wife."

My eyes remain locked with Kostas's as he fucks me hard and deep, reminding me who I am. Who I belong to. And by the time we're both coming, I'm screaming out the name of the man who owns every single part of me.

"Add Phoenix to the approved list," I tell Kostas after the waiter sets down our plates of food.

Kostas's jaw clenches. "You're going to want to rethink how you speak to your husband, *anóito korítsi.*" *Foolish girl.* "Otherwise, I'm going to be forced to remind you again who you belong to, but you aren't going to be screaming my name in pleasure this time."

Not wanting to argue with him, I take a calming breath and try again, this time nicer. "Can you please add my brother to the list of approved people who can speak to me?"

Kostas glares my way but nods. "It's already been done."

"Thank you."

"How was your first day of school?"

"It was good. The first performance in my theatre class is *Macbeth.*

Guess which part I'm trying out for." I bat my lashes playfully, and Kostas chuckles.

"Let me guess, Lady Macbeth," he answers dryly.

"Yep. I think I'll make a great Lady Macbeth. She's strong and ambitious. Determined."

Kostas barks out a laugh. "She's cunning and ruthless and manipulative. She repeatedly questions her husband's manhood until she pushes him to the edge, forcing him to commit murder. Then she can't handle it and takes her own life." Kostas puts his fork down and stares at me with a mixture of humor and seriousness. "You know what would've saved her life? If she had let her husband handle shit."

I roll my eyes. "You're such a caveman."

"Doesn't Lady Macbeth have to kiss Macbeth in that play?" Kostas asks thoughtfully.

"I don't know." I shrug. "If she does, it's only for pretend. It's a stage kiss. It's not real."

Kostas lets out a growl. "I'll be damned if my wife is kissing another man, staged or not."

"Caveman," I repeat.

"Careful, *Lady Macbeth*. You will hate the outcome if you drive your husband to the edge and he's forced to commit murder." Kostas's lips curve into a wicked grin as fear shoots through my veins like some deadly hit of a drug I want no part of.

Any other man and I would take his threat as a joke, but with Kostas, I have a feeling he's being dead serious.

chapter thirty

Kostas

THERE ARE TWO THINGS THAT RILE MY WIFE UP. ONE, TELLING her no. The other, her motherfucking raging hormonal period time. This morning, the stage is set for a nuclear meltdown. For once, I'm eager to send her ass to school so I can get a moment of fucking peace.

"Say it again," she seethes, her face turning red.

I scrub my palm down my face in frustration. "You're just mad because you're on your period." She had Tadd and Michael run her by the drugstore after school yesterday, so I know this is half of her problem.

"What did you say?" Her voice is deceptively calm, but I can see the figurative claws coming out.

"I'm saying it's why you're being irrational."

She picks up a vase and heaves it at me. I don't even have to duck out of the way because she throws like shit. My wife's favorite things to throw are vases, so I keep having them replenished in our home. It crashes behind me and her chest rises up and down with fury.

"I am not being irrational, Kostas. I'm not being hormonal. You're being a psychopath!" She's too pissed to cry. Nothing but rage ripples from her. Normally, I like to pin her down and fuck the anger out of her, but she's on the rag and isn't into it.

I stalk over to her and grip her jaw, smushing her cheeks so her lips pucker out. "You married me knowing I was a psychopath. Don't act surprised now, Mrs. Demetriou."

She hisses like a fucking cat. "I'll be Lady Macbeth, and I'll kiss him! It's what my grade requires me to do!"

Just thinking about her kissing that motherfucker makes me see red. I'd been proud when she auditioned for the part and got it, but the moment she reminded me she'd have to kiss the guy, I wasn't having any of it.

"And I told you what I'd do if he kissed you," I bite out, rubbing the tip of my nose against hers and pinning her with a hard glare.

"You can't cut off his lips, you fucking freak!" she cries out, her emotions finally winning out over her anger. Tears well in her pretty blues and I hate that I caused them, but I won't back down on this.

"I will. Tell your teacher you can pretend to kiss him. But I won't have him taking what's mine," I tell her simply.

"You're impossible," she snaps. "I'm leaving."

"How long is this Theater practice?" I ask, not releasing her pretty face.

"Two hours." She rolls her eyes. "I know the drill. Come straight home. Don't pass Go. Don't collect two hundred euros. Just come back to the dungeon so my psychopathic husband can put me back in my cage."

"Get over yourself," I grumble, letting her go. "I swear, I ought to put you in a cage one week out of every month."

Her lip curls up in fury. "I hate you."

"Mhmm."

"You can't keep me pressed under your thumb forever," she threatens, her lip wobbling slightly. "I won't stand for it. You know this, Kostas."

I grip a handful of her blond hair and kiss her pouty lips that keep spewing so much hate today. She doesn't kiss me back, which really fucking pisses me off.

"You'll stand for it because you have no goddamn choice," I bite out and press a soft kiss to her forehead. "Have a nice time at practice."

She pulls away and glowers at me for a moment before turning on her heel and stalking off. I should go after her, yank her back into the room, and make passionate love to her so she'll calm down…period be damned. But I have a meeting with my father and I don't have time to pacify her like usual.

"Don't wait up for me," she sasses over her shoulder.

"S 'agapó, ómorfi gynaíka mou." I love you, my beautiful wife.

The door slams before I even get the words out.

I'll let her cool off and then I'm going to spend all weekend teaching her how to behave. A little duct tape. Some rope. Naked and at my mercy. It'll be hard to be pissed when she's had countless orgasms.

Sometimes I think Talia likes to fight with me just so we can make up. We're really fucking good at making up.

Father was in his bedroom when I arrived, laid up in his bed. For a man who months ago ruled with an iron fist he is weak now. So fucking weak. My mother made him that way. I helped him dress, along with his live-in nurse, and then wheeled him down to the dining room where his cook had made a fantastic lunch spread. An hour passes before we finish our meal and get down to whatever it is Father called me here for.

"How's married life treating you?" he asks, his features hardened.

"Splendid." He doesn't need to know that Talia pushes every fucking button I have, but I secretly like it. Our fighting is foreplay. Father definitely doesn't need to hear about that.

"Hmmm," is all he says. "Where's your brother?"

I pull out a phone and check for any texts.

Aris: On my way. Sorry I'm late. Selene's mouth needed to be punished.

Rolling my eyes, I set my phone down on the table. "He'll be here soon."

One of Father's servants walks in with a tray, bringing us some cookies and coffee. While she busies herself with setting everything out, I scroll through my phone checking on emails. I fire off a text to Talia.

Me: I miss you even when you piss me the fuck off.

I smirk, imagining the way her nostrils will flare and her blue eyes will darken with anger.

"The wind is fucking horrible," Aris calls out as he strides into the dining room looking disheveled. "Tropical storm coming through?"

He and Father discuss the weather while I stare at my phone. The servant brings out a plate of lunch for Aris. After ten or fifteen minutes of them gossiping about the weather like two old fucking men, I let out a huff and set my phone down. My gaze finds Aris and I notice his bitch literally got her claws into him. His neck is red where she scratched him. Selene is a skank, but Aris seems quite taken by her. When he catches me staring, he flashes me a lazy grin.

"Where's Niles?" Father demands, dragging my attention his way.

I grit my teeth. For someone who has to have a nurse twenty-four-seven, he sure is a demanding motherfucker. "He's hiding like the rat he is."

Aris snorts. "His son sure as hell isn't."

Father lifts a brow at me in question. "Phoenix sniffing around?"

"I married his sister. It's not unheard of for annoying brothers to stick their noses where they don't belong." I level Aris with a glare that makes him bark out a laugh.

"Can we shake out information from him?" Father asks, his shrewd eyes narrowing at me.

"He doesn't know anything," I grit out.

Father blinks at me before shaking his head. "He does. And you could get it out of him. But you won't. Why is that, my son?"

"Father, you're out of line."

"Me?" He scoffs. "You're the one acting like a piece of ass is more important than this family."

"Enough!" I roar, slamming my fist down on the table. "She is my wife. And just like you respected my mother, I will respect her. He's her brother. I'm not going to torture answers out of him. We'll find Niles another fucking way."

Aris smirks as he watches our exchange.

"Talia is a distraction. She makes you soft," Father growls. "You're not fit to lead."

I rise from my seat and sneer at him, motioning at his wheelchair and the fucking salmon-colored afghan blanket in his lap. "Too bad you don't make those decisions anymore."

"Kostas Angelo Demetriou!" Father bellows, but I'm already storming away from him.

Father can meddle all he wants, but I know what the hell I'm doing. I have men all over sniffing out Phoenix's moves, hunting for Niles, and following every Galani roach left all over Crete. Just because I don't blab to my brother or my father every damn time I do something doesn't mean I don't spend all goddamn day piecing together the puzzle that is my life.

I climb into my Maserati and zip down the streets, anger buzzing through my veins. By the time I reach the hotel, it's ten minutes after when Talia gets out of class. Her not texting me back means she's super pissed. I shut off the car and dial a local flower delivery company. Women like flowers and Talia is no exception. Once the flowers are ordered, I text her again.

Me: I'm sorry, zoí mou.

I'm still staring at my phone when Tadd calls.

"Boss," he grunts out, his breathing heavy. "We've got a problem."

A chill races down my spine.

"What kind of problem?" I growl.

He curses. "A big one."

"Where. Is. My. Wife?"

A long pause.

"We don't know. She left the auditorium to go to the bathroom and never came back."

I pull up the tracker I have on her phone. "It shows she's on campus. She's pissed, Tadd. We fought. Find her ass wherever she is hiding and call me. Check the campus coffee shop or the library. I'm on my way."

Without wasting a second, I haul ass to her school and dial Aris.

"Hey," he grunts in greeting.

"You heard from Talia?" I demand, pressing my foot down on the accelerator.

"Not since dinner the other night with Selene. Why? She pissed at you again?"

I don't have time for his taunting shit.

"Can you call her and see if she answers?"

He sobers up. "Is she missing?"

"Went to the bathroom and never came back."

"Fuck," he hisses. "She wouldn't just leave. Phoenix?"

I knew adding him as an approved person was a bad idea. "I don't know. Call him. Find him."

We hang up, and I try dialing her number. It rings and rings. Next,

I call Adrian and send him to the airport since that's where she first ran off to.

Fuck.

As soon as I pull into the parking lot, I throw my car into park and take off running toward the building. Tadd greets me with a worried expression. Michael is nowhere to be found.

"Where's Michael?" I demand.

"Checking the school again."

"And you're sitting out here with your thumb up your ass?"

He frowns. "I was waiting for you."

If I wasn't worried about my damn wife, I'd cut this lazy dumbass's throat.

"Go get in your fucking car and find my wife," I snarl. "Your neck depends on it."

He gives me a clipped nod and runs off. Michael comes out of the building holding a young woman by her arm. Her eyes are wild when she sees me.

"Tell him," Michael barks at the girl.

She flinches and stammers, "I, uh, before rehearsal, she was crying. She was upset."

I already fucking know that. I pissed her off.

"And?" I snap.

"Uh," she whimpers. "She kept saying she just needs to see her mom."

My blood runs cold. She wouldn't just bail on me. Not now. Not with all the people who could hurt her. She knows better than this. Right?

"She seemed really upset," she says, "and then she grabbed her purse to go to the bathroom. Never came back. I thought she went home for the day."

I turn my glare on Michael. "You were to watch her every move. What the fuck were you two doing?"

"Jesus, boss," Michael grunts. "We didn't follow her into the bathroom. We stayed in the auditorium. The bathroom was just outside the doors."

I'll deal with these two pussies later once I've found Talia.

I *will* find Talia. I always do.

I pull the tracker app back up on my phone to check it again. "It still shows she's on campus." What the fuck? Did she leave her phone here? "Go check every damn classroom, every bathroom. That phone is somewhere on this damn campus. Find it. Find her."

My phone rings, and I answer it on the first ring. "What?"

"I asked Selene if she's spoken to Talia," Aris grits out. "Fuck. She's worried about her. She said last night in the middle of the night, she called asking to borrow some money. I didn't even know Selene left my villa to meet her with the money." And I didn't know Talia left ours. Fuck.

"Money for what?"

"Selene said she seemed as though she had her mind made up about something. She lent her the money and didn't think much of it until I called."

"So you're saying she willingly left me?" I growl into the phone.

Aris sucks in a sharp breath. "You and I both know we can't go on that assumption."

The line goes quiet before he lets out another heavy sigh.

"Some of the men at the hotel said they heard Estevan Galani finally recovered from what you did to him on your honeymoon and is here in town." Aris huffs. "What if…"

My blood turns ice cold.

I knew I should have killed that motherfucker.

"If he has her," I rumble out, "he's a dead man."

"Kostas, if he has her, she's a dead woman."

Fuck.

Fuck.

Fuck.

I have to find her.

Her life may depend on it.

playlist

Head Above Water by Avril Lavigne
Complicated by Avril Lavigne
I'm a Mess by Bebe Rexha
Broken-hearted Girl by Beyoncé
Reason to Stay by Brett Young
Never be the Same by Camila Cabello
Consequences by Camila Cabello
The Scientist by Coldplay
Let it Go by James Bay
In Case by Demi Lovato
i hate u, i love u by Gnash
Desire by Meg Myers
Stay by Rihanna
Back to You by Louis Tomlinson
Bad Things by Machine Gun Kelly and Camila Cabello
Love on the Brain by Rihanna
Rock Bottom by Hailee Steinfeld
The Monster by Eminem
So Good by Zara Larsson
Remind Me to Forget by Kygo & Miguel
Him & I by G-Eazy & Halsey
Bad Blood by Taylor Swift
Mad by Ne-Yo
I'm a Mess by Ed Sheeran

stolen
lies

To the brave readers who are back for more. We promise not to put *too* much strain on your heart.

chapter one

Kostas
One Year Later

Lies.

All fucking lies.

Both of the assholes lie straight to my face. I'll kill them both. An evil laugh erupts from me, making them both wince in exactly the same way at exactly the same time.

"Is that your final answer?" I ask, grinning.

"Y-Yes," the fuckface says. "M-My final answer."

The room spins and I close my eyes. Blood. Sweat. Piss. The scents emanating from this cellar have my bile rising. Fuck, I'm going to puke.

I slice through the air and miss them both. Irritated, I stomp over to the table and grab my bottle of tequila. Adrian clears his throat as I guzzle down the liquid, but I ignore him. The burn races down my esophagus and then hums through my veins.

"I hate liars," I mumble and take another swig. "You're a liar."

The man—some Galani idiot cousin whose name doesn't even matter to me—whimpers. "Please," he begs. "Please don't kill me. I told you everything."

Ignoring his pleading, I swipe the air again. This time I get them both right across the chest. This makes me laugh. His cries of pain are fucking entertaining.

"Sir," Adrian says.

Swiveling around, the room spins, and I stumble at the movement.

When everything slows to a stop, I find two Adrians too. Both scowling at me. What the fuck is his problem?

"Got something to say?" I demand, my voice a husky slur.

He shakes his head. "Nope. Just fucking hungry."

What time is it?

What fucking day is it?

Fury burns through my chest hotter than the tequila. These days, I'm losing sight of myself. My purpose. Everything.

Don't think about it.

Don't think about it.

Blond hair. Blue eyes. Pouty as fuck lips.

Pain chases away the anger and the ache inside my chest threatens to rip me in two. I grit my teeth so I don't do something stupid like throw myself onto the floor kicking and screaming like a goddamn toddler.

She's gone.

Been gone for a motherfucking year.

All leads are dead ends.

Even this slimy asshole tonight was a dead end. He knows nothing. Nothing of value. I've sliced enough of his skin that if he knew the answer, he would've given it up already. But he hasn't because he doesn't know shit.

Where are you, Talia?

Someone took her. I can feel it in my bones. But all the usual suspects are quiet and in hiding. Everything feels so normal. As if I imagined my wife—imagined holding her luscious curves and driving into her tight heat. Sometimes I wonder if I did. Was it all a fucked-up dream? Am I in some unknown level of hell?

I swing out again, missing the Galani roach and his double. Squinting, they become one. Ugly motherfucker. Him and his blurred phantom twin.

Everything turns black for a moment and I stumble. I'm just blinking away the confusion when Adrian forcefully grabs my knife.

"Let me finish up here, Boss." He pins me with a hard glare. Why the fuck does he have four eyes?

"What'd I miss?" Aris asks, clomping down the stairs. "Yuck. A fucking mess is what."

"Kostas was just heading up to grab some coffee and a bite to eat," Adrian says. "You came just in time."

Aris rakes his gaze down my form and his lips purse together in disappointment. Same fucking way Mamá's did. My heart fucking hurts. His stare softens as he grabs my arm and hooks it over his shoulders.

"Come on, bro," Aris mutters. "Let's get you back home."

My home is empty and cold. I hate it.

"Wanna swim?" I slur, leaning heavily into him.

He chuckles. "And watch your ass drown? Maybe later."

"Let me guess," I grumble. "You gotta get home to your wife."

A snort escapes him. "Selene is not my wife."

"Yet."

"Yet," he concedes. "But she sure as fuck acts like one, always bitching if I don't get home at a decent hour."

I laugh. "At least you get laid."

"If I get home in time," he jokes.

We stumble up the stairs and he helps me into his Porsche. The drive back to my villa makes me nauseous. I'm about to puke when the car finally comes to a stop. He helps me out of the car and into my villa. I groan when I scent lemons. The maid's been by, which means she had to clean up after my latest rage. Everything has been replaced and put back together again. I fist my hands, eager to destroy it once more.

"Dude," Aris groans. "You have got to quit trashing your villa. Do you know how much money we've spent on fixing this room? I thought we were past this."

I'll never be past this.

Talia.

Just fucking gone.

"She's dead," I tell him, my words choking my throat.

He sighs. "You don't know that."

"She is."

With a grunt, he drops me onto my sofa. I fade in and out of consciousness as I hear the microwave beeping. Something savory makes my stomach grumble. Aris sets down a plate of microwaved pizza on the coffee table.

"Eat, man. You're wasting away."

I shrug. "I'm not hungry."

He crosses his arms over his chest and levels me with a serious glare. I roll my eyes as I take a bite of the pizza. My, how our roles have reversed. I think Aris secretly likes taking care of me as I wallow in my fucking misery. I'd say he gets off on it, but his concerned eyes that are exactly like Mamá's don't lie. And because of that, I eat the damn pizza.

"I really do need to bail," he mutters. "I hate leaving you like this, but Selene can be such a bitch."

"Married life," I say with a grunt.

"Not yet." He laughs. "Hell, maybe not ever."

"You bought a fucking house for her." I scratch at my jaw. "Am I an embarrassment?"

"Truly, you are," he taunts, his brown eyes lighting up with playfulness.

"Fuck off. You never have me over."

"You've been preoccupied. You think I want to rub in your face the fact I'm happy with Selene and thinking about popping the question while you're dying over here in despair? Hell no. I may think you're a dick, but I'm not going to do that shit to you."

I chew the pizza and frown before swallowing it. "Don't tell me you let her decorate."

He winces. "The kitchen is seashell themed."

"Jesus," I say with a laugh. "Mamá would be rolling over in her grave."

We both sober up momentarily.

"I miss her," Aris rumbles. "I miss her so fucking much."

I, however, have mixed feelings on the matter. She fucked over my dad. Sure, he can be a dick. Like me. But did he deserve to be cheated on for a damn decade? Did he deserve to be shot because he was angry about the affair? He sure as hell didn't deserve to lose his ability to walk because she couldn't keep from having sex with Niles Fucking Nikolaides.

Is that what happened to Talia? Did she run off with her secret lover? No one fucking knows. Especially not me.

"Maybe when you're not getting fucked up, you can come over for dinner one day. Make some décor suggestions to Selene."

"Maybe," I grumble. We both know I'm not leaving this fucking hotel to go give interior decorating advice to my brother's whore wannabe wife.

Aris leaves the room and returns shortly with a glass of ouzo. He smiles as he sets it down next to the plate. "My peace offering."

"Who knew you could be so cordial, brother?"

He grins. "Someone has to take care of your broody ass."

I suck down the ouzo and then slam the glass back down on the table. "You out?"

"Yeah. I'm out. See you tomorrow."

"Any leads?"

A frown mars his features. "If I had any, you'd be the first to know." He lets out a heavy sigh. "We'll find her, Kostas."

Bones in a ditch.

Hair hanging from a vat of acid.

Her big diamond ring at the bottom of the sea.

That's how I imagine we'll find her one day.

I hate that I'm losing faith we'll find her alive. It's been so long. Her mother is devastated. Phoenix is damn near crazed. And me, I'm fucking destroyed.

A year.

A motherfucking year.

It's not getting better. It's getting much, much worse.

"If you want me to stay with you and talk," Aris says, "I can tell Selene we're working more leads. I don't like that look in your eyes." He clenches his jaw. "You can't do to me what Mamá did to us. Don't leave me with our damn dad all alone."

He thinks I'm going to kill myself.

It's like he doesn't know me at all.

I don't want to kill myself…

I want to kill anyone and everyone involved in the disappearance of my wife.

And if Talia left me of her own accord, well, I'll deal with her ass when I find her.

"Go," I grunt. "Go play house."

He smirks. "You're jealous."

"Jealous you're going to get your dick sucked? Fuck yes. But by Selene? Hell no. Sorry, Aris, but she's a snotty bitch."

Rather than be offended, he shrugs. "She gives good head."

We both laugh and then he lets out a sigh.

"One more peace offering and then I'm gone," he grunts. "You can get your lazy ass up off your couch if you want any more. Tomorrow, come to the office sober and we can shake up some more leads."

He disappears and once again returns with my glass refilled with ouzo. With a tip of his head, he leaves me with my alcohol and my depressing thoughts. After I suck down the drink, I stumble into the bathroom, shedding my bloody clothes along the way. I take a long, hot shower and lean my head against the cool tile. My hand rubs at my dick, but between the ouzo and my shitty attitude, it's not interested in release.

"What the fuck ever," I grunt out.

Once I'm dry, I wrap my towel around my waist and fall onto the bed. I reach into the drawer, pulling out my iPad. Turning it on, I open the pictures app and find ones I have saved of Talia.

In the photos, her blue eyes are alight with fire. She was so alive. She loved to challenge me. I loved it right back. Loved her.

Now?

I still fucking love her, which is why this shit hurts so bad. I let her leave that day pissed at me when I should have dragged her back to bed to leave love notes with my mouth all over her body. I should have spoken those words. Maybe it could have made a difference. Maybe she would still be here with me.

Scrolling past several pictures, I find my favorite. One of her lying in bed, her hair messy and her tits exposed. They're red from my mouth and her nipples are hard. The sultry look on her face just begs me to come back to bed and fuck her again. Again and again and again. That's not the look of someone who'd willingly leave. Deep down, I feel that in my heart. But my head? My head wonders if she was acting all along.

Refusing to think badly about her when all I want is to fucking come, I undo my towel and fist my cock that's come to life upon seeing her picture. She's still my wife. Until I know she's dead or left me, I'll go on the assumption she's alive somewhere out there missing me. I stroke and stroke, fixating on her plump lips. Her full tits. Her hooded eyes.

Closing my eyes, I remember back to how tight she felt when I'd push into her slick cunt. How her tits would jiggle and she'd moan so fucking sweetly. Her fingernails would scrape down my shoulders and she'd beg for release. I groan when my nuts seize up. Heat splatters on my stomach and my chest heaves. When I reopen my eyes, I realize I've accidentally slid to the next picture. It's one of her at the opening of Pomegranate that her mother took. I stole it from her mom's social media like a fucking creepy stalker.

God, she's beautiful.

She's still out there.

She has to be.

As my eyes droop, I silently make a vow.

I'm coming for you, moró mou. *I'm always coming for you.*

And one day I'm going to find you.

chapter
two

"IN THE UNDERWORLD, PROSERPINA HAS GROWN TO LOVE PLUTO, who treated her with compassion and loved her as his Queen. As she would have up in Olympus, she remained eternally beautiful in the Underworld. Pluto admired her kind and nurturing nature. However, Proserpina missed her dear mother greatly and wished to spend time on earth with her. When Hermes reached the underworld, he requested that Proserpina come back to earth with him to rejoin her mother and father." I turn the page of the book, and a tiny hand swats out at the page, wrinkling it slightly.

"No, no, sweet girl," I tell her gently. "We have to be nice to the book." She looks up at me with her radiant bright blue eyes and giggles, and my heart feels as though it's thumped straight out of my chest. But I guess that comes with the territory. My mom used to always tell me being a mom means removing your heart and giving it to your children.

Wiping a drop of liquid emotion from my cheek, I continue to read my favorite part of the book. "Pluto knew he could not refuse the commands of Zeus, but he also could not part from his beloved Proserpina." A golf ball sized lump fills my throat, and I have to set the book down for a minute to gather myself together. It always happens when I get to this part. Thoughts of *him* surface and I have to force them away. It's the only way.

With a deep breath, I continue to read the story. "Before she departed from the underworld, Pluto offered Proserpina a pomegranate as a farewell. This was, however, a cunning move by Pluto. All the Olympians knew that if anyone ate or drank anything in the Underworld they would be destined to remain there for—"

"That book again?" a shrill voice, equivalent to nails grinding on a chalkboard, says, ruining story time.

Without turning to face the owner of the voice, I close the book and stare out at the blue waters of Mirabello Bay. From up here, I can't smell the salt water, but I can still see the waves lapping up at the shore, and sometimes when I close my eyes, I can imagine being down there, lying in a hammock, smelling the scent of—

"You know it doesn't understand anything you're saying, right?" the annoying voice continues, snapping me out of my daydream. "It's a baby," she snarls.

"And that's why I'm the mom and you're the maid." I give my daughter a kiss on her forehead and inhale her fresh baby scent that's mixed with chlorine from our swim in the pool earlier. "*She's* not an *it*. And she's almost six months old. She's sitting up and crawling. She laughs and…" I turn around to face *the maid*, annoyed at myself for allowing her to work me up, but I can't help it. Every time she speaks of my daughter as if she's some alien, it riles up my mama bear instincts and I pounce.

When my eyes scan down her body, I notice she's dressed in a skimpy shrimp-colored dress and white heels, her face full of makeup, like she's about to go to the club instead of rotate the laundry. Her collagen-filled lips are pursed together in a mixture of hate and confusion, and I roll my eyes. I don't know why I even bother to try to explain anything to her. She doesn't have a single maternal bone in her body. I pity anything—plant, human, animal, mineral—she attempts to care for. It will be dead within days.

I shake my head, giving up on explaining to her for the millionth time, my daughter is probably smarter at six months old than she is at… however old she is. It's hard to tell. Her voice is screechy and whiny, giving off a young vibe, but all the makeup makes her appear to be older. "Never mind. What do you want?"

"Dinner's ready." Oh, dear Lord, please tell me she's ordered something. If I have to eat one more of her home-cooked meals I'm going to throw myself off this cliff. I'm going to seriously have to have a talk with

Aris when he gets home. Just because she's decided she wants to try and play house, doesn't mean I have to be punished.

"I'm not hungry. I'll eat later." I open the book to read more of the story to my sweet girl.

"I wasn't asking," she informs me. "I was telling you. Aris brought dinner home and he's waiting." She rolls her eyes, obviously annoyed that the man she's in love with doesn't feel the same and would rather have my company than hers.

"Fine," I snap. "I'll be there in a few minutes."

She turns on her heel to head back up to the house, when I call her name. "Oh, and *Selene*, my daughter would like her sweet potatoes pureed with only a *hint* of butter. The last time you made them there was enough butter in them to give a grown man a heart attack."

She huffs, but doesn't argue. *Damn right, bitch, know your place.*

"You ready to eat dinner, sweet girl?" I coo at my daughter, who throws her chubby little arms in the air and giggles. It's the most beautiful, melodic sound in the world.

After taking one last look down below, I stand and carry her into the mansion of a house. With at least ten bedrooms, and even more bathrooms, it would take a map to find your way around the entire place. But lucky for me, the only room I need to be able to find is my daughter's, which is on the first floor attached to mine. I give her a quick bath to get the chlorine off her body and then feed her a bottle. When I'm done, I head to the dining room.

"Nice of you to finally join me, dear." Aris stands and makes his way over to my daughter and me.

"I had to feed her first," I explain. "But I'm here now."

"And how is my daughter?" Aris asks, taking her from me before I can stop him.

"*Zoe* is perfect," I tell him, opening the lid to her high chair, so he can set her in it. "Selene!" I call out. "I need Zoe's dinner now!"

Aris chuckles, but doesn't say a word. He never does. The only reason why he keeps her around is because he knows how obsessed the woman is with him, which means she'll do anything he asks of her.

"And how was your day?" Aris asks after pulling my chair out for me and then sitting at the head of the table. Selene saunters into the dining room, her heels *click-clacking* against the marble floor. She drops Zoe's sweet potatoes down in front of me and they spill out of the cup. They look overcooked and gross. Good thing I never planned to feed these to her.

"Actually," I tell her, stifling my smile, "she's not that hungry. She just had a bottle." I reach over and grab Zoe's container of fruit and place some on her tray. "You can take this away." I lift the bowl of sweet potatoes and wait for her to take them. Which she does. Because she's the maid.

I begin eating my chicken and realize it's from Pomegranate, the restaurant I built from the ground up. Aris is probably hoping for a reaction, but he's not going to get one.

"I asked how your day was," Aris repeats.

"Fine."

"Just fine?" he prompts.

"That's what I said."

Selene sits at the table across from me, on the other side of Aris. "My back hurts," she complains. "I swear that baby accumulates so much laundry. Can we please hire someone?"

"That's what we have you for," Aris snaps, and I snort out a laugh.

"But, Aris…" she whines.

"No buts," he tells her, shutting down the conversation.

After dinner is over, I grab one of the cupcakes from the pantry I made for today. Snagging a lighter and candle from the drawer, I take everything with me onto the veranda. When I go back inside to grab Zoe, Aris has her in his arms. It's not often he holds her…

"Can I have her, please?" I extend my arms to grab her and she shifts her body toward me. *That's my girl…*

Aris doesn't hand her to me, but instead walks outside. "A cupcake?" he asks, even though he knows the drill.

"She's six months old today." Closing my eyes so the tears that are burning my lids don't fall, I take in a deep, cleansing breath. But when I open my eyes, a couple traitor tears fall. Aris, of course, mistakes them for me being a sentimental mother.

"Don't be sad, Talia. Growing up is inevitable."

"Can I borrow your phone to take a picture?" I ask. Aris chuckles.

"How about you hold her and I'll take the picture?" He hands me back Zoe.

I light the candle and Aris snaps a picture of the two of us before I blow it out and make a wish. A wish… Every birthday when I was growing up my mom would tell me to make a wish using the candles on the cake. I used to wish for trite things like a new bike, the bracelet I wanted. For my mom to let me go to the movies with my friends. Now, though, even though they're technically Zoe's wishes, every time I blow out the candle for her, I make the same wish. For—

"Talia," Aris says, breaking me from my thought. "Selene is going into town with me tomorrow. Make sure you make a list of anything you need."

My eyes snap to Aris's, but I quickly school my features, not wanting him to have any clue what I'm thinking.

"I'll make a list. And can you please have that picture printed for me?" I point to his phone, holding the picture of Zoe and me.

"Of course. Anything for you." He pulls me into his side and kisses my temple. "Anything for you."

chapter
three

Kostas

MY HEAD THROBS LIKE A MOTHERFUCKER. THERE WAS A TIME, when Talia disappeared, that I was clearheaded and hell-bent on finding her. I exhausted every resource I had into looking into what happened. Nothing ever came of it, though. She just fucking vanished.

Just like Michael and Tadd.

I remember torturing those incompetent fools because someone had to pay. It was their job to protect her. They had one fucking job and they failed. Adrian and Basil brought them in, strapped them to chairs, and handed me weapon after weapon until I drained them of every ounce of life.

It didn't make her reappear. She was still gone.

Leaning back in my office chair, I ignore my phone as it buzzes. Another call from my father. It drives him insane that he's stuck at his house in forced retirement. Aris and I visit him to share meals on occasion, but whenever he tries to talk business, we shut him down. I can thank my brother for that much—having my back against our father. Father is out of touch. It's Aris and I who deal with the business day in and day out. In fact, now that I've given Aris more responsibility in the past year, we've thrived. Money just fucking floods in.

Unfortunately, I don't give a shit about money.

I'm obsessed with finding Talia.

For the millionth time, I wonder about Alex. The scuzzy American fucker she dated before she came to be my wife. I know everything about the asshole. His flavor of the week. His favorite restaurant. His shitty taste in music. I follow him on every social media outlet because I figure one day he's going to slip up. One day I'll learn he has her hidden away while they play house together, laughing at the fact I'm finally out of the picture. In those dark fantasies, I slaughter Alex and make Talia watch. Then, I fuck her back into submission. It's easier being angry with her. At least there's hope threaded in with my anger. Hope that she's alive and I'll find her one day. It's a helluva lot better than the alternative: her being dead.

My eyes drag from my phone over to the bottle of ouzo sitting on my desk. I practically shake with the need to drink. I'm not stupid. I'm well aware of the fact I'm drinking myself into oblivion. And the more I drink, the further from finding her I feel. But when it's staring me in the face, it's hard to push it away. At least when I'm drinking, my body goes numb. The bleeding in my fucking heart stops.

Ignoring the ouzo, I grab my phone and pull up Alex's Instagram. He's back in Florence with a brunette tucked under his arm. His eyes are hooded as he smiles crookedly at the camera. It boils my blood that Talia was once with this idiot. I've often thought about dragging him here to my hotel so I could cut off every part of his body that may have once touched her. Adrian's eyes grew wide at my suggestion, which is the only reason I didn't follow through. I know Adrian looks out for me and with one wild expression, I knew I was acting like a madman and not like the cunning mobster I am.

But so help me if that fucker Alex has Talia or knows where she's at…

I scrub my hand down my face and begin scrolling through my contacts. I find Talia's mother, Melody, and stare at her name. This woman used to hate me, but now we share a common goal: find Talia. Melody wears her heart on her sleeve when it comes to her daughter. If she were hiding her or knew where she was, I'd know about it. I put the phone on speaker and dial her. She answers on the first ring.

"Kostas," she greets, her voice tight with concern. "Any word?"

She always answers right away, hopeful I've found Talia.

"No," I grunt out. "Any news on your end?"

A heavy sigh escapes her. "None."

We share a long moment of silence, both of us brooding.

"Emilio hasn't heard any chatter?" I'm always hopeful with his governmental position and contacts with the police, he might hear of some organization somewhere bragging over the fact they got Kostas Demetriou's wife.

"Nothing," she says. "I spoke with him today and nothing. Niles?"

I wince at his name. "Still missing also."

Another long moment of silence. It's a theory we've discussed before. Niles taking her and hiding her away. The motive is unclear, but it's one that makes a lot of sense. She is his daughter and he hates our family. It could be a way to stick it to us. He's just not smart enough or rich enough for that shit. It doesn't add up.

"I will be visiting Phoenix soon," I tell her. "I'll see what I can find out."

"Don't hurt my son."

I smirk. She's like Talia in that sense. Bossing around a crime lord like it's not a big fucking deal. But, because it reminds me of her daughter, I give her allowances I shouldn't. "We'll see."

She must not hear any threat in my words because she lets out a relieved sigh. "What about on Crete? My father said not long before she was taken, Ezio had an attempt on his life by the Galanis. Could they be behind this?"

It irritates me she knows so much about our world, but again, she's her daughter's mother. I can't fault her for being dedicated to plucking up every stone to see if it leads to her daughter. I'll take all the help I can get at this point.

"Most of the Galanis are gone," I bite out. "The dickless one is still out and about, but he doesn't have the spine to do something grand like kidnap my wife. Plus, he'd love to gloat. If he had her, he'd torment me with that fact. Since everything is silent, it tells me it's someone new or someone who couldn't care less about taunting me, but maybe someone with their own agendas."

"She's such a beautiful woman," her mother breathes. "What if someone kidnapped her and sold her into a sex trafficking ring? Do you know people who do that sort of thing?"

No, but your ex-husband does.

"I doubt that's it." I fucking hope that's not it. "But to be safe, I'll bring it up to Phoenix at our meeting. Niles admitted to allowing passage with some new clients who were into that shit."

She lets out a ragged breath. "Kostas, we have to find her. If she's with sex traffickers…" A loud sob escapes her. "I worry we'll never get the Talia we know and love back."

I scrub my face in frustration. "Whoever has her will fucking pay," I growl. "I will skin them all alive."

My words don't frighten her. "Good. They deserve it for taking my baby girl."

Voices echo down the hallway just outside my office and I sit up straight. "I need to go."

"Okay, *cara mio*, take care and let me know if you learn anything new."

I hang up and let her words sink in. Lately, she calls me *her darling* like I really am her son. And fuck if I don't correct her because it makes me miss Mamá.

Frustration churns in my gut. I rise from my chair and stalk outside onto the veranda. This afternoon, the air is warm and the salty sea scent evokes memories of my honeymoon. Taking Talia on the beach for the first time. The look of pure adoration on her pretty face as I made her mine. It's times like these, when I'm sobering up, everything feels so crystal clear. I think back to that week when we located Estevan Galani in that apartment building. How he'd eyed up my wife like she was trash he wanted to burn. The fact he survived his injuries I gave him wasn't surprising, but the fact he remains in hiding and not fucking with me is a disturbing fact. It feels important. Like I need to pursue why he isn't fucking with me. I shot his dick off, for fuck's sake. If someone shot my dick off, I'd try to destroy them, and would die doing it too.

Think, Kostas.

My mind wanders to the day she disappeared. We fought like fucking hell, but it wasn't a relationship ending fight. Too many times I've allowed myself to blame it on that. That she was pissed and finally left me. She'd met up with Selene and asked for money. Another big mystery.

I'd assumed she took the money and used it to get away.

But what if she was being blackmailed?

Rushing back inside, I sit at my desk and unlock my computer. When she went missing, I made sure the backups of our security footage were being stored in another place. I've scoured through tons of it, but often, I get frustrated sifting through hours and hours of footage that leads to nothing. The footage that never made sense was the night she supposedly took the money from Selene. I want to view it again. I pull back the footage to that night and find where we last enter the villa. Then, I skim through the night, waiting for her to leave. It eventually skips to the next day when she storms out to leave for school. I check all the cameras surrounding the villa, and nothing shows up.

Selene claimed Talia borrowed money from her, but it didn't happen that night.

She never left.

Which means either Selene confused the events or lied to me.

Why?

I assess Selene's behavior over the past year. She's obsessed with Aris. I bet she was even jealous of Talia, even though Talia was my woman and not Aris's. Would she lie to us to make Talia seem like a bad person who left me? And why?

She's a catty cunt, but she's not smart enough to pull off some grand kidnapping of my wife and keep it from me all this time. Most likely she just wanted to make Talia look bad. Regardless, I'm going to find out why the fuck Selene would lie because it doesn't help me get to the bottom of this shit with her meddling.

"Frown any harder and your face may stick that way," a familiar voice booms from the doorway.

As soon as I see my brother, I click out of the video footage and pop open Google on my browser before turning to him. "This is my face. It's been stuck this way since I turned thirteen."

He snorts. "I can't believe Dad actually gave us lessons on how to look fierce and intimidating."

"You failed," I grunt out.

"And you passed with flying colors. But seriously? What kind of father teaches their kids that?"

I shrug and glance at the clock, before watching every tick of my brother's face. "Want to have dinner?"

His brown eyes flash for a second before he schools his features, not taking my bait. "Of course."

"Actually," I mutter. "I need to get ready for my trip to Thessaloniki."

Aris's shoulders relax slightly. "Raincheck then. We could always go visit Dad and have dinner with him."

It's sad how much he desperately tries to gain Father's favor. Even now. Even with Father being practically an invalid and meaner than a snake. My mother's death has killed him more than he'll ever let on.

"Sure," I tell him with a shrug.

"Anything new?" He walks over to the wet bar in my office and pulls out two tumblers. After he fills them with ice and a little water, he heads back over to my desk. I'm silent as I watch him fill them with ouzo. He pushes a glass my way and then he proceeds to sip his.

Not touching the glass, I cross my arms over my chest and lean back in my chair. "Nothing."

His lips purse together. "We'll come up with something eventually."

My stare on him must unnerve him because he waves a hand at the ouzo. "Drink up, man. I have to get home to Selene soon or I'll never hear the end of it."

"Sure are pussy-whipped," I say, picking up the glass and swirling the ice around in it.

He snorts. "She knows her place."

"Where is Estevan Galani?" I ask, setting my tumbler down.

His eyebrows hike in surprise at my question and then he gives me a one-shouldered shrug. "Your guess is as good as mine. Went silent after you blew his cock off."

I scrub at the scruff on my face. "Galanis aren't known for their silence. They have the biggest goddamn mouths on Crete."

His lips press into a thin line. A worried line. It makes me scrutinize him further. "I'll look into it."

"Good," I grunt. "So will I."

"Cheers to dealing with the Galani infestation," he says, raising his glass and imploring me to drink.

I rise from my seat and walk over to the door. "I'll never toast to a fucking Galani. Go on and get out of here before your viper girlfriend tries to make a meal out of your balls."

He drains his glass and slams it down with a hard clunk. Then, he stands, shooting me an unreadable expression. With a deep breath, he inhales and then exhales whatever was threatening his composure. A wide grin spreads across his face.

"Have a good night, Kostas," he says with a smug grin. "My night will be a helluva lot better than yours, I can assure you."

He walks out without another word.

I glance over at my untouched ouzo and straighten my spine. I've been a cloud for far too long.

It's time to wake the fuck up and find my goddamn wife.

chapter four

Talia

"I NEED MORE FORMULA," I YELL OVER THE SCREAMS OF MY PISSED off daughter.

Selene glares my way. "I was just in town a few days ago. Aris told you to make a list." She eyes me accusingly, but I just shrug nonchalantly, not bothering to settle Zoe down. Her screaming always flusters Selene. For the sake of the human population, the woman should be sterilized so she can never reproduce.

"I did make a list." Zoe's screams get louder. "But Zoe had a growth spurt and I ran out sooner than I expected. Babies grow," I challenge.

"And you don't have any left at all?" she questions. I can see it in her features, she's about to reach her limit. Her hands are shaking, and her eyes are twitching. Come on, bitch…

"If I did I wouldn't be asking. Look, if you don't want to go, I can." I shrug with a smirk that I know will piss her off. "Zoe isn't going to stop crying until she's fed." As if on cue, Zoe's screams get louder. Every wail from her squeezes my heartstrings, but it's for the greater good.

"Jesus!" Selene shouts over the loud crying. "Fine. I'm going." She knows damn well she'll be in trouble if my daughter is unhappy in any way. A pissed off Zoe leads to a pissed off Aris. And a pissed off Aris never ends well. We've both learned that the hard way. The only difference is Aris actually cares about me since I'm the mother of his daughter, whereas with Selene, he views her as nothing more than a human pincushion. Poking every hole when he feels like it. The thought has me gagging. Better her than me, though.

Frustrated, she quickly unlocks the key box right in front of me, just as I hoped she would. Seven-two-two-four. She grabs a set of keys, slams it closed, then heads over to the garage door. I watch as she types in the code. Four-nine-nine-five. The light flashes green and she opens then closes the door behind her. I wait until I hear the garage door open and close and then I run into the kitchen. I type in the code to the key box and it clicks open. Grabbing the pair of keys, I pull one off the ring and put the other one back. As I'm closing the box, I spot Selene's cell phone on the counter. Holy shit! She forgot her phone.

Grabbing it, I tap the screen. It comes to life, but there's a password. No problem since I know it. Four-six-three-six. I type it in, but it's wrong. What the hell! I type it in again, but it's still wrong. I saw her type it in myself. This has to be right. The phone prompts I only have one try left before it locks.

I hear the garage opening back up. Damn it! She must've realized she forgot her phone. What do I do? Then it hits me. I bring up the passcode screen and hit the emergency button. The car door slams closed as the call connects.

"What is your emergency?"

I run with the phone in one hand and Zoe in the other to hide in another room. "My name is Talia Demetriou and I need you to—"

Before I can finish my sentence, my head is yanked back and the phone is snatched from my hand. "You bitch!" Selene yells. She raises her hand to slap me, but I duck. Zoe is now screaming bloody murder, and I'm running to get away from Selene so she doesn't inadvertently hurt my daughter. I make it into Zoe's room and slam the door just before Selene can touch either of us.

The door doesn't lock, so with my weight against the door, I grab the rocking chair and wedge it under the doorknob so Selene can't get in. Once I know we're safe, I make Zoe a bottle and feed it to her. She calms down right away, and once she's full, falls asleep in my arms.

Since there's no way I'm going back out there until Aris gets home, I use the time to go over my list. Stealing Selene's cell phone wasn't my original plan anyway. I just saw it on the counter and figured it was worth a try. Pulling the small diaper bag out from under my bed, I double-check everything I've accumulated over the last several months. Formula, bottles, diapers, wipes, clothes for Zoe and me, three knives, over two hundred euros. Reaching into my pocket, I add the spare keys I stole to Aris's SUV. Selene and Aris will be so focused on me trying to steal her phone, they won't even think about the fact my entire purpose was to steal his keys.

Not wanting to risk the bag being seen, I shove it back under the bed. While Zoe naps, I read a book, and once she wakes up, I spend the rest of the day playing with her in her room. It isn't until I hear Aris's voice on the other side of the door, I move the chair and open the door.

"I heard you've been busy today," he says, eyeing me with annoyance.

"I was scared for my life," I cry out. "Selene is psycho, Aris. The only reason I tried to call the police was because I was scared." Tears prick my eyes, but Aris just rolls his.

"Stop your shit, Talia. Your little stunt today was stupid on your part." Aris smirks. "Want to know why?" I don't bother to answer. I know he'll tell me. "Since I now have to worry about you trying shit, I had to give Selene a gun." Jesus fucking Christ. Is he serious?

"If you try anything, she's been told not to hesitate." Aris steps forward and grabs ahold of my ponytail, jerking my head up to look him in the eyes. "I don't give a shit if you live or die, Talia," he hisses. "The only reason I keep you around is so you can take care of Zoe. You're her mother and I didn't want to take you from her. But if you're going to become a problem…" He lets his sentence linger, releasing my hair. "Now, dinner is ready. Let's try to have a good night. I've had a long day at work. My brother has become a raging alcoholic and I'm now having to do both of our jobs." Aris rolls his eyes then walks out of the room.

Kostas has become an alcoholic… My heart squeezes in my chest at the thought of what he's been going through this last year. It's hard to believe anything that comes out of Aris's mouth. I knew the night he raped me, he was a wolf in sheep's clothing, but I had no idea just how deadly of a bite he had until the day I was taken.

I'm sitting in the auditorium, waiting for rehearsal to begin. I've only been here for a few minutes, but I want to go home. When I left this morning, Kostas and I were fighting. I know part of it is my fault. I'm overemotional and haven't told him why yet. Mostly because I'm scared of how he's going to react. But it's also his fault because he's so damn jealous. I have to kiss Macbeth in the play and I know Kostas is going to kill him if I do, which means I'm going to have to either tell my professor I can't play the role as Lady Macbeth or figure out a way to fake-kiss my partner, so my husband doesn't rip his heart from his chest. I want to be mad at him for being such a possessive asshole, but then he sends me a sweet text and I turn into a pile of mush.

Kostas: I miss you even when you piss me the fuck off.

Okay, well, sweet for Kostas… It's crazy to think how quickly he's become my entire world, and not because I was forced to marry him, but because I love him. The problem is, while I'm not sure if Kostas loves me back, I do know he wants to own and possess every part of me. At this rate, there is going to be no me without Kostas, and I'm scared of what will happen when I can't put him first. When I can't give him all of me. Will he still want me? Will what I can give him be enough? Or will he do what my father did and stray? The thought has me wanting to throw up.

"You are going to make the craziest Lady Macbeth," Penelope says, sitting next to me. When I glance up at her, she frowns. "What's wrong?"

"Nothing." I shake my head. "I'm okay."

"No, you're not," she insists. "You're crying." She reaches over and swipes a tear off my cheek I didn't realize was there. "Talk to me."

As if the dam that was holding back my flood of emotions caves, I let out every thought and feeling without holding back. Penelope wraps her arms around me and listens as I pour my heart out to her. She doesn't say anything the entire time as I tell her about everything I'm feeling and how much I miss my home and my family, especially my mom. When I'm done, she hugs me tightly.

"What is it that will make you okay right now?" she asks.

After a moment of thinking about her question, I say, "I-I think…" I hiccup through my sobs. "I think I really just want my mom." We both break out into a fit of giggles at how much of a child I sound like in this moment.

"Moms do make everything better," Penelope agrees.

I stand and wipe the tears from my face. "I'm going to go use the restroom and wash my face. Thank you for listening. Honestly, I think I just needed a good cry." I choke out another laugh and Penelope joins in.

Grabbing my purse, I throw my phone into it and walk through the side stage doors that lead to the bathroom. Setting my purse down on the sink, I wet a paper towel and wipe under my eyes until I no longer look like a raccoon.

Leaving my purse on the sink, I head into the first stall to go pee. I hear the bathroom door open and then a masculine voice yells, "Talia! You in here?" Aris? What the hell is he doing in here?

I swing open the door and find him standing in front of the door.

"We need to go now."

"What? Why?" I'm so confused.

He grabs my arm and yanks me from the stall and out of the bathroom. "I'll explain once we're in the car. Kostas sent me to get you. There's been a threat and he needs to know you're safe."

"What about Michael and Tadd?" My head is spinning.

"They are the threat," Aris says as he opens the side door to the building. Something isn't right here.

"Aris, wait!" I shout, but he doesn't listen. I reach for my phone and realize it's still in my purse…in the bathroom. Shit! "Aris, I want to speak to Kostas," I demand, but he ignores me. When I dig my feet into the grass, refusing to walk, he turns around and whips a gun out.

"Get in the fucking car, Talia," he says.

Instantly, my hands go to my stomach, fearful not only for myself, but for my baby. "Okay," I tell him. "Okay, just please don't shoot me."

The entire drive, my only thoughts are that there's a good chance I'll never see or speak to Kostas again. My last words to him were said in anger. He texted me to tell me he misses me, but I never texted him back. He'll never know how much I love him, and that I'm pregnant.

chapter five

THE ENTIRE THREE-HOUR FLIGHT FROM HERAKLION TO Thessaloniki was difficult. Being trapped in my private plane with nothing but a stocked bar and a building rage, I was about to explode. I wanted to drown out my thoughts, but something keeps niggling at me—something I need to keep a clear head for. Like the answer is right in front of me, but I can't seem to put my finger on it.

Aris.

I want to say Aris has something to do with it, but he's afraid of me. Deep down, I know he is. Where he might willingly sleep with my wife just to show he could, he'd never kill her. And hide her away for a year, that's just bullshit Aris couldn't keep from me. I see him every day, all day. If he was hiding something huge about Talia, I'd know.

Wouldn't I?

When she was taken, I was blinded by determination to find her. Then, anger that I hadn't. Now, drowning in grief also known as fucking alcohol. Alcohol that Aris has no qualms about offering me anytime he's around.

Which is exactly why I need to keep a clear head. For the first time since she's been gone, I feel alert and aware. I didn't get to where I am today for being a blind fool.

I'm brooding on my thoughts while we hit the tarmac. The staff on the plane is accommodating, but I'm distracted by Talia. Always Talia. Once I step out of the plane, I'm irritated to see Phoenix leaned against a door-less Jeep. He's dressed casually in a pair of jeans and a black T-shirt showcasing all his tattoos and looking like a fucking escaped convict. I hate how much he looks like Talia. It's a painful reminder of my loss of her.

"Where's my car?" I grumble.

Phoenix shrugs and hops inside. I follow suit and climb into his metal death wish. I'm sure I look out of place in my Armani suit.

"Where are your men?" he asks, nodding at the plane.

"Where are yours?" I challenge back.

"I don't need them," he sneers, side-eyeing me like I'm a minnow he can easily scare away.

"Same," I bite back like the shark I am.

He smirks as he throws the Jeep into drive. We haul ass down the road into the city. It's been a while since I've come to meet him about the taxes. In the beginning I did, right after he took over for Niles, but then, when I was losing my ever-loving mind over Talia, Aris took care of business.

"Where are we going?" I demand upon realizing we're not headed toward the city where his office is.

"We can do business anywhere with our phones," he grunts out. "I'm hungry and I figured you are too."

It's noon and I didn't touch the refreshments on the flight. He's right, but I won't tell him that. He takes us to a small restaurant outside of the city. It has horrible curbside appeal, but the moment we exit the Jeep and I get a whiff of the savory garlic scents in the air, I know looks will be deceiving.

He greets the man up front and then ushers us to a dark corner booth. When he orders ouzo for the both of us, I change my order to water, which gets a lifted brow of surprise from him.

"Got a problem?"

His nostrils flare. "Nope."

As soon as the waiter runs off to fetch our drinks, Phoenix crosses his arms over his bulky chest and glowers at me.

"What?" I demand.

"Nothing," he sneers. "Just finally looking at the man who let my sister get taken. The same man who can't find her." He's pissed and his jaw muscle keeps flexing. If I had any thought that he'd taken her, it's squashed in this moment.

"You're looking at the man who will cut your throat for fucking disrespecting him," I growl, cracking my neck. "Watch your tongue, Nikolaides. Seems you forgot who you were talking to."

He grinds his teeth but relaxes his posture. "I just don't see how after all this time you haven't found her." His eyes narrow. "Unless you don't want her to be found."

"Me?" I snap. "If I wanted to get rid of her, I would have, and I'd gladly fucking tell you. I don't play little girl games."

"Then where the fuck is she?" he bellows, leaning forward, fire gleaming in his eyes. "Where the fuck is my sister?"

"Maybe she's with your father," I bite out. "Since you can't find him and all. Maybe they're in the same magical hidden realm of the earth."

"What are you, a fuckin' fairy?" He shakes his head in frustration. "Dad is quiet, but if he had her, I'd know about it. For one, she'd drive him insane. He'd make me deal with her. Dad and Talia haven't gotten along in some time. I'm the peacemaker between the two."

The waiter brings our drinks and we order from the menu.

"What about those men who were supposed to be guarding her?" he asks bitterly. "Could they be in on it?"

I crack my knuckles before picking up my water and chugging it down. With a slam of the glass on the table, I level him with a hard glare. "We can't exactly ask them because I skinned them alive."

His brows furrow, but his eyes flash in appreciation. "Mom keeps yapping at me about the Galanis. You two chat an awful lot."

Fucking Melody.

"I want answers," I grit out.

"And Mom has them?" he challenges.

"Fuck no, she doesn't have them."

"Then why do you call her?"

Because she reminds me that Talia was a good woman who wouldn't just leave me.

"I check every lead." I lift my chin and meet his glare. "Can I say the same for you? What about the traffickers your dad was letting come through?"

"That shit ended when I took over. And I look for her every damn day, Kostas. I think that's the only fucking thing we have in common. Well, that and the inability to find her." He lets out a heavy sigh. "We'll find her."

I hate that we have a common goal. Nikolaides and Demetrious working together. It's a shitshow, clearly.

"*I'll* find her," I amend, my fierce stare begging him to argue.

"Glad you put the bottle down, man. I was tired of dealing with your arrogant brother. At least with you, I know what the fuck you intend to do. With him…" He frowns. "With him, I don't know what to think."

I'm not about to buddy up to Phoenix Nikolaides of all people and share a drink gossiping like two teenage girls over how much my brother is a sneaky bastard. No, I can think about that all by myself.

"Where's my money?" I demand, putting an end to all things Talia related.

He rolls his eyes like the fucking teenager I pegged him for and pulls out his phone. "I'll wire it over right now."

"I know, Selene," Aris grits out, his voice booming from his office. "I said I know, dammit."

Her annoying, screeching voice can be heard all the way into the hallway. I lean toward the door, hoping to catch her end of the conversation, but I hear nothing.

"Is that all?" he asks in a bored tone. "I have shit to do."

She must end the call because he slams the phone down on his desk and curses. I choose that moment to saunter in. He shoots me a weary look and then sighs heavily when I sit in front of his desk.

"Trouble in paradise?" I ask as I rest my ankle on my knee and lean back.

Ignoring me, he stands and checks the clock. "Your meeting with Phoenix went quickly. Back before five? Was he even there?"

"We had lunch and took care of business. He's not a cheating bastard like his weasel father."

Aris is rigid as he pours two drinks. When he sets down the tumbler with amber liquid in it, I pick up my glass and inhale the familiar scent.

"What's the special occasion?" I ask, swirling the alcohol around in the glass, eyeing him.

"Can't a man enjoy a nice bourbon with his brother and not need an excuse?" He knocks back the drink and dips his head, indicating for me to do the same.

I set it down and push it across the desk to him. "You look like you need it more than me."

His jaw clenches and he picks up the glass, slamming it back as well. "What do you want, Kostas?"

"My wife."

He tenses. "What the fuck do you want me to do about it?"

I shrug. "You asked me what I wanted. I told you. No need to get defensive."

"I'm not defensive," he growls.

I grew up with you, motherfucker. Don't play games with me. I taught them to you.

"Hmm," is all I say. "How come you never invite me over for these wonderful dinners your blow-up doll wannabe wife is always making?"

"I've invited you more times than I can count over the past year," he bites out. "Not my fault you chose to drink your dinner instead."

"Yes."

"Yes, what?"

"I accept your dinner invitation."

His gaze hardens. "You called my future fiancée a blow-up doll. Consider the invitation officially rescinded."

I lean forward in my seat. "Are you hiding something from me, brother?"

"Fuck off," he scoffs. "If you want to come to dinner, come to fuck-ing dinner. Don't say I didn't warn you that Selene is a terrible goddamn cook and you'll probably die of food poisoning. Just make sure you give me a proper warning so she can get to the store and buy what she needs."

I stare at him for a long moment, watching him intently. Each facial tick. Every twitch of his lips. The slow reddening of his skin. Finally, once I've infuriated him to the point his carotid bounces along his neck, I stand.

"I'll let you know." I give him a wide grin that I know unnerves him. "Tell Selene I said hello."

Walking out of his office, I wonder how exactly he and Selene have made it this long. What does she offer him that makes him stay? He doesn't like her. At best, he barely tolerates her. Sure, she has tits and dick sucking lips, but you can find nicer women with those same physical attributes who don't sound like a donkey in heat.

I'm going to find out.

I settle back in my own office. Back to scouring video surveillance footage from the time Talia was with me around the time she was taken.

Taken.

I know it deep in my gut.

She wouldn't leave me.

Talia Demetriou may have been pissed as fuck, but she loved me. She may have never spoken the words, but I felt them. Now that my head is clearing, I remember that part of our relationship without a doubt. With each look, each caress, each kiss, I knew.

And whoever took her will pay so fucking dearly for every second I've lost with her.

"I'm out of here," Aris says, peeking his head into my office. "Sorry about earlier. Selene is a bitch and she pisses me off."

"She must give amazing head," I say with a wicked smile.

He sneers. "I wish."

With a wave, he bolts before I can taunt him anymore.

So, the blow-up doll doesn't even suck cock well. Again, I wonder what the fuck sort of value she provides my brother with. He can get any fucking woman into his bed with his stupid smiles and charm. He certainly doesn't hang onto any woman for very long, much less a bitch like Selene. It's more than sex with my brother. It always is. I've seen him fuck the wife of a local gangster just to piss him off. I've seen him fuck around with the Minister of Police's daughter just to anger our father. I've seen him flirt with my wife and grab her ass because he wants to irritate me.

But Selene?

What's the end game?

Marriage, babies, white picket fence.

Yeah, fucking right.

I don't buy it for a second.

Swiveling around in my chair, I decide to dig into Selene a little. I'll find out what the blow-up doll has been up to. If the past year has taught me anything, it's that I can be quite the resourceful stalker when I want to be. I will tear apart Selene's past and present. I'll learn every damn detail about her. Who her family is. Who she's connected to. How she remains tethered to my brother.

And then I'll invite myself to fucking dinner.

chapter six

Talia

TODAY IS THE DAY. I'VE SPENT THE LAST YEAR LEARNING everything I can about where I am and what it will take to get out. I can either keep waiting, or I can make my move. At this point, I don't think there's any more preparing I can do. If it weren't for my precious cargo, I would've already tried to run, but with her in tow, I have to be twice as careful. I can't risk anything happening to her.

I'm sitting on the lounge chair out by the pool like I always am. Zoe is sleeping on the chair next to me on her belly, under the umbrella, sucking on her pacifier. My little girl loves the pool and sun. I bet she'll love the beach as well.

"I'm leaving for work," Aris says. "Do you need anything while I'm out?"

"I can have Selene pick up anything I need." I wave him off, knowing full well he won't let that happen anymore.

"She's not running any more errands for you," he says, just like I knew he would. "I'd hate for you and Selene to get into it again, and I come home to a bloodbath, so whatever you need, I'll pick it up."

Exactly what I was hoping he would say.

"Zoe hasn't been feeling well. Can you stop by the pharmacy to pick her up Tylenol?"

Aris's gaze lands on Zoe.

"She's teething," I add.

Her body shifts, and her pacifier falls from her lips, landing on the ground. I lean over to grab it, but I can't reach. "Can you hand me that, please?"

Aris picks it up off the floor and offers it back to me.

"It's dirty now." I shake my head. "Just throw it in the sink on your way out. I need to clean it before I give it back to her."

He shoves it into his front pocket. "What the hell does teething mean?"

I roll my eyes at his lack of parental knowledge. "It means she has teeth coming in and it hurts. Tylenol will help the pain."

"Fine, whatever. I'll pick it up on my way home."

"What time will that be?" When he glares, I add, "There are a lot of different kinds. I need you to take a picture of the different ones and send them to Selene so I can let you know which one."

Aris groans. "All right, I'll send her the pictures when I'm there. It probably won't be until five or six o'clock. I have a late meeting."

Perfect!

"Thank you," I say, dismissing him.

I wait for him to acknowledge his daughter before he walks away, but as always he doesn't. He never hugs or kisses or gives her any attention. Not that I'm complaining. I'd rather him stay the hell away from both of us. It's just that I find it odd. I think back to when I told him I was pregnant. In life, we have choices to make, and a lot of times when making a choice, it isn't about which choice is the right one, but which one will keep you alive…

"What the hell is wrong with you?" Selene screeches.

I lift my head from the inside of the toilet and glare at her. "Get out," I demand.

When she doesn't leave, I reach over and slam the door in her face, so I can finish throwing up in peace.

A few minutes later, I hear yelling in the other room. Aris must be home and he and Selene must be arguing. They're always arguing. Tiptoeing out to eavesdrop, I listen to what they're saying.

"You never said you planned to keep her here forever!" Selene whisper-yells. She's meaning to whisper, but her screeching voice carries.

"It's not forever," Aris explains. "It's only until my brother completely

loses his shit and I take over the business. It's only been a month and my brother is already on a downward spiral."

"Then what are you going to do with her?"

"I haven't decided yet."

"Why don't you just kill her?" Selene whines. When Aris doesn't say anything, she says, "Aris…you don't like, like her, do you?"

"No, I don't like her, but I'm not going to kill her. Then I would be as much of a monster as my brother and father. Plus, she's pregnant, and it's either my baby or my brother's."

Oh my God! He knows! He knows I'm pregnant.

"She's what?" Selene screeches.

"Are you that fucking stupid?" Aris accuses. "Haven't you seen her throwing up since we brought her here?"

"And it could be yours?" Selene sounds like she's crying.

"Yes, now stop asking fucking questions. I need to go check on her. When I come back, you need to be waiting for me in bed, with your legs spread and your mouth closed."

Footsteps across the wood floor have me scrambling back to my room. I've just dropped onto my bed, when Aris enters the room.

"Did you hear all of that?" he asks. My eyes widen in shock. "Good, then I don't have to repeat myself. You're pregnant. You know it and I know it. The question is, who is the father?"

I have a choice to make…right here, right now. If I tell him the baby is his, he can take it from me after he or she's born. If I say it's Kostas's, his hatred toward his brother can lead to him hurting it. Either way, I'm possibly screwed…

"It's yours," I admit.

"I call bullshit."

"Call it whatever you want." I shrug.

"If I find out you're lying, you will pay," he threatens.

"More than what I am now?" I challenge. "How long do you plan to keep this up, Aris? You know I heard you…you're not going to kill me, so what are you going to do? Keep me prisoner forever?" I scoff. "It's not like Kostas loves me. It was an arranged marriage." But even as I say the words, I refuse to believe them myself.

Aris chuckles darkly. "If you believe that, you're either dumb or blind.

Until you, I didn't think my dear brother was even capable of loving anyone besides our mother, but I was wrong, which is why I took you."

"You took me because you think he loves me?" I don't get it. There has to be more to it.

"I took you because my brother destroys everything he touches and he's not going to get a chance to destroy you the way he destroyed our mother."

"Aris…" I begin, but I don't even know what to say. I hate him. He raped me. He hurt me. He stole me. But my heart still breaks for the man who lost his mother. He's grieving and he's broken. He's not thinking clearly. My only hope is that he'll eventually come to his senses and let me go. And hopefully before this baby is born.

That was a year ago. He was a monster the day he took me, but now, it's as if he lives for destroying Kostas. He feeds off it. He's never going to let me go, which means I have no option but to run.

Zoe's tiny body stretches, telling me she's waking up. Her fisted hands rise above her head, and her chunky little body rolls to the side. Her beautiful blue eyes open and she grants me the most beautiful smile.

"Mommy's going to get us out of here, *cara mia.*"

After I feed her and give her a bath, I get dressed in a comfortable outfit. I don't have any tennis shoes, so I make do with the pair of flip flops I have. I tie my hair back in a ponytail and then pull my bag out from under my bed.

When I tiptoe out of the room, I spot Selene on the couch watching TV. I need to be smart about this. Aris's dumb ass gave her a fucking gun. If I play this right, that gun can become an asset to me, but if it goes the other way, it can be the very thing that kills me.

I spot the gun on the end table next to her. Laying my bag down behind the counter, near the garage door, I set Zoe in her high chair. "Be a good girl," I whisper, placing a few cereal puffs on her tray.

"Hey, Selene," I call out.

"What?"

"Aris is supposed to text you a picture of the different Tylenols for Zoe when he's on his way home. Has he texted you yet?"

"No." Good, that means he's still at work. I have time.

Grabbing a frying pan from under the sink—yes, I'm about to be cliché as hell—I tiptoe up to Selene. I'm not sure if the pan will actually knock her out, but my intention is just to knock her off her game long enough to grab the gun. Once I have it, I can make a run for it and she won't be able to stop me.

I spot her phone in her lap. I want to grab it as well, but the gun is more important. Raising the heavy item to the side, I swing it as hard as I can at the side of her head.

"Ahhh!" she screams, falling from the couch and onto the floor. Without looking back at her, I snatch the gun off the table, dart back to the dining room, grab my daughter and bag, and haul ass. I quickly type in the code to the garage and it works! Using the key in my hand, I hit the fob to unlock the doors. The SUV lights up and I throw Zoe into the seat next to me. I hate that I don't have a car seat for her, but there's nothing I can do. With a click of the garage door, it rises, and we're free.

chapter seven

Kostas

"**B**ASIL?"

Adrian nods at my question as he pulls into the driveway of my father's estate. Once we're in park, he levels me with a hard glare. "Basil is loyal until the end."

There was a time when I almost questioned Basil's loyalties. When he did my brother's bidding. But when I'd looked in his eyes, I'd seen he was simply doing his job. For me. At the time, it felt like betrayal, but he was only doing what I'd asked long before.

Keep the enemies close.

And since I've always seen Aris as an enemy who happens to share my blood, my two best men, Basil and Adrian, have always kept an extra close eye on him.

"Any news from Basil then?" I ask, climbing out of Adrian's SUV.

He follows me and lets out a grunt. "Just normal comings and goings to and from the hotel. His house is pretty quiet during the day. On occasion, his slut leaves to grocery shop and shit."

"Galani? Niles? Does anyone besides the skank go in and out?"

"Nope, just her."

I don't like it. Feels too easy.

"Call him and have him see if he can find anything out from the hotel staff. I want this quiet and discreet. He'll need to do it in person."

"I'll text him and send him that way," Adrian assures me. "You sure dropping in on your dad like this is okay? What if we're interrupting his nap?"

I bite back a snort of laughter. Adrian, even though he's one of my best men, has always been more like a brother to me than Aris ever was. He's the only motherfucker I'll allow to get away with making fun of my father.

"Good to keep the old man on his toes," I say with a chuckle.

We walk through the massive estate looking for him. Things are strained with my father. He thinks I should run things differently than I do, but I do them the way I want and there's nothing he can do about it. He is my father, though, so I don't disrespect him by just ignoring him. I make sure he's taken care of and check in on him from time to time like a good son does.

When I hear moans coming from down the hallway, I pause to shoot Adrian a confused look. I stalk down the hall to the source of the sound. At my father's door, I hesitate for a fraction of a second before pushing into the room. The sight before me has bile crawling up my throat.

Some young blond bitch is riding my father in my parents' bed. He may not be able to walk, but his big hands dig into her pale ass as he urges her to fuck him. She moans and rocks her hips. All I can do is see fucking red. My mother has barely been dead a year and he's fucking sluts in their bed.

"Father," I boom. "What the fuck?"

The woman cries out in surprise and slides off him. Her big tits bounce as she scrambles to find her dress that's been discarded on the floor. I stand there glaring at my father, who looks like a pathetic old man with his dick at half-mast.

"The money's in the usual place, Lyssa," he grumbles out, his eyes cutting to mine as he pulls the covers over himself. "Why the hell are you here unannounced?"

Money?

My father is fucking a goddamn prostitute?

I block the doorway when the blonde comes my way. She casts a glance over at Father, as if to ask him what she's supposed to do.

"A whore, Father? Really?" I guess it's better than him actually dating so soon after my mother. The fact it's just sex seems to soften the blow a little. Still pisses me off. Feels like just yesterday my mother was buried.

"Lyssa is more than a whore," Father bites out. "She's a friend. We go way back."

Pull the fucking brakes. "What?"

"What'd I miss?" Aris demands from behind me, finally gracing us with his presence. "Fucking gross. Do I smell pussy in Dad's room?"

Father's face burns red with fury when Aris scoots past me and into the room. My brother shakes his head.

"Why are you two here?" Father barks out.

"Kostas said we should meet with you," Aris says, his gaze raking down Lyssa. "Who are you?"

"Father's whore," I hiss.

"Another one?" Aris asks.

I snap my head his way. "What do you mean another one?"

Aris sneers at me. "Why are you acting like this is the first one you knew about?"

Darting my eyes back to my father, I fist my hands. "So Mamá dies and you fuck as many whores as you can? I didn't think your dick even worked anymore."

Aris snorts. "Since Mamá died? Where the hell have you been all our lives, man?"

All our lives?

He's fucking with me.

Our mother may have cheated on Father, but my father was loyal to her. He's the whole goddamn reason why I'm so obsessed with loyalty. It's been drilled into my head for as long as I can remember.

"Lyssa's been on the payroll for years, Kostas. Don't be obtuse." My father scowls my way.

Obtuse?

Don't be fucking obtuse?

The woman in question shrugs as if it's no big deal to fuck a man three times her age who can't even go to the bathroom by himself.

"What about Mamá?" I hiss.

Father's face softens. "I know you're having a rough time since your wife left you—"

"She didn't fucking leave me," I roar, making the woman jump.

Aris seems pleased as hell to see me lose my shit over our father's indiscretions. The smile is wiped off his face when his phone rings. As he scrambles to pull his phone from his pocket, something hits the floor and bounces. A pacifier. For a baby. I stare at it in confusion as he picks it up and shoves it back in his pocket. He answers the phone in a hateful tone that makes me wonder, again, if he even likes that woman he's shacked up with. His dumbass bitch can be heard screeching on the other line. He pales and then pure fury morphs the charming Demetriou prince into a dragon. For a split second, his hateful eyes find mine, and if they had the power, he'd slay me where I stand.

"Emergency with Selene," he growls out as he pushes past me, knocking his shoulder into mine on the way out.

Lyssa takes his exit as her cue to leave as well. As she steps past me, I grab her bicep. She shoots me a panicked look.

"You fucked him while he was married to my mother?" I demand in a cold tone.

Her eyes flicker over to my father, but he doesn't save or defend her. I can see it in her eyes. The answer is clear as day. Yes.

"Lyssa is a tigress in bed, son. You can't tell me you haven't fucked anyone since Talia left."

"She. Didn't. Leave. Talia was taken."

"And with all those pretty maids walking around, you're telling me you didn't get your dick sucked not once this entire time?"

"I'm fucking married, Father!"

He snorts. "Marriage is something for everyone else to see. It's an illusion of happiness. Everyone fucks around. Even me."

But what about loyalty to your motherfucking wife? He's drilled loyalty into my head since I was old enough to learn what the word meant. It was all a fucking lie.

"Adrian," I bark out.

His heavy footsteps thud down the hall. "Sir?"

"Take Lyssa home. The *long* way."

He doesn't argue or balk at my orders. Adrian's a good man. Without explanation, he'll do what needs doing and that's burying this dirty little secret today.

I release her once he has her in his grip. He stalks away with her. My gaze falls to the stack of bills on the dresser—money she'll never touch again.

"You lied to me," I tell him, bitterness creeping into my tone. "My entire life I thought you were devoted to my mother."

"Don't be an idiot," he bites out. "You know your mother slept with Niles fucking Nikolaides of all people."

I couldn't understand it before. How she'd even step out of her marriage in the first place. But now I wonder. Did she know about my father's whores? Was she trying to hurt him like he hurt her?

"When did you take your first whore after marriage?" I ask, my voice deadly and cold.

He glowers at me and his jaw clenches. My eyes skirt over to the pillow beside him. My mother's pillow. A smear of Lyssa's lipstick taints the pillowcase. A framed picture of my mother on the nightstand faces the bed as though she's punished even in death to take my father's abuse.

"This is none of your business," he says, cutting through my thoughts.

Slamming my gaze back on his, I crack my neck. "Everything's my business now."

His nostrils flare at my words. The double meaning behind them. "I'm still in charge here," he seethes. "You're my son, but you mustn't forget who built this empire from the ground up."

His skin is grayish and his muscle tone is gone. Father is nothing but a decaying bag of bones. It's a wonder his dick still works because his legs sure as fuck don't. He's a pathetic excuse for a man lying in his bed, unable to do a goddamn thing but listen to what I have to say.

"You're not in charge," I state coolly. "I've been running this shit ever since the accident last year."

"Accident? Your mother's attempted murder was an accident?"

"You provoked her," I bark.

"You're insane, boy."

I crack my neck again before sliding my jacket off and draping it over the back of his wheelchair. His eyes track my movements. When I unbutton my shirt at the cuff, he narrows his gaze.

"You're going to beat an old man up? What kind of son are you?" Despite his rage, fear glimmers in his eyes.

I slowly roll my sleeve up to my elbow. The muscles in my forearm flex and the veins throb with the need to inflict pain.

"You're my father," I hiss. "I'd never strike you."

He relaxes some, but his weary gaze remains fixed on my actions. I take my time rolling up my other sleeve as well.

"This is my empire, Kostas. *I* am the Demetriou name. You can't forget that," he tells me with false bravado.

"What happens when you're gone?" I ask, already knowing the answer. "That's right, everything goes to me."

"To both my sons," he lies.

Now that I don't have the alcohol buzzing through me and wreaking havoc on my brain, I took the time this morning to analyze every facet of my life. According to our family attorney, I'm still listed as sole heir to the hotels, the Demetriou fortune, everyfuckingthing.

"I used to think loyalty was the backbone of our family name." I make a tsk of disapproval. "I was wrong. It's lies. Lies are woven into every aspect of our lives like fucking snakes in a garden." I smile at him. "It's time to cut the head off the biggest viper in the nest."

"You won't cut me open like I'm one of our victims in the cellar," he growls. "I know you better than that, Kostas. In case you've forgotten, I'm your father. We're exactly the same."

"You're right," I admit. "I won't make you bleed." My gaze drifts to my mother's picture. "But where you're wrong is that we're not the same. You may have destroyed Mamá, but you will not destroy me." I flash the picture a sinister smile. "This is for what you couldn't finish, Mamá. I heard your dying wishes loud and clear. I won't let you down."

"What the f—"

Father's words are silenced when I reach across him to grab Mamá's pillow that's stained with another woman's lipstick. I shove the fluffy pillow down on his face. His attempts to drag the pillow away and then trying to hit at me are futile. I'm a monster. A motherfucking fire-breathing beast. He's a lowly snake in the grass waiting to be stomped on. With my eyes on my mother's picture, I smother my father with her pillow. He should have died when she shot him. It's my duty to end the disloyal bastard's existence. My father struggles for longer than I expect given his weakened state. I'll give him that. At one time, I thought he was the most powerful man in the world. I fucking looked up to him. And the way he looked after Mamá and loved her was admirable.

Lies.

All lies.

Mamá may have broken my heart when she killed herself, but she opened my eyes. She tugged on the veil of deception my father had slipped over my head. She made me see there was more to life than money and mayhem.

Love.

She wanted me to see that love was more important than so called loyalty.

It was hard to believe considering she'd deceived my father, but now learning he was the root of everything, I feel as though I finally understand her message.

Love is everything.

Love is loyalty and forgiveness and hope.

The rest is just bullshit.

I'm not sure how long I hold the pillow over Father's face, but when he's stopped moving for some time, I pull the pillow away and gently put it back where it goes beside him. His eyes are glazed over but still open. I slide my fingers down over his lids, closing them. When I check his pulse, I learn he's, in fact, dead.

I feel nothing.

Not victory or sadness.

Fucking nothing.

Once I undo my sleeves, I pull my jacket back on. I grab the picture of my mother and then head downstairs. As I wait for Adrian to return to pick me up, I make some coffee and sit in the kitchen on a barstool. My mind drifts to times when Mamá would busy herself in here, despite the fact we had a cook, and try to give us some semblance of a normal life. She'd sing and teasingly brush flour on my nose as we baked together whenever Father was away on business. I loved those simple moments with her. When I forgot I was destined to be a mob boss and could just be her little boy. Back when I would dream of racing cars in Monte Carlo and surfing with sharks. I was innocent and my father ripped that innocence away from me no matter how hard my mother clutched me to her, trying to preserve it.

I'm not innocent anymore.

But it doesn't mean I can't be the man my mother would have wanted me to be.

I'll never be good, that's for damn sure. I'll be good enough for love, though, just as she would have wanted. I'm good enough for Talia. And one day soon I'll find her.

"Good afternoon," Tammy, a nurse of Father's, greets as she enters. "How's Ezio?"

I clench my jaw and think about my mother. About how devastated I was when she pulled that trigger on herself. Real emotion shines in my eyes as I regard the nurse.

"He went to be with Mamá during his nap," I choke out.

"Oh, honey," Tammy cries out. "He died?"

I nod and the woman hugs me. I let her. To be honest, it feels good to be drawn in a motherly hug. Resting my chin on top of her gray head, I let out a heavy sigh.

"You know Father. He's so proud. It was his wish to keep his death quiet when the time came. Cremation. No service."

She pulls away and furrows her brows as she cups my cheeks. "I'm discreet, honey. We'll get it sorted together. Just tell me what I need to do."

"Let me be the one to tell my brother," I mutter. "To tell everyone."

"Do what you have to do, dear. I'll go upstairs and make sure he's decent."

"Thanks, Tammy. Don't worry about not getting paid. I'll have Aris wire you a bonus as a thank you for all you've done."

She smiles at me. "The Demetriou men are good men. I'm proud to have worked for this family."

We're bad men, but I don't want to spoil the moment with the truth.

I give her a nod, dismissing her. I sip on my coffee as I watch out the window for Adrian. It takes a quick call to Franco to have him come deal with Father's body, and another call to the family attorney, Thomas, to inform him of the official change of power. The next person to know needs to be Aris. And it'll need to be told in person. No one wants to hear their father is dead over the phone.

I'll go back to the office, deal with some other affairs, and then drop by this evening to deliver the news over dinner. Kill two birds with one stone. It's time to see what lies Aris has been telling, and if I know my brother, the lies are plentiful. I've just never really cared too much until now.

But now?

Now I care a whole lot.

I'm going to uncover every hidden truth.

And once everything is all laid out on the table, I'm going to make those who've been playing games against me pay.

Blood. Sweat. Tears. Limbs.

They. Will. Pay.

Every last one of them.

chapter eight

Talia

As I drive down the driveway, the winding road takes us to the front gate. I hold my breath, praying it opens from the inside. Over the last year, I've planned the best I could, but because I couldn't see this far, I could only plan to leave. As the gate slowly moves to the side, I spot a black SUV driving up behind me. What the hell? There's no way Selene caught up that fast. When I glance in my rearview mirror, I spot a man in the driver's seat.

Without waiting for the gate to completely open, I press my foot on the gas, refusing to let this guy, whoever he is, catch up to us. Damn it! How did I not see him? Aris must have someone guarding the house, but he's never been where I can see him. I've checked so many times.

Zoe sits in the passenger seat, babbling to me, as I drive down the curvy roads. I have no clue where I am or where I'm going, but my goal is to get to the city so I can ask someone for help.

I look in the mirror again, and the SUV is catching up to me. There's no way I'm going to make it out of these hills unless I pick up my speed. I glance over at my little girl and she smiles up at me. I need to protect her. I need to get us to safety.

With one hand on the wheel, I reach over and grab the seatbelt, drawing it across her lap. It's not ideal, but it's the best I can do in a shitty situation. I press my foot harder on the gas and increase my speed, but when I glance back, the SUV is less than a car away from me now. I'm never going to make it.

All this work, all this planning, and I missed something. I slam my fist against the steering wheel. I was so fucking close. Aris is never going to give me this much leeway again. I had one chance and I messed it up.

The front of the SUV hits my back bumper and the vehicle swerves. No!

My eyes briefly fly to Zoe to make sure she's okay before they're back on the road.

I can do this. I can get away.

He lays down on the horn. He wants me to pull over. I make it around the bend before his bumper hits mine again. Zoe lurches forward and I use my hand to hold her against the seat. I can't keep going. Whoever this guy is isn't going to stop until I pull over, and I can't risk him driving me off the road. I can't put my daughter's life in jeopardy.

Prickly tears of defeat burn in my eyes as my heart rate races.

I don't want to give up. I'm not ready to give up.

When my gaze flits back over to my little girl, my eyes land on the gun in the center console, and my thoughts go to Kostas. He wouldn't even hesitate. If he were in my shoes right now, he would kill this asshole. It's me and Zoe or him. And I'm choosing me and Zoe.

I can do this.

I am Talia Demetriou, wife of a fucking mob boss.

I pull over on the side of the road and get out, not wanting him to make it over to where my daughter is. I flip the safety off and wait for him to exit the vehicle. And when he does, I'm momentarily stunned. Estevan Galani. The man my husband shot in the dick. Of course Aris would hire a damn enemy to guard his house. Those two roaches deserve each other. At least one of them is about to be exterminated. Kostas can deal with Aris.

Pointing the gun right at him, I pull the trigger.

Pop!

The gunshot echoes loudly, making my ears ring and Zoe scream. He stumbles back, but doesn't fall. Fucking damn roach. Crimson swells where I clipped his shoulder.

"You bitch!" he growls, pulling his own gun out.

Before he has a chance to hurt either one of us, I pull the trigger again and again and again. Until he hits the ground. I stare in shock at the bullet holes littering his chest.

I shot him.

I fucking shot him.

My hands are shaking, and my body is numb. I just killed a man. One who would've done the same to me, I remind myself. As I turn around to run back to my vehicle, I run right into a hard wall. No, not a wall…

"That wasn't very smart," Aris says.

I lift the gun to shoot him, but before I can, he snatches it out of my hand.

"Get your daughter from the vehicle, now," he barks, "and get your ass in my car."

My eyes dart around me, wondering if there's any way I can still escape. There are woods on both sides, but there's no way I'll make it to grab Zoe and run without Aris stopping me.

As if reading my thoughts, he snarls, "Don't even think about it. Get your fucking ass in the car."

We walk a few feet, when I hear a moaning sound. That asshole is seriously not dead?

Aris hits me with a hard glare, then stalks over to him. With the same gun I used, he points it at Estevan's forehead and shoots. His brains explode, and I lose everything in my stomach.

Everything's a blur as I pull Zoe from the seat and clutch her to my chest. I can feel the tears falling, but I'm numb to them. I sit in the front seat of Aris's Porsche and inhale my sweet baby's hair.

Please don't hurt us.

Please don't hurt us.

Zoe is no longer crying now that I'm soothing her, and she babbles to Aris when he falls into the front seat. He says something to her before peeling out and taking us back in the direction we came. When we get back to the house, Selene is sitting on the couch with an icepack pressed to the side of her head.

"You fucking bitch!" she hisses.

"Enough!" Aris booms. "I have to go clean up the fucking mess you made," he says to me. "And since you can't play nice with Selene, and I can't risk you trying to escape, you can now consider yourself a prisoner."

"Oh, *now* I can?" I scoff. "I've been your damn prisoner for the last year."

Aris smirks wickedly. "No, Talia, you were my guest. Now, you're about to see what it means to be my prisoner." He forces me into my room and I set Zoe in her crib, so I can deal with him, but when I turn around, the door is slammed shut and it's locked from the outside. Motherfucker! I race through the bathroom to see if that door is unlocked, but as I twist the knob, the lock clicks in place. He locked me inside! With a hopeless sigh, I slide down the door and press my head against the wood. This was it. This was my one chance. And it's gone. And now we're worse off than before.

Zoe's babbling has me standing and going to her. Lifting her out of her crib, I bring her over to my bed and lay her next to me. Holding her tight, I stroke her soft black hair until her eyes flutter closed and she falls asleep, and then I let myself fall asleep as well.

Knock. Knock. Knock.

My eyes shoot back open.

Knock. Knock. Knock.

Is someone knocking on the door? Nobody ever knocks on the door. Carefully edging off the bed, so I don't wake Zoe, I go to the window to see who's there. I can't see the front door, but I can see part of the driveway.

Maserati GranTurismo.

Charcoal-gray.

Black on black tires.

It can't be… There's only one man I know who has that exact car…

Kostas.

He's here. He's going to save us.

And just like that my hope is restored. Like a sliver of light illuminating my dark world, I can finally see again. I'm chasing it. Running toward the brightness.

I don't bother trying to open the window because I already know it's nailed shut, but I watch the vehicle, refusing to look anywhere else. The house is quiet. Selene must be outside talking to him. Does he know I'm here? I listen with bated breath until I hear the front door close.

Is he in here? I can't decide whether to abandon the window to go bang on the door, or stay by the window to catch a glimpse of him. Before I make a decision, though, I see him. In his signature suit, he stalks back to his car. Strong, powerful, handsome. I miss him so much it hurts. My palms hit the glass, hoping he will somehow hear me.

"Kostas!" I cry out, knowing it's futile.

His hand freezes on the handle, and he turns. Did he hear me?

"Kostas!" I yell again, my palms smacking so hard against the window, they're stinging. "Kostas! I'm here!"

His eyes assess the area before he opens the door and folds himself into his car. And then he's gone. And as quickly as the light came, it's now gone. Leaving me stumbling through the darkness alone.

A flood of tears gush down my cheeks as I watch my fucking husband's headlights get farther and farther away until they're completely gone.

One year and he's never been here. And when he finally does show up, I'm locked in my fucking room. He must know something. That's why he came here. He's looking for me. I know he is.

Oh, Kostas, you're so close. Don't give up, please. I'm here, waiting for you.

Crawling back to my bed, I snuggle back up with Zoe. She's awake now from me yelling, but as soon as I comfort her, she falls back asleep. Such a good girl. She deserves more than this. More than being held prisoner.

"It's okay, *cara mia*, we're going to be saved."

"Wake up," Aris barks. His voice startles Zoe and she lets out a loud cry. I glare daggers his way, but he doesn't care. "It's time to eat."

"I'm not hungry. I'll eat later."

"You'll eat now, or you won't eat at all," he threatens.

After changing Zoe's diaper, I grab a bottle to bring out to the table. When I get out there, Selene and Aris are both at the table, already eating their dinner. Steak, broccoli, and potatoes au gratin. He must've brought it home because Selene can barely make grilled cheese without burning the shit out of it.

When I walk past the table, Aris's hand lands on my thigh. "I'm going to grab a jar of food for Zoe."

"I'll get it," he says. "Sit down."

"Fine." I set Zoe in her high chair and place a bib around her neck. She giggles her delight, slapping her tray in excitement.

Aris brings over a jar of sweet potatoes and a spoon and sets them in front of Zoe before sitting back down. Zoe grabs the spoon and bangs it against her tray. "Da-da-da," she babbles. Aris's eyes meet mine. "Da-da," she continues. She's too young to know what she's saying. She's just making random noises, but the thought that she's calling him da-da has me feeling sick to my stomach.

I open the jar and begin feeding it to Zoe, when Aris finally speaks. "Until further notice, you will be locked in your room while I'm not home."

"Are you seriously going to keep me and your *daughter* locked in a room for hours at a time?" I shoot him a glare.

"Or I can have Selene take care of her and just keep *you* locked up…" Aris smirks with a shrug.

Selene huffs, and when I look at her, the entire side of her face is black and blue. I can't help the grin that splays across my face. That pan got her good.

"Fuck you," she spits. "Hope it was worth it."

"Oh, it was," I volley. "Looks like you're going to be needing another visit to the plastic surgeon. Probably for the best since they fucked up your face the first time around anyway."

"Aris, haven't you had enough of this bitch? Your brother was here today! He's snooping around and he's going to find her."

My gaze swings over to Aris, whose eyes widen.

"Kostas was here?" he growls, venom in his tone. "Why the fuck didn't you tell me?"

"I just did!" Selene screeches. "And he was asking questions. How long until he figures out you have his precious Talia? Just kill her already. We can take your baby and run."

At her words, I snatch the steak knife off the table and dart around behind her, putting her into a headlock before she can even think about what to do. With the knife against her throat, I meet Aris's gaze. "You let this woman touch my fucking baby and I will slice her throat."

"Enough," Aris stands. "Put the damn knife down." He steps toward me and I press the blade against Selene's throat.

"Aris!" she cries.

"Talia, calm down." Aris's eyes dart over to Zoe. When he steps toward her, I have no choice but to let go of Selene.

"Don't you touch her." With the knife still in my hand, I lift my daughter out of her high chair.

"She's my daughter too," Aris sneers. "And if I want to fucking touch her, I will."

He steps toward me and I take a step back. When he doesn't make another move, I continue backing up until I'm back in my room.

"We'll deal with this tomorrow," Aris says. "Clearly shit needs to change around here."

Without saying another word to him, I slam the door in his face, and then I pray to God that Kostas comes back for me and Zoe. Because if he doesn't, I'm not sure how much longer Aris is going to keep me alive.

chapter nine

Kostas

I'M SEEING SHIT.

Losing my goddamn mind.

It. Was. Her.

I pinch the bridge of my nose and debate on what to do next. Either I can drive my ass back over to Aris's house and find out for sure, or I can sit here like a pussy wondering.

I'm just downing the rest of my dinner in a restaurant between the hotel and Aris's, when my phone rings. I could answer it and tell him right now that Father is dead. Most days, I'm a dick, but even I won't do that to him. No, I'll do like I intended when I drove over there earlier and tell him to his face. I send his call to voicemail. Seconds later, I get a text.

Aris: Did you come by?

The next text comes immediately after.

Aris: What did you need?

Aris: Want to meet up?

I groan and before I can reply, he continues blowing up my phone.

Aris: Selene said you had something important to talk about.

Aris: I don't hit her if that's what you're wondering. She fell.

Fell?

I'm not stupid. That bitch did more than fall. Someone bashed her fucking head in.

My mind drifts to earlier.

"What do you want?"

I lift my brow and sneer. "Excuse me?"

"How did you even get on the property?"

"I used the fucking code," I growl. "Were you trying to keep me out?"

Selene has the sense to stand down once she remembers who she's talking to and shakes her head in vehemence. I'm not some pushover like Aris. I will drag her skinny ass back to the cellar by her fake-red hair to remind her if I need to. Luckily, she replaces her snotty expression with one of healthy fear.

"What'd you do to your face?" I ask, nodding to indicate the giant ass bruise that looks fresh and is forming beneath her swollen-red flesh.

She purses her fat lips before letting out a huff of exasperation. "I fell."

Says every woman hiding the fact she's being hit by a man.

"The floor must fucking hate you."

"And I hate the fucking floor too," she snarls out. "Aris went to…run an errand. Is there something I can help you with?" Her venom bleeds away as her green eyes skim down the front of my body in appreciation.

"Nah," I grunt out. "I'll come by another time."

When I turn to leave, she grips my bicep. "Call him first."

I glower over my shoulder at her. "Are you his keeper?"

"W-What? No. He's just always busy and rarely home. You should call him first so you don't miss him."

"Hmmm," is all I say before breaking from her hold and walking away.

The door slams shut behind me. I'm almost to my car when I feel eyes on me. Stopping, I turn and look back toward Aris's massive house.

Blond hair.

A woman.

Talia?

But when I squint, the vision vanishes. That's all she is to me now. A fucking ghost.

God, I miss her. I'd give up my entire fortune to have her in my arms just so I could inhale her hair. I don't know that I even remember what she smells like anymore. The fact I'd give up everything to see her once more is disappointing. I'd always thought of myself as someone powerful. Someone who doesn't need anyone else.

Like my father.

Turns out, I was never like him.

I was always like my mother.

After I pay my bill, I leave the restaurant and inhale the early fall air. The sun has gone down. It's only just hitting me that my father really is gone. I extinguished him from this earth. Remorse or guilt should flood through me, but all I feel is relief. I was never allowed to figure out who the real Kostas was. He bred me into his monster. For his favor over my brother, I gladly heeded every instruction. And now I'm nothing but a shell. I don't want to do anything but fill up my entire being with her.

My wife.

Fuck, I'm losing it.

I need to tell Aris Father is dead and then move the fuck on. At some point, I will have to accept that Talia probably is too. A year is a long time—too long in my world—to be missing without a word. If she'd run away, I would've known about it. Someone would have tattled.

She's dead.

It's a hard pill to swallow.

One I have trouble choking down because too much uncertainty rattles around inside my head.

I pull up to the gate and punch in the same four digits Aris uses for everything. It'd been a no-brainer when I'd come earlier, but after the way Selene acted, it made me wonder if they were trying to keep me away.

So I wouldn't see that he beats on her?

Like I give a shit. She probably runs her fucking mouth too much and earned that knock to the head. We're villains, not goddamn heroes. Who am I to judge?

No, if they wanted to keep me away, it's for other reasons.

Reasons that niggle and tug at me, desperate to be thrown out in the open.

I pull up to the house and park in the driveway. Lights shine from a window in front of the house and then some upstairs. Climbing out, I pause to listen. Nothing but the breeze picking up as a fall storm rolls in. The wind whistles and I scent the promise of rain.

As I walk toward the front door, my eyes drift of their own accord to the window where I'd thought I'd seen someone. When a figure stands in front of the glass, the light shining around them, my heart does a squeeze in my chest.

I blink several times to clear my vision.

Still there.

Blond hair. A woman.

I'm storming over to the window before I can stop myself. Wide, teary blue eyes meet mine. Familiar blue eyes. Her blue eyes.

No. Fucking. Way.

"Zoí mou." My life.

Her bottom lip trembles—lips I've ached to kiss for so long it's maddening. This can't be real. She can't be staring back at me from behind the glass of Aris's fucking house. It makes no sense. I'm truly losing my goddamn mind.

"Kostas."

The voice of an angel carries through the glass, shattering what little bit was left of my heart. She's alive. She's alive and well and standing right in fucking front of me.

"Open the window," I rumble, my words barely a whisper.

She looks over her shoulder and shakes her head. "I can't."

Fury swells up inside me to incredible heights. "Open the fucking window."

Tears race down her cheeks as she moves her plump lips rapidly, speaking in hushed tones that are somehow supposed to send me away.

I'm not going anywhere.

Bending, I try to open the window, but it's locked shut. I point at the lever and thump the glass hard. "Talia, unlock the window."

"I can't."

I slam my fist on the window, making her cry out in surprise.

"I said open the window or so help me I'm coming right through it," I growl. "Open it. Talia, open it!"

When she steps away, turning to look toward the door again, I lose it. With a swift swing of my elbow, I bust out a pane of glass. I reach my hand inside and flip the lock. It still won't open.

Talia rushes back over to me and reaches her hand through the glass pane. Her touch is soft as she runs her fingertips along my cheek. "I can't, Kostas. It's nailed shut."

Nailed shut.

What in the actual fuck?

I grip her wrist in a tight grip and then lean in to kiss her palm. I'm afraid to let her go because she might just fucking vanish again, but I need to get to her. I need to hold her.

"Stand back," I order.

She jerks her hand back and steps away from the window. I could go beat on the front door, make my brother answer, and demand he hand her over, but right now I'm on a one-track mission. Get to my fucking wife. Hiking my leg up, I kick hard along the metal strip along the middle of the window.

Crunch. Crunch. Crunch.

I kick over and over until the metal frame of the window is mutilated and folded in, glass broken all over at my feet. Once I've weakened it enough, I slam my shoulder into what's left of the window and send it and myself careening to the floor. I'm on my feet in the next second, prowling after Talia.

Anger. Betrayal. Sadness. Confusion.

My emotions spin around and around like a fucking tornado. I'm ready to cause massive destruction. I want to destroy everyone.

Gripping Talia's throat, I walk her back until her ass hits the door. I bury my nose in her hair, inhaling the scent of her shampoo mixed with her natural sweat. The growl rumbling through me is a possessive one bordering on rage. My thumb traces along the vein in her throat that's pulsing rapidly.

"Why?" It's the only word I have. It's a loaded question.

"I don't know."

I pull away and glower at her. "You want to be here?"

She shakes her head, fat tears rolling down her red cheeks.

"You're trapped here?"

A sob escapes her. "We have to get out of here."

I'm distracted by her bottom wobbly lip, and now that I know she's a captive for some fucked-up reason, I need her like I need my next breath.

"*Zoí mou*," I whisper over her lips. "I've fucking missed you."

Slamming my lips to hers, I take the kiss I've been craving since the moment I let her walk away from me after our fight. I slide my hand up to her jaw, gripping her tight so she can't escape me as I ravish her perfect mouth. She moans as I devour her lips and tongue. Her fingers thread through my hair, cradling me to her. My other hand finds her hip and I slide it to her ass that's fleshier than I remember. I want to strip her down right here and inspect every part of her body to see if she's changed. A choked sound escapes her when I rotate my hips, rubbing my aching cock against her body.

"Da-da-da-da."

I freeze mid-kiss. When I hear an excited shriek, I yank away from Talia, my head darting around to find the source. My eyes land on a baby. A fucking baby. With bright blue eyes like Talia.

Talia steps toward me. "Kostas, listen—"

"A baby?" I growl, snapping my head back to look at her.

Her chin is tilted up and her watery eyes are fierce. "My baby."

I stumble back, feeling as though she's kicked me in the gut. A baby. Her baby. And Aris's? The baby makes another sound and I can't help but look over at her.

"Kostas," she says, walking over to the baby and picking it up. "Her name is Zoe."

All the air is sucked from my lungs as I snap my eyes back to the little girl.

Zoe.

Zoe.

Zoe.

"Zoe, *zoí mou*?"

Tears well in her eyes and she nods rapidly.

Holy shit.

Our baby.

We had a fucking baby.

All happy thoughts come to a screeching halt. I'm going to murder them. Slaughter both Aris and Selene. Right the fuck now.

"Kostas," Talia says, her voice shaking as she rushes over to me. "We have to go. Now."

The baby—Zoe—grabs the lapel of my suit and tries to pull it her way. I'm stunned for so many fucking reasons. All I can do is lean forward and inhale her dark hair.

Mine.

She's fucking mine.

They both are.

I'm eerily calm as I say, "I'm going to kill them."

"And I want you to," she whispers. "But we need to get Zoe someplace safe. Selene has a gun and she's not afraid to use it."

My mind wars with what I should do. The mobster inside me craves violence and blood and vengeance. The husband—*and father*—in me has an overwhelming urge to protect what's mine.

I can't have both.

Not in this moment.

So I choose them.

Pressing a soft kiss to Talia's lips, I murmur, "Let's go."

She hands me Zoe and I freeze. I've never held a damn baby. But Talia doesn't give me a chance to argue. The moment the tiny flailing thing is in my arms, Talia starts throwing stuff into a diaper bag. I can't help but hold Zoe close to me, kissing the top of her head.

Those motherfuckers kept this from me.

My wife. My baby. My goddamn family.

Rage surges violently inside of me, but I don't unleash it. Talia's right. I need to get them out of here and make a plan. I'll get the full story of what's happened and then shed blood when my family is safe. Within minutes, Talia is packed and we head out the broken window. She rushes over to my car and tosses the bag into the backseat. Then, she takes Zoe from me and sits in the front seat. As soon as I'm seated and the engine fires up, the reality begins to sink in.

They're here.

I have them.

My first instinct is to call Melody. She doesn't know she has a granddaughter. The fact I want to call her should be alarming, but it's not. Not after spending the last year leaning on this woman for emotional support under the thin veil of questioning her on the whereabouts of my wife.

"Hurry," Talia says. "I didn't make it very far last time."

Despite her words, I don't gun it like I normally would. The baby doesn't have a seat. I finally understand the term precious cargo.

"You escaped?"

"Today," she breathes. "Finally. But he caught me." A pained sound rattles from her. "I shot someone, Kostas. I was protecting me and Zoe. H-He's dead. I'm sorry, but I'd do it again and again to protect her."

Reaching over, I give her thigh a squeeze. "I don't know what the hell has been happening right under my goddamn nose, but I want you to tell me everything." I shoot her a hard look. "And don't ever apologize for protecting our little girl."

Our little girl.

I'm in fucking awe right now.

A dad. I'm a dad.

And I have my wife back.

<h1 style="text-align:center">chapter
ten</h1>

Talia

FOR THE FIRST TIME IN OVER A YEAR, I CAN FINALLY TAKE A DEEP breath of relief. Oxygen can enter my lungs without a lump the size of a boulder blocking my airway.

Because Kostas is here.

He didn't give up on me, and he found me and Zoe, and we're finally safe.

Thunder booms and lightning strikes, lighting up the entire sky. The clouds open above us, and rain begins to pelt the windshield. It almost feels metaphorical, as if the rain is washing away every bad moment from this past year, hydrating the life back into us. For the last year, I've felt dead inside, but now, with Kostas here, I feel like my body is finally thriving once again. I was struggling to make it through each day, pieces of me slowly dying, but now I'm alive and can breathe easy.

Zoe's head lands on my shoulder, her body snuggling into my chest. When she babbles softly, Kostas glances over at the two of us, and for a brief moment our eyes meet. His hazel eyes tell me everything I need to know. Everything is going to be okay. He's going to make sure of it.

"When we get home, you're going to tell me everything that's happened," he says.

But my thoughts are stuck on one word. *Home.*

We're going home. Where we belong. Where we should've been this entire time.

And then it hits me. Home is the Pérasma Hotel. The hotel Aris part owns.

"We can't go back there." I sit up straight, and Zoe whines. It's late and she's exhausted. "Please, Kostas. We have to go somewhere else. Somewhere far away." My blood pressure is rising, and my heart is thumping against my ribcage.

"*Moró mou*, calm down." Kostas squeezes my thigh.

"Don't tell me to calm down, please." I'm working myself up. My head is feeling fuzzy, and it's hard to breathe again. "I can't risk Aris getting to Zoe and me again."

Kostas pulls into the parking garage, swings the car into his spot, and slams on the brakes. "Nobody is fucking taking you again. They're not going to live to have a chance."

Kostas pulls his phone out of his pocket and dials a number. Because we're still in the car, it rings over Bluetooth.

"Boss," Adrian says, answering on the first ring.

"I found Talia," Kostas says. "At Aris's house."

"Fuck."

"He and his bitch were holding her and my daughter captive."

Adrian curses under his breath again, but doesn't question anything Kostas is saying.

"I need you to go there and get *both* of them. Bring them to the cellar. Call me when it's done."

"Yes, sir."

Kostas hangs up, and after grabbing the bag I packed for Zoe, walks around and opens my door for me.

When we enter the villa, it's as if time has stopped. Everything is the same as it was the last time I was here. My flip-flops are still by the door where I left them. My favorite blanket to cuddle with is still thrown over the back of the couch. My school papers I left on the table in the foyer are still in the same spot. My purse I left in the bathroom when Aris took me is under the table. Kostas must've found it.

When I walk into our bedroom, one side of the bed is made. *Kostas's side*. The other side is how I left it. Messy sheets thrown about because I was in a rush to get to rehearsal that morning. My robe is still draped over the sitting chair. My pajamas are still on the floor next to the hamper because I missed when I tried to throw them in and told myself I would pick them up when I got home.

Only I never came home.

Because I was taken.

Because Aris fucking took me.

Took a year of my life.

"Kostas," I begin, in shock. "Did you live here while I was gone?"

His eyes meet mine, and with one look, I can feel everything he doesn't need to say. Pain. Loss. Confusion. Relief. I assess his features. There are dark circles under his gorgeous, glassy eyes. He's still as beautiful and captivating as he was a year ago, but he looks exhausted. Like he hasn't slept since I was taken.

"I couldn't do it," he admits, stepping toward me. Zoe's head is back on my shoulder. When she's nervous, she snuggles into me. And this is the first time she's ever been away from the only place she knows as home, so she's nervous.

Gently, Kostas rubs the top of Zoe's head and gives it a kiss before he leans over her and kisses my forehead as well. The sweet action has me momentarily closing my eyes, relishing in his touch. My body thrums, needing more of him.

"I looked for you every fucking day, *zoí mou*," he says softly. "At first, I was too pissed to sleep in here. I thought you ran. So I slept in the guest room. Then every day I searched, the signs pointed to you more than likely having been taken. I looked everywhere. I didn't think I left a single stone unturned." He curses under his breath. "I didn't even think to look in my brother's house." His jaw clenches in fury. "Fuck, he's been helping me look for you." He rubs his knuckles down the side of my cheek, his hand trembling with rage. "I couldn't bring myself to sleep in here. To move anything of yours. It would mean accepting you might not ever be back. I told myself once I got you back I would sleep in here again with you."

Be still, my heart.

This man. So powerful and controlling and cold. Shows zero mercy for anybody he comes across. And he couldn't sleep in our bed without me.

"Every day Aris would come home from work and tell me things about you. That you were a drunk and you stopped caring. That you had moved on. I didn't believe him, Kostas." Tears leak from my eyes. I'm finally here. Back in my home. With my husband. "I knew you would find me."

"It took me a fucking year, *zoí mou*. I failed you and our daughter."

"No, don't say that. You found us." He can't blame himself for this. The guilt will eat him up inside. I need my strong Kostas.

"After you put Zoe to bed, you're going to tell me every fucking thing my *brother* did to you and our daughter, every lie *he* told you, and I can promise you, I will make him regret every single goddamn thing he did and said."

If words weren't so matter-of-fact, the steely look in his eyes would tell me he means exactly what he says. When he finds Aris, he's not going to quickly kill him. He's going to slowly torture him for every day he held me prisoner, every lie he told me, and the thought has me almost smiling.

"I want to be there," I tell him. "I want to see Aris and Selene get what's coming to them."

Kostas grins. "Fuck, I've missed you." He gives me a chaste kiss on my lips.

Zoe stirs in my arms and it reminds me… "I don't have anywhere to lay her down." I glance at the bed. I suppose I could lay her in the center and line pillows along each side…

Kostas, of course, is already calling someone. "Thomas, this is Kostas Demetriou. I need a portable crib brought to my villa right away." He hangs up, and one side of his lips tip into a playful smirk. "The perks of owning and living in a hotel."

While I'm feeding Zoe, Kostas makes several phone calls in the other room. He's barking orders left and right, cursing and making threats like the mob boss he is, and my heart tugs in my chest. You don't realize how much you love your life until it's taken from you. And this life, the one with Kostas yelling at people, while our daughter snuggles in my arms, is all I want.

"What the fuck do you mean?" My body stills at his words and tone. Something is wrong.

Zoe knocks the bottle out of the way and climbs up into my lap. Kostas enters the room and points to the sitting room attached to our bedroom for the gentleman to set up the crib. He quickly rolls it in, pops it open, and scurries out.

"Let me tell you something, my fucking wife was locked in that fucking house for the past goddamn year. Are you telling me you had no idea?"

"Kostas, who is that?" He shoots a glare my way and I give him one right back. At one time, his glare would've scared me, but now, it only turns me on. "Kostas." He ignore me, which pisses me off. I understand he's mad, but I am too. I was the one taken. "Kostas!"

"It's Basil," he barks out. "They got to the house and they're gone." The blood running through my veins goes cold. My eyes dart around us, and I find myself hugging Zoe tighter. They got away. Kostas wanted to take them out right then and there and I begged him to get us to safety first. And now they're missing. They can be anywhere. On their way here…

Kostas puts him on speakerphone. "Go ahead, Basil. Tell my wife how you were assigned to watch over that house and you never managed to find out she was in there."

"Boss, I swear," Basil sputters. "I never saw anything out of the ordinary. They came and went like everything was normal."

"Kostas, there's no way he would know," I tell him. "I was never allowed to leave the house. I even gave birth there." At my words, Kostas's eyes go to our daughter, and they soften slightly. "Unless Basil was able to get inside, he couldn't have seen me. Aris even had Selene drive across town to buy Zoe's stuff. I didn't even know that guy…Estevan, the one you shot his dick off, was guarding the place."

At my words, Kostas roars, "What in the actual fuck. Did you hear her?" he barks at his men. "Estevan was there?" he asks me, needing me to confirm.

"I heard her," Adrian says. "We'll find him."

"He's the guy I shot," I admit. "Several times. And then Aris finished him off. He's dead."

"Jesus fucking Christ," Kostas growls. He scrubs one of his hands over his face in frustration.

"Several of their drawers are empty," Adrian speaks. "And stuff is missing from the closet."

"They took both vehicles," Basil adds. "They're gone."

"Dammit." Kostas punches a hole in the drywall. Zoe jumps and starts crying. "Shit, I'm sorry." He gives her a pleading look, trying to convey how sorry he is.

She snuggles her face into the crook of my neck. "It's okay. She just doesn't know you yet." My words aren't meant to hurt him, but I can see it in his eyes how much they do.

"Adrian, you still there?" he growls.

"Yeah, Boss."

"Call the Minister of Public Order. Tell him I've found my wife and it was Aris and his cunt girlfriend who took her. I want every goddamn man searching for them. Every fucking available badge. They couldn't have gotten far," he barks out before he hangs up.

While I change Zoe's diaper and get her ready for bed, I can feel Kostas's eyes on us. I double-check the locks on the windows in the bedroom. With Aris and Selene missing, I'm scared they're going to show up here.

"Nobody is getting in here," Kostas vows.

"I know. I just need to make sure."

Once Zoe is comfortable in her temporary bed, with her pacifier in her mouth, her eyes roll back in her head. I laugh softly at how fast my baby girl falls asleep, and Kostas smiles.

"We made her," I tell him.

"She's perfect."

"That's because she's the best part of us."

"Let's talk." Taking my hand in his, Kostas leads me out to the living room. I glance back at the bedroom, but Kostas squeezes my hand, telling me it's okay.

When he sits on the sofa, I stay standing, needing to double-check the rest of the locks myself. Kostas watches as I go from the front door to each window, unlocking and relocking every lock. "I'm scared, Kostas," I tell him once I'm done, sitting on the sofa next to him. "They could be anywhere, planning their next move, and Aris thinks Zoe is his daughter."

"Why the fuck would he think that?" Kostas barks. Huh? Oh, shit! There's only one reason a man would think a baby is his. "You two had sex? When?" His eyes burn into mine. "While you were living under my roof? Fucking me? You were also fucking my brother?" Kostas tries to stand, but I grab his arms to tug him back down and climb into his lap, needing to be close to him. I can't let him push me away. I only just got him back. "What the fuck, Talia."

"Stop yelling, please," I beg, glancing back at the bedroom. "You're going to wake up Zoe." My hands frame his face. He hasn't shaved in some time, so his cheeks are all stubbly just the way I like it.

"I don't give a fuck," he says, but I know he does because his voice is now several notches lower than it was a minute ago. "Tell me why the fuck my brother, even for a second, would believe our daughter is his. Did you fuck him, Talia?" His eyes plead for me to tell him no, but I can't lie to him. It's time for the truth to come out. Maybe if I had told him the truth from the beginning, Aris never would've had a chance to take me.

"Kostas…" My heart is pounding like a drum in my chest.

"It's a yes or no. Tell me. Did. You. Fuck. My. Goddamn. Brother?"

I need to explain, but he's not giving me a chance to. "Kostas, please just let me explain," I beg. "It's not that simple."

"Yes or no!" he roars.

"Yes!" I blurt out, "Yes, I had sex with your brother."

chapter eleven

Kostas

Her words chill me to the bone. But they're wrong. The words don't match the pain in her eyes. Despite the rage thrashing at me, I can't unleash it.

Talia is here. Straddling my thighs. Imploring me to understand.

I reach up and grip her delicate neck. Her bottom lip trembles as a tear races down her cheek. Tightening my hold, I draw her close to me until our lips nearly touch. I almost kiss her but pull away, hardening my glare.

"Take off your shirt and show me what he touched that's mine," I growl.

She stares at me for a long moment before grabbing the hem of her shirt and pulling it away. Her tits are full and nearly spilling from her plain black bra. I give her a nod to continue. She unhooks the bra, freeing her perfect breasts. The nipples are peaked and a lovely rosy color. I want to suck them until they're an angry shade of red.

"Did he touch you here?" I ask, cupping her breasts and running my thumbs along her nipples.

Another tear races down, dripping from her jaw. "I don't remember."

"One time?"

She gives me a clipped nod.

That. Motherfucker.

"It was your first time." I can barely contain the hate surging through my veins, burning just under my flesh begging to blaze.

"Kostas," she chokes out. "My first time was with you." More tears leak out. "You told me that. I need to believe that."

I close my eyes.

He raped her. He fucking raped her.

Before our honeymoon at some point. This whole time I thought it was some asshole she dated. Not my own goddamn brother.

"H-He, uh, he was d-devastated after your mom k-killed herself. Y-You were gone and I w-wanted to help. I went to check on him." A sob escapes her. "He was c-crying and I was crying. And…and…"

I open my eyes and slide my hands to her hips. "And…"

"I had t-to get the b-blood off him," she sobs, trembling. Her hands frantically cup my face. "I had t-to help him."

Sweet, innocent fucking Talia.

"Kostas, don't hate me." Her face crumples. My heart crushes.

I hastily swipe away something wet on my cheek. The ache that settles in my muscles dulls the fury. He hurt her. He hurt my fucking wife.

"Kostas," she whimpers.

I grip her throat again and pull her close. Our lips brush against the other. "Tell me all of it."

Her fingers slide into my hair as she steals a kiss. Soft. Sweet. Apologetic.

I hate it. I hate the apology in her kiss. It's dirty and wrong.

"Tell me," I whisper. "Talia, fucking tell me."

She needs to say it and I need to hear it.

"I was worried about him," she whines. "And then…I don't remember how it happened. He was j-just on me. K-Kissing me. The towel was g-gone and…"

Her body wracks with sobs. My fingers trace over her ribs and then my palms slide to her back, pulling her closer. She rests her forehead against mine. Salty tears fall on my face, mixing with my own.

He broke her.

He broke my fucking Talia.

And in doing so, he broke me.

"Tell me," I plead. I need her to say the words. To hand me the proverbial sword. I need to destroy and wage war. I need blood. I need fucking vengeance.

"He was so strong," she breathes. "I was scared."

Her lips press to mine, attempting to distract me. I nip at her bottom lip in warning.

No distractions. No more lies.

I need the truth.

"And then…and then he forced his way in." She sucks in a sharp breath before breaking down. "It hurt s-so bad, K-Kostas. I hated it. I was scared you would hate me."

I grip her jaw and kiss her hard before pulling away. Our eyes lock. Intense. Vicious. Feral.

"I could never hate you. I love you, goddammit," I growl, enunciating every word. "I love you so much it's killing me to hear this."

"I wanted to tell you," she whimpers. "But he said you'd kill me."

My chest feels like she cracked it open, shoved her hands inside, and scooped out my fucking soul.

"Talia…" My voice is low and deadly. I need her to understand me. "I would never fucking hurt you. Ever. Even if you slept with the motherfucker of your own free will. Fucking. Never. Don't you see? I'm under your goddamn spell. You got inside me. It was so fucking dark and, Jesus, Talia, you were all light. I wanted that light so bad I could taste it." I kiss her supple lips. "I'd never hurt you. Do you hear me? Never."

Her kiss is frantic—thankful and desperate—as she claws at my tie. I rip her pants roughly down her ass as she sits up to aid in my effort. We're both clumsy and overly eager as we yank off our offending clothes that stand between us. I manage to get my jacket and tie off by the time she pulls away her pants and underwear. She works on my slacks as I pull hard on my shirt, and the buttons go flying. As soon as my cock is free in her hot, soft hand, I grab her hips, pulling her to me. My hand wraps around hers to hold my cock as she slides down over my length. With a hard thrust, I drive into her from beneath her. We both groan in unison.

"Kostas," she cries out. "I missed you."

Our lips crash together as her fingers claw at my bare skin on my chest. She pushes the fabric down over my shoulders so she can dig her nails there too. My fingertips bite into her hip as I guide her to fuck me rough and fast. Being inside her is the best fucking feeling in the world.

Sliding my free hand between us, I find her clit to offer her some quick pleasure. I won't last long. Not after a year of celibacy. I'm going to come like a teenage boy. Soon.

Her pussy clenches around me when I rub her clit in firm, rough circles. I hiss in pleasure, spiking my hips up harder. She bites on my lip and rakes her nails down over my pectorals.

"Fucking come, Talia," I bark out. "I need you to come before I embarrass myself in front of my wife."

She smiles against my lips and rocks her hips in unison with the way I rub her. When sweet whines begin climbing out of her throat, I know she's finding ecstasy with me. I pinch her clit in the way she used to love and am rewarded with a full-bodied shudder. My name screeches past her lips as she comes wildly. The frantic, feral way in which she does it is enough to send me over the edge. I lean forward and suck on her neck hard enough to mark her as my nuts seize up. Grinding up into her, I groan as I flood her with a year's worth of pent-up release.

Her arms circle around my neck as she hugs me to her. I bury my nose against her flesh, inhaling her sweaty, unique scent. I lick her salty skin and brand her with my teeth. I'm already hardening again like I'm fifteen years younger.

Fuck.

She does this to me.

I stand with her in my arms and kick out of my slacks and shoes. She holds on, worshipping me with her kisses as I carry us to our bed so I can return the favor. We fall into the bed—where we fucking belong—and I kiss her deeply. She helps me rip my shirt off the rest of the way and then I'm driving into her slowly, my eyes glued to hers.

I want to see her.

I want to look at her for-fucking-ever.

We spend hours tasting and teasing and fucking. I can't keep my dick out of her. We're sweaty and messy and fucking exhausted. And yet, we can't part ways. It isn't until we've showered and I'm about to bend her over the bed again that we're dragged from our sex-fest haze.

"Da-da-da-da-da."

The baby babbling in the other room warms me to my soul.

"I'll get her," I grunt as I yank on some boxers. Talia grabs one of my T-shirts from the drawer to wear as I leave to get our baby.

When I turn on the light, Zoe watches me with wide blue eyes. Fuck, she's so damn perfect. I stalk over to her and pluck her from the crib. Hugging her to me, I inhale her hair.

"I love you, *agapiménos*," I whisper. "I will kill that motherfucker for stealing you and your mother from me."

I consider telling her all the horrible ways I will torture that monster, but then I figure that's not a fatherly thing to do. It's something *my* father would do. And I'm not him.

Carrying her back to the room, I can't help but smile when I see Talia cozied up in our bed. She's so fucking beautiful with her hair wet and messy. Her lips raw from kissing. Purple bruises from my mouth littering her skin.

I settle on the bed and adjust the little one so she's nestled between us. On my side with my arm propped under my head, I admire the cute as fuck kid we made. Talia mimics my position and smiles proudly at our daughter.

Aris—my goddamn brother—took from me.

Took and took and took.

Never again.

As soon as I find him, *and I will find him*, I'm going to take from him.

Skin. Hair. Teeth. Organs.

I'm going to take from him until there's nothing left to take.

A slap to my face erases all murderous thoughts. The little angel with the blue eyes and brown hair swats at me again as though she's trying to touch me. Leaning in, I let her abuse me. She's vicious as she grabs a handful of scruff and tries to pull me to her mouth.

"She's hungry?" I ask because I know fuck all about babies.

"She's been teething, so it could be that. Or she's curious. Usually she cries when she's hungry."

"What do I do?" I grunt. "Fuck, she has a good grip."

Talia laughs and untangles the tiny fingers clawing at me. "For one, don't offer your face as a chew toy."

Zoe's face pinches and she lets out a pouty cry.

"But she likes it," I argue.

"She also likes hair and blankets and shirts."

I grin down at my baby. "Don't listen to Mommy. You can eat my face if it makes you happy."

Zoe coos and wriggles more, attempting to grab at me. I offer her my thumb and she sets to trying to pull it to her mouth.

"I'll make her a bottle," Talia says with a laugh.

While she's gone, I stare at my perfect daughter. How is it this afternoon I was wallowing in despair and murdering my fucking father with my mother's pillow and hours later I have my wife back and a daughter I never knew about? I feel like I'll blink awake and this will be some cruel as fuck dream.

The baby swats at me with her other hand.

"You're distracting like your mother," I grumble but smile at her.

Talia walks in, messy hair, perfect nipples poking through the thin shirt, and bare legs on display, carrying a fucking bottle.

"Distracting," I whisper to Zoe. "You're both bad news for the bad guy."

Talia grins as she hands me the bottle and climbs onto the bed, flashing me her naked pussy beneath her shirt. "Out there you're the bad guy. In here, you're Daddy." She leans in and kisses me. "And spoiler alert, he's the good guy."

chapter
twelve

Talia

THE SOUND OF MY DAUGHTER BABBLING HAPPILY FROM BESIDE me wakes me from my deep slumber. I open my eyes and find Zoe lying on her back, her feet in the air, and her fists in her mouth. Kostas's side of the bed is empty, but in his place are a dozen pillows entrapping Zoe. I laugh, imagining him building a barricade to keep her safe in the bed. He doesn't know she's fully crawling and could climb right over that wall if she wanted to.

"You're awake." Kostas walks through the door, freshly showered and shaved, dressed in his power suit. God, he's so sexy. Zoe spots him, and wanting off the bed, turns over on her belly and crawls toward him. Kostas's eyes widen, and I laugh.

"Yeah, she can crawl." I nod toward the makeshift wall. "That wouldn't stop her, but that was a good try." I stretch my arms over my head. For the first time in over a year, I feel well rested. It's been too long since I've felt safe enough to get a good night's sleep. "I slept so well," I tell Kostas. His lips curl into a boyish grin.

"I did too."

"I missed this bed," I joke, and he laughs good-naturedly.

"Is that all you missed?"

"No," I admit, "I missed lying next to you… Too bad when I woke up you were gone." I pout playfully.

"I've had a busy morning," he says, picking Zoe up. She reaches for his scruff, but it's gone, so instead she pats the sides of his face.

"Any news?" I sit up, suddenly remembering that this feeling of safety and comfort is only an illusion.

"Not yet," Kostas says. "But I've removed Aris's name from all the accounts, so other than his personal account, which he can't use without leaving a trail, he has zero access to any of the Demetriou funds." He glances down at Zoe, who is chewing on her fist again.

"She's hungry." I climb out of bed to grab a bottle for her. When I'm done making it, I take Zoe from Kostas and sit in the chair near the window to feed her. "What does your dad have to say about all of this?" I know he's not a fan of me. He used me to get back at my dad for having an affair with his wife, but it backfired when Kostas and my marriage became real.

"My dad is dead and he left me in charge of the organization. He no longer has a say."

My eyes fly to meet Kostas's, but he's not looking at me. He's standing in the same place, glancing down at his phone nonchalantly, like he didn't just tell me his father is dead.

"What?" I ask in shock. "Your dad is dead?" When he doesn't look up, I say, "Kostas, look at me." His eyes lift from his phone. "Stop what you're doing for two damn seconds. Since when is your father dead? Aris never mentioned that. He would've mentioned it. Did he know?"

Kostas tucks his phone into his pocket, finally giving me his undivided attention. I can hear his phone vibrating from over here, but he ignores it. "You almost sound like you care about how Aris might feel…"

"Don't go there." I shoot him a glare. "It's just the last year, every time Aris would go on one of his rants, if it wasn't about you, it was about your father. He was obsessed with bringing him down. When he finds out he's dead, he's going to lose it." Instinctually, my eyes graze the room. If he can't focus on destroying his father anymore, his entire attention will be on destroying his brother.

"He's not going to touch you," Kostas growls. "I'm going to kill him, just like I killed my father. Only, unlike Father's death, which was quick and painless, Aris's is going to be drawn out. He's going to feel every ounce of fucking pain we felt this past year from him taking you and our daughter."

Oh, shit! *He* killed his father? What the hell happened while I was gone? "You killed him?" It should worry me that I'm more shocked than upset that my husband killed his own father, but it doesn't. I know Kostas, and if he killed his dad, there was a reason why. My husband might be cold and cruel when he needs to be, but he's also smart and calculating. Everything he does is for a reason.

"Turns out he and my brother have far more in common than anybody thought. He was cheating on my mom for years before she had her affair with your dad. And Aris knew the entire time." He scrubs his hand along the side of his face in frustration. "He instilled loyalty into us from the time we were born, but he was anything but loyal to his own wife. I walked in on him yesterday getting fucked by some whore in the bed my mother slept in, so I made sure the last breath he ever took was in that same bed."

Yesterday… "That was why you were at Aris's. To let him know your father is dead."

"He invited me to his house a million times over the last year, but I always declined. Didn't care to hang out with him and his skank. But I felt I owed it to him to tell him in person. Showed up unannounced and that's how I found you. I saw you looking out the window. Thought I lost my fucking mind." Wow, the death of his father was what led Kostas to finding me. Had he not killed him, he may not have ever found us. No, I refuse to believe that. It was only a matter of time.

"I'm glad you killed him," I blurt out, and Kostas grins. "Because it meant finding us," I explain.

"I would've found you," Kostas says, his tone filled with conviction. "But yes, I suppose his death was meant to be."

Zoe finishes her bottle and bats it away, sitting up and then crawling off the chair and onto the floor. When she gets to Kostas's shiny expensive shoes, she scratches her tiny nails along them, curiously. Kostas picks her up and gives her a kiss on her cheek, and my heart warms. This is all I ever wanted, and now we're so close to having it. All that's in our way is Aris and Selene still on the run.

"It's Aris's entire purpose to make you and your father pay," I tell him, remembering all the times Aris told me how much he despises them.

"He can try." Kostas shrugs, as if my words barely deserve acknowledgment. "But now he has limited resources to do so. It won't matter anyway because I have every man out there searching for him. We'll find him soon."

"Like you found Niles?" I accuse. I shouldn't poke the hornet's nest, but I can't help it. He's so sure he's going to find Aris, yet my father has been underground for even longer and he still hasn't been found.

Kostas glares. "I don't give a fuck about finding Niles. He's a waste of air. Your brother has taken over and is turning a nice profit. But finding Aris will happen, and when I do he will regret ever fucking with what's mine." He gives Zoe another kiss on the top of her head.

"And until you do? What if it takes months or even years? Are Zoe and I going to be held captive here as well?" If my dad was able to hide out, I can't even imagine what Aris is capable of.

Kostas glances over at me. "You will never be held captive again. I have men surrounding the villa, and if you want to go somewhere, we go. I'll make sure you're safe."

"I'd like to take Zoe to the beach." I stand and walk over to them. Her gaze flits over to me and she leans toward me, so I can take her. "Every day I was stuck in his house, I would watch the waves and wish I were back down here. We spent a lot of time at the pool, but it wasn't the same. There were walls holding us in. I want Zoe to feel the sand between her toes. To feel the waves hit her body. I want her to know what it's like to be free, even if she's too young to understand it."

"Then to the beach we'll go. But first, you need to call your mother and brother. They've been almost as worried about you as I was." Kostas pulls his phone out of his pocket and hands it to me.

Wow, things have changed. Kostas is telling me to call my family… "Have you spoken to them?" I ask, taking the phone from him.

"Your mother and I speak almost every day," he says. "I guess you can say we formed a sort of truce. We both wanted to find you. And your brother is nothing like your father. He actually handles business the way it should be handled."

"Thank you." I bring myself up on my tiptoes and give Kostas a kiss.

"For what?"

"For finding and saving us." I give him another kiss. "For loving us."

After calling my mom, who cries when she finds out I'm safe, then cries even harder when she finds out she's a grandma, then tells me she's coming to visit, and Phoenix, who—without the tears—also promises to visit soon, Kostas, Zoe, and I head down to the beach. Since Zoe doesn't have a suit, we grab one from the hotel store.

I notice a few men following us, and Kostas notes they're our guards. I still can't help but glance around. Maybe this wasn't a good idea after all. But I still keep walking toward the beach. After a year of being held prisoner, I think I just need a moment to feel free.

Kostas has one of the cabana boys set up lounge chairs and umbrellas for us. I throw a blanket down, and Kostas sets Zoe down on it. We watch as she crawls to the end and reaches for the sand. She fists a handful and is bringing it up to her mouth when Kostas swoops in and saves her.

"No, no, *agapiménos*," he says softly. "That will taste bad."

Zoe's face scrunches up in confusion, and Kostas laughs. It sounds so carefree, so unlike Kostas. Being a father really does bring out the best in him. All she has to do is look at him and he transforms from hard to soft. "So curious, just like your mother." He taps her nose with his finger and she giggles.

Grabbing his phone from the blanket where he tossed it along with his shirt, I open the camera and take a photo of the two of them. When Kostas leans in and kisses her cheek, I snap another one.

I don't realize I'm crying until Kostas looks over at me and frowns. "What's the matter?"

"Nothing." I wipe the falling tears. "Everything is perfect." I step toward the two people who are my entire world. "Every day when I was stuck in that house, I would imagine what it would be like when you found us. But my imagination didn't do it justice. Getting to see you hold our daughter in person is better than anything I ever dreamed of."

When I click on the photos I just took, I notice a tattoo I didn't see before. Glancing from the phone to Kostas, I spot it on the side of his ribcage. "That's new," I point out. Dropping the phone onto the blanket, I step toward him and bend so I can get a better look at it.

"I got it a few months after you disappeared," he says. The tattoo is of a grenade, cracked open at the seams, and inside of it are bright red beads…no, not beads. Seeds. From a pomegranate. "I thought you left me," he admits, and I stand back up.

"What?"

"We were fighting that morning and then you disappeared. I thought you left me."

I glance back down at the tattoo. I'm almost positive the seeds symbolize Proserpina—me—being forced to stay in the Underground, but… "What does the grenade mean?"

"My world being blown apart." Kostas swallows thickly. "The day you went missing my entire world exploded." And just like that, I fall even deeper in love with my husband.

The day is spent playing in the sand and swimming in the ocean. We order lunch to be brought down, and only when Zoe is so exhausted, she can't keep her eyes open, do we go back up to our villa.

After laying her down in the new crib—yes, while we were at the beach, my crazy husband somehow had an entire nursery of furniture brought in—I find Kostas on the phone in his office. It reminds me of the time he fucked me on his desk, and that thought has me wanting him to take me there again. We've lost so much time together. All I want is to spend all my time with him. Create new memories to push away every memory that was created this past year.

When he spots me in the doorway, he abruptly ends his phone call.

"That was rude," I joke. "Won't whoever you were talking to wonder why you hung up on him?" I saunter over to him and he spreads his muscular thighs to let me in. He's still in his swim trunk sans shirt, and I take a moment to memorize every hard ridge, every tattoo on his body, including the tattoo he got while I was gone.

"I'm the boss," he says, running his hands up the sides of my hips. "I answer to no one."

"Do you answer to me?" I ask, my voice flirty.

His fingers find my pebbled nipples through my thin bathing suit top and he pinches them roughly. Waves of pleasure shoot through my entire body.

Kostas lifts me up and sets me on his desk. Papers crinkle under my weight, but he doesn't seem to care. "You and me aren't business," he says, pushing the material aside. He leans in and wraps his lips around my nipple, and the coolness of his breath sends a shiver straight down my spine. "But yes, *zoí mou*, I answer to you." He bites down on my nipple, then darts his tongue out to lick it, as he continues to pinch and pull at the other one. When I let out a low moan, tugging on his messy hair, he glances up at me with a wicked smirk. "I may not know a lot about this whole marriage thing, but I do know one thing…"

He pulls my bottoms down my legs, dropping them onto the floor, and I spread my legs so I'm completely exposed to him. "What's that?" I prompt, needing him to get to his point before I lose all my focus.

"Any smart man knows his wife is in charge." With his hands pushed against my thighs to keep me open, he dips his face down and swipes his tongue up my center.

"You're wrong," I tell him through a moan. He sucks my clit into his mouth and bites down playfully. "You do know a lot…" Kostas pushes two fingers into me, and I arch my back, craving more. Always more. "You're a really good husband…" I breathe. He adds another finger, stroking my insides in a way that has me squirming in pleasure. With every touch, every lick, every stroke, he works my entire body into a frenzy, until I'm coming all over his face and fingers, screaming his name.

"You only think I'm a good husband because I make you come." He smirks playfully as he stands and pushes his swim trunks down. I can't help but laugh. I love when my husband is playful.

"That's not the only reason." I reach forward and grip his hard cock. It doesn't need any preamble, but I stroke it a few times just because I want to.

Kostas watches for a few seconds before he loses his patience.

With my hand still gripping his shaft, he steps closer, allowing me to guide him inside of me. As he slowly enters me, his thick, long length stretches me until he's buried to the hilt. "Fuck, *moró mou.*" He groans. "I've missed your sweet cunt so fucking much." His hands land on either side of me, and with his strong arms caging me in, he fucks me hard and deep.

His mouth finds my neck and he suckles on my flesh. I can smell myself on his breath, and it sends me over the edge once again. Kostas's head lifts, and his eyes meet mine. "I'm never letting you out of my sight again," he vows. And with one last thrust, he finds his own release.

His movements still momentarily, and then he pulls out. Glancing down, I spot his cum dripping out of me and onto the desk. "Kostas," I breathe. We were too wrapped up in each other last night, and then again just now… "I'm not on birth control."

Kostas smirks, his gaze focused on the mess that's now dripping onto the floor. I try to close my legs, but he grips my knees, forcing them to remain open. He swipes at the liquid, gathering it onto his fingers, then smears his cum along the hood of my clit, as if he's claiming me all over again. The thought has my insides clenching in need. "Kostas," I repeat breathily. "I could get pregnant…"

"That's good, *moró mou,*" he says, looking me dead in the eyes. "Because I intend to knock you up again as soon as fucking possible."

chapter thirteen

Kostas

I FLICK THROUGH THE SCREENS OF THE VARIOUS CAMERAS ON MY app. My newest obsession. Nothing. Nothing is better than something. It's been nearly a week since I got Talia and Zoe home, but we're on edge. Not Zoe, of course. She's cute as fuck and learning the lay of the villa. I didn't know babies could be so goddamn fast. I've been tempted to build her a little cage to keep her safe from furniture and decorations and tiny things she seems to find on the floor to put into her mouth. Talia says no to cages.

My phone rings, and I answer Adrian's call on the first ring.

"Anything?" I grunt out. I swivel around in my chair to glower at the rain. My beach babies are restless stuck inside. Thank God Melody and Stefano showed up yesterday. Otherwise, I'd never get any work done. Now, they can visit and catch up with Talia while I hunt down the motherfuckers who hurt her.

"There's some chatter…"

I stand abruptly, nearly crushing my phone to my ear. "Spill, Adrian."

"With Estevan's body turning up, his people are pissed. They're not loyal to Aris like Estevan was. Estevan kept them in check because Aris's dime insured that. Now that he's gone, the roaches have scattered. Basil and Bronn have been following one of his men named Gutter."

"Gutter?"

He snorts. "Rats. Roaches. They're all pieces of shit. Anyway, Gutter seems to be planning something. Rallying his troops."

"To do what?"

"Not sure. I've been fed information that maybe they're waiting for you to fly out to Thessaloniki again. Might try to take out the private jet or put a hit on you while you're there."

"Why not here and now?"

"You're vulnerable there because you travel with minimal security. Here, at the hotel, it's a fuckin' fortress."

"Is Gutter calling the shots or is Aris still pulling strings? Aris is a sneaky sonofabitch."

"Aris is a ghost. But…"

"But what?"

"I got a tip about an older man who fits Niles's description staying about thirty minutes from here."

My entire body tenses. "What the fuck, Adrian? You could have led with that."

"It's just a tip. Nothing's confirmed. I was going to check it out. Didn't want to leave the king of the fortress unprotected."

I smirk. "The king can handle himself. Plus, security on the hotel is extra beefed. I'm about to head back to my family. Call me if you get Niles. Bring him to the cellar. Tell Basil and Bronn to keep me informed."

"Later, Boss."

We hang up and I stride through the hotel. It's pouring down rain and I hate to get out in it, but I miss my wife and our precious little angel. I grab one of the hotel umbrellas and pop it open as I step outside into the nasty weather. Wind hits hard from the west, soaking my slacks with rain. I grumble as I stalk along the pathways toward my villa. When I arrive, Melody and Stefano are just leaving.

"The weatherman said it's only supposed to get worse," Melody says in greeting. "Stefano and I are going to call it an early night. Maybe order room service. Breakfast tomorrow, though?"

"Pomegranate has an excellent brunch menu. We can meet there in the morning," I agree. "Stay dry."

Stefano holds the umbrella over her as she leans in and hugs me. I'm stiff as I accept her embrace.

"You two made a beautiful baby," she says. "Thank you for being such a wonderful husband to her. I knew you had it in you."

Stefano nods at me as she pulls away. Then, they disappear into the rain. Once on the front stoop of the villa, I close the umbrella and prop it against the wall. I mash in the code and then push through the door. It smells like coffee and Talia. Two warm, comforting scents.

I kick off my rain-soaked shoes and then walk through the villa on a hunt for them. I find Talia in Zoe's bathroom, running her a bath. Zoe splashes from her little seat inside the tub. With Talia's blond hair curtaining her face as she looks down at the little angel below her, I can't help but think she looks like an angel herself. *And Daddy is from the depths of the Underworld.* Somehow, our opposites attract. When she sees me, she grins, and her brilliant blue eyes glitter with love. It's a punch to the chest every time she knocks me over with her intensity. There's no questioning our feelings anymore.

"Someone is soaked," Talia says, smiling. "Why don't you go grab a hot shower and we'll eat after? I'll preheat the oven to cook a frozen lasagna once I'm done with her bath. It won't be homemade, but it's better than getting out in that weather."

I walk over to her and kiss the top of her head. I ruffle Zoe's dark hair. "I'll make it quick."

"Any news?"

"A lead on Niles. Maybe some other shit, but I won't know until Basil and Adrian check it out."

She purses her lips together. "Are we safe?"

"Of course."

Her brows pull together as though she doesn't believe me. It makes me bristle, but I don't let it get to me. After the hell she's gone through, she's allowed to have anxiety. One day, hopefully, it'll fade completely. I quickly shed my soaked clothes and breeze through a shower. Since we're not going anywhere, I pull on a pair of gray sweatpants, some socks, and a white T-shirt. Talia likes it when I'm dressed down. With my hair still wet and messy, I pad through the house to find her in the kitchen, Zoe propped on her hip.

"Here, hold her," she instructs.

I take my baby, who now smells sweet and clean, bouncing her in my arms as Talia peels the plastic film away from the lasagna and sits it on a tray. She then busies herself with making a salad while the oven preheats. Zoe and I walk over to the window where the storm seems to worsen.

Boom!

Thunder crashes loud and hard enough the windows rattle.

"That was intense," Talia exclaims from behind me. "This storm—"

Boom! Boom! Boom!

My blood runs cold. Thunder doesn't sound like that. It doesn't hit that quickly either. What the fuck?

"Get in the closet," I bark out, grabbing Talia's arm and rushing her through the villa as the booms continue.

"Kostas," she cries out. "What's happening?"

"We're being attacked."

"W-What?"

"Turn the lights off. Hide in the closet," I bellow as I grab my phone from the bedroom. I dial Adrian and he doesn't answer. When I call Basil, he picks up. "We're being fucking hit."

"We're five minutes out and I have Caymon on the other line. He says Aris's Porsche is at the front. Explosives are going off near the front entrance. Bold ass motherfucker," Basil huffs. "Want me to take him out, Boss?"

"No kill shot. He's mine. I want him in the cellar," I bark out.

Basil says something to Bronn and then grunts, "Bronn says Caymon's men have the Porsche surrounded."

"I'm on my way." I hang up and shove my phone into my pocket.

I stalk into the closet to find Talia and Zoe watching me with wide eyes. I shove my feet into a pair of tennis shoes and shove my suit jackets aside to get to my gun safe. After punching in the code, I pull out a Glock, check the magazine, and then hand the weapon to Talia.

"Shoot first, ask questions later," I hiss before turning to pull out my AR-15. "They have Aris's Porsche surrounded."

"Be careful," Talia cries out. "Please."

I rush over to her, planting a kiss on her lips and then one on Zoe's soft head. "Shoot anyone who walks through that closet, Talia. I have my phone. Call me if you need me. I'll be back as soon as we have that motherfucker detained."

As I leave, I turn off all the lights, to keep them safe under the cover of darkness. The doors are all locked and I slip out the front into the pouring rain. Wind violently whips at me, slashing me with rain and soaking me to the bone. I sprint through the downpour, racing toward the front of the hotel under the cover of shadows and between buildings. I'm not letting my guard down for an instant.

"Boss," Caymon hisses from between a building. He stumbles out, holding his side. "It's a fucking—"

His head explodes in front of me as he collapses to the dirt. I lift my AR and turn toward the direction the bullet came from. Spraying bullets into the trees, I try to mow down the attacker. This isn't Aris's style, which means he has his men doing his dirty work. Someone grunts from the trees and I charge after them.

I tackle the man and lay a hard punch to his kidney. He groans, attempting to roll away from me, splattering us with mud, but I'm stronger. I flip the man and shove the barrel of my AR against his Adam's apple, making him gag and cough.

Niles motherfucking Nikolaides.

The urge to shoot his head right off his spine is strong, but I need answers. I kick him hard in the stomach, making him howl.

"Get the fuck up and walk," I bellow.

He groans and unsteadily makes his way to his feet.

"Turn." As soon as his back is to me, I poke the gun in between his shoulder blades. "To your left." My phone buzzes and I quickly answer it. "What?"

"It's Adrian," he barks out. "Where are you?"

"Walking Niles to the goddamn cellar. Where are you?"

"Standing behind the Porsche. We can see them inside. A man and a woman. Call it and I'll put a bullet in their heads."

"No," I growl. "I want my brother alive. I'm going to tie down this fucker and then I'm on my way."

"Hold on," he bites at me as he talks to someone. "No fuckin' way. Basil has Phoenix."

That traitorous motherfucker.

"Tell Basil to bring Phoenix to the cellar to keep his daddy company and to watch them both. You keep Aris there."

We hang up just as I storm into the groundskeeper's house with

Niles leading the way. The groundskeeper sits on the sofa, soaked to the bone, holding pressure to his stomach as blood blooms over his hands. He gurgles out something to me, but it's too late. Hot pain slices through the back of my arm, just as I'm turning. Whoever nearly stabbed me in the goddamn back, missed a deadlier hit when I moved at the last minute, but it still hurts like a motherfucker. With my gun still trained on Niles, I swing out with my leg, taking down my assailant. They hit the ground with a loud grunt.

I sling the AR to the guy's face and pop him right in the mouth with three bullets. Niles tries to run, but I crack him hard in the back of the head with the butt of the AR. He falls hard on his knees but doesn't go completely down.

"Get your ass down those stairs or I'll kick you down them," I roar, shoving the barrel into his back. "Move."

He groans and curses all the way down to the cellar. I force him into the chair and tie him tight enough around his wrists, his hands turn purple. I'm about to head back upstairs when Basil and Bronn manhandle Phoenix down the steps. His face is beat all to hell, but he's raging like a beast. Not taking any chances, I stay until they get him subdued with an elbow to the face and tied down.

"I'll be back soon with my brother and his bitch. Don't let them go anywhere."

Basil and Bronn both nod as I take the steps up two at a time. My arm hurts like a motherfucker, but I'm high on adrenaline. I've thirsted for vengeance for what feels like forever. I'm finally getting it. Fucking finally.

I run through the rain toward the front gate with my AR raised and ready to fire. My staff are trained in the event we're ever attacked, so the guests should be fairly safe, although it's going to be a helluva PR nightmare. I'll have Josef pissed as fuck having to cover our shit, but there's nothing money won't buy—even the Minister of Public Order's compliance.

When the Porsche comes into view, flashes of light can be seen in conjunction with pops of gunfire. My men are shooting into the vehicle against my orders. What the fuck!

Racing toward them, I nearly mow down Adrian in the process.

"They shot him against direct orders—"

"Something isn't right, Boss!" Adrian barks out.

I shove past him toward the Porsche. Pushing a guy out of my way, I fling open the door. A man and a woman are slumped over, the entire interior splattered with their blood. The guy is an older man with his hands tied behind his back. The woman has gray hair and her arms are bound too.

Fuck.

Fuck.

Talia.

Bullets spray at me and I dive down into the mud, wincing at the pain searing through my hip where I've been clipped. The guy I'd pushed away splats beside me, his head blown off.

"Boss," Adrian calls out from nearby. "Stay the fuck down. I'm gonna get the bastard!"

Rolling onto my back, I wince when my arm screams in protest and my hip burns like a motherfucker. I strain my neck, searching for the shooter. The rain is relentless and it's dark as fuck. I work myself into a squat and rush around to the back of the car. Popping can be heard just north. I see Adrian's big form not far away. We make eye contact and I nod at him, pointing in the direction of the shooter.

We're coming for you, asshole.

And you're going to wish you'd never been fucking born.

chapter fourteen

Talia

With Zoe clinging to my chest, I listen to the front door slam closed. Zoe, the six-month-old that she is, squirms, wanting to play in the closet. She doesn't understand what's going on, or that she was born into a world where the villains and monsters I read to her about, the ones who always get taken down by the white knights, are real, and they don't get taken down as easily in real life as they do in her books. Sometimes, in fact, they don't get taken down at all.

Once upon a time I thought Kostas was a monster. But now that I've seen Aris in action, I know the difference. Whereas Kostas is powerful and smart, and makes calculated decisions, Aris is cruel and vindictive, and makes decisions based on his emotions. His need for revenge. Kostas may not be like the knights in Zoe's books, but he's still *my* knight. And I know without a doubt my dark knight will do everything in his power to make sure his princesses are safe.

Where is he?

What's taking so long?

The booms we heard sounded like explosions. I pray Mom and Stefano are safe someplace. I should try to call and check on them, but not until Zoe and I are in the clear. Kostas would lose his mind if I left the closet to look for them. I have to trust my stepdad will take care of Mom.

Fear clings to me and I can't shake it off. An ominous feeling washes over me. I'm not safe here in this closet. Deep down, I know it's Aris. He can't let his brother win. It's all he's bitched about for a year. Destroying him. Toying with him. We're Kostas's weakness and Aris is smart enough to know that. He'll hunt us down. Nothing will satisfy him until he has us.

Over my dead body.

I'll shoot him in the face before I let him take us again.

I can't live as a captive ever again. I won't do that to Zoe.

"Ba-ba-ba," Zoe babbles around the pacifier I keep trying to push back into her mouth to keep her quiet. She's getting annoyed that I won't let her loose to play. In a few minutes, she's going to get frustrated and will soon be screaming her tiny little head off. My daughter doesn't do well with being confined. Hopefully, whatever is happening, will be over by then.

Hope is worthless at a time like this. My brain trumps the hope flittering in my heart. These people are mobsters, not normal men. That means hope is useless, unlike the gun beside me.

Feeling around in the dark, I find a shoe and try to hand it to Zoe to distract her. She takes it for a second before she drops it to the ground and wriggles, trying to get free.

"Ba-da-da," she babbles some more, frustration evident in her tone.

Come on, Kostas.

We don't like being alone without you.

"Shh, baby, let's go night-night." It's close to her bedtime, so maybe she will go with it. Lifting her into my arms, I start to rock her back and forth, when I hear something shatter. Zoe hears it too because her head, which was lying against my arm, pops up, smacking me in the face.

Crunch. Crunch. Crunch.

Footsteps on glass.

Oh, God.

Someone's in the house.

Grabbing the gun from beside me, I'm preparing to do as Kostas said—shoot first, ask questions later.

I strain my ears, hoping it's just the storm. But I can hear voices inside. Whispers. Something crashing to the floor. A door slams and more voices. The bedroom light turns on and shines in under the crack of the doors.

People are here.

They're going to find us.

My body trembles with fear and adrenaline courses through me. If we can be quiet, maybe they won't think to look in the closet.

"Ba!" Zoe screeches, and I wince. If someone is in here, Zoe's voice just gave us away.

"Shh," I whisper. "Shh, baby."

But she's not quiet and starts to screech as she squirms.

Come home, Kostas!

When the closet door swings open, momentarily blinding me with the new light shining in, I let out a choked sound of horror. I have no clue who is standing there, but if it were Kostas, he would've made his presence known. So, with Zoe wrapped tightly in one of my arms, I raise the gun with my other and shoot.

Bang. Bang. Bang.

Three shots go off, making my hand go numb and my ears ring.

My eyes adjust just in time to see Selene stumble back. I hit her somewhere based on her howling, but she's still alive.

"You fucking bitch," she screams, stalking toward me like one of those crazy zombies who can't be brought down. "You shot me!" Blood seeps from her lower abdomen and it's hard to tell if I got her good or just clipped her.

I aim again, hoping to hit her in the heart, and—

"It's over." Aris comes out of nowhere and tackles me. Still trying to hold Zoe in my arms, I hit and kick at him. But he's stronger and quickly disarms me, before pinning me to the floor. Zoe is flung out of my grip, and before I can grab her, Selene plucks her off the ground.

Blood curdling screams.

Zoe! My baby!

She's screaming for me and I need to get to her.

"No!" I wail. My drive to get to my daughter takes over, and grabbing the first thing I can get my hands on, I plow it into Aris's face. He's caught off guard long enough that I'm able to roll over and get out of his grip. I'm about to stand, so I can run after Zoe, when Aris tackles me from behind. With his weight on top of me, my arms give out, and my chin hits the hardwood floor. Something metallic swarms my mouth.

Zoe's screams go louder, spurring me to focus on her instead of the pain.

My baby. I need to get to her.

But before I can move forward, Aris's strong hands grip my biceps, and he flips me over onto my back, smashing the back of my head in the process. He crawls up my body, wrapping his legs around my torso. With him hovering above me, I can make out his features.

His eyes scream hate. Fury. Revenge. But the way he's smirking, it sends shivers down my spine. He's enjoying what's happening. Just as I thought he planned all of this, and he's confident enough to believe he's going to win.

Not if I can help it.

"Did you really think I would let you and that baby leave that easily?" He chuckles darkly.

"Fuck you!" I spit the blood that's been building up in my mouth in his face.

"Been there, done that." He cocks his hand back to hit me, but I see it coming. And lifting my butt into the air, I knee him in the back, forcing him to fall forward enough to lose his balance.

Taking advantage of his current state, I slide my body backward then knee him in the dick as hard as I can. He groans and rolls to his side, as I roll to mine, determined to get to my daughter. We're both on our feet, running out the bedroom door, when something heavy smacks me in the side of my face.

I fall forward, my face catching the side of the end table.

Gray. Blink. Gray. Blink.

Everything fades so quickly as the sounds grow muted.

"Payback's a bitch," Selene screams as my vision goes blurry and then fades to black. I try to fight it, but I can't.

Wake up!

Open your eyes!

But I can't. Oh God.

The last thing I hear before everything goes silent is the sound of my daughter, *zoí mou*, crying for me. Needing me. Needing to be saved. And I pray that Kostas is somewhere close. And that, just like in Zoe's storybooks, the monsters lose, and the dark knight saves the princesses.

But sadly, we all know too well that reality rarely imitates fiction.

chapter fifteen

Kostas

MY MIND IS ON ONE TRACK. FIND AND KILL THE MAN SHOOTING at us. The quicker I can eliminate this threat, the quicker I can find my fucking brother.

"Radio to everyone," I hiss out to Adrian, though I can't see him. "I want this place surrounded. No one leaves."

The static of his device can be heard as he makes the command. My phone buzzes in my sweats' pocket, but I can't answer just yet. Not when I'm crouched and running between vehicles hunting down a man.

Pop! Pop! Pop!

Bullets whiz past me, but I duck down just in time. It's dark and pouring down rain, so most likely he's just shooting in our general direction rather than having eyes on us. Something crunches ahead and then a man makes a grunting sound as though he fell. I charge his way. A form is rising to his feet and I don't waste any time.

Pop!

My bullet hits him in his lower stomach and he groans from the impact. He drops his weapon to apply pressure to the wound. Adrian flies up out of nowhere and tackles the fucker.

"Get him to the cellar," I growl. I'm blinded by the rain that's running from my hair into my eyes and everything fucking hurts. I'll need to get my shit dealt with because I won't be able to run on adrenaline forever.

I stumble a little, my hip screaming in pain, but manage to keep myself upright. My phone buzzes again. "I need to check on Talia," I bark out at Adrian. "Let's get this asshole there for questioning. Aris is still missing." My blood runs cold with fear that he might have gotten to her.

Men are staked out around the villa.

Aris would have to go through an entire army of men to get to her.

She has a gun and knows how to use it.

It provides some semblance of relief, but not much. Just as we push into the groundskeeper's house, I dig my phone out of my soaked pants pocket. Adrian hauls the fucker to the cellar while I wait in the living room. My hands are shaking and it takes a few tries before I'm able to enter my code to open it.

The door flies open behind me. I'm on autopilot as I sling my AR around, ready to spray bullets into my assailant. As soon as I see who it is, I nearly fall to my knees in relief.

"Kostas!"

It takes me all of two seconds to take in her appearance. She's soaked to the bone from the rain, but so many things click into place all at once.

Blood smeared all over her teeth and running down her chin.

Blond hair matted to her face and clothes clinging to her form.

Giant bruise on the side of her face.

Sobbing. Sobbing. Sobbing.

Gun shaking hard in her grip.

No baby. No baby.

No. Fucking. Baby.

"Where's Zoe?" I demand, terror burning through me like accelerant to an already out of control inferno.

She falls against me, nearly knocking me over. I toss the AR to the couch to hug her to me.

"Talia, where the fuck is our daughter?" My chest hurts and violence thrums through me.

"T-They took her," she sobs. "You said we were s-safe. We were n-not safe."

Guilt and fury wage war inside me.

I left them alone. I thought I could eliminate the threat.

"Who?" I ask, my voice low and deceptively calm.

She looks up at me, her bottom lip wobbling. "Aris and Selene."

I should have known Aris wouldn't storm the gates so brazenly. That he'd have a plan of attack that would throw me off.

"Adrian," I bellow. "Get a car and let's go."

Three seconds later, Adrian storms into the living room. I don't have to say the words because he takes in our appearances and mutters out, "Motherfucker!" He rushes out into the night as I walk Talia out the door to wait for him to bring up a vehicle. Soon, he arrives with an SUV and I pile into the front while Talia jumps in the middle row seating behind us.

"Where to?" Adrian demands.

I scrub my palm over my face to swipe away some of the water. The asshole hid from me for an entire year right under my nose. He's a sneaky bastard like that. But now it won't be so easy. He'll have an infant in tow and a mouthy bitch. Someone will see him. I need every goddamn person looking for him.

"Airport," I utter, though I'm not sure he'll try that. The jet is always fueled and ready. At the very least, I want to make sure he's not leaving Crete Island.

Adrian hauls ass through the dark. My fingers tremble as I dial Basil.

"Yeah, Boss?"

"Make them talk, but don't kill them. I need answers." I close my eyes and breathe heavily. "They took Zoe."

"Aris?" he growls.

"I need you to have the men eliminate the threat at the hotel. Get the bodies out of there and make sure the hotel guests are okay."

"Minister of Public Order?" he asks.

"I'll call Josef. Just clean up the fucking mess and keep the roaches on a leash in the cellar. I want to know anything, no matter how insignificant."

"Talia?"

"She's safe with us but have someone check on her mom, please."

Talia squeezes my shoulder from behind in thanks.

"On it, Boss."

After we hang up, I dial Josef. My body feels cold and I fight a tremble. Awkwardly, I fumble for the heater. Adrian shoots me a worried look before swatting my hand away to do it for me.

"This better be good," Josef growls. "I have everyone blowing up my goddamn phone."

"Terrorists after a politician," I lie. That's the lie he'll spin for me too and he'll be paid handsomely for it. "Set up a press release for the morning. They took my daughter."

He barks out some orders to someone before saying, "No shit?"

"I need…" I suck in a deep breath, blinking away a wave of dizziness. "I need you to have your men out there looking for my brother."

"Aris did this shit? Your father would be disappointed."

No, Father would have already found him and put a bullet through his skull. I'm softer than Father and it shows. I can't hold onto anything precious to me. Not my mother, not Talia for so long, not my daughter.

"Have the police looking for her. Brown hair. Blue eyes. Six months old. I'll text you a picture to send to your men."

"I'll keep it discreet. We'll find her."

I wince as I adjust my position in the seat. Blackness eats at my vision.

"And if we don't by the time of the press release tomorrow…" Josef trails off.

Adrian shakes his head at me in warning.

"Then what?" Josef asks.

"We go wide with it," I bite out. Tell all my enemies I have something I want back, even it if means presenting to them my weakness.

Josef is silent. I pull the phone away to make sure we're still connected before pressing it back to my ear.

"You heard me?" I rasp out.

"That puts a big target on your most vulnerable possession."

My heart pumps fast and furious. "Right now, I need that target to find her. Make it happen."

"Of course," he says with a sigh.

We hang up and I fade in and out the entire trip to the airport. Adrian keeps getting calls and barks out orders. My phone buzzes a few times with texts from Basil. Eventually, he sends me a text with a picture of two very freaked out looking people, but they're alive. I lift my phone to show Talia and she sobs in relief.

Melody and Stefano are okay.

My phone slips from my grip and tumbles to the floor. Talia picks it back up. Her hand is warm as it brushes along mine.

"Kostas," she cries out in alarm. "Your hand is like ice." She runs her palm along my cheek. "What's wrong with you? Are you hurt?"

"He's been hit," Adrian alerts her. "Took a bullet outside and not sure what got his arm."

"Knife," I hiss out.

Talia practically climbs onto the console to look me over. Adrian pulls up to the airport and exits the vehicle.

"You're bleeding everywhere," she whispers. "And you're so pale."

"I'll be fine," I grunt out.

"We need to get you to a hospital."

"Fuck that," I snarl. "They'll hold me when I need to be out here searching for Zoe."

Her lips press together in a worried line. "I want her just as bad as you do, but we can't look for her while you're dying on me. I need you." Tears leak from her eyes and her chin wobbles.

"But Zoe," I choke out.

"Aris never hurt her or was cruel to her," she assures me, though I hear the doubt in her voice. "He still thinks Zoe is his. We have to have faith she's going to be okay with him."

I close my eyes, suddenly very tired. "I'm sorry I failed you."

Hysterical sobs escape her and she slaps my face, forcing my droopy eyes back open. "Don't you dare fucking take the blame for what your brother did. You have done nothing but try to protect us."

Lifting my weak arm, I swipe away her tear. "He fucking hit you."

"I hit back," she tells me icily.

"Good girl."

"I shot Selene," she whispers. "But she got away anyway."

Energy surges through me. "You put a bullet in that bitch?"

"Yes."

Gripping her neck, I pull her to me and kiss her mouth that still tastes of blood.

"You're so cold," she whimpers. "You've lost too much blood."

"I'll be okay," I assure her as I text Josef.

Me: Selene—Aris's bitch—got hit. She might need medical attention so keep eyes on the hospitals.

A wave of dizziness has my head thunking against the window. Talia slaps my face again, rousing me.

"Wake up," she says firmly. "Tell me what you need me to do."

"I need Basil to…check the footage…" I blink hard.

She grabs my phone and dials Basil. "Check the footage. See what they drove off in. Send the information to Josef."

Fuck, she listens well.

Basil says something to her and she huffs.

"If they find him, I want to see his face," she hisses. "And then I want to stab him to fucking death."

Adrian climbs back in and shakes his head. "Nothing. They didn't come here. What now?"

"We neeeed toooo," I slur, my head pounding as I try to make sense of what I'm trying to say.

"Get back to the hotel. He needs medical attention. Call his doctor because he already nixed the hospital idea. Basil's pulling up the video footage to get the make of the vehicle to send to Josef. We're going to go torture fucking answers out of the men you guys caught. And then we're going to find my baby."

"Damn," Adrian says as he peels out of the parking lot. "You've been busy."

"Oh," she sneers, "and when we find Aris, I'm going to kill him."

Adrian snorts. "You got it, Boss."

Her warm lips press to my cheek as blackness pulls me under. Hot words are whispered against my flesh that have me relaxing. "Rest, baby. I need you to get better so we can fix this. Until then, we'll take care of what we can."

I didn't marry a weak Nikolaides.

I married a goddamn mafia queen.

A Demetriou in heart and now one in soul.

chapter sixteen

Talia

THE DRIVE FROM THE AIRPORT BACK TO THE HOTEL IS SPENT WITH me begging Kostas to stay awake. Scared if he falls asleep he might not ever wake up. His forehead is glistening with sweat, and his skin is cold and sticky to the touch. He needs a doctor sooner rather than later. I can't make out exactly where he's been shot, or how extreme it is, but based on his pale complexion, I have a feeling it's bad.

A myriad of emotions are running through me. Fear that I'm going to lose my husband and daughter. Anger that Aris would stoop this low to involve Zoe in his revenge plan. The man barely even paid attention to her the entire time we lived with him. What I told Kostas was the truth. Aris was never cruel to Zoe, but he also barely acknowledged she existed. The only reason he was keeping us there was to get back at his brother. He never even once tried to have sex with me or spend any time with Zoe, even thinking she was his daughter. Zoe and I are nothing more than tools to him. Tools to hurt his brother.

What I don't get, though, is why he didn't take me this time around… Taking me would mean hurting Kostas. And then a thought strikes me. Selene wanted me out of the picture, so the two of them could play house. Did he only take Zoe so he could keep her for him and Selene to raise? But he can barely even stand Selene. He treated her more like she was a warm body to sink his dick into when he was horny than like a potential wife.

Maybe he's hoping to use Zoe as a bargaining tool, and it was easier to take her than the both of us. Kostas did cut him out of all the business assets. Maybe he's planning to get somewhere safe and then he'll contact Kostas to make a deal. But even as I consider that, I know deep down Aris cares more about revenge than making a deal. Unless the deal involves Kostas losing everything and Aris ending up with everything.

Would Kostas give up everything he's worked his entire life creating to make sure our daughter is safe? Of course he would. But hopefully it won't come to that. I would rather find Aris and Selene and put a bullet through their cold, black hearts than hand anything of value over to them. They don't deserve anything. Not a single dollar. And definitely not the business. Hopefully whoever Kostas and his men caught will have some answers.

Kostas groans softly, his head lulling to the side, and I'm brought back to the present. Before we can do anything, we need to make sure Kostas is okay.

Adrian pulls in front of the groundskeeper's house and jumps out of the car. Basil comes running out, and between the two of them, they carry a stumbling Kostas into the house and lay him across the couch. While we wait for the doctor to arrive, I grab a knife from Basil and cut open Kostas's shirt, needing to see how bad the damage is. As I'm assessing his body, the doctor and his assistant walk in. I've met them both when we first got home. Kostas wanted to make sure Zoe was healthy since Aris wouldn't let anyone see her. The doctor was helpful and gave her the necessary vaccines she needs.

"He has what looks like a bullet wound to his right side and a large knife gash on the back of his arm," I tell him.

He nods once and sets to work. Opening his duffle bag, he seems to have everything he needs. He begins working on Kostas's side, just above his hip, while his assistant helps him, grabbing various tools and such.

Needing to feel like I'm doing something, I grab a washcloth from a cabinet and wet it with cool water. Without getting in the way, I sit next to Kostas's head and pat his forehead with the cool washcloth.

His eyes flutter open just long enough for our eyes to meet before they close again, and my heart squeezes in my chest. I've never seen Kostas look so vulnerable and weak. He must be in so much pain.

"Did you give him pain medication?" I ask, worried he's suffering.

"Yes," the doctor responds. "But only the minimum. He doesn't like to be sedated."

His words make me realize this isn't the first time he's had to fix my husband. And that thought has me wondering how many times he's come close to dying. How many more times will his life be at risk? How long do I have with him until one day his life—or mine—is taken? I married a powerful man, who many people would love to see brought down. Every day I spend with him is on borrowed time.

The thought has me choking back a sob. If I were with a man like Alex, this never would've happened. We'd be safe at home, running lines for an upcoming play. No, that's not true. If I were still with Alex, we would've already graduated.

But then I would've never met Kostas. I would've never known what it's like to fall in love with a man who has the ability to consume every part of my mind, body, and soul.

I would've never found myself. My sense of purpose. What I had with Alex, might've been safe, but it was boring. Alex didn't make my heart pound against my chest the way Kostas does. Going to school was fun, but it didn't pull the passion out of me like creating Pomegranate did. Alex was sweet, but he didn't challenge me the way Kostas does.

I would've never had Zoe. With her dark hair identical to her father's, and my blue eyes, she's the perfect mixture of the two of us. She's only a baby, but I can already see both of us weaved through her. My sass and determination, and Kostas's strength and bravery.

I didn't understand it at the time, but it wasn't until I married Kostas that I finally found my place in this world. It's not spitting lines in a play-house, or traveling with friends. It's right here on this island, at this hotel with my husband and daughter. I love being Kostas's wife, being Zoe's mom.

And all I want is to be given the chance to continue to be both. Which means I need my husband to live, and I need to get my daughter back.

Right now, the only possible lead we have to go on are the men being held in the cellar. If Kostas doesn't wake up soon, I'm going to have to interrogate them myself. There's no way Kostas would want everyone sitting around waiting for him to get better while that asshole and his evil sidekick are getting farther and farther away with our daughter.

Moving the washcloth off Kostas's forehead, I lean down to give him a kiss. "I love you," I whisper. "I need you to be okay."

Kostas groans. "You're not getting rid of me that easily." He gives me a lazy smirk that shoots straight to my belly. Butterflies. Even hurt, he can still manage to turn my insides out. He just has that effect on me.

I watch in silence while the doctor works on Kostas's side and then turns him slightly over to work on the back of his arm. After what feels like hours, the doctor sits straight and pulls off his latex gloves, handing them to his assistant.

"All done," the doctor says. "The bullet that entered his side has been removed, and he's been stitched up. An inch more to the left and it would've hit a kidney." He hands me a bottle of pills. "Here's an antibiotic for him, so it doesn't get infected."

"And the arm?" Kostas asks, shocking me when he opens his eyes and attempts to sit up.

"Whoa," I chide. "You can't move." I place my hand on his arm, and thankfully, he doesn't try to sit up anymore.

"It was deep, cut through some muscle," the doctor says. "Needed twenty stitches. But it could've been worse. Could've hit a lung." He turns his attention to Kostas. "You are very lucky. It's going to take some time for it to heal." Kostas nods in understanding. "Try to make sure not to use that arm too much while it's healing."

His assistant hands me a tiny bottle. "There's some healing cream. Apply it to both areas. The stiches will dissolve on their own in a couple of weeks."

I take my first deep breath of relief. Kostas is okay. "Thank you," I tell them both.

"Thanks, Doc," Kostas adds.

"I'll walk you out," Adrian tells them.

When Adrian returns a minute later, he reaches for Kostas, who extends his arm.

"What are you doing?" I hiss. "Lie back down!"

"Like fucking hell," Kostas says. "I've been through worse."

Stupid, stubborn fucking man!

Adrian helps my husband to his feet.

"Anything?" Kostas asks him, already back to sounding like himself.

If it weren't for seeing him wince in pain, I wouldn't even know he was recently shot and stabbed.

"Nothing. None of them will speak," Adrian says. "Phoenix is still claiming he wasn't a part of it."

Phoenix? Oh my God! Phoenix was coming to visit. "You can't possibly think my brother had a part in helping Aris kidnap our daughter. She's his niece!"

"And what about Niles?" Kostas grunts. "He was brought in as well, after trying to take me out."

What the hell! "Niles is here?" I glance around, even though I know exactly where he is. "He's here, in that fucking cellar?" I shout, my blood boiling.

Kostas nods, his dark eyes flashing with violence.

"I want to see him now." I don't wait for Kostas as I stomp down to the cellar. I swing the door open and find Basil and a few of Kostas's other men standing guard. In the center of the room are three men, all tied with thick rope to their chairs. The first one I recognize as my brother. His flesh is bloody, and his head is quirked to the side, like he's slightly out of it. His eyes are closed, but I can see his chest heaving up and down. He's still alive.

The second is Niles. His face is also covered in blood, both eyes puffy and black and blue. His eyes are also closed, but he's not breathing heavy like Phoenix, so it takes me a second to determine he's still alive. For now.

The third guy I don't recognize, but he's in just as bad of shape as my brother and Niles. His eyes are open and he's glancing around him, as if trying to figure a way out. Not happening, fucker.

"Niles, wake up!" I kick his legs and his head pops up. The moment his eyes meet mine, my body trembles with anger. "You fucking asshole." I stalk closer to him and slap him across the face. "How dare you!" I cry. My hands are shaking, and my heart is beating erratically against my ribcage. How could he do this to me? To his own flesh and blood? It wasn't bad enough he used me to pay off his debt, but now he works with Aris to help steal my daughter?

"Sunshine," Niles cries out, and the nickname he used to call me has me seeing red.

"Don't you ever call me that!" I backhand him this time, and his face whips to the side. "Do you have any idea what you just did?" I grab his chin between my fingers and force him to look at me. "Do you?"

"I had to," he chokes out. "Aris has been holding me captive. It was either help him bring down Kostas or die." He thinks he chose his life over Kostas's…

"You didn't help take down Kostas," I spit. "You helped kidnap my daughter!" With no outlet for my built up aggression and frustration, I smack him across the face again. "He took my baby! And you helped him!"

Niles's eyes go wide. "Kostas's men said you had a baby, but I didn't know. I swear, Talia, I never knew anything about a baby. Aris never said a word."

I stare into his eyes for a long moment to gauge his reaction. He's telling the truth. I can see it in his eyes. The pain of knowing he helped take my daughter. It doesn't excuse what he's done, but it means he's no help. Useless.

"He doesn't know anything," I whisper, mostly to myself. Niles not knowing anything means there are only two other people in here who might know something about where Aris and Selene have taken Zoe.

I turn my attention to my brother. "Phoenix." When I say his name, he lifts his head. I don't even need to ask him. I know my brother. He loves me and would never do anything to help Aris in taking my daughter. I heard his voice over the phone. He was excited to be an uncle.

"You know damn well I wasn't a part of this," Phoenix growls, his voice strong and deadly.

"And why the fuck should we believe you?" I turn around to find Kostas standing behind me. "It won't be the first time you've followed in your daddy's footsteps," Kostas sneers. I'm not sure how long he's been here—I was too focused on Niles—but his color is almost fully back, and he's wearing a new shirt.

"I would never do that shit to my sister," Phoenix hisses.

"Kostas, I don't think he would do this," I tell my husband, needing him to believe me. Otherwise he's going to kill my brother. Phoenix might have spent his entire life working for Niles and the business, but he would never purposely put my life or my daughter's at risk. I believe that with my entire being.

"I didn't do it," Phoenix says again.

"Then prove it," Kostas says, his eyes locked on Phoenix as he slowly walks over to him. Once he's standing in front of him, he glances at Basil. "Hand me your knife."

Adrian steps forward. "Boss…" I know what he's silently not saying. *Let me handle this.* Kostas is too weak to torture anyone. But if Adrian says it out loud it will make Kostas appear weak. And Kostas would rather die than ever appear weak in front of his men, or especially, his enemies.

"I got it," Kostas hisses. He snatches the knife out of Basil's hand and slices the rope holding Phoenix down. Then he slices the rope holding his hands together. "You say you didn't have a part in helping my brother kidnap my daughter… Okay. But your fucking father did. Caught him red-handed with a fucking gun, shooting at me. You have a choice to make."

Phoenix clenches his jaw, and his furious gaze flits from Kostas, to me, and then to Niles, who is now wide awake and staring at his son.

Phoenix stands and stalks over to Kostas, until their chests are practically touching. "I don't have to prove shit to you," Phoenix says.

I hold my breath in fear of what's to come. If Phoenix doesn't do something, Kostas will kill him without hesitating.

Phoenix's hateful glare leaves Kostas, and he turns toward Niles. "You did this shit to yourself," he says in a lowly, distant voice.

"Son, please," Niles begs. "I didn't have a choice. You have to believe me."

"Shut your fucking mouth!" Phoenix roars. "You chose yourself over your fucking daughter for the last time." My brother stalks toward the guard standing closest to Niles, grabs the gun from his holster, and aims it at Niles's chest.

"This is for everything you've done to Talia."

Pop!

Crimson bleeds through Niles's shirt as he cries out in shock. He hit him in the stomach, not the heart—keeping him alive. Before he can beg Phoenix not to kill him, Phoenix aims the gun at his forehead.

Instinctively, I slam my eyes closed, already knowing what's coming.

"And this is for Zoe."

Pop!

I open my eyes back up. Nile's head has been blown to bits. Several of the guards have blood splattered on them. My stomach roils at the sight, but I force the bile down, refusing to look weak in front of all these men. He got what he deserved.

My gaze goes to the third man. He's staring at Niles, his eyes wide-open in shock and fear.

"What do you know about Aris taking my daughter?" I ask him.

"I don't know anything!" he exclaims. "I was just told to come here and kill as many men as possible."

"He doesn't know shit," Kostas growls. "Nobody fucking does because Aris was too smart to let anybody know."

Kostas pulls the gun out from behind him and shoots the guy dead in the heart. His life ends so quickly, his eyes remain open as if he's frozen in place.

My eyes flit back and forth between the two dead men as reality hits. "Kostas," I cry. He turns his attention to me. "If nobody knows anything, how are we going to get our little girl back?"

Kostas walks over to me, and as tightly as his broken body can, he wraps me in his arms as I sob into his chest. We have no more leads. There are no breadcrumbs to follow. Nobody knows anything. It's as if Aris and Selene have vanished with Zoe. "Shh," Kostas coos, his body shaking from the pain he must be in. "We're going to find her. I promise."

chapter seventeen

Kostas

I STARE AT MY REFLECTION AS I BRUSH MY TEETH. COLD. FURIOUS. A monster. Certainly not one who looks like the father of a small, perfect baby. Or the lover and husband of a beautiful woman. I'm ruthless. My father's son. Every bit the Demetriou I need to be to face the media.

Because *they* will see.

My enemies.

And I need them to see who the fuck they're dealing with.

Talia enters the bathroom as I angrily scrub the film off my teeth. I barely slept two hours, but the press will be here at eight sharp this morning, and if I have any hope for making it through today, I need coffee and a motherfucking bagel.

"I've never heard anyone growl while brushing their teeth before," she says, her eyes squinting and her voice gravelly from sleep.

I spit, then rinse, before drying my mouth off. I've already showered for the day, which was agony on my wounds, and am in just a towel. My wife looks stunning somehow in one of my oversized T-shirts. Her blond hair is in disarray. But what has me seeing red is the awful bruising and split lip. The entire side of her face is dark purple and blue.

He touched what's mine.

He *has* what's mine.

Aris always thought he could battle with me, and because he was fucking blood, I played his games. Enjoyed taunting him whenever I could. In a way, it was our screwed-up way of bonding. But then he crossed the line. Raped my goddamn woman. Stole her and kept her from me. And now he took my child.

Loyalty means nothing to that Demetriou.

Loyalty means everything to me.

This means fucking war.

When Talia was gone, I drifted. Lost in a fog of confusion and anger. Aris played me. Dangled me by his strings and reveled in my torment. Talia made me soft. I *wanted* to be soft for her. Only for her. But clearly, I softened in a way that exposed my weakness. I may as well have given Aris a fucking gun and said, "Point and shoot here."

For the last year, he's had a "blind me" on his side. He had money and resources. He had my lack of knowledge.

But now he's no longer battling a brother, he's in a war with a monster. He thought he could sneak into my compound and get away with this shit. Sadly, he was mistaken. I will gut Greece. Burn it to the motherfucking ground. I will fill every hole with gasoline and light it on fire. Every roach will come out of hiding and I will smash them until I find the rat.

Aris will be mine.

And I'll get my daughter back.

"Kostas," Talia says, her brows furrowing. "Are you okay?"

I gently grip her jaw and tilt her head to the side so I can inspect every dark shade of the abuse she endured yesterday. With the barest of a kiss, I whisper it over her sore flesh. My words of hate are breathed against her skin.

"He will pay for this."

She shivers and grips my wrist. I turn slightly to find her lips. Despite the cut on her lip, I kiss her hard enough to split it back open. The sweet, metallic taste of her mixes with the minty toothpaste, making me hunger for her more than any bagel this morning. If I had more time, I'd turn my aggressions into passion so I could whisper all my evil promises against her skin—promises to take out our enemy and bring home our treasure.

My phone buzzes and I nip at her sore lip once before I pull away.

Adrian: Press is already lined up at the gate. Josef is waiting, too. Where are we doing this?

Me: Hotel lobby. Send Josef to my office. I want to meet with him before we go public.

Adrian: On it.

"I have to meet with the Minister of Public Order. Then, I'll be doing a press release." I stroke my fingers through her hair that hangs in messy, natural-dry waves after the shower she took alone last night while I crashed into bed. "I need you to look the part of an angel."

Not that she'll have any trouble doing so.

Her brows furrow. "Why? What's going on?"

My perfect Talia and her never-ending quest for answers.

I drop my towel and nod at her to follow me while I dress. Throwing on some boxers and socks, I then make my way into our closet. The mess had been cleaned up by hotel staff before we went to bed, but the feeling of failure washes over me.

Zoe was taken from this very closet.

Talia lingers in the doorway, no doubt feeling sadness over last night and what went down in here. As I dress in a suit, she runs her fingers over one of her white dresses. She pulls it off the hanger and holds it up.

"This one?"

I rake my gaze down the serene, silky white material. "Perfect. And don't you dare cover up what he did to you. They need to see."

Her blue eyes dart back and forth. "Who? Who will need to see?"

Snagging a blue tie that matches her eyes, I slide it around my neck and begin knotting it. Once I've tightened it at my throat, I let out a heavy sigh of resignation.

"You are married to the monster Greece knows. Well, at least the one all the scum knows. *I* will reach them. I'm a Demetriou, it's what we do. But you," I say with a smile as I grab my jacket off a hanger. "*You* will reach the regular people. Every man, woman, and child in all of Europe. We're going to hit them from all sides. Just be you and you'll do exactly what I need you to." I step into my shoes and then walk over to her. "And you're going to have to let me be me."

"What exactly does that mean?"

"It means, I'm soft with you. In here, with our family, soft is good." My features morph into something wicked and furious. "But out there,

I need to be a blade forged in stone. I need to be unbreakable. I need to be powerful." I start to put my jacket on, but my arm winces in pain.

She purses her lips before dropping the dress in favor of helping me. She takes the jacket and holds it open so I can gingerly slide my bad arm into the sleeve. Once I have it pulled on and buttoned, I turn to regard her.

"You're hurting," she breathes. "Physically and in here." Her palm presses to my chest between my pectorals. "It's okay to be vulnerable. Our daughter is gone. They hurt us."

Sweet, innocent, pure angel.

I slide my fingers beneath her chin and tilt her head up. Blue eyes sparkle at me. She's so fucking strong. Only a woman like Talia could ever have the backbone and fire to be able to stand beside a Demetriou. She's fearless and determined. A fucking storm.

"Out there, I can't be. It's the only way to get Zoe back. The public needs an angel and the Underworld needs a fiery, unstoppable king." I kiss her nose. "Are we in this together?"

She smiles. "Since the day I saw you in that courtyard."

"You tried to run," I say, in a slightly playful tone.

"I wanted you to catch me."

Reluctantly, I pull away, needing to get a move on the day. "Make sure you grab something to eat. Basil will escort you. There'll be coffee and bagels in the lobby if you want that."

"I was thinking fruit. A pomegranate sounds good."

She pulls off her T-shirt, revealing her round tits and rosy nipples. Fuck, she does my head in when all I need is to focus.

"A pomegranate?" I ask, my voice husky as my dick strains in my slacks.

She bends to pick up the dress from the floor and holds it to her chest. Her blond hair cascades over one shoulder as she tilts her head to the side. "An angel can live in hell."

"Not without getting burned."

Sauntering over to me, she stands on her toes and kisses the corner of my mouth. "The devil wouldn't allow that."

"He already has," I growl, my palm finding her hip and squeezing possessively.

"But he won't let it happen again."

So confident and sure.

She's right.

"Go be the badass we need right now," she says, pushing on my chest to break us apart. "I'll be at my restaurant sucking on seeds until you let me suck on you later."

"Are you trying to kill me?"

"You'll need to relieve some tension and then you'll need a nap." She shrugs. "Because then we're going to go get our girl."

"Damn right."

I let my stare linger on the swell of her breasts and then up her slender throat before I latch my eyes to her parted lips. Fuck, how I want to yank her to me, drag her to the floor, and drive into her wildly. The desire to claim and own is fierce, but we have more pressing matters to attend to. And once we have our daughter back, I'll demand my fucked up happily ever after, one orgasm at a time.

Adrian flanks my right and Josef is on my left as we walk into the hotel lobby as a united front—the mob and the police coming together for the same agenda: take down Aris and find a baby. Talia will enter soon with Basil. I need to say what I need to say without her weakening my resolve. As soon as the press sees us, flashes start going off like rapid gunfire. The lights blind me, but I ignore them as I make my way to the podium that's been set up. Josef steps to the microphone first.

"Dear citizens of Crete Island," he starts, holding up his hand to end the buzzing chattering of questions being barked our way. "We're not here to answer questions, but to instead deliver a series of statements."

More flashes snap.

"Last year, good men and women of Cretan General Hospital were gunned down in a tragic terrorist event. The Demetriou family, while dealing with their own familial tragedies, were instrumental in eliminating the threat at that time." Josef gives me a grim smile to which I nod so he'll continue. "His father, the late Ezio Demetriou, was a friend to me and a pillar in this community. The philanthropic donations of this family have been what's kept the island profitable and successful. With…" He flashes me another look and I nod. "With Ezio's recent, natural passing—something the family had wished to keep quiet so they could grieve in private but are no longer able to—we are faced with terrorism once again. There are those who see the Demetrious' efforts as something to destroy, making these attempts when they are down. Last night, they tried to do exactly that. But they are wrong. Our people and the Demetrious aren't broken so easily. We will fight for peace and profit."

He steps away from the podium and gestures for me to take his place. I keep my features cool and impassive. Whenever I lock stares with a reporter, they cower under my gaze and look away.

"My family is the proud owner of the Pérasma Hotel. Last night, men stormed our gates and tried to destroy what we built." *Men ordered by my brother.* "Because we take security extremely seriously, none of our guests were hurt or even saw the terrible situation unfold. We lost a few good men protecting the people at our hotel."

More flashes go off as reporters demand to know the names.

I raise my hand, effectively silencing them all. "They were hired on to do a job for the Demetriou family. And they did it well. But now we need for you all to do your job."

A flash of white in the back of the room indicates Talia has arrived. She's clutching a soft pink blanket and a newly framed picture of Zoe. Basil escorts my wife past the curious onlookers and to the podium with me. I pull her close, sharing the microphone with her.

"I'm a private man," I say, my voice hard as steel. "I keep my personal life out of the spotlight. Because of my influence in Greece, people think they can use my personal life as a weakness against me." I lean over to inhale Talia's sweet scent before kissing the top of her head, earning more pops of flashes. I turn back to the crowd, my glare once again affixed. "Last year, I wed the woman I loved in a secret ceremony for just the two of us. But then she was taken from me." People demand to know by whom, but I ignore them. Everyone underground knows it was Aris and that's all that matters. "When I found her again, she brought home a Demetriou princess. My strong, resilient wife survived the atrocities of capture, delivered our daughter while in captivity, and found the strength to make her way back to me."

Talia starts to cry and clings to me, which sends the media into a frenzy.

"Last night, while we worked to keep our people safe, the terrorists came in and took our daughter."

The press starts shouting, horrified and demanding answers.

"She's…" I trail off and swallow hard. "My wife, Talia, would like to speak about her."

She sniffles as she pulls away slightly. "Our little girl Zoe was kidnapped." Her body trembles as she holds the blanket to her and shows the crowd the picture. "She's sweet and curious and laughs and…" A sob chokes her. "Oh God, I just want her back in my arms."

I stroke my fingers through her hair in a possessive way while staring down every camera in the room, commanding them with one look. *Find my fucking daughter and bring her to me alive.*

"I beg of you," Talia pleads. "If anyone knows anything, please help us. We need her. She doesn't deserve this."

"Our fine Minister of Public Order has set up a call center to take any and all calls. Calls leading to the finding of our daughter will be handsomely rewarded," I say into the microphone. This is for the normal, everyday citizens. They'll look for her because that's what good people do, money or not. They want to reunite a child with their family.

But I need the bad people looking too.

"Fifty million euros."

The room explodes with excitement.

"She was last seen with Aris Demetriou and Selene Vincent." The crowd gasps again. I ramble through their physical descriptions while deliberately leaving off the fact Aris is my brother. They all know this. I don't need to fucking say it. Everyone underground will see this as one concrete fact: Aris Demetriou is dead to me.

"Twenty-four hours. If she's found within that time frame, I'll reward the finder additionally in ways I see fit." Meaning, they will get a favor with the Demetrious, which is priceless. "Thank you all for your help."

The group goes wild with questions, and seven of my men have to flank us to get us away from the crowd. Once we're safely inside my office, I give Adrian a nod to clear the lobby of the press and tell him to apprise me of any new developments. The moment I have the door closed and locked, I collect my emotional wife in my arms.

"You did great," I murmur against her hair. "We need everyone's help in finding her."

"I miss her," she whimpers.

"Me too, *moró mou.*"

She tilts her head up to look at me, her eyes red and swollen from her crying. "The people who hate you know everything now. That your father's dead. That you're married. That you have Zoe. That your brother betrayed you. You showed your hand, Kostas."

I sweep my palm delicately over her bruised cheek and then run my fingers through her hair. "It was the only way to get her back. We *will* get her back."

"What if someone hurts her to get back at you?" she whispers, a fat tear rolling down her cheek.

I kiss the wetness on her skin and close my eyes. "We have to trust that money talks. The only one who cares about revenge over money is Aris. The citizens of Crete Island and every piece of scum who knows the Demetriou name will be hunting for our little girl. There's no way we can know where Aris went and turning over every stone would take precious time we don't have. All we can do is let the people do what we can't. We have to trust this will work."

"What if it doesn't work?"

"It's our only option, Talia."

"I'm scared."

"I know," I breathe against her soft lips. "I'm doing the best I can."

"I know you are and I love you for that."

Her lips press forcefully to mine as a fierce growl leaves her throat. The kiss takes me by surprise, especially when her hands begin frantically sliding my jacket off my shoulders and sending it to the floor before yanking at my belt. My cock—ever ready to play with his favorite pussy—stiffens in my slacks. Pre-cum leaks from me as the desperate need to fill her overtakes me. She pulls my dick from its confines and kneels before me.

"Talia," I rumble, my fist grabbing into her hair, ready to pull her back up to my level. I pause to admire how fucking gorgeous she is.

Her blue eyes are intent and dark with lust as her tongue slides between her plump lips and flicks against my wet tip. A hiss rushes past my teeth as I stare at the angel queen who bows before her evil king. Pure wickedness gleams in her eyes as she circles my slit with her hot tongue, her expression equal parts hungry and taunting. I could pull her up to her feet and fuck her senseless, but I'm mesmerized by her devious stare and pretty mouth that's stained the color of pomegranate from breakfast. She slides her mouth over the crown and a growl rumbles from me. I close my eyes, dizzied by the bliss. Her mouth bobs up and down over my length as she desperately feeds my cock into her hungry mouth. When her teeth scrape my tender flesh as she tries to take me deep in her throat, the need to have her completely overwhelms me.

"Stand up," I command. "I need to be inside you."

Her mouth pops off my dick as she shakily rises to her feet. I waste no time grabbing her full ass and lifting her. She fuses her swollen lips to mine and kisses me just as she was my dick a moment ago. I shove her against the wall as I reach between us to grip my cock. She moans when I slide my tip along her wet slit over her panties, seeking the tight warmth only her body can gift to me. I push the head of my dick under the side hem of her panties to tease her bare flesh with my own and seek entrance. With a painful flex of my hips, I drive all the way into her, her wet panties rubbing along the side of my dick as lubricant. As I fuck my wife against the wall, I can feel the burn as my stitches tear free. I could opt for a better position, but only one goal is in my mind.

Take Talia.

I grip her ass with one hand and squeeze her tit with the other as I drive into her hard. Her mouth owns mine as she fucks my mouth with her tongue. Her thighs tighten around my waist, only further irritating my wound. I'm about to come, but a wave of dizziness has me struggling to keep Talia upright. With her still on my dick, I carry her over to my desk. I sit her ass down on the surface and then push her back, breaking our kiss. She whimpers at the loss.

"Pull your dress up your hips and let me see what I'm fucking," I rasp out, ignoring the pain lancing through my body.

She yanks up the material, fisting it just under her breasts that jiggle each time I drive into her. Her heels rest on the edge of the desk and her thighs are parted open in a dirty, inviting way that makes me want to recreate this moment later when our life is back to normal and I can call her filthy names like my "needy little slut." Names I know will turn her on while getting nasty in my office, but names that don't quite fit the moment.

"Touch me," she commands, her blue eyes intense as she drags me away from the fact that our daughter is still missing and nothing will be normal until she's found. "Right now, it's just us, Kostas."

Failure and loss fade for the moment as I run my fingers along her throbbing clit over her panties. She cries out in surprise when I rip the fabric apart and toss it away. Her hips lift and she clenches around my cock. I easily circle my fingers in a way that strums my wife into having the most beautiful sounds leave her lips.

Someone knocks on the door and we both grind out words at the same time.

"Go the fuck away!"

"We'll be out in a minute!"

Our eyes lock and I thrust hard against her, pinching her clit in tandem with each glide inside her. When I notice blood on her leg, I run my free fingers through it, marveling at the smears along her tanned flesh. Her body seizes with pleasure and her breasts jut forward as her back arches. I'm captivated with how wild and so damn beautiful she is as her pussy squeezes the fuck out of me. I groan, nearly collapsing as my balls tighten and then my release spurts furiously inside her. Cum leaks out as I slide in and out of her, filling her with everything I have. When I'm wrung dry, I slip from her hot body and stagger back, trembling and my still-hard dick dripping.

"Fucking gorgeous," I hiss, my eyes raking down her perfect body and settling at her pussy.

Bright red and raw from being fucked hard.

Thick, white cum runs down her used slit toward her ass crack.

Shaking thighs as she recovers from her orgasm.

I step closer despite the spinning around me and collect my cum on my finger. Our eyes meet when I push it back into her needy body. She whimpers and squirms as I fuck my jizz back into her cunt with just my finger. Once I'm sure it's deep inside where it belongs, I curl my finger up and seek out the part of her that'll make her scream. She shakes her head as though she can't take any more, which only urges me to show her she can. I add another finger and press the hot, throbbing spot inside her until she grips the edge of the desk with both hands and bellows my name. Her hips ride up, doing their own little dance to meet the movement of my fingers until she comes down from her high. I slip my hand away from her and admire the dark, pink depths that remain open and inviting to me. With one clench, she hides that part of herself from me, sending more cum pushing out of her pussy.

"I need…" she whispers, closing her thighs. "I need to shower and change and eat and…oh my God, you're bleeding!"

I shrug as I glance down at my white dress shirt that's seeping with blood. "It was worth it."

She sits up and then stands in front of me. Her dress falls into place and I want to pout over the fact that I can't watch my cum slide down her inner thighs. "Let's go home and get cleaned up so we can find our girl."

"Talia," I growl as I grip her throat and draw her to me. I press my lips to hers. "I love you."

Her lips break into a smile—one that's been missing the past twelve hours. "I love you too."

"We're going to find her."

"I know we are."

<h1 style="text-align:center">chapter eighteen</h1>

Talia

IT'S BEEN FIVE DAYS SINCE KOSTAS AND I STOOD IN FRONT OF ALL of Greece and pleaded with the people to help locate our little girl. Five days since he offered them millions of euros to locate Aris and Selene. And it's been five long as hell days of sifting through the thousands of leads that end in nothing but dead ends. Everybody wants a chance at the money, which means everybody thinks they've seen our little girl. I've sat in Kostas's office with him and his men for hours upon hours, clicking on lead after lead, blowing up image after image, hoping to spot one of them. I've seen several dozen redheaded women, hundreds of men in suits, and I've looked at enough babies that they all have blurred into one of the same. But none of them are the people we're looking for.

It wasn't until my eyes were itchy and I felt like I was going cross-eyed that Kostas ganged up on me with my mom and made me go home to take a break. I begged and pleaded, but they insisted.

"*Cara mia*," Mom coos. "Please, you have to eat something." She pushes the homemade chicken soup closer to me. The aroma fills my nostrils and my stomach growls in hunger. I can't even remember the last time I ate something besides an energy bar. "You need to be strong for your little girl, and in order to be strong, you must take care of yourself."

She leans in and rubs her thumbs along my cheeks and then under my eyes. "You have dark circles under your eyes. You need to sleep."

"I have slept," I argue, pulling my face out of her grasp.

"More than a couple hours," Phoenix adds. He's been staying at the hotel, helping to check out any leads that come through that Kostas feels are worth investigating further, which is almost all of them. My husband is determined to find our daughter, and if there's a slight possibility someone's lead could be the one that takes us to her, he wants it investigated. He has hundreds of men scouring the country on top of the thousands of leads that are being emailed and called in.

And with each passing hour, each lead that hits a wall, I get more anxious that Aris has disappeared where nobody can find them.

"Talia, please," Mom begs. "Just a few bites."

Not wanting to argue with them, I bring the spoon to my lips. But before I can take a bite, I imagine my daughter locked up somewhere with Aris and Selene, hungry and tired and cold, and a sob racks through my entire body. I drop the spoon back into the bowl, and hot liquid splashes out, burning my hand. "How am I supposed to eat when I don't even know if my little girl is being fed?" I push the bowl away. There's no way I can eat until I know she's safe in my arms and her tummy is full.

I stand at the same time Mom does. She envelops me in her arms and I breathe in her floral scent. "What if she's hungry?" I cry out. "Or lonely?" My entire body shakes against my mom's as she holds me tight. I can feel an anxiety attack coming on, but I already know I won't be able to stop it. I've been having them every day since Zoe was taken. "What if they've hurt her…or worse…" I can't even finish my sentence. My words are cut off with my cries. My head pounds so hard it feels like my entire body is vibrating. My heart is racing, and my legs feel like noodles.

"Talia, you have to calm down," she says as I begin to hyperventilate. She walks us over to the couch and helps me to sit. I try to take in gulps of air, but it's hard to breathe. My sweet little baby is somewhere out there with two crazy psychos who don't love her. They don't even care about her. Anything can happen to her, and every second she's gone is less of a chance of ever finding her alive.

Stefano appears in front of me with a glass of water. "Here, sweetheart, take these." He extends his hand with two pills, but I shake my head.

"No, I need to be awake and lucid in case a solid lead comes in." The last thing I want is to be out cold when my daughter needs me.

"Talia, you can't keep going like this," Mom demands. "Please, it will help you to calm down and rest. If a lead comes through, we'll wake you up. Kostas is handling it."

I want to argue with them, but they're right. I haven't slept in what feels like days. My body is over exhausted and shaking like a leaf in a storm.

With trembling hands, I take the glass and pills from Stefano. After swallowing them, my mom pulls me back into her side and rocks me until my body gives up and my eyes close.

My eyes flutter open, and when I look around, I see I'm in my bed. I listen for Zoe. The villa is quiet. Is she sleeping? What time is it? Does Kostas have her? And then I remember she's not here. She's missing. And my heart cracks all over again.

My phone vibrates on the end table and I grab it to see who is calling. Kostas. I check the time. It's ten o'clock at night. I've been sleeping for almost eight hours thanks to the pills Stefano gave me.

I quickly answer the call, hoping he has good news. "Have you found her?"

"No, there's been no leads that have panned out."

My heart falls into my stomach. No leads. In a couple hours, it's going to hit midnight and it will be another day without my baby girl.

"I was calling to check on you," he adds. His voice sounds worried. My mom must've told him I had another anxiety attack.

"Are you in your office?" I ask, sitting up and throwing the blankets off me.

"I am, but you need to get some sleep," Kostas says softly.

"I've been sleeping all afternoon. I'll be there in a few minutes."

I shower quickly, get dressed, and brush my teeth to get rid of the bad taste in my mouth. Then, I head to Kostas's office, Basil hot on my trail. I'm thankful for my ever-present shadow. Mom and Stefano must've gone back to their villa for the night.

On the way, I see Phoenix walking down the pathway. He gives me a sad smile. "I was checking out another lead," he says. "Another dead end."

"Thank you for helping." I wrap my arms around his waist and give him a hug.

"There's nowhere else I would be," Phoenix assures me. "We're going to find her, Talia."

I want to believe him, but with each passing day, my hopes are shattered more and more. None of it makes any sense. If Aris wanted money, he would've contacted us by now. If he wanted to use her as a bargaining chip to steal the business from Kostas, he would've reached out. And since Kostas made sure to announce publicly that Ezio is dead, Aris has to know by now that his father is no longer alive.

But he's been completely silent. And that's what worries me. If he took her with the intent to keep her, he could be anywhere by now, and we may never see her again. At least if he took her with the purpose of using her to negotiate, we could give him what he wants and get our daughter back. The problem is Aris believes Zoe is his. A lie I told at the time to save us, but now regret.

As I walk through the doors of the office, I see Kostas and a thought hits me. "Kostas." He glances my way and walks toward me. "You told the world that Zoe is your daughter."

"Yeah…" Kostas gives me a confused look.

"Aris thought she was his. If he heard your speech, he knows she's not his." My hands cover my mouth as I remember what Aris said to me when I told him Zoe was his.

"Talia, talk to me," Kostas demands.

"Aris warned me that if he ever found out the baby wasn't really his, I would pay." I lied to him for over a year, swore up and down the baby was his… "What if he took her to use her as a bargaining chip, but once he found out she wasn't really his, he changed his mind?" My heart begins to race, and my head feels cloudy. Another anxiety attack is surfacing. "He could be keeping her just to make me pay." This could be all my fault. I never should've lied to Aris.

"Talia, calm down," Kostas says, taking me in his arms. "It doesn't matter what Aris knows or doesn't know. It changes nothing. You told him what he needed to hear to keep you and our little girl safe. We're going to find her."

"Boss," Adrian calls Kostas over. "Check out this image." He blows up a picture on the computer screen. It's of a man who meets Aris's description carrying a baby, but we can't see any faces.

"Where was this taken?" Kostas asks.

"The airport about thirty minutes ago," Adrian says.

"He wouldn't just walk through the airport," I say out loud. Aris is too smart for that, even if the man holding the baby looks almost identical to him.

"Probably not," Kostas agrees. "But we're following every possible lead."

He looks over his shoulder. "Phoenix," he barks. "Airport." Without asking any questions, Phoenix comes over and gets the information from Adrian then takes off.

We spend the next couple hours going through emails and calls of leads. When it's nearly four in the morning and I can tell Kostas is dragging, I tell him we need to go home. He looks like he wants to argue, but doesn't.

When we get home, he takes a quick shower and meets me in bed. With his arms around me, I snuggle into the crook of his neck. "Six days," I whisper. Tomorrow it will be a week.

"We're going to find her," Kostas says for a millionth time, his voice filled with as much conviction as the first time he said it.

As my eyes are closing, his phone rings loudly throughout the room. He leans over and answers it. "Yeah." He sits up straight, knocking my head off his body. "You sure?" I can't hear who he's speaking to, but whoever it is, is talking fast. "I'll check right now."

Kostas places the phone on speaker and pulls up his email app. Peering over, I look to see what was emailed, and right there in color is a picture of Selene holding our daughter.

"That's her!" I gasp.

chapter nineteen

"O N MY WAY," I GROWL, SLINGING MY BODY OUT OF THE bed on a frantic hunt for clothes. "Pick me up in front of my villa in two minutes."

Talia flies out of the bed and starts dressing. "I can't believe they found her. Is it close? How long until we get there—"

"Not we," I bark out as I button my jeans and yank on a white T-shirt. "Me."

"Hell no," she screeches as she throws on her own clothes. "I'm going."

I don't have time to fight with her on this. All I do have time for is to grab my Glock from the bedside drawer and stalk out of the bedroom. Talia comes trotting after me. When I open the door, Basil is standing beside Adrian's SUV, talking to him.

"Hold down the fort," I bark out to Basil.

He nods before stepping away. I open the rear door and assist Talia in getting in before climbing into the front passenger seat.

Talia starts to sob in the back seat. When I glance back, I see that Adrian already loaded up the car seat. He feels it too. We're bringing her home. Thank fuck we have the cover of the dark, early morning. The last thing I need is for someone to tip Aris off.

Adrian hauls ass out of the hotel property and gets onto the main road. When he'd emailed me the pictures, he also emailed the location. Two hours from here on the other side of Crete Island near a small airport. Aris may have thought about trying to leave via plane but decided against it at the last minute because he has to know I have eyes everywhere, especially ports and airports. The motel we're headed to is a piece of shit one that hookers and johns use. I cringe thinking what sort of cesspool my baby's living in right now.

"Who'd the tip come from?" I ask as we drive.

"A maid."

"Just a maid?"

"Just a maid."

"Good," I grunt. "We won't owe any roaches shit. You'll have to get the maid to safety. The moment we wire her the money, she'll have a target on her back."

"Zoe first, maids later," Talia offers from the back seat.

I look over my shoulder and smile. "Zoe is always first."

The two-hour drive is tense and quiet. I answer calls and check in on different people. My main concern is Aris and Selene getting tipped off before we arrive. Soon, we're creeping through a small town twenty minutes from the coast. The sun has risen and a few restaurants blink their signs offering hot breakfast, making my stomach growl.

Zoe first, coffee and bagels later.

"It's up here," Adrian says.

"I'll go around front and you check the back," I order to him.

"I'm going with you," Talia says, trying her shit with me again.

I whip around and reach for her hand, pulling her close to me. With my eyes burning into hers, I kiss the back of her hand. "Not today."

"But—"

"I need you safe inside the SUV ready to drive off. Understood, *moró mou*? If Adrian and I should get injured, I need to be able to pass Zoe off to you and you get the fuck out of here. Please, for once in your stubborn fucking life listen to me." My words are spoken harshly to her, but I can't keep my wits about me if she's behind me. No fucking way. I need to be able to act without question.

Fat tears well in Talia's blue eyes, but she nods, sending them loose from her lids and skating down her cheeks.

"I love you," I whisper to her. "I *need* you to do this."

"I *can* do this," she says fiercely, swiping at her tears with her free hand. "I love you too."

I kiss her hand once more before releasing her to pull my Glock out of the center console and readying myself to act. Adrian parks a little ways up the road where we can see the small, aging, and decrepit motel, pointed toward the main road for a fast getaway. Several cars litter the parking lot.

"Which unit?" I demand.

"The maid said room six there on the end of the east side."

"We'll walk over to the west side and split around the building from there. Shoot first, ask questions later. At this point, put a bullet in Aris's skull. We can't risk him getting away. Zoe's safety is our primary concern." As much as I want to torture the fuck out of him, I can't let it cloud my judgment.

Adrian and I climb out of the SUV. When I glance back, I can see Talia scrambling to the front seat. Good girl. With my Glock ready, I nod at Adrian and then quietly walk along the front of the motel. He disappears around back. I pass by rooms one through three without incident, but when I get to the fourth room, I hear muffled crying not far off.

Zoe.

Panic swells up inside me and I quicken my pace, no longer worried about hiding. My sole focus is my daughter, whose crying gets louder the closer to room six I get. When I make it to the door, I press my ear to it.

"Shut up, stupid baby! Just shut the fuck up!"

When I hear what sounds like a slap, I step back and kick the door in. It slams against the wall and I charge inside, my gun drawn. Selene has Zoe in her arms and picks up a gun beside her. Zoe is red-faced and squirming, clearly pissed at being struck by this psycho cunt.

"Give me my fucking baby," I bellow, my gun aimed at Selene's face.

She presses the gun against Zoe's side. "Get the hell out of here!"

I don't move. Quickly I take stock of the situation. It smells like dirty diapers and hard liquor. Beside Selene on the end table are several empty bottles of alcohol. Between those are a few of Zoe's used bottles. My daughter wears a diaper and it's full of piss, hanging off her little body. A red handprint on her little thigh makes me want to bash Selene's head into the corner of the nightstand.

"Put Zoe down and I'll let you live."

"Liar," she snarls. "That's why I'm keeping this baby." When she digs the barrel of the gun into Zoe's side, she screams bloody murder.

Fuck.

I could put a bullet in her head, but she's holding Zoe too close to her. With the way Zoe flails and squirms, I could accidentally hit her. I can't take that chance.

"Money? You want money?" I ask, my gun still trained on her. "I'll give you money and ship your ass to another country. You don't fucking deserve it, but that'll be my trade. It's the best goddamn offer you have."

Her eyes dart to the window, her brows furrowing. "I need this baby. I need him."

She looks like shit. Her red hair is dull and stringy and she's not wearing makeup. A big blackish purple bruise mars her throat. Someone grabbed her neck hard enough to leave a mark. If I had my guess, it's that my brother's been hitting the bottle and lost his temper on her. I just hope they didn't hurt Zoe. The red mark on her leg is infuriating enough. I can't imagine more.

Zoe's screams get louder and louder. She's pissed. I'd like to think it's because she hears my voice and wants me, but she's only six months old, so that's probably not right. I don't know much about babies. What I do know is she'll be one happy kid the moment she's in her mother's arms rather than this cunt's.

"He doesn't want you," I grind out. Delusional bitch. "You were always a cover for him." That much I realize now. Had I thought he was remotely interested in Talia, I would've shaken him down a lot sooner. But the fact he pretended to love Selene and I thought he wanted to marry her, he was able to fool me.

"He does want me!" she cries out. "He loves me and one day I'll give him a baby of our own. We won't need that stupid bitch's baby anymore!"

This is taking too long.

Adrian is probably outside wondering what's going on but won't enter, especially if he overhears me trying to talk her down. But Talia? She's probably panicking. I know her. The last thing I need is her flying in here like a loose cannon upsetting the situation even further.

"Put the gun down," I command, my voice loud and sharp.

Crash!

The motel shakes as something explodes nearby. It's enough to distract Selene to jerk her head toward the sound, dropping her guard.

Pop!

I put a bullet on the part of her body farthest from my daughter. Her foot. She screams, dropping Zoe, who rolls to the floor with a loud thud. My daughter screams—which is music to my fucking ears considering the drop to the floor—and I stalk forward. She's okay. Selene raises the gun and I put a bullet into her shoulder. Another one pierces her throat. I want to make her hurt. She gurgles, grabbing her throat as blood sprays. With my eyes on her, I scoop up Zoe, tucking her under my arm like a football. Selene gapes at me as she tries and fails to stop the blood flow.

Pop!

I hit her in the stomach. I want her to bleed to death, thinking about what she did. How she struck my goddamn daughter. How she hurt my wife. How she aided my brother in an unimaginable crime.

Tucking my gun into the back of my jeans, I pull Zoe to my chest and kiss her sweaty head. "Shh, I've got you."

Selene has slumped against the headboard of the bed, but she's still alive, trying desperately to hold onto her life. I stalk over to her and grab a handful of her greasy red hair. Slamming her head down, I connect it with the corner of the end table, ending her misery early. Her skull cracks and she'll be dead in seconds. If I had more time or if I didn't have my daughter in my arms, I would've tortured her.

Turns out, I'm a family man now.

Torture can't happen at every enemy encounter. Sometimes I need to be quick and efficient to get back to what's important.

"Let's go see Mommy now," I coo to Zoe. "Daddy's here. No need to be upset."

Zoe grabs my shirt and screams, still super pissed at being slapped, screamed at, and then dropped. Fuck, I'd be pissed too. Holding her to me, I step outside the door I kicked in and frown when I see Adrian's SUV rammed into the unit beside this one. Talia is sitting behind the wheel looking every bit like a mafia queen. Wild eyes. Furious stare. Protective motherly aura rippling toward me in hot waves.

"What did you do to my fuckin' car, woman?" Adrian gripes as he comes up behind me.

"I stayed in the car!" she yells out. "I obeyed! Now bring me my baby!"

Zoe screams harder and tries to flip out of my grip.

Someone wants their mother.

chapter twenty

Talia

MY FIRST THOUGHT WHEN I SAW KOSTAS STALKING TOWARD the SUV with our baby in his arms was that she's alive and safe and I can finally breathe again. My second thought was how fucking sexy my husband looked holding our daughter to his chest like she's his entire world. Those hands that are capable of killing and torturing are also capable of being gentle and loving. When his eyes met mine, I could see the hardness in his light eyes—quite the contradiction—but the moment he looked down at Zoe, who was crying, his eyes went soft. The same way they go soft when he looks at me.

Once I stop staring at his eyes, and how precious our little girl looks in his arms, I notice the blood. Blood everywhere. All over their clothes, and splattered across their flesh.

"Is that blood?" I jump out of the driver's seat and run around the back, needing to get to Zoe and Kostas. "Is she bleeding?" I snatch her out of Kostas's hands and start checking her for injury. Her face is red and swollen from crying and there's a handprint mark on her thigh, but there're no cuts.

"It's not hers," Kostas says. "We're both okay."

"Who the fuck slapped her?" I bring her thigh up to show him. I'm seeing red. I don't see Selene or Aris anywhere. Did those fuckers touch my baby and then leave her here? That blood better be theirs.

"Selene did," Kostas says through a growl, his jaw tightening.

"Please tell me that bitch is alive," I hiss. "I'm going to fucking kill her."

Kostas shakes his head. "She's dead."

"Did she at least suffer?" I rub my daughter's thigh while holding her close to my chest. Her crying is already calming down.

"This is her blood," Kostas tells me. "I made sure that bitch was in pain before I ended her life."

"And what about Aris?" I glance around, suddenly realizing we've only been discussing Selene.

"He wasn't here," Adrian says.

"What?" I screech. Zoe jumps in my arms, and I remind myself I need to stay calm. "He can be anywhere." My gaze flits around us, hating that we're standing outside. He could be about to pounce.

"We're going to find him," Kostas promises. "Right now, we need to get our daughter home."

Kostas is right. Zoe's diaper is filled to the brim and leaking. She probably has a diaper rash. Who the hell knows when she was fed last. If that bitch wasn't already dead, I would torture and kill her my fucking self. Aris better run far because when I get my hands on him, I'm going to make sure he suffers for the both of them.

"We need to find a hotel," I tell the men as we climb into the SUV. Luckily, when I drove into the front of the building, hoping to create a diversion, the siding was rotted wood and no major damage was done. "We need to get her diapers and clothes and formula. She can't go two hours like this. I need to give her a bath."

The heaviness of everything that's happened is hitting me like a two-ton weight on my chest, and it's hard to breathe. "We need to get her to a doctor," I say through a sob. "What if…what if they hurt her?" I'm supposed to put Zoe in her car seat, but I can't let her out of my arms. She's clinging to me like a little koala bear.

Kostas tells Adrian to stop at the store, and while he runs in to grab stuff for Zoe, Kostas calls a local hotel and makes a reservation. The entire time, Zoe's tiny, chubby arms are wrapped around me with her face snuggled into my chest.

Oh, God, I finally have her back in my arms.

My heart is racing.

I need to get her as far away as possible. To somewhere safe.

What if Aris is following us? Waiting to make his move. What if this is all a trap?

I'm so tired, and all I want to do is snuggle up with my baby, but I need to make sure she's safe.

As I watch her, I notice she's fighting sleep. She's probably too scared. Whatever those pieces of shit did to her has my baby too scared to let herself go to sleep.

When we arrive at the hotel, Adrian checks us in and then both men flank me as we ride the elevator to the top floor. Only my husband would book the Presidential suite when we're only going to be here for a couple hours.

Adrian remains outside, while Kostas and I head inside. While I give Zoe a bath, checking to make sure there's nothing visibly wrong with her, Kostas rinses off as well. Adrian must've gotten him clothes because when he gets out, he's in a plain white T-shirt and a pair of gray sweatpants.

Once they're both cleaned up, I sit on the couch with Zoe while Kostas makes her a bottle. I hold her close and take in her sweet baby scent, thankful to have her back in my arms.

Her eyes are almost closed at this point, most likely exhausted from everything she's been through, but she's still fighting to stay awake.

My strong fighter. Just like her daddy.

The second the bottle touches her lips, she sucks it down. Her eyes begin to droop, and her stiff body loosens in my arms.

"She was so hungry," I mumble, trying hard to stay strong for my daughter, but inside I'm a mess.

Something worse could've happened to her.

We could've lost her.

"She's a baby," Kostas says. "She'll soon forget what they did to her." He runs his fingers through her head of soft dark curls.

"I'll never forget," I tell him.

And I won't.

Not until the day I die.

Every thought in my being is fueled by the urge to hunt Aris down and punish him for this.

For putting my baby in harm's way.

One day we're going to find him, and when we do. I will make him pay.

"As soon as we get home, we're going to get shit organized and find Aris," Kostas promises. His words hit me. *Home.* The hotel. The villa where Zoe was taken. The thought of bringing her back there has my heart racing.

"I can't go back there," I blurt out, and Kostas's eyes widen. "I know it's your home, but…"

"*Our* home," Kostas growls out without letting me finish.

"Kostas…"

"If the next words out of your mouth are to tell me you're leaving me, so help me fucking God." Kostas stands, towering over me. Zoe's bottle is empty and she's sleeping soundly in my arms. "You're my fucking wife, and that's our daughter, and if you think I'm going to let you leave me, you better think twice," Kostas chokes out. "I know I fucked up, Talia. Her getting taken is on me." He pounds his fist against his chest, and his eyes bore into mine. "But you aren't fucking leaving me. Ever."

"Kostas, that's not what I was going to say." I consider laying Zoe down, but I can't do it. So instead I stand, still holding her, and walk over to him. "I'm not going anywhere without you."

Kostas's shoulders drop slightly in relief. "Tell me what you need, *zoí mou.*"

"A place where we'll feel safe. A home where Aris hasn't touched and soiled. Maybe one with a pool, so I can take Zoe swimming. But it needs to be secure so nobody gets to us." I just need a damn break. A moment to be at peace with my family without living in fear. It can be months or years before we find Aris, and the hotel no longer feels like my safe place since it's where he stole our daughter. There's no way I'm going to be able to sleep at night, knowing that's where she was taken from.

"I'll handle it," Kostas assures me, already pulling his phone out. "Why don't you and Zoe go lie down and rest and once she wakes up, we'll head out."

Before I head to the room, I step closer to Kostas, and with Zoe sleeping between us, give him a soft kiss. "I don't blame you for any of this. Never think that. I blame Aris and Selene."

Kostas nods once, but I can tell by the way his eyes flinch slightly, he'll always in some way blame himself for not keeping Zoe safe. And I get it, because I'll always blame myself as well.

When we pull up to the house—no, house isn't the right word, more like castle—Kostas gets out and unbuckles Zoe. She's awake now and goes willingly with him. Unlike where Aris kept us, this place is backed up to the beach. I can smell the salt and hear the waves. My heart already feels steadier. My body already feeling lighter.

Surrounding the home is a tall block wall with a wrought iron fence running along the top. From what I can tell, it runs around the entire perimeter of the property. The house is at least three stories tall.

"Nobody is getting in or out of here without my knowledge," Kostas says. "The home is owned by a well-known politician. It's equipped with cameras and has a surveillance room. Once Adrian sets it all up, we'll be able to see every inch of this place right from our phones. And those fences"—he points to the walls—"they're wired with five thousand volts of electricity. One touch and it will knock a person the fuck out."

"Thank you," I tell him, feeling like the weights have been removed from my chest and I can finally breathe again.

"Let's go inside."

The inside is completely furnished. Beautiful shades of cream and bright blue. White wash wood everywhere, giving the entire place an up-scale beachy vibe. To the left is a huge living room and dining room—a massive floor-to-ceiling fireplace separating the two. To the right, from what I can tell, is the kitchen. In the middle is a stunning white wash spiral staircase that leads to the upstairs.

"Can we stay here forever?" I joke.

Kostas doesn't laugh, though. "If you want to."

My head whips around to face him. "Are you serious?"

"If this is where you'll feel safe, then it's yours." He shrugs like it's no big deal, when it is in fact a huge deal. This house must cost millions, and he'll buy it just because I love it.

It doesn't matter what I ask for, he always makes sure I get what I want. He said it in his vows that he would make sure I'm always happy, and while I didn't believe them at the time, I know now he meant them. Even back then, when we barely knew each other, he was promising to put my happiness first.

Before I can say anything back, the front door opens and in walks Mom, Stefano, and Phoenix.

"Oh, *miei cari*," Mom cries out. *My darlings.* She runs straight toward Zoe and me and wraps her arms around us. "I was so worried," she cries, which makes me cry.

"We're okay, Mom. Zoe is okay."

Zoe wiggles in my arms and her bright blue eyes pop open. She grants my mom the most beautiful gummy smile, and Mom's and my tears fall even harder.

"Da-da-da," she coos, and Kostas laughs. Of course the only sound she's still making sounds like *Dad.*

"She already knows who she needs to call to get whatever she needs," Kostas says, taking her from me and holding her to his chest.

I sigh, watching him whisper something to our daughter. I don't think I will ever tire of watching him hold her.

"This house is gorgeous," Mom says. "How long are you staying here?"

"Until we find Aris," I tell her at the same time Kostas says, "As long as Talia wants."

We spend the day by the pool—yes, the house has a stunning infinity pool and Jacuzzi—enjoying Zoe. Kostas frequently takes calls, no doubt determined to find Aris. For the first time in months I feel safe and don't even bother to ask him for updates. I'm simply content living in this temporary bubble.

For dinner, Kostas has one of his men pick up groceries and Stefano grills burgers while my mom and I make the side dishes. Everything feels so normal. I know being with Kostas means nothing will ever really be normal, and there will always be threats. My husband is a powerful man who runs a dangerous organization. But seeing another side to him today—him sitting on the lounge chair in his swim trunks, eating a burger and baked beans, and swimming in the pool with Zoe—gives me hope that after we find and kill Aris, we will be able to finally start our life as a family.

After dinner, everyone leaves, and it's only Kostas, Zoe, and me. While we were out back, he of course had her furniture brought over. Her room is upstairs, directly next to ours, but he also had a portable crib put in our room for now.

"Thank you for putting a crib in here." I lay Zoe in her bed. "It's going to take some time until I'm comfortable with her sleeping in her own room." She's been fed, has a fresh diaper, and is sucking on her pacifier, already half asleep.

"She'll stay with us until you're ready," Kostas says. "But I promise you, she's safe in this house." He locks our bedroom door. "Come shower with me."

When I give him a look, silently asking why he locked our door, he says, "I want to make sure none of my men accidently walk in and see my sexy wife naked. Then I'll have to kill them."

I laugh even though I believe he really would do just that.

With my hand in his, he guides us into the bathroom. From here, we can still see Zoe's crib.

I watch as he pushes his trunks down his muscular thighs, and his thick cock springs free. His eyes meet mine, and the love that shines in them takes my breath away. I've always thought Kostas was sexy, but seeing him as a father, interacting with our daughter, makes him beautiful. And when he looks at me the way he is right now, knowing that underneath all that darkness is a lightness only reserved for Zoe and me to see, makes my heart swell.

I strip out of my bikini, keeping my eyes on Kostas as his heated gaze runs over every inch of my body. If looks could burn, I would be on fire.

"Come here, wife," he demands. He turns the water on and steps into the shower first. There are several showerheads raining down on us, so no matter where we stand warm water hits us.

"How are you feeling?" he asks, framing my cheeks with his strong hands. Our bodies are flush against one another, and he has me backed up against the wall.

"I'm good," I tell him honestly. My eyes flit out of the open shower and into our bedroom, thankful I can see Zoe. "I'm not sure I'll ever be able to let her out of my sight."

"Does that mean when she's a teenager, we can keep her locked up?" Kostas asks, his lips twitching in amusement. I love every side of him. The serious, the sweet, the silly.

"Don't rush my baby growing up." I pout, and Kostas grins.

With his thumb and finger on my chin, he tilts my head up and his lips descend on mine. My arms cling to his neck as our mouths tangle and our tongues duel with one another. Tasting. Coaxing. Getting lost in each other. I didn't realize how much I needed his touch, to feel him until now. We kiss until the water turns cold, and then after quickly washing our bodies, Kostas carries me out of the shower.

With both of us dripping wet, he sets me on the sink and spreads my thighs. His mouth goes right back to mine, his tongue massaging mine. His hands grip my hips, and he pulls me toward him. My hot center rubs against his pelvis. My fingers wrap around his hard shaft, and I stroke it, getting it hard, before I guide it into me.

Kostas's mouth leaves mine to watch as he enters me slowly, filling me with every inch of him. We both watch as we become one. When I'm filled to the hilt with him, he pulls out slowly.

"Do you see this?" he asks, already knowing I do. "Your cunt was made just for me." My insides tighten at his dirty words, and he smirks. He pushes himself back into me, hitting my G-spot.

"Faster," I beg, desperate to find my release. My breasts are heavy and my nipples are painfully erect. I need more, but he's refusing to give it to me.

"There's no rush, *moró mou*," he purrs, continuing to push in and out slowly. Every time he enters me, the head of his cock hits me deep. Little by little, like a hurricane on the horizon, my orgasm builds higher and higher. With every thrust, I can feel it getting closer, gaining momentum.

Kostas finds my clit, and he massages it in circles, still watching as he enters me deeply and then draws out slowly. In and out. Bringing me to the precipice and then taking me away from the edge before I can fall.

"Kostas, please," I beg. Can one die from being denied an orgasm? I'd rather not find out.

When his eyes meet mine, his gaze is filled with lust and love. Heat and desire. My back arches slightly, and my breasts are thrust in his face. He takes a nipple between his lips, and when he bites down on it, my body convulses in pleasure.

His thumb leaves my clit, and he cages me in, somehow filling me even deeper than before. That's all it takes for my body to detonate. His mouth covers mine, muffling my screams of pleasure as he drives into me. My hips rise to meet his thrust for thrust as we both come completely undone.

My legs are shaking, and my body has gone limp. It takes a few minutes to calm my heavy breathing. Kostas pulls out of me and smirks at what I'm sure is his cum dripping between my legs. There's no doubt he's going to have me knocked up soon…and I can't fucking wait.

chapter twenty-one

Kostas

"YOU KNOW WHAT? FUCK HIM." I SCRUB MY PALM DOWN MY face before leveling Adrian with a hard glare. "I'm done going after him. It's what he wants."

"No," Adrian argues. "What he wants is to toy with you."

It's been days since we rescued our daughter. Days since we've used up all our energy looking for my brother. I'm over it, dammit.

"With what resources?" I demand. "I get that he could do that shit when he had access to the Demetriou fortune. When he had a bitch who worshiped the ground he walked on. When he had a fucking car. But now? He has fucking nothing. I'm done wasting precious time with my family to hunt down this motherfucker."

"I'll have Basil continue to probe his contacts. Just because you don't want to actively search for him doesn't mean we can't still keep an eye out for him," Adrian says.

A year ago, I would've fucked over a man with just my knife if he'd undermined my authority. Now, I think a little differently. Besides, Adrian means well and has my best interest at heart.

"You got anyone besides Basil?" I ask, irritation clipping my tone.

Adrian's brows knit together. I know they're like brothers, but brothers can fucking turn on you. I of all people know this. "Wesley is there. He's one of my best and most trusted."

"Give Wesley the same job. Then, we can compare notes on what information they give back to us."

Adrian is clearly annoyed, but he nods before texting. While he busies himself with the affairs of the dark side of my business, I have to deal with the legit side. I call and make arrangements with the hotel manager, Carla. She'll get started on hiring a construction crew to repair the damage Aris and Selene inflicted upon the hotel while also updating some areas of the hotel that need it. We'll be down for the season, but our other hotels in Crete and Santorini will bring in plenty of profit.

"Where's Phoenix?" I ask once he's done firing off messages.

"Last I saw, he was out by the pool with the girls."

I exit my office and make my way to the back door. As I exit, one of the men, Fowler, bows his head in respect. Phoenix stands by the pool like a sentry, looking more formidable than the five guards I have placed all over the backyard. He's dressed in a suit that fits his style unlike that shitty stuff he and his father always wore. It's like he belongs here. And I know he'd do anything to protect Talia.

Which makes him perfect for what I need him for.

Pushing through the door, I nod to him before walking over to the edge of the pool. Melody waves to me from a pool lounger. I crouch to give my wife a kiss and to grin at my daughter. She lets out a squeal of laughter, melting away all my anger and irritation. If I didn't have so much shit to do, I'd go swimming with them. But, even bad guys have to fucking work.

"My beautiful girls," I say before leaving them to play. I click my tongue and nod into the house, motioning for Phoenix to follow me. "Watch them," I bark out to Fowler.

"Always, sir," Fowler says back.

As soon as we're in my office with Adrian, I close the door and pull out the ouzo. I'm not the lush I once was, but now that I have my family back, I can relax with a drink from time to time. I make the three of us a drink and then settle in my office chair. Phoenix is guarded but stoic. I study him for a long while and decide that both he and Talia have Melody's strength. I tapped into her strength when Talia was missing, so I know this firsthand. With Niles gone, it's easier to note the similarities between the siblings. He's lucky. The fucker is growing on me. Talia sure as hell did.

"Your duties in Thessaloniki are over." I sip my ouzo and watch for his reaction.

His jaw ticks, but he doesn't show anger. "Is that so?"

"It is." I reach into my drawer and pull out a set of keys. "The Land Rover in the garage is yours. Trade it in for what you want."

He lifts a brow. "Okay. You going to elaborate?"

"Your father is dead. Your sister is here. What more do you want?"

"Not bullshit answers," he grumbles, frowning just like my fucking wife.

I let out a heavy sigh. "My brother betrayed me. You'd die for your sister. I need someone like that on my team. Someone who would give up anything to protect my wife. Is that someone you?"

"You want a Nikolaides to come work for a Demetriou?" He scoffs, shaking his head. "Never thought I'd see the day."

Adrian snorts out a laugh. We never saw this coming either. But here we are.

"Technically, you already did work for us in case you've forgotten," I grit out. "Again, are you willing to trade your glorious life back in Thessaloniki for one on Crete Island? You'll be paid handsomely."

"Like I've ever given a fuck about the money," he bites out. "All I care about is my family."

"Then that will be your reward, Phoenix. You'll have unlimited access to both my wife and my daughter. I'll bring you into the fold—erase your fucking Nikolaides past, and give you a Demetriou future. But once you're in, there's no getting out."

He leans back in his chair and gulps down his ouzo before setting the glass down hard. "What do you want me to do? Guard my sister?"

As much as I would love that added layer of protection, I need Phoenix for more.

"You've handled the taxes quite nicely. You have a flair for numbers, correct?"

He nods. "Dad sure as hell didn't. I learned at an early age how to run numbers to help his ass out."

"Good. I've just lost my numbers man." My chair creaks when I lean forward, placing my elbows on my desk and steepling my fingers. "The moment you're given the key to the castle, there is no turning back. If

I even sniff one ounce of you turning coat, I will fucking destroy you, Phoenix. I will make Talia cut into you and remove each organ for me. Are we clear?"

Adrian laughs again, earning a scowl from Phoenix.

"You're such a fucking psychopath," he grumbles. "And, no, I'd never do that shit to my sister. You have my word."

"Wonderful. Now run along and go trade that expensive ass car in for another stupid Jeep. We have to go over a mountain of shit. The sooner you get back, the sooner we can get to it." I wave him off with a flick of my hand.

Phoenix rises and gives Adrian an incredulous look. "Does he talk to you like that?"

"He grows on you," Adrian says with a snort.

"Right," Phoenix grumbles. He stops mid stride and turns to glower at me, making me tense. "And Jeeps aren't stupid. They're practical."

Adrian laughs. "Go on, boy, before you get bitch slapped."

"You assholes can fucking try," Phoenix says with a smirk that reminds me of Talia. Ornery fucker.

As soon as he's gone, I pull up my laptop and dive back into business, both legit and nefarious. A villain's work is never done.

I wake up in the dead of the night to my phone ringing off the hook.

"What?" I snarl into the line.

"Your father's place," Adrian barks out. "I'm on my way. Meet me there."

He hangs up on me. What the fuck? I slide out of bed and start throwing on clothes.

"Where are you going?" Talia asks, her voice raspy from sleep.

I lean over the bed and kiss her mouth. "Business. Phoenix and the men will be here. Your gun is in your bedside table. Use it if you need to."

As I start to pull away, she grabs my wrist. "I love you."

"Love you too."

Within five minutes, I'm dressed and locking the bedroom door behind me. I stalk down the hallway to the guest room where Phoenix is staying before pushing inside. When I flick on the lights, he snags his Glock and has it aimed in my direction. Good reflexes.

"Need you to keep an eye on Talia and Zoe. Something's happened at my father's place," I tell him before turning on my heel.

He pads behind me. "Another diversion?"

I stalk into the spare room where we have a gun safe and turn the dial on the lock. "I don't know, but we can never be too sure. Just in case"—I toss him an AR-15—"use brute force to protect them."

In nothing but boxers and socks, Phoenix still manages to look formidable with a Glock in one hand and the AR in the other.

"You think he's coming out of hiding?" he asks.

"Nah," I grunt as I push past him. "He's just fucking with me. It's what he does."

"He'll slip up one day, Kostas," Phoenix calls out after me. "And we'll make him fucking pay."

"Damn right we will."

The drive to my father's is quick as our new home isn't too far from there. I'm less than a mile away when I see what the fuck happened. That asshole set our childhood home on fire. I push back memories of my mother and me in the kitchen. Many nights when I was small and she'd read stories about heroes to me. The scent of her perfume that still lingered even a year after her death.

Fuck Aris.

It was his mother too.

This just proves to me he's nothing but a sociopath. All he cares about is number one. Himself. And his favorite way of pleasuring himself is to fuck with me. Sick bastard.

By the time I reach the home, it's completely engulfed in flames. The firefighters are already doing their best to control the fire so it doesn't spread elsewhere. I pull up next to Adrian's SUV and hop out.

"What the hell?" I snap, trotting over to him.

He scowls at me. "Aris."

"No fucking shit."

"And, Boss…" He pinches the bridge of his nose. "I can't get ahold of Basil."

My blood runs cold. "It's the middle of the night. Understandable."

"Wesley says he never came back to the hotel last night."

"Aris took him?"

Adrian's features pinch. "He packed his shit, man."

A rat. I had a hunch before and I was right. Unfuckingbelievable.

"Put Wesley in charge at the hotel. I want you on point hunting Basil down."

"I thought we were done hunting," Adrian huffs, irritation making his voice gruff.

"Aris. Basil is a different story. We find Basil, we'll find Aris. Find out where the fuck he went, when he went there, and why he thought fucking me over was a smart plan. We find Basil, and I'll bleed out every detail he knows about Aris."

Adrian scowls but nods. "Yep."

I clutch his shoulder and give it a squeeze. "Brothers can turn. But you and I? We don't fucking turn. You feel me, Adrian? We're better than brothers."

"I'm gonna find his ass and haul him in myself. This shit will end soon," he vows. The exhaustion from this entire Aris debacle over the past year has worn down on my longtime friend.

As soon as he gets in his SUV and leaves, I pull up my security cameras. Talia is asleep in the bed and she's moved Zoe with her. Phoenix paces the hallway right outside their door dressed all in black, the AR slung over his shoulder. Thank fuck. The rest of the men are stationed around the perimeter of my house. At least they're safe.

But they won't be until I deal with my fuckface brother.

I'm going to find his crazy ass and end him because I'm getting too old for this shit. Can't a man just settle the fuck down and have one goddamn week to be a normal fucking husband and father?

Until I drag Aris's ass into that cellar, I won't.

I need to start thinking like him. If I were Aris, what the hell would I do next to fuck with me? Cars are a dime a dozen. He doesn't know the location of our new home. That leaves the hotel. I text Adrian to secure the property from every angle. Next, I text Josef.

Me: I want every cop hunting down Aris Demetriou. Every fucking one of them.

Josef: And compensation?
Me: Money. Lots of it.
Josef: And?
Me: Reelection.
Josef: Done.

If Josef leads me to Aris, I'll get him into any political position he so fucking desires. My next text is to a low-level punk gangster with a big mouth—someone I pay to get messages out.

Me: Aris Demetriou to me alive. 50 mil. Spread the word.
Jaws: Poppy needs a new pair of shoes. On it, Boss.

I don't care if my brother drains me dry. I'd gladly lose every dime if it means having him strapped to a chair in the cellar. Every goddamn dime. Because once he's dead, I'll just make more fucking money. I'm a Demetriou. It's what we do.

chapter twenty-two

Talia

"Guess what today is?" I ask Zoe as I pick her up out of her crib. She flails her chubby arms and babbles like crazy, excited to see me.

Last night was the first night in her own room and I swear I got up thirty times throughout the night to check on her. I know she needs to sleep in her own room, but it's hard to be away from her.

With Aris having burned down their family home recently, Kostas has our home on lockdown. Nobody is allowed to come or go except for him and his men. Stefano had to leave for Italy to get back to work, but my mom has extended her stay. Thankfully, we have a beautiful pool house, complete with its own kitchen and laundry room, so while she's here, she's staying there.

"What's today?" Kostas asks, stepping behind me. I lay Zoe across her changing table so I can change her diaper and get her dressed.

"Today, Miss Zoe is seven months old." I lean over and blow raspberries on her belly. Her giggles ring out through the room. "Every month when I lived with…" I stop myself, not wanting to bring up Kostas's brother. With Aris still missing and wreaking havoc all over town, Kostas's frustration has been at an all-time high. The last thing I want to do is add to that.

"What?" he prompts.

"Never mind. She's seven months old today, that's all."

"Talia." He picks Zoe up from the changing table then turns to face me. "Whatever happened while we were apart, I want to know. It fucking kills me that I missed out on everything. Your pregnancy, Zoe's birth, the first six months of her life…"

He's right. I can't help what happened while I was being held captive by Aris. And stopping my tradition just because it began while I was at Aris's house only gives him power he doesn't deserve.

"I started a tradition when Zoe turned a month old. I would bake cupcakes and after dinner, I would light a candle in one and make a wish. Then afterward, I would take our picture. I would make Aris get it printed and I put each one into a scrap book."

Kostas smiles softly. "What did you wish for?"

"For you to find us." I take a breath, not wanting to cry. I started my period this morning, so I know I'm being overly emotional. We're home and safe, and there's no reason to cry.

Kostas steps toward me and pushes a wayward strand of hair out of my face. "Looks like this month you'll have to make a new wish." He bends slightly and kisses me. It's sweet and quick, but it still lights my belly on fire.

"Do you still have the scrapbook?" he asks.

"I do. I snatched it when I grabbed our stuff."

"You'll have to show it to me," he insists.

When he steps back, I notice he's dressed in his suit. "Are you leaving?"

"I need to handle a few things at the office. Handle my parents' house."

"Will it be able to be saved?"

"No, but it was fully insured. I need to meet with the agent today to go over everything." He gives Zoe a kiss, then hands her to me. "I should be home for dinner. Save me a cupcake." He winks playfully, and I laugh at how damn sexy he is when he's playful.

After seeing him out, I head into the kitchen to make the cupcakes. My mom comes in as I'm setting them in the oven with a cup of coffee in her hand.

"Did you sleep okay?" I ask, grabbing my own cup of coffee and sitting at the table across from her. Zoe is sitting in her high chair, playing with her new sippy cup and eating her cheerios.

"I slept very well." She smiles. "That bed is so comfortable. I'm going to have to tell Stefano to buy us one." She glances into the kitchen. "Baking this early?"

"They're Zoe's seven-month cupcakes. I make them every month to celebrate her birthday."

Mom grins from ear to ear. "Kind of like your birthday pancakes?"

"Yeah." I laugh, remembering when I was growing up I would insist Mom make pancakes like every day. Not wanting to make them all the time, she would say they were only for special occasions. So, every time I would ask, I would make up an excuse, like it was my twelve-year, two-month birthday. She could've totally told me I was full of shit, but she never did. Instead, she would make them every time.

"How's Kostas doing?" she asks. I hate that I was gone for over a year, but I love that something good came from the shitty situation. A friendship of sorts was formed between Kostas and my mom. And not just between them, but also between Kostas and Phoenix. Well, maybe not a friendship between Kostas and Phoenix per se…but definitely a mutual understanding. Kostas even gave him a job and a place to live at the hotel.

"He's okay. Just stressed. Aris is still missing, and instead of keeping quiet, he's apparently trying to create destruction at every turn to bring Kostas down."

"Has he done anything else since he burned down their parents' home?"

"Last night they think he tried to burn the hotel down. Some wires got tripped, but Kostas was ready for him and they caught it quickly, so no damage was done. But, of course, they didn't see who did it. So, now Kostas thinks there's a rat."

Mom huffs in disgust. "I hope they catch him soon."

"Same, but until they do, I think it's safe to say Kostas will be on edge. I just wish there was something I could do."

Mom takes a sip of her coffee and when she sets it down, she grins. "What if I take Zoe to the pool house with me tonight, so you can make him a romantic dinner? You can spend some time just the two of you."

My first thought is there's no way I'm letting Zoe out of my sight, but then, after I take a deep breath, I remember the pool house is only a few yards away and my mom did raise me. She's great with Zoe.

"I'll even ask Phoenix to come over," she adds, obviously sensing my reluctance. "I can spend some time with my son and granddaughter, and you can have a nice, peaceful dinner with your husband."

The buzzer goes off, indicating the cupcakes are done, so I head over to the oven and take them out.

"What do you think?" she prompts.

"I think that would be great." I open the fridge to see what we have. Upon inspection, I find I have everything I need to make Kostas's favorite: chicken parmesan.

"But not overnight," I tell her. "Once we're done, I'm coming to get my baby back."

She laughs and shakes her head. "It's so hard to believe that *my* baby is all grown up." She stands and walks over to me, enveloping me in one of her comforting hugs. "You've grown into such a beautiful woman, Talia," she says. "A loving mother and a devoted wife. I'm so proud of you."

"Thank you, Mom." That means a lot coming from her because she's not only my mom, but my best friend, and growing up, I always wanted to be just like her.

After cleaning up the kitchen, we get changed into our swimsuits and head out to the pool. It's a perfectly sunny day with not a cloud in sight.

While Mom holds Zoe, I swim some laps, and once I'm done, I take Zoe around in her little inflatable boat that has an umbrella top on it to provide shade. She giggles and splashes in the water. Only getting out of the pool to eat her snacks and drink her juice.

When lunchtime rolls around, I give Zoe back to Mom, so I can grab us something to eat.

"Need help with anything?" a masculine voice asks. Bending to grab my towel, I glance over my shoulder to find Fowler standing right behind me with his gaze pointed directly at my butt.

Since Basil has gone MIA, Kostas and Adrian are out more, so that leaves Fowler and the team watching over us. At first, when I would catch him checking me out, I thought I was seeing things, but the more he does it, the more I realize he's a fucking perv. And a dumbass because once I tell Kostas, he's going to kill him. I almost feel bad.

I stand back up and turn around. "Nope, I got it."

"You sure?" Fowler steps closer and the small hairs on the back of my nape rise.

"Well, if you really want to help, you can start by watching *my family* instead of watching *me*."

I know he gets what I'm insinuating because he smirks. It's smarmy and sends chills up my spine. I glance around, hoping to see another one of Kostas's men, but it's just us. I know they're all over the grounds, but only one usually stays with us inside the house or out back.

"Sorry, I'm a flirt by nature. Nothing meant by it." He shrugs, not even bothering to look guilty, despite his words, for staring at my body. "It's hard to focus when you're dressed like that." He grins boyishly and nods toward me. I'm wearing a two-piece bikini, and sure, it might be on the small side, but I'm in my own home, and even if I weren't, I should be able to wear whatever the hell I want without being ogled by Kostas's men.

Just as I'm about to give this asshole a piece of my mind, I hear my husband call out my name.

Perfect timing.

"*Moró mou*," Kostas says, pulling me into his side. He kisses my temple then addresses Fowler. "How's everything?"

Fowler's gaze flits from me back to Kostas and I swear I see a hint of a smirk playing on the corner of his lips. *Does this guy seriously want to die?* "Absolutely perfect," he says.

"Kostas, can I talk to you for a minute?" I ask.

"Of course." He turns his attention back to me.

When Fowler doesn't take the hint, I add, "Alone."

Kostas's brows knit together. "What's the matter, Talia? If there's an issue, Fowler needs to know as well. Did something happen?"

"No, nothing happened." I glance over at Fowler, who's still standing there, with his arms crossed over his chest, and his eyes roaming my body. Is this guy for real? "Well, actually something did happen." I look pointedly at Fowler. "This guy keeps checking me out, and it's making me uncomfortable."

Kostas's brows dip further. "Is this true?" he asks Fowler. "Are you checking out my wife?"

"Sir, it wasn't like that," Fowler sputters. His back goes straight, and finally, his eyes are no longer on me.

"Either you did or you didn't check my wife out. It's simple."

"She's wearing a skimpy bikini, sir, and I might've noticed. I didn't mean any offense."

I scoff at the way he's downplaying this. He was totally perving on me.

"Where's Greg?" Kostas asks him.

"In the security room," Fowler says.

"And Kip?"

"Guarding the front."

Kostas steps toward Fowler, and since Kostas is a good half a foot taller, he looks down at him. "I don't give a fuck if my wife is naked, you don't ever look at her in any way other than to make sure she's safe. Understand?" His voice is calm, but I can see it in the way his jaw is ticking, he's about to lose his shit.

Good! Serves that asshole right.

"Yes, sir," Fowler says like the good soldier he is. Gag.

"Go take over for Kip and tell him to get back here."

What? That's it? He's just assigning him to a different location?

After Fowler leaves, Kostas's eyes swing back over to me. "Talia, is that the only bathing suit you have?"

Oh, no, he didn't.

"No, but—"

"Go change into something more appropriate, please."

I glance over at my mom, who is lying on a chaise lounge with Zoe in her arms. I can tell by the look on her face she can hear everything that's happening.

"I'm not changing," I tell Kostas, crossing my arms over my chest in defiance. "This is my home, and I'll wear whatever the hell I want."

Kostas's brows rise in shock. "Talia, it wasn't a suggestion. Go fucking change. I'm not going to have you prancing around here so my men can ogle what's mine."

What's his? Like I'm a goddamn piece of property!

"You're a chauvinist pig, and if you don't walk away right now, I'm going to push your ass into that pool." I walk around Kostas and over to Mom. I take Zoe out of her hands, so I can lay her down for a nap.

"Talia," Kostas growls, but I ignore him, because if I don't, we're going to fight. And I'm choosing to chalk his dumb ass remarks up to stress because of Aris.

"I'll see you tonight!" I call out behind me.

"So, that's it?" he shouts back. When I keep walking, he says, "Real fucking nice, Talia. I'm so glad I came home to see my family for lunch."

Too pissed, and afraid I'll say something I might regret later, I don't bother answering him. And the smart man he is, doesn't follow me.

While I'm laying Zoe down, I think about everything he said. While he's in the wrong, he also made a valid point about being appropriate in front of his men. Not wanting to fight with him over something so trivial, when I get back downstairs, I look for him to apologize, but he's already gone. Great, now I'm going to need to make sure this dinner is extra perfect because if I know my husband, he's going to come home cranky as hell later.

Chicken Parmesan-check.

Pasta and sauce-check.

Salads-check.

Wine-check.

Oh! The bread.

Remembering I placed it in the warmer, I run back into the kitchen to grab it. Since my mom has Zoe, and I'm making this dinner for Kostas, I frosted Zoe's cupcakes and put them away. I figure we can make our wish tomorrow. One day won't make a difference. Plus, with Kostas being all growly, I figured the best way to calm him down will be to ply him with his favorite food, since I'm on my period and can't have sex with him. If he's extra cranky, I'll give him head. That always softens him up.

I hear the door open then slam shut, and then Kostas's voice booms throughout the house.

Great, just as I thought…he's cranky.

"I don't give a fuck what he said," he barks into the phone. "I've had enough of this back and forth bullshit. I want answers!"

With the bread basket in my hands, I'm stepping into the dining room, when I see Kostas already in there. He yells some more at who-ever he's on the phone with, and then, like it's happening in slow motion, his fist comes out and swipes at the items on the table. The wine glasses shatter, the chicken parmesan splatters, and the salads fly through the air.

I gape at the destroyed table, my eyes fixated on the red sauce that will stain the wall it's slowly trekking a path down. The entire meal I just spent hours making is completely ruined.

Kostas's eyes meet mine, and he looks around, as if now realizing what he did.

"Talia," he breathes.

"My mom's watching Zoe for us… I made you dinner," I choke out. "And it's ruined." I don't have to feel my cheeks to know I'm crying. I know it's just food, but I worked hard on it to make him feel better and with one swipe, he destroyed it all.

"Shit." He scrubs his hands over his face in frustration. He's always frustrated. Always mad. When he found us, it was supposed to be the beginning of our life together, but instead, because of Aris, it's as if our life is on hold. Kostas tries so hard not to let this side of him show in front of Zoe and me, but I've been watching it build and build, and he's finally reached his boiling point.

"I didn't mean to," he says, stepping toward me, his brow furling and his eyes shining with remorse. "It's just…it's been a bad fucking day."

chapter twenty-three

Kostas

TALIA RUSHES OFF AND I FEEL LIKE A FUCKING ANIMAL. I SCRUB my palm over my face and laugh bitterly. Aris has infected every part of my relationship with Talia straight from the beginning. He's like a bite from a zombie and as time passes, I'm becoming infected too.

I want to hack him away from me.

Sever him like a diseased limb I'll be better off without.

We're at war, my brother and me, and it's fucking bloody.

But I will win.

Winning means keeping my wife happy. Because when we're happy, Aris has lost. The loser in a game where he didn't get the girl. Even when he stole her, she was never his. She will never be his.

I can be pissed as fuck at my brother, but allowing him to creep into our evening time alone and ruin our dinner is too much. He doesn't deserve that win. And my wife deserves more than that.

With a heavy sigh, I clean up the mess. Sure, we have people to do this, but I need to be the one to do it. To smell the heavenly sauce I won't get to eat. To curse over the expensive bottle of wine that's ruined and never tasted. To face the consequences of my destruction. And to clean it all up.

Talia is next.

I'll kiss her and make it all better.

Once the dining room is cleaned up, I grab a bottle of vodka from the cabinet and set it on the counter. Then, I pull out some salami, several cheeses, crackers, and grapes. After arranging them on a giant plate, I locate the can of leftover frosting in the fridge. Shoving a spoon into the top, I then place it in the center of my plate of apologies. I tuck the vodka under my arm and grab up the plate. I don't find her right away because she's not in our bedroom. Eventually, I locate her in the theater room. Sitting in the dark. Crying. Fuck.

I turn on the lights and she buries her face in her hands. Setting down the plate and alcohol on the table beside a vase filled with fresh Gerber daisies, I pick up the remote to turn on the giant eighty-five-inch screen. It takes some scrolling through Netflix, but I find a version of *Romeo + Juliet* I can handle. Leonardo DiCaprio and Claire Danes. I kick off my shoes and sit down beside her.

"I know you don't want to hear me tell you I'm sorry again," I say softly, gripping her thigh and squeezing. "So I'm not saying it. You don't respond to that shit anyway."

She hisses at me. "Fuck you!" she bellows, kicking out and sending the goddamn vase on the table flying across the room. Her fucking periods will be the death of me.

"What I mean," I growl, staring at yet another broken vase, "is you do better with actions. I made you a charcuterie board."

"You can't win me over with your fancy cheese plate," she bites out. "Not after you threw my dinner to the floor, Kostas Demetriou."

I snort, which earns me another hiss from her. "You didn't even look at it."

She peeks out between her fingers that still cover her face. "Is that chocolate icing?"

I'm a smart fucking man.

"I bet the grapes taste good dipped in the chocolate icing," I offer, reaching over to pluck a grape from the vine, and then run it along the fudgy sweetness. "Should I taste it first?"

She pops her lips open like a petulant toddler finally giving in to receiving her medicine. I pretend to put the grape to her mouth, but then replace it with my lips at the last second. Her gasp is one of surprise, and before she can push me away, I nip at her bottom lip.

"I love you," I murmur before finally treating her to the chocolate grape.

"Mmm," she moans, her eyes fluttering closed. "I still hate you, but just a little less."

"Then I better keep feeding you."

"You better."

"I put your favorite movie on," I tell her.

She laughs, but it's a mean laugh that gets my dick hard. "I hate this version."

"But you know all the words," I argue. "Your eyes light up when you watch it."

"It's cheesy," she grumbles.

"I'll show you cheesy."

"Oh my God." She fights a smile as I pile salami and cheese onto a cracker. "You're totally cheesy. This is ridiculous. Twenty minutes ago you were furious and slinging shit around our kitchen. Now you're telling me dumb dad jokes and watching corny chick flicks? This is why I hate you."

"You love me," I explain as I shove the whole cracker in her mouth to keep her quiet so I can speak. "You love me because I am nothing without you."

Her brows crash together as she chomps on the cracker in such an unladylike way it makes me want to lick every single crumb that falls onto her thighs.

"You make me want to be better than I ever thought I could be. I never cared to be *better* until you. Now, this villain thinks he can be your hero." I lean my forehead against hers. "I'm going to be really honest here. I'll suck at it at first. You'll hate me at least once a week. But I'm fucking trying, Talia. For you. For Zoe. For our family."

She swallows and pouts. "You make it sound like I don't appreciate you. I do, even when you're an asshole."

"I see your pretty face and every horrible thing I've ever done is forgotten. All that matters is you and our daughter. I fucking bask in your presence, whether you're beaming at me or burning me with your anger. As long as you're the one doing it, I fucking want it. All the warm, happy moments and the raging, hot terrible ones. You, Talia. I want you."

"I want you too. I hate that we're being deprived of our happiness because of him."

I grip her jaw and kiss her softly. "I'm going to try harder. To leave the stress at the door. By bringing it in our home, I'm letting him win. I'll be damned if I let that weasel win."

"We win," she tells me firmly. "You and me, Kos. We're a team. A filthy king and his adorable queen." She laughs and it sounds like music.

"Accept my apology," I demand, nipping at her bottom lip. "Now, woman."

"You're such a prick," she says with a sigh. "My prick."

I grip her hand and run it over my cock. "Your prick's right here."

"Your prick is being punished," she tells me primly. "Go on. Feed me some more. I'm enjoying the groveling." She leans forward to grab the vodka and makes a seductive show of unscrewing the lid before wrapping her dick sucking lips around the bottle.

With my eyes on her so I don't miss the way her throat bobs as she swallows down the burn, I fix her another cheese and meat cracker. The movie plays in the background—the soundtrack working in my benefit to seduce my wife. As the food disappears and the bottle empties, I warm my woman up. All anger has dissipated as giggles take over.

"What's so funny?" I murmur, my lips tracing kisses along the side of her neck. "Romeo and Juliet is a tragedy."

"This version is," she snorts.

"A man tries to be romantic and this is how he's rewarded." I bite her warm flesh. "Maybe I should stop wooing you and just ravish you instead." When I slide my palm up her bare thigh to just under her dress, she lets out a sharp breath and grips my wrist.

"I'm on my period, remember?"

"So?"

"Kostas!"

"You think I'm afraid of blood?"

"Don't be gross."

"Nothing about fucking you on your period is gross."

She gapes at me when I push her dress up her hips.

"Lie back," I order.

"Kostas…"

I reach under her dress and grip her panties. Her breath hitches when I tug them down her thighs. Once they're tossed away, I kiss up her naked thigh.

"Kostas," she whines. "I have a tampon in. This is weird."

Ignoring her half-ass pleas to get me to stop, I run my tongue up her inner thigh. She moans when I suck on the apex of her thigh. Gripping her knees, I spread her open. The string of her tampon remains within reach, but I leave it alone to seek out her clit.

"I like the way you smell." I lick her clit, loving the way she shudders. "I like the way you taste. You think I was a vampire in another life?"

"Do not go there," she breathes. "Please."

Maybe not today.

There's always next month.

"Can I go here?" I ask, circling her clit with my tongue.

"Y-Yes. Go there. Mmm."

Smiling against her pussy, I tease her bundle of nerves until she's squirming on the sofa. I listen to the sounds of her breathing and pay attention to the way her hips lift each time she gets close to orgasm. When I know she's about to fall over the edge, I suck hard on her clit. She screams in pleasure as her whole body detonates. I press kisses to her perfect pussy as I tug on the string of her tampon.

"What are you doing?" she hisses, her chest heaving.

"This." I gently pull until her body releases the bloody plug. With my eyes searing hers, I drop the thing onto the empty cheese plate and then yank at my belt. Her pussy is open and inviting.

A little blood doesn't fucking scare me.

I'm a goddamn villain.

Blood turns us the hell on.

I unfasten my pants and pull out my aching cock. After I shove my pants down my thighs and rip at the buttons on my shirt, I prowl over to her, deciding that's enough stripping. I want inside her before she changes her mind.

"See this pussy?" I ask, teasing her opening with the tip of my dick.

She nods, frowning.

"It's mine," I growl with a hard thrust of my hips.

My dick slides into her warmth and I groan. Her lips are parted, her eyes soft. I want to fucking devour her. She cries out when my lips crash to hers. I kiss her hard and urgently, making her feel my apologies for what I've done and my hope for how I want to be. She kisses me back, equally as passionate.

Talia meets my fire with gasoline.

She taunts and draws out the beast inside me.

And rather than being fearful of the man I can be, she lets me own her with my mouth and punish her cunt with my cock. Begs and moans for it. Fucking loves it.

The sounds coming from her body are juicier than normal and it makes me hard as stone. It takes everything in me not to come without at least attempting to make her come again. Luckily, my girl is needy and tipsy, and the moment my fingers touch her clit, she clenches around my dick as she yells my name. I thrust into her several more times until my balls draw up, desperate for release. With a groan, I spill my seed in her bloody cunt. What a fucking mess we are. A beautiful mess.

With a peck to her lips, I pull out slowly, loving the way her blood is smeared over my thickness. If I didn't just come, I'd have the urge to wrap my hand around my dick and use her blood as lubricant, bringing myself to climax. Talia fucking undoes my mind.

"I can't believe I let you do that," she complains, but her voice is breathless and happy.

"Believe it. Because in about five minutes, I'm going to regroup and do it again in the shower."

"It blew up last night."

You've got to be fucking kidding me.

"Planes don't just blow up," I growl to Adrian. "Fucking Aris. What did airport security say?"

"They're investigating and looking through video footage to see what happened."

"We know what happened. Aris wanted to fuck around with me."

He lets out a heavy sigh. "I'll look into it. But good news is, I have a lead."

"Oh?"

"Wesley said the vehicle Basil took had less than a quarter tank of gas."

I lean back in my office chair. "And?"

"And all the service stations have been checked. He never arrived to refuel."

"So it means Basil is close. Aris is close."

"Any hideouts within fifty miles or so?" he asks. "I could start checking in on some."

We pretty much own everything worth owning within that radius. My mind flits to a few motels that we don't. One particular shithole is known for shady motherfuckers staying at. It would be stupid for Aris to go there, especially with a fifty-mil price tag for his head, but that doesn't mean he wouldn't try it.

"Let's check it out," I order.

After a quick kiss to Talia and Zoe who are napping, I grab my keys. I find Phoenix in a heated discussion with Fowler, but I don't stick around to break it up. Phoenix has taken command over these men, so if Fowler with the wandering fucking eyes needs an attitude adjustment, who am I to step in and interfere.

Adrian and I climb into my Maserati before zipping through town toward the shitty motel. Fifteen minutes later, we creep up to the building. On the side, a vehicle is parked with a blue tarp covering it.

"Basil's car," Adrian growls, jumping from my car before I get it in park.

We didn't have a plan coming here, just following yet another lead. Most leads are pointless. It's surprising as fuck this one might lead us right to Aris.

"I want at him before you kill him," Adrian hisses over his shoulder. "Give me that. I want to ask him straight to his face why he'd turn on his best friend."

I follow him along the sidewalk. We creep, listening in at each door. Nothing seems of interest until I hear him. Moaning. Lifting my leg, I kick in the door hard. Adrian rushes past me, his gun drawn. When he stops suddenly, I slam into his back.

"What the fu—" My jaw drops, ending my words.

"No," Adrian whispers. "No."

Basil, in nothing but his boxers, whimpers at the sound of our voices. Aris, that sick motherfucker, did this to our friend. A friend who we wrongfully thought was a rat was nothing more than a victim. He's lying on the bed, his torso cut from throat to groin. His body has been pulled apart to expose his organs. I step closer and notice that he's been freshly packed with ice. Lots of it.

"He's here," I hiss.

"N-No," Basil croaks. "Gone."

Adrian jolts from his stupor and sits beside Basil on the bed. I mimic his actions, coming up on the other side. As Adrian grabs Basil's hand and lets out a choked sound, I drag my stare over his open torso. His intestines have been pulled out some and hang over the sides of his ribs, dripping in sticky blood. He has to be in agonizing pain.

"We need to call an ambulance," I mutter, fixated on the horrific sight.

Adrian jerks his head my way. "That shit isn't fixable, Boss." His cheeks are wet with tears. "I thought he was a rat."

I sit down next to Basil and frown at him. "We didn't think you were a rat," I explain. "We just figured you were with one. And we were right. Where's he headed next? Give me anything and I'll put you out of your misery."

Basil's face scrunches. "H-He wants b-back at the h-hotel…"

"Why?" I growl. "We've not even been there."

"Info…info…" He groans.

"Information?"

"Yesss," Basil whispers.

Aris is nothing without his numbers and he wants them back. Makes fucking sense. Over my dead body.

"You served me well," I tell Basil. "Say goodbye to Adrian."

Adrian makes a growling sound of a pained animal. He leans forward and presses his forehead to Basil's. "I love you, brother," Adrian tells Basil. He sighs hard and then he's gone, leaving me alone with Basil.

"Thank you," I mutter, pulling out my Glock. "A promise is a promise."

Holding the barrel against his temple, I stare into Basil's dark eyes so he doesn't have to die alone, and I pull the trigger.

Aris will pay for this.

His time is running out.

chapter twenty-four

"How are you doing?" I ask Kostas. He's standing in front of the mirror, tying his tie, and looks like he's a million miles away. When he got home last night, he filled me in on everything. His private plane has been blown to bits, and Basil was found in a shitty motel, alone and dying.

I didn't know him well, but from what I've seen, Kostas, Adrian, and Basil were all close. As close to friends as three men in this world can be. The way he looked at me, with sad, distant eyes when he told me about his death, had me wanting to hold him close.

Kostas won't ever say it, but I think he blames himself for Basil's death. If he had looked harder, maybe he would've found him in time. My poor husband has suffered so much loss in his life, I don't know how he even gets out of bed in the morning. If I were knocked down as many times as him, I don't think I would be able to get up.

But in typical Kostas fashion, he quickly schooled his features and pretended like everything was okay. He made love to me slowly and told me no less than a dozen times he's going to catch his brother.

"I'm okay," he says for the millionth time, glancing at my reflection in the mirror. "How about I pick up dinner on my way home to make up for the one I fucked up the other night?"

He walks over and sits on the edge of the bed where Zoe and I are still lying. Zoe likes to wake up at the crack of dawn, have a bottle, and then come back to bed with Kostas and me for early morning snuggles.

I warned Kostas the first time she did it, she would keep doing it. He just shrugged and said he hoped so.

"You already made up for that dinner." I smile, recalling the way he made up for it several times. First with his tongue, and then a couple more times with his cock.

Kostas smirks, knowing what's running through my head. "Still, I'll pick up dinner." He leans over and kisses my lips. Groaning into his mouth, I grab his lapels and try to pull him back into bed.

He chuckles and stands. "Not happening, *moró mou*. I have another appointment with the insurance adjuster."

"For the plane?"

"Yeah." He pecks my lips one more time. "I should be home early. Behave."

A little while later, Zoe wakes up drooling and cranky. I think another tooth is coming in. After she's changed and fed, I give her to my mom to hold so I can find one of the men to go to the store to pick up medicine.

As I'm opening the front door, I run straight into Fowler. Our bodies collide and his hands land on my hips. Not wanting him to touch me, I move out of his reach, but his fingers are digging into my skin, preventing me from moving.

"Let go of me," I hiss, swatting at his hands.

"Would you rather I let you fall?" He smirks evilly.

Anger burns through me and I'm seconds from clawing his face apart.

"Get your fucking hands off my sister," Phoenix growls, walking up behind Fowler. "Now."

Fowler stares me down in an arrogant way that leads me to believe he thinks he's powerful and untouchable. But based on the fury rippling from my brother and when Kostas gets wind of this, this asshole will learn his place in my home—in my world.

"My bad." He releases his hold on me and raises his palms into the air.

"Why the fuck were you touching her?" Phoenix accuses. "Didn't we already talk about this?" He steps into Fowler's face.

Fowler grins wide, as if they're two old friends in on a joke. "Bro, I didn't touch her—" Fowler begins, but Phoenix cuts him off.

"I'm *not* your bro."

Fowler just laughs. "Look, *man*, she ran into me and I caught her so she didn't bust her ass. Next time I'll just let her fall." He shrugs and walks around Phoenix.

"Two strikes," Phoenix calls over his shoulder.

He says it loud enough that Fowler can hear him, but he keeps walking, pretending he doesn't.

"That guy seriously rubs me the wrong way," I tell Phoenix.

"Yeah, he's a punk."

"What's with the two strikes?" I ask, curious.

"Three strikes and he's out." He looks over his shoulder then back at me. "Why were you coming out here?"

"Zoe is teething. I need someone to run to the store to buy her pain medicine."

"Is she okay?" Phoenix's brows furrow in concern. I never imagined I would ever have my brother in my life, let alone my daughter's. And I definitely never thought Phoenix would be such a hands-on uncle. Growing up, I only got to see him for a short time over the summer, or for the holidays when he would visit. I always assumed he was just like Niles—selfish and irresponsible. But he's actually nothing like him. His only fault was that he was loyal to his dad—until he wasn't.

"She's fine. I just want to make sure she's not in pain. She's whining and being cranky."

"Sounds a lot like her mom." Phoenix smirks.

"Hush it." I push his shoulder playfully.

"I'll send Fowler to go get it." He laughs. "He's not doing shit anyway, so he can play errand boy. Make himself useful."

"I think it's time for me to go home," Mom says. We're sitting on the floor in Zoe's nursery, watching as she crawls all over the place, knocking blocks over and smashing the keys to her soft play piano.

"Already?" I pout. I love having my mom here with me. Once she goes back to Italy, who knows when I will see her again.

"Already?" She laughs. "I've been here for a month."

My pout deepens, my bottom lip jutting out dramatically. "But I'm going to miss you, and so is Zoe."

"I know, *cara mia*, but Stefano isn't good at fending for himself. He's complained every day that the cook isn't making what he likes." She rolls her eyes in mock annoyance. "Imagine if you were away from Kostas for a few days? Or a week?"

I laugh at the thought. Kostas would never let that happen. He'd be all growly and then demand he either goes with me or I don't go. "I get it. So how much longer do I get you?"

"Stefano found a flight for next week. So we have a little more time together." She gives me a soft smile.

"Okay, I'll take it."

Zoe stops banging on the piano and turns to me. Her eyes well up with tears and she shoves her tiny fist into her mouth. Fowler should be back by now with her medicine.

"I'm going to go see if Fowler is back with Zoe's medicine yet. Can you hold her?"

"Of course," Mom says, taking Zoe into her arms. "You know, when you and Phoenix were babies, we just rubbed whiskey on your gums."

I bark out a laugh. "I think we'll stick to good old Tylenol."

I run downstairs and spot one of the men on the phone in the kitchen. Not wanting to interrupt him, I head out the front door. The vehicle Fowler uses is parked in the driveway, so I go in search of him. I find him standing on the side of the house. I'm about to call out his name when I see he has his phone pressed up to his ear. Instead, I walk forward a few steps so I can listen.

"The plane is totaled," he says then stays quiet, listening to whoever is on the other line. I'm curious as to who he's speaking to since all of Kostas's men already know the plane is totaled.

"The bitch and the baby? That's going to cost you big time. Last time I checked you don't have that kind of money. If you want me to grab them, I'm going to need to see the money first."

Oh my God! The bitch and the baby? There's only one bitch around here with a baby, and that's me. I consider sticking around to hear whatever else he's going to say, but decide I've heard enough to know this guy is bad fucking news. It's why he doesn't give a shit about anything Phoenix or Kostas threaten. He's not working for them… He's working for Aris. He's a damn rat!

Needing to get to my daughter and mom to make sure they're safe, I turn and run back into the house and up the stairs. The first thing I need is my gun. There's no way I'm chancing that asshole kidnapping Zoe and me and bringing us back to Aris.

Since my bedroom is before Zoe's, I pop in there to grab my gun from the nightstand. But as I'm grabbing it, I hear footsteps behind me, and a chill runs up my spine. Somehow Fowler knows I heard him.

Not chancing him either killing or kidnapping me, I quickly flip the safety off and turn around with the gun aimed directly at him. He has his aimed at me as well.

"Easy, girl," he starts, an evil glint in his eye as he steps forward.

Pop!

I choke on a gasp as the blood swells, blooming like a flower. Holy shit. His eyes widen as he grabs his side. He wasn't expecting me to be packing and he sure as hell didn't expect me to shoot. He should've, though. I'm married to the most powerful mob boss in the country. Of course he's going to make sure I can defend myself.

Pop!

I waste no time squeezing on the trigger again. This bullet goes through his arm and he drops the gun.

We both go after it at the same time, but as I'm diving down to grab it, Fowler drops to the ground. When I look up, I find Phoenix standing in the doorway with a gun in his hand.

"Thank you," I breathe. I glance over at Fowler and he's knocked out, the side of his head bleeding. Phoenix must've hit him with the butt of his gun.

"I'll always have your back, sis," he says, reaching his hand out to help me up.

"How did you know?" I ask, standing and handing him the gun.

"Overheard him talking on the phone. Saw you listening as well, but I didn't want to draw attention to you. As soon as you ran, he turned around, and I knew he saw you." He kicks Fowler in the stomach so he rolls over onto his back. He's bleeding heavily onto my carpet. Great, I'll probably never get that stain out.

"I'm so glad you're here." I run into Phoenix's arms.

"Eh, looks like you were handling yourself just fine." He kisses the top of my head.

"I need to go make sure Mom and Zoe are safe," I tell him. "I don't know who we can even trust. I'm going to have her lock herself in the room. Can you tie this fucker up and call Kostas?"

Phoenix's lips curl into a wide grin.

"What?" I ask, confused.

"Nothing." He shakes his head. "I just hope one day I find a woman like you. Kostas got himself a good one. He better treat you right."

"He more than treats me right," I tell him. "He treats me like his queen."

When I get to Zoe's room, the door is closed and locked. "Mom," I call out.

"Talia! I heard a gunshot! Are you okay?" she says through the door.

"Yes, I'm okay. You can open the door." I want to make sure nobody is in there. I knew something was up with Fowler. Who knows who else is a rat.

When she opens the door, I sigh in relief at the sight of my daughter bouncing up and down in her crib. "Go ahead and lock the door again. Phoenix has Fowler, and Kostas will be on his way shortly. Don't open the door unless it's one of us."

"Okay, be safe, sweetheart." She gives me a kiss on my cheek.

I get back to the room to find Phoenix has Fowler propped up in my reading chair and has used my robe belt to tie his hands. He's awake, but his head is hanging down. I bet he has a massive migraine. The thought makes me laugh. When my husband is done with him, a migraine will be the least of what he feels.

"What the fuck are you laughing at?" Fowler hisses. "You think tying me up is going to stop Aris from getting to you again?" He laughs wickedly, and I take a step back. Gone is the pervy flirt, and present is a ruthless mobster. "That man is on a revenge mission, and he ain't gonna stop until he has everything Kostas cares about. Mark my fucking words."

The room chills several degrees like a cold storm has surged into our bedroom, ready to destroy everything in its path.

"My brother will get to my wife again over my dead fucking body," Kostas says, entering the room. He saunters over to Fowler like he doesn't have a care in the world. But I can see the darkness in his usually light eyes. He's pissed and he's going to make Fowler pay…after he makes him talk.

"We can make this easy or difficult. Are you going to tell me where my brother is, or am I going to beat it out of you?" Kostas cracks his neck to one side and then to the other, the bones popping in an intimidating way.

Fowler laughs. "I'm not saying shit." He spits at Kostas. "I already know my death warrant's been signed. I'm not going down a fucking rat."

Kostas glowers at him as he sheds his jacket and rolls up his sleeves. "The hard way it is." He turns to me, and I give a look that tells him I'm not going anywhere. I'll be damned if I don't get to see this asshole get what's coming to him. Kostas simply shakes his head, not even bothering to argue.

Kostas unbuckles his belt and pulls it through the loops. For a second, I wonder if he's going to whip Fowler with his belt, but instead he wraps it around his neck, tightening it so tight, Fowler's veins in his neck and face bulge. He doesn't stop until Fowler's face is bright red.

"This is for teaming with the wrong side." He tightens it some more, and I worry he's going to kill him before he gets any information out of him.

"And this is for even *thinking* you would try to take my daughter and wife from me." Kostas tightens the belt, and Fowler's survival instincts kick in. He tries to wriggle his body to get free. His head lashes back and forth as his face color turns to a deep crimson.

"Sis, you sure you wanna be here for this?" Phoenix asks, his tone laced with worry.

"She's not going anywhere," Kostas says, answering for me. "Your sweet little sister has quite the dark side in her." While still choking Fowler, he looks back and shoots me a knowing smirk, causing my belly to flutter with butterflies. Jesus, I think I might be as crazy as my husband.

chapter twenty-five

Kostas

WHEN I'D GOTTEN THE TEXT FROM PHOENIX, I'D SEEN RED. But thankfully, Talia's brother is one of the few people I can trust around here. He'd been onto Fowler's bullshit already and had his eye on him. And when the fucker thought he could hurt *my fucking wife*, she shot him.

Good girl.

Good goddamn girl.

The prick is whining and hissing against the leather belt that has him in a chokehold, but all I can do is admire my wife. She looks borderline angelic in her yellow sundress and sunny hair that hangs down her back in what she calls beach waves. Even the smile on her plump red lips is serene. It's the eyes, though.

Brilliant and blazing.

Wickedly blue.

A monster who teases my own.

If I didn't have this dickhead to torture, I'd bend her over my bed right now and take her bloody cunt. I'd smack her ass in the way bad girls get their reward and use my crimson-soaked dick to push between her cheeks, taking her where she doesn't bleed but sure as fuck will feel like it.

Having a hard-on with a rat in my presence is inconvenient.

"Take him to the garage. This shit is going to get bloody." I nod at Phoenix. "Don't kill him yet."

While Phoenix handles him, I grab Talia's wrist and haul her into our giant closet. I close the door and then pounce on her. My lips crash to hers as I grab her ass.

"I was fucking terrified something happened to you," I growl, nipping at her bottom lip. "And here you are, ruling over your mere mortals like the queen you are. You make me proud, *zoí mou*."

She kisses me hard and works at my tie. "You can't wear your good tie to cut off limbs, husband."

"And sundresses are meant for the beach, not stabbing rats," I tell her, ripping at the fabric and pulling it down one shoulder so I can kiss her bare skin. "As much as I want to fuck my gorgeous wife, I need to get down there and find answers."

She grumbles as she grips my dick through my slacks. "You can't go down there with this." She squeezes me. "You'll accidentally poke someone's eye out." When she drops to her knees, I groan in pleasure. Her wicked grin is back as she tugs at my zipper and reaches into my boxers to free my cock. She pulls it through the zipper hole and admires it with exaggerated excitement.

Little brat.

Playful and sexy in a time where we need to be ruthless and evil… and yet I want to make them wait for five goddamn minutes so my wife can suck my dick.

Her pink tongue darts out, wetting my tip, and she circles it in a teasing way. I grip a handful of her blond hair and pin her with a fierce stare.

"Wrap your fat lips around my dick," I growl.

She scowls. "Fat?"

Oh, Jesus, fuck.

"Plump. Juicy. Perfect. Your lips were made for sucking dick, Talia. Fucking own it."

This earns me a smile and then she wraps those lovely lips around my thick, veiny cock, ravishing me with her hot mouth. I grunt and flex my hips, slightly fucking her mouth. Her teeth scrape along my flesh and her blue eyes dart up to mine, a warning gleaming in them. I take her challenge and buck again. She gags and purposefully drags her teeth up my shaft to the crown. Her cheeks indent as she sucks on the crown, hard and unyielding, as though she can bleed me dry of cum with such a simple maneuver. It nearly fucking works. A growl rumbles through me and I thrust again. Her throat constricts when my tip slides into its tight, warm depths.

She's so fucking pretty when her blue eyes water when she tries to swallow me whole.

"I'm going to come down your throat and then tonight I'm going to come in your ass," I tell her smugly, daring her to challenge me.

She doesn't because it's hard to argue with a nine-inch dick for a lollipop down your throat. Her slender fingers massage my balls before she twists slightly, reminding me of the fact that just because she's on her knees, it means nothing.

She. Fucking. Owns. Me.

Seeing her so goddamn powerful on her knees with a monster's balls in her grip has me snarling with my release. She takes me deeper in her throat the moment that first burst of cum hits her throat. I hiss as my dick is swallowed down her needy throat. I flex my ass cheeks as I milk the rest of my cum into her hot mouth and then I pull away abruptly.

Talia rises to her feet and kisses my lips as she tucks my wet cock back into my slacks.

"Good boy," she purrs. "Now let's go torture that motherfucker."

It's true love with this one.

Talia leans against the wall, quietly watching, while Phoenix paces the floor in front of Fowler. Adrian has Fowler's phone and is already tracing numbers to locations. He'll work his tech side to get information while Phoenix and I do it the good old-fashioned way: by brute force.

Fowler's shirt has been removed and someone poured superglue in his gunshot wounds to keep him from bleeding out. That shit has to hurt like a bitch. Exactly what we wanted, too. It's only going to get worse from here.

"Where's Aris?" I ask coolly, fiddling with the tip of my knife.

He spits at Phoenix's feet. "Fuck you."

Phoenix bitch slaps him, making Fowler cry out in surprise. These men can take punches, but a slap to the face like a fucking girl is jarring to them. He gapes at Phoenix incredulously.

"You tell me where my brother is and we'll let you live." I snort. "Man, I can't even say that with a straight face. How about this? We'll let you die quicker if you tell us where he is."

"I won't tell you shit," Fowler snaps.

"So you don't need your tongue then?" I step forward, loving the way his eyes widen marginally so.

"He didn't get a chance to tell me before your cunt wife—" Fowler starts.

Phoenix bitch slaps him again and snarls at him. "Her name is Talia. Use her name."

Fowler is pissed, but he rethinks his fight because he grits out his words. "Talia interrupted."

"Give us something," I say calmly. "Anything."

"What will you give me?" Fowler attempts to negotiate. "Maybe I'll tell you what I know, but I need something in return."

"You give me the information and I will cut you loose." I smirk at him. "Trust me?"

"I *don't* trust you, though," he says, scowling.

"You don't have many options," Talia reminds him.

Fowler snaps his head her way and glowers at her, but not before raking his eyes boldly down her body. This fucker has a death wish. He thinks he has the upper hand. That if he'll be openly salacious against her, I'll just end him now and put him out of this misery. When he licks his lips suggestively, I consider it, but Phoenix bitch slaps the look right off his face.

"What the fuck man?" Fowler bellows. "Stop fucking slapping me."

Phoenix smirks at me. "This is the most fun I've had…ever, frankly. Every time you open your bitch-ass mouth to spew more bullshit, I'm gonna slap the words right out of it. Man the fuck up, Fowler. Tell us what you know and you'll die like you have a pair of balls between those legs."

"Agia Fotia. There's a hotel there that the Galanis used to hide out in. You know it?" Fowler asks.

I give him a clipped nod and then cut my eyes over to Talia. She slips from the room, hopefully to pass on the news to Adrian.

"Yeah, I know it. Is he there?" I demand, stepping closer.

"Fuck if I know, but he mentioned a hotel there in our last conversation. Didn't say if he was going there or not because your cunt—"

I press my blade to his lips, glaring down at him. "Careful, rat. We're not done talking and if you keep calling my wife a cunt, I'm going to cut your tongue from your throat. I'll make you learn goddamn sign language to finish this conversation. Don't fucking test me."

Blood trickles down his chin and I pull the blade away.

"We never got to finish our conversation," he gripes, before licking the new cut on his bottom lip.

Talia returns and gives me a nod before mouthing, "Adrian," to me. At least he can be checking our contacts there before this dick sends us on a wild goose chase.

"What's he planning next?" I ask.

"I don't fucking know." Fowler glowers at me.

"What do you know?"

"Nothing else."

Well, I guess our time here is over.

"Look at my wife," I order.

Now the greasy motherfucker tries to disobey me. Phoenix steps behind him and grabs his hair, yanking his head to the side.

"Boss says look," Phoenix growls, "you fucking look."

"And when Boss says keep your eyes to yourself, you keep them to your fucking self." I whistle for Talia. "Come here, woman, and hold my knife."

I sense her hesitation, but she won't undermine me now. She walks over to us and takes the knife from me. Fowler watches her with pure hatred that burns hot through my veins. He thinks I'm going to make her cut him or stab him. She's not fucking touching him.

"Like what you see?" I purr, my voice deceptively calm.

"Looks like a spoiled, used cunt—AHHH!"

I dig my thumbs into his eyes hard, cutting past the inner membrane inside his lower eyelids. His screams are otherworldly as he thrashes in his chair. Phoenix holds him in place as I rip through the flesh beneath his eyeballs. Vomit spews out at me when I pull my thumbs away and blood gushes down his cheeks. I flip my palms up and push three fingers into each hole beneath his eyeballs before curling them up around the back side of his eyeballs. He sputters and gurgles and hisses. With a hard yank, I relieve him of his wandering eyes, leaving two bloody, gaping holes in his head.

Talia has retreated, her back now against the wall. Good. I want her away from this sick fuck. I open my palms to look at the rat's eyes. Beady and fucking useless now. I toss them on the ground and Phoenix stomps them with his combat boot. Fowler has officially been renamed Howler because he's crying out like he's a fucking wolf lost from his pack.

Adrian enters the garage and his dark eyes gleam with approval. He hates this fucker too. When he nods at me, I know the intel is good. We'll need to leave soon.

"Toss me the knife," I say to my wife.

She throws it at me and it clatters at my feet. I pick it up and then begin sawing Howler free. He squawks and carries on like the little bitch he is.

"What now?" Phoenix asks, violence gleaming in his eyes that match Talia's.

"A promise is a promise," I reply, shrugging. "I told the fucker I'd cut him loose if he gave us information." Then, I grin at Phoenix. "But you, man, you didn't promise him a damn thing. He's all yours. I need you here protecting Melody and Zoe. Talia and I are going on a second honeymoon."

After we showered, changed, and packed some weapons, Talia and I headed out to Agia Fotia Beach with Adrian following behind in his new Jeep. Fucking Phoenix corrupted him with that corny-ass Jeep shit. But, since my wife smashed Adrian's car, it was only fair I bought him a new toy. Even if the toy is meant for a man twenty years his junior.

To an outsider, Talia and I in my Maserati look like any other rich couple. Carefree and happy. We're happy, that's for damn sure. And we'll be carefree the moment I have my hands around my brother's throat. Until then, we'll keep hunting his awful ass down.

"We're almost there," she says, yawning. "Are we really going to stay at the beach house?"

"You mean the Cliffside monster stairs home?"

She laughs. "Remember when I made you carry me up all those steps?"

"Remember when I fucked you on four hundred rocks and made you mine?"

We both smile.

"It won't always be like this," I promise her. "The people in Greece know they can't fuck with me. They can try and I'll hunt their asses down. If they're smart, they'll pay their taxes, do my bidding, and be fucking merry."

"Is that all?" she asks dryly. "Want them to suck your dick too?"

"That's your job," I tell her with a smirk.

"You have to admit, you like it when I negotiate using blowjobs."

"Your blowjobs are the true secret behind world peace. Too bad you only give them to a tyrant."

She taps at her lips and feigns a thoughtful look. "Maybe I should spread the love around."

"Maybe I should spread you over my lap and make you fuck me the rest of the way."

"I did not come through all this to die in a ditch because my sex freak husband wanted to have more period sex while driving a million-dollar car."

Three mil, but who's counting.

"There's always the ride home," I tease, gripping her jean-clad thigh.

The rest of the trip we drive in contented silence. I know she's nervous about finding him, but I'm eager as hell. It's long overdue.

Rather than going to the hotel the Galanis always stayed at, I take her straight to the Cliffside home. It's my first destination. We pull into the driveway and I lean over to kiss Talia.

"How long will it take to find out if Aris is at the hotel?" she asks once we park.

"He's not there," I state as I climb out of the car.

She follows me, grabbing my hand. "What? What do you mean?"

"If there's one thing I know about my brother, it's that he likes to play games. He doesn't trust anyone. You think he'd give such an obvi-ous clue to his man?"

Talia stops to frown at me. "No."

I caress her cheek. "No, because if the man was found out, then he'd tell me. And if Aris knows me, he had to know I'd find out because I'm not fucking stupid."

Her plump lips purse, making my dick thicken with need. Not now, but soon, I'll have those lips on me again. "He wanted to lure you to the hotel." She lets out a rush of relieved breath. "So we outsmarted him then?"

"Did we?" I muse aloud, darting my eyes to the house.

Her blue eyes flicker with fear, but I shush her with a kiss. "He knew we'd stay here if we came looking for him at that hotel. He'd attempt to catch us off guard."

She pulls away, whirling around. "Where's Adrian?"

"Don't worry about that," I say with a grin as I lead her over to the front door. "Let's get you inside. I want to fuck you in the hot tub."

Her shoulders are tense, but she trusts me as I guide her into the home. As soon as we walk inside, we see Aris. Gun in hand and evil fucking smile on his face.

And then Adrian tackles him from behind.

Aris's eyes blink open slowly. He looks like shit. I'm not sure he's show-ered recently and the scruffy beard he's sporting doesn't make him look refined. It makes him look like trash.

That's what he is to me.

Trash.

Ready to be kicked to the goddamn curb. Indefinitely.

"The almighty Demetriou reigns," Aris snarls, finding his venom past the haze of recently being knocked out.

I snort. "Nothing's changed, little brother."

His brown eyes dart to Talia, who's perched in my lap like a fucking goddess waiting to be worshiped. Rather than worshiping his queen, he spits her way. She flinches and I hate that he holds some sort of power over her.

Not for long.

Adrian is still as a statue, leaned against the wall like a fucking gargoyle. All it takes is Aris to move the wrong way and Adrian will pounce on him, gutting him like he gutted Basil. The violence ripples from Adrian in waves like heat from the sun. Powerful, malevolent, unforgiving.

"You didn't think you'd go on terrorizing me and not get caught in my web eventually, did you?" I stroke my fingers through Talia's blond hair, my eyes fixed on him. "You're caught now. Nothing but a useless fucking moth, struggling to get free." I flash him a smug grin. "You, Aris fucking Demetriou, are a victim now. Something to be destroyed and ruined. Forgotten."

"Fuck you," he snarls. "Your theatrics are boring, Kostas. Get the hell on with it."

"Personally," Talia pipes up, her voice wavering slightly. "I find his *theatrics* quite charming."

"You always were a dumb bitch," Aris growls, fighting against his restraints.

"They're mouthy as fuck when they're looking death in the eye," Adrian bellows from across the room, making the three of us look his way. His hateful glare is fixated on Aris. I should let him deal with my brother, but that wouldn't be fair to Talia. She suffered too. This is her vengeance.

"I've been planning your death for a while now," I tell Aris. "I imagined all the ways I'd cut you and drain you of your blood. How I'd make you suffer slowly. But then I realized it's not up to me." I pat Talia's thigh. "It's up to her."

She rises from my lap and I rake my eyes down her perfect jean-clad ass.

"I trusted you," she says, her voice small as she picks up the knife from the table. "I tried to comfort you."

"Aww," Aris taunts, his nostrils flaring. "You thought your magical pussy would make me all better? Sorry, princess, but your cunt is just like every other cunt out there. Although, you squealed like a little pig when I shoved my dick in it."

She freezes and I'm tempted to leap over the table to crush his fucking skull. But I won't. Not unless she asks me to. And my brave wife doesn't ask for help. She slowly approaches him, like a viper ready to strike. The knife in her grip gleams in the light.

"You raped me," she accuses, her voice breaking. "You took advantage of my kindness and then you took advantage of me."

He laughs hatefully. "It didn't feel like rape when you were impaled on my cock. It felt like vindication." He sneers at me. "How does it feel knowing I popped that cherry, big brother? Does it burn you up every night knowing your brother's dick has been inside your wife? Does it— what the fuck?"

Blood runs down his cheek from the slash of the knife. Her body trembles as she stares down at him.

"It was rape and you know it," she seethes. "Admit it and I'll let you keep your cock."

"My cock belongs to you, though, bitch," he taunts. "You damn near begged for it the whole time I had you holed away from Kostas. If Selene weren't there, you know we would've already made another baby."

She slashes again, this time ripping through his bottom lip. Blood runs thick down his chin. His eyes turn wild as he realizes he's dying in this living room. Tonight. At the hand of the one he brutalized.

Eye for a fucking eye.

Even Howler learned that lesson.

"Say it," she orders. "Say it or I'll cut you a thousand times. Don't fucking test me, Aris. I will. I'll cut you for every time I lied to your face and told you Zoe was your daughter."

His nostrils flare. "I raped you because I could," he sneers. "I haven't deflowered a virgin since I was a fucking teenager. I should have taken your ass instead."

She turns her head to look at me, tears gleaming in her blue eyes. Even had he not admitted, I knew the truth. But this was something she clearly needed to hear. To confirm. For me to know without a shadow of a doubt. This is her vengeance, not mine.

Yes, he took and took from me, but he didn't take that.

He stole her virginity and her freedom. He stole her happiness.

For that, she will make him pay.

I give her a nod of support and a wink.

"You thought you could bring down my husband, but you couldn't," she whispers, turning back to him. "You couldn't because you were always the weak one. The unloved one. The least favorite. Poor little Aris. Only Mommy loved you, but even still, she loved you equal to your brother."

"Fuck you," he roars. "Don't ever talk about my mother."

"Your mother is rolling in her grave because the man she hated most is the man you turned out to be," Talia continues, her body vibrating with power. "You turned into him. Ezio. You're that spineless bastard, weak and afraid."

"I am not like that motherfucker!" he screams, his face turning purple with rage.

Aww, someone still has daddy issues.

"You always did look more like the gardener," I muse aloud.

Talia laughs. "How does it feel to be powerless? You only had the illusion of power for a short while there. Your brother always wielded it and it drove you fucking crazy. He got the empire, he got the girl, and he got the kid." She slashes again, this time slicing a big gash on the side of his neck. "What do you have, Aris? A mediocre cock in your pants and a burning desire to be him?" She points her knife at me. "Well, you're not him. Not even close."

"Go to hell," Aris slurs, his skin quickly paling with the blood loss that's pouring like rivers down the side of his neck.

She straddles his thighs and presses the tip of the blade against his chest, right over his heart. "You soon will." Her body trembles, but she doesn't make the move.

"Talia?" I ask, rising to my feet.

A sob chokes her. "I want to, but…"

Walking over to her, I stare down at my brother she's singlehandedly ruined with her knife. I could end him right now. Hell, we could leave him and he'd bleed to death within minutes. That won't bring her peace, though. She needs to do this.

I lean forward and wrap my arms around her. My hand grips hers on the hilt of the knife. Nuzzling her hair with my nose, I inhale her sweet and sweaty scent. I kiss her hair and murmur my words against her head.

"Ready, *zoí mou*?"

"Yes," she breathes.

I use my other hand to cover the top of the hilt of the knife and drive it forward. Her hand flexes beneath mine, but she doesn't squirm away. Together, we push the blade past his flesh and into his chest. Together, we pierce his heart. Together, we breathe raggedly as we watch the life quietly drain from the monster in our lives.

Releasing the knife, I hook my arms around her middle and pull her away from him. I walk her outside so Adrian can deal with the body. She turns in my arms, sobbing against my chest. I stroke her hair and kiss her head. The waves crash down below.

"It's over now, *moró mou*. You can be happy."

She pulls away and places her blood-splattered hands on my cheeks. Her blue eyes are watery as she regards me. "I am happy, Kostas. With you, never doubt that."

"I love you," I murmur. "My beautiful, brave, fiery wife."

"I love you more."

"Impossible," I growl, nipping at her juicy lip.

A smile tugs at her lips. "Then prove it."

"Anything."

"Give me a piggyback down to the beach."

All those stairs. All. Those. Fucking Stairs.

"Aww, I'm only teasing," she says, laughing. "You should have seen your face!"

With a growl, I scoop her into my arms.

I carry her down all those goddamn stairs. Every last one of them. And when I've fucked her in the warm sea and made her scream my name in pleasure, I'll carry her back up all those motherfucking steps. Every grueling one.

I'll carry her anywhere.

To the ends of the earth. Through heaven and hell. And into the next life.

She's fucking mine forever.

epilogue

Talia
One Year Later

"Mommy, what's this?" Zoe asks, pointing at the exquisite fountain in the middle of the courtyard.

With me almost two weeks overdue, we decided to drive over to the Pérasma Hotel with Kostas today to hang out, swim a little, and get some sun while being waited on.

When Zoe asked if we could go for a walk, I figured it would be the perfect opportunity to try to walk my overly-pregnant behind into labor. Big mistake. Because now I've plopped myself onto the wicker lounge chair to relax for a minute, and there's a good possibility I may never get back up.

Not wanting to tell her what she's pointing to is Bernini's *Rape of Proserpina*, I go with a more childproof answer. "It's a statue of a man and a woman."

"Not just any man and woman," a masculine voice says, catching my attention. I glance over and spot my sexy husband sauntering over. Unlike the first time I saw him in this very spot, dressed casual in khakis and a button-down shirt, today he's sporting his power suit. I would take him either way, but truth be told, my favorite Kostas is the one without any clothes on in our bed.

Kostas picks Zoe up and she squeals in excitement. "This statue is of Pluto and Proserpina," he tells her as if she can understand. He always talks to her like she's an adult. It's oddly adorable.

"Pluto?" she questions. "Like the doggy?"

He gives me a confused look.

"Pluto is the cute puppy on Disney," I explain.

He laughs and shakes his head. "No, this Pluto was a very powerful god." He gives me a knowing look. "He stole Proserpina and brought her into the Underworld. And because he loved her so much, he tricked her into staying by tempting her with delicious food. She, of course, took the bait and was sentenced to remain with him for the rest of eternity."

I grin at his version of the story. It was my version. The safe version. The one that made Pluto out to be the bad guy and kept Proserpina innocent. But as I look at my handsome husband holding our daughter in his arms, I realize my view of the story has changed. That I've changed.

"He didn't trick her," I say out loud.

Kostas's eyes gleam with excitement. "No?"

"No, that would be giving him too much credit and her not enough," I admit. "I think you were right before. If she didn't want to stay, she wouldn't have eaten the seeds. But she did so because she wanted to."

I attempt to stand, but my big belly weighs me down.

"*Moró mou*," Kostas says. "Let me help you." He sets Zoe down, who runs over to the fountain to dip her hand in the water.

As he helps pull me into a standing position, my stomach tightens, and I cringe slightly at the pain that shoots down my back. "I made Proserpina out to be the damsel in distress," I tell him. "The victim, but maybe she wasn't. Maybe she was just scared and he helped her come to the realization of what she already knew."

"And what's that?" Kostas asks, gripping the curve of my hips and leaning over to kiss my lips.

"That she was always meant to be loved by Pluto and to be the Queen of the Underworld."

I can imagine how she felt. When she met Pluto, there was no turning back. She fell for him the moment she laid eyes on him. He didn't have to drag her there, because she belonged there. She just needed to come home.

Another pain shoots down my back and then it feels as though I've peed myself. I glance down and liquid is dripping down my legs under my bathing suit.

"Talia, are you okay?" Kostas asks, his eyes widening in fear. It's not often I see my husband appear to be scared.

"Yeah." I nod with a smile. "But our baby is finally coming."

Kostas

Fuck. Fuck. Fuck.

Fuck. Fuck. Fuck.

Fuck. Fuck. Fuck.

"Stop saying fuck," Talia seethes, "or I will rip your tongue out of your mouth."

The doctor smirks at me from between her legs and I tense. Clearly I've been chanting the words that have been running inside my head from the moment she was put into this hospital bed. I wonder if she heard the other ones.

She's brave and resilient and strong.

The best mother in the world.

Beautiful beyond reason.

"A real Casanova, that one," the nurse says to Talia, winking.

I look down to find Talia's eyes watering. "I love you," she whimpers.

Leaning down, I kiss her plump lips. "I love you too. You're doing great."

"Oh shit," she whines. "I can't do this."

"You've done it before," I remind her.

"And her head wasn't as big as Nora's either!"

I can't help but grin at her. The moment we found out we were having another little girl, Talia asked if we could name her after my mother. It broke my heart and healed it all at once. Of course I said yes. My mother would be so fucking proud of me. She would've loved those girls with everything she had. Thankfully, we have Melody and she does the job of two grandmas at once.

"I see dark hair," the doctor says, his eyes crinkling with delight. "The baby is coming. Want to watch?"

I dart my eyes to Talia, who nods. I missed Zoe's birth, so seeing Nora's is a gift. Releasing Talia's hand, I shuffle down to the end of the bed.

"Holy shit," I utter, completely transfixed to see the head of my daughter trying to come through the small hole. "Talia, she's almost here."

"Another contraction," the nurse says. "That's it, honey, push and hold."

Talia bears down and the head begins to push out. When she can't push anymore, the dark hair disappears some. Another contraction hits right after the other and my incredible wife pushes harder. I'm awestruck by how strong she is—scrunched face in determination, purple flesh as she uses every ounce of strength she can muster, sweaty hair stuck to her forehead.

"There we go," the doctor says, drawing my attention back to our daughter.

Fuck. Fuck. Fuck.

Fuck. Fuck. Fuck.

"STOP SAYING FUCK!" Talia warns through gritted teeth.

I gape in part horror, part fascination as I stare at the head sticking out of my wife's body. A film of something covers her face and she's as purple as her mother. Birthing a baby is a fucking miraculous thing.

I gently caress Talia's thigh. "I can see her head, *moró mou*. She's so perfect."

Talia sobs but then she's pushing again. And again. And again. Until the baby seems to slide out of her body and into the doctor's waiting arms. Bloody and messy. Screaming at the top of her little lungs.

"Big baby girl," the doctor praises as he shuffles the squirming infant onto Talia's stomach. Blood is everywhere. The good kind of blood. The blood of miracles.

Talia's whole body trembles as she cries and admires our daughter.

"Want to cut the cord?"

I snap my eyes over to the doctor, who offers me a pair of scissors. Sure enough, the thick umbilical cord that's attached to our daughter needs removing. Will it hurt if I cut it? Can Talia feel it?

"Cut the cord, Kostas," Talia urges, her words no longer laced with violence. They're gentle and sweet and encouraging.

Frowning at the doctor, I shakily accept the scissors. "Are they going to feel it?"

"No, son, they're not going to feel it," he says, chuckling.

I've cut off limbs and eyeballs and every other body part imaginable.

So why the fuck do I feel like I'm going to pass out?

It's a cord. A tiny passage of nutrients our daughter no longer needs.

With bile rising in my throat and sweat coating my flesh, I start to snip through the cord. But it doesn't cut smooth and easy. I have to hack through the thick rope.

Fuck. Fuck. Fuck.

Fuck. Fuck. Fuck.

This time, Talia laughs.

"Baby ears are listening," she teases.

I manage to sever the cord, making Nora officially ours to take care of and protect. The weight of the responsibility nearly crushes me. But I've managed to do it with Talia and Zoe. What's one more?

As they continue to deliver the placenta, I abandon the scissors and opt not to watch that part. I may be a fucked-up mobster who's seen some shit, but I haven't seen that, nor do I fucking plan on it. No, I'd rather keep my eyes glued to our perfect daughter and her adoring mother.

"Zoe is going to be so proud," Talia tells me tearfully. "You think she's giving Uncle Fee hell?"

I snort. I hope so. Phoenix is a pussy-magnet player who's corrupted Adrian with his manwhore ways. When they're not working, they tear up the fucking town looking for women. I'm glad one little girl owns his heart. Now he'll have another one soon wrapped around his finger.

"I hope she tells him the names of all her stuffed animals," I say with a chuckle.

She has tons. Too many. Talia and I both have been the victims of her lengthy sessions of telling us the name of each and every one of them. If you interrupt, she starts over. If she forgets a name, she starts over. I've tortured many a men, but Zoe has invented a form of torture all on her own.

I'd say she got it from me, but that has Talia written all over it.

We admire her until they take her away to clean her up a bit and run some tests. Then, they hand our daughter back, bundled in a warm blanket.

"Want to hold her?" Talia asks, her smile serene.

I nod as I pick up the tiny thing. She weighs nothing. So light and fragile. As I pull her to my chest and cradle her, my eyes burn with emotion. I'll protect this little one like I do her sister and her mother. With everything I own until the day I die.

Nora scrunches her face and makes a crabby whining cry that has me chuckling. She's so damn cute. When I glance over at Talia, her bottom lip wobbles as tears streak down her cheeks.

"What's wrong?" I demand, alarmed at her crying.

She shakes her head. "Nothing, Kostas. Everything is right. Better than right. It's perfect."

I let out a relieved sigh and kiss my daughter's forehead. "I love you, *prinkípissa*." *Princess.*

"You're a good man," Talia mutters, reaching her hand out for me.

Taking it, I give it a squeeze. "Only for you."

Our eyes lock and a million emotions pass between us.

Talia and I are the earth, the sun, the stars, and everything in between. We're evil and good, wrapped in one complicated ball of love. She challenges me. I provoke her. Vases get broken and words get said. Sometimes we fight like hellions straight from the bowels of the Underworld.

But we love hardest of all.

Fully. Passionately. Dangerously.

Our love is violent and messy, destructive for those who dare near it. It slaughters and slays. Powerful and intimidating to those around it. Love between a Demetriou king and queen is chaotic like the tropical storms that often ravish our seaside properties. We're a pull of two forces of nature, only working when orbiting the other.

Fate drew us together—victims of a complicated history of our parents.

Love kept us there.

"What are you thinking about?" Talia asks, her blue eyes gleaming with adoration and utter loyalty.

"You. Always you."

The End

playlist

Head Above Water by Avril Lavigne
Complicated by Avril Lavigne
I'm a Mess by Bebe Rexha
Broken-hearted Girl by Beyoncé
Reason to Stay by Brett Young
Never be the Same by Camila Cabello
Consequences by Camila Cabello
The Scientist by Coldplay
Let it Go by James Bay
In Case by Demi Lovato
i hate u, i love u by Gnash
Desire by Meg Myers
Stay by Rihanna
Back to You by Louis Tomlinson
Bad Things by Machine Gun Kelly and Camila Cabello
Love on the Brain by Rihanna
Rock Bottom by Hailee Steinfeld
The Monster by Eminem
So Good by Zara Larsson
Remind Me to Forget by Kygo & Miguel
Him & I by G-Eazy & Halsey
Bad Blood by Taylor Swift
Mad by Ne-Yo
I'm a Mess by Ed Sheeran

about
K WEBSTER

K Webster is a *USA Today* Bestselling author. Her titles have claimed many bestseller tags in numerous categories, are translated in multiple languages, and have been adapted into audiobooks. She lives in "Tornado Alley" with her husband, two children, and her baby dog named Blue. When she's not writing, she's reading, drinking copious amounts of coffee, and researching aliens.

Keep up with K Webster
Facebook: www.facebook.com/authorkwebster
Blog: authorkwebster.wordpress.com
Twitter: twitter.com/KristiWebster
Email: kristi@authorkwebster.com
Goodreads: www.goodreads.com/user/show/10439773-k-webster
Instagram: instagram.com/kristiwebster

about
NIKKI ASH

Nikki Ash resides in South Florida where she is an English teacher by day and a writer by night. When she's not writing, you can find her with a book in her hand. From the Boxcar Children, to Wuthering Heights, to the latest single parent romance, she has lived and breathed every type of book. While reading and writing are her passions, her two children are her entire world. You can probably find them at a Disney park before you would find them at home on the weekends!

Reading is like breathing in, writing is like breathing out.– Pam Allyn

Contact Nikki Ash

Facebook: facebook.com/authornikkiash
Twitter: twitter.com/authornikkiash
Instagram: instagram.com/authornikkiash
Amazon: amazon.com/author/nikkiash
Website: www.authornikkiash.com

Nikki Ash's reader group:
www.facebook.com/groups/booksbynikkiash

Subscribe to Nikki Ash's newsletter:
bit.ly/NikkiAshNewsletter